C.A. RUDOLPH
DIVIDED WE STAND

BOOK FOUR OF THE WHAT'S LEFT OF MY WORLD SERIES

Copyright © C.A. Rudolph 2018. All rights reserved.
Cover Art by Deranged Doctor Design
Formatting by Deranged Doctor Design
Edited by Sabrina Jean
Proofread by Pauline Nolet

Featured on the cover:
Darja Filipovic of Deranged Doctor Design

ISBN-13: 978-1981659142
ISBN-10: 1981659145

No part of this book may be reproduced, scanned, or distributed in any printed or electronic form without permission. Please do not participate in or encourage piracy of copyrighted materials in violation of the author's rights. Thank you for respecting the hard work of this author.
This is a work of fiction. Names, characters, places, and incidents either are the product of the author's imagination or are used fictitiously, and any resemblance to locales, events, business establishments, or actual persons—living or dead—is entirely coincidental.

FOR CYRUS

Luke will never replace you—no dog ever could. But he reminds us so much of you sometimes, it's as if you never left us. We love you and we miss you, and we think of you often. You will never be forgotten.

"The reason why the world lacks unity, and lies broken and in heaps, is because man is disunited with himself."

Ralph Waldo Emerson

AUTHOR'S NOTE

The term *divided* is the key expression used throughout the pages of this book. The word is used repeatedly, and it is my intention for you, the reader, to comprehend how the word applies to the story on a myriad of levels, and comparatively to the current state of our country and the world in which we live independent of the story, both of which are far from being fictional.

The nonlinear timeline I routinely utilize to support randomly occurring flashbacks has also been divided, not only within this particular volume, but between books as well, making things a little more complex. In short, various chapters within *Divided We Stand* shadow the same timeline as those found in the preceding book of the same series, *We Won't Go Quietly*, dating back to November 30th in Chapter 15. As such, many characters left behind or 'missing' scenes from book three were written into this book in parallel.

To generate even more disunion, chapters contained within this book, while not necessarily flashbacks by any means, will alternate between current and preceding dates as the story moves forward. So be sure to watch or listen for the 'present day' cues.

This note is simply a preemptive reference, written as a forewarning to some readers and listeners who might otherwise have a tougher time following along.

Thank you for being a fan and for procuring *Divided We Stand*, my fourth installment in the *What's Left of My World* series. Enjoy the story.

~ Chad 'C.A.' Rudolph
June 2018

PROLOGUE

IT WAS FIFTEEN MINUTES BEFORE FOUR o'clock in the afternoon, and her bus was right on schedule.

Lauren Russell sat in her seat, bright-eyed and resplendent, her body eagerly slanted toward the aisle, watching as her stop drew closer through the windshield. Although tempted to stand and scuttle to the front, thereby shortening the distance between herself and home, she held back, recognizing that doing so while the bus remained in transit was frowned upon.

Lauren was known for questioning most things up to and including authority, but she didn't want to risk it and chance being reprimanded by the driver again for 'jumping the gun' like she had in the past. The weather was far too agreeable today, and there were more important matters for her to attend to.

During her half-hour ride home from school, Lauren focused on what passed by on either side through the windows and remained inobtrusive and somewhat listless while the adjacent juvenile majority carried on like a three-ring circus. In her silence, she couldn't help but overhear the other children nearby gab and rattle off at the mouth about random topics, most of which she considered inane and petty.

Lauren just couldn't help it. Most of what her fellow classmates chattered about was of no interest to her. Elementary school thus far had been a breeze. Her grades had been exemplary. But the fifth grade had been a learning process for her, seemingly less concerned with education, and more connected with popularity and acceptance.

It was one big party. A contest in which one could only be subjugated by showing off, engaging in the oftentimes cruel intimidation of others, and being the loudest, most infantile-acting member in the band. Lauren had zero interest in any of those behaviors.

The loudest ones in the room, or *bus*, in this case, were the weakest. *They're the least of my worries,* Lauren thought.

At least that was what her father had told her, though not verbatim, a couple of years before—his own words entangled and aligned with cherry-picked quotes from movies. Lauren had grown to find confidence in it and accept the axiom as true, but not before finding the need to test it.

Peering across the aisle, she flashed a friendly smile at a girl in bright pink plastic-framed glasses. Her generous blond locks were pulled into pigtails that fanned out at the ends as if static electricity were actively tugging on each strand of hair. Eliza was a grade below Lauren, and they had met earlier in the year when Eliza's family had moved in a few doors down after her dad's job had relocated him to the area.

Eliza was busily darting her eyes around, passing off askance looks at the other children on the bus. She was an incredibly intelligent child, but also quiet and backward, unsure of herself, making her no match for the other first-string players in the ongoing popularity games. As such, she'd initially been bullied by several of her classmates, and Lauren had been the first to stand up for her, bloodying a boy's nose and blackening another's eye in the course of it, and finding herself in a bit of trouble as a result.

"It's the quiet ones you need to look out for, L...They will be the ones to rise up—certain to astound us all someday. So watch out for them and stand up for them, even when no one else does. God made all of us equally, and popularity is just as pedantic as it is impermanent. So be kind to others as often as you can, especially to those no one else cares to, like the quiet ones. Always root for the underdog."

Lauren blamed her father for her integrity and for always feeling the need to do what was right—especially if it found her in some sort of trouble as a consequence. But each time she performed a good deed, helped someone along, or defended what she felt was right and honest, she could feel herself becoming a better person. She was ascending a stairway into an honorable maturity, unlike so many others in her generation. Lauren was merely just beginning to understand the source and significance of her undying sense of right and wrong, and regardless of her dad's involvement or influence, it wouldn't be long before she would learn to take ownership of it.

The sun was shining brightly today, and the air outside was warm and comforting. A gentle breeze was blowing, offering a pleasant, ideal climate for outdoor activities, and all Lauren could think about was changing into a pair of shorts and flip-flops and heading outside to play so she could feel the sun's warmth on her skin. But she wanted to finish her math homework first.

At the point the bus was heard screeching to a halt at the intersection with her street, Lauren slid out of her seat and traipsed to the front of the bus while hurdling over an assortment of legs, feet, and bookbags.

She waved bye to Eliza after hopping off, assured her she'd be back outside in about an hour, then headed for the driveway, surprised to find her dad's car in its normal spot. It wasn't unusual to see him home at this hour, but it wasn't exactly customary either, and Lauren rushed to the house after briefly checking the mailbox to see if anything inside was addressed to her.

As she approached the front door, she could hear the school bus pulling away while another similar-sounding engine was pulling up. As the noise drew closer, Lauren turned to see a UPS truck veering on to the edge of her driveway.

She pulled her hand away from the door, turned, and hopped down from the porch as the driver stopped his engine and disappeared into the back. A moment later, the brown-uniformed man opened the rear door and jumped out, sliding several boxes to the edge and stacking them onto a dolly.

Lauren remained wary, inching her way closer while keeping a semblance of a safe distance away from the driver and his truck. After a quick glimpse at the boxes, she distinguished a familiar yellow, rectangular logo. It contained the business name Carolina Readiness Supply in an easy-to-read, luminous, vivid red font.

On each box, a personal note had been inscribed with a black Sharpie, thanking her father for his patronage. They were even signed by someone calling herself 'Jan'.

Great, Lauren thought. *More prepper crap.*

After the driver had finished stacking and arranging his load, he angled the dolly and pulled on it energetically, sending Lauren a warm smile as he wheeled past her. "Afternoon, young lady. Is this your stuff? I might need you to help me with it…It's heavier than it looks. You look pretty strong to me."

Lauren didn't respond, but coldly scrutinized his stares at her arms.

He shrugged while regarding the house and driveway. "Are your folks home? Or are you alone today?"

Lauren knew full well never to offer a reply to such questions, no matter how innocent the situation felt or appeared. The answers provided far too much information to the inquiring person. She was a lanky eighty-five pounds, barely four and a half feet tall, and the UPS driver was every bit of three times her age and twice her size.

Even if she was home alone, it was always best for everyone, excluding family and trustworthy friends, to be none the wiser. It was a mindset both her parents had drilled into her for as long as she could remember. The world was an expressly dangerous place for young people and was worsening by the day, even if it didn't appear to be on the surface. All that was needed for the most unsuspecting of persons to engage in immoral acts was opportunity.

Lauren rolled her eyes at the driver while facing him and shuffling her feet carefully in the direction of safety. She'd seen him delivering packages in the neighborhood before, and therefore didn't consider him a danger to her. But that didn't obstruct her from calling him out. "Don't you think that's an inappropriate question for an adult to ask a kid?"

The UPS driver tilted his head, a bit taken aback. "Sorry…I was just trying to be friendly. I suppose you're probably right about that, though. My bad."

"My parents work from home, by the way," Lauren said. "They're always here."

"That's good, I guess." The driver turned to scan the boxes with his tablet. "I've been making a lot of deliveries to this address lately. If you don't mind me asking, is your dad a prepper or something?"

Lauren didn't miss a beat. "I *do* mind you asking."

The driver turned to her with an awkward smile, hesitating before handing her the tablet, allowing Lauren to scribble her name on the screen.

The driver pressed a few buttons on the tablet while verifying Lauren's youthful John Hancock. "I didn't think you kids still knew how to do cursive." He paused a second, smirking at Lauren. "What's your dad's first name? I gotta have it for my records."

Lauren turned away, heading back to the porch. "Alan. And you can just leave those beside the garage door."

After going inside and locking the door behind her, Lauren strode to the kitchen to drop off her backpack and grab a drink. A glass of her favorite pulp-free orange juice in hand, she scanned the house for signs of her father and, upon finding none, guessed he was probably in his office, where he could normally be found when no one else was home. She removed the homework folder from her backpack and cradled it under her arm, and with OJ in hand, she bounded the stairs, heading for her room.

Along the way, she passed by the door to her father's office. It was closed, but Lauren could hear indiscernible noises and chattering coming from the other side. She assumed he was playing with his radios again, something she didn't fully understand and never really cared to before. The subject just seemed so way over her head and far too complicated. It was definitely nowhere near as fun or exciting as riding a bike, taking a run through the woods, playing on the swing set with her neighborhood friends, or even digging in the dirt, looking for buried artifacts or perhaps even worms.

Placing her ear to the door, Lauren eavesdropped for a moment, trying to determine what she was hearing. It sounded akin to static or white noise of some kind, but the static was being interrupted by recurrent beeping tones, which sounded rhythmic at times. They carried their own cadence, similar to that of a human heartbeat or a pulse.

Lauren had other things to do, but she needed to let her dad know about his packages. She took a step back and knocked on the door.

"Friend? Or foe?" Her dad's voice beckoned through the door's amalgamated, hollow structure.

"Foe."

"The door is open, L. Come on in. Just be mindful that I'm armed and relatively dangerous."

Lauren smirked at the response. This wasn't their typical daily exchange, but she knew her father was the type of person who took pride in keeping everyone guessing, even her.

Alan's eyes were immediately drawn to her over top his computer monitor upon her entry. His expression became pliable, and he smiled at Lauren proudly. "Hey, you. Home from school already?"

"I get home from school at the same time every day."

"Good point."

"And I should be the one asking *you* why *you're* home so early."

"Another good point. Company meeting today. They were kind enough to send us on our way after they got done divulging how profitable we were, how awesome we've been for the year, and how happy our customers are with us…along with a bunch of other lies."

"Hmm…sounds like fun," Lauren said. "UPS delivered a package for you—*another* one. It's outside in front of the garage. I signed for it."

"Cool, I appreciate that, L. Who's the package from?"

"Some *Carolina Readiness* store," Lauren muttered, a snide tone marking her words. "It's more of that prepper cra—stuff of yours."

Alan nodded. "Probably that food sampler I ordered a few days ago. I want to take it with us on our next outing so we can test it out."

"So we can see if it's…palatable?"

Alan snickered. "Flavor *is* pretty significant, don't you think?"

"Hmm…I think you use mom and me as your guinea pigs," Lauren mused. "The last stuff you bought tasted bland…like sawdust. Of course, I've never actually eaten sawdust."

"In point of fact, L, you very likely have, along with the rest of modern society," said Alan. "Check the ingredients next time for something called cellulose. It's wood pulp, an FDA-approved food additive."

Lauren's face bunched up. "Eww. Gross."

"At least it adds fiber to your diet."

Her interest in what she was hearing but not able to see was steadily increasing. "So, what are you doing? Sounds weird. I could hear it from out in the hallway."

Alan offered a hand, waving her in. "Don't just stand there…curiosity may have killed the cat, but not in my house. Come see for yourself."

Lauren circled her father's desk and moved in closer to him. Just as she had predicted, he had a radio turned on. But instead of a microphone, he was holding a computer mouse in his hand.

The monitor displayed a window of a brand of software she didn't recognize. In the middle of the window was a zigzagging line with multiple colors cascading underneath in a constant moving spectrum.

"What's this?" she asked, pointing at the screen. "I don't think I've ever seen it before."

"That's because you haven't. It's called *Fldigi*. That stands for 'fast light digital modem'. It works with my computer's sound card. You can do a lot with it, but I've been using it as a visual aid."

"Visual aid for what?"

"I'm getting older, L, and my mind doesn't work in the same way yours does—especially when learning a new language."

Lauren looked curious. "What new language?"

"Why am I not surprised you're asking me that?" Alan grinned. "It's continuous wave."

One of Lauren's brows elevated. "That sounds more like a surfing competition or a movie about a killer tsunami."

"That's just a term some ham radio guys call it on occasion. Sometimes they refer to it in shorthand as CW, which stands for continuous waveform."

"Okay, thanks…for the info. But what is it?"

Alan gestured to the radio. "You're listening to it right now."

Lauren turned her head away from him and gazed at the radio while she listened intently to the beats reigning over the static noise floor.

Alan slid a sheet of paper to her from the other side of his desk, which displayed letters and numbers in a table, each corresponding to a series of dashes and dots, or decimal points. At the top of the paper, the title written in bold lettering read 'Morse Code'.

"Why didn't you just tell me you were trying to learn Morse code?" Lauren asked quizzically. "I know what *that* is."

"CW existed before Morse code came about, and they're not exactly one and the same. Morse is interrupted continuous waveform used to convey a message. I tried learning the code when I was your age around the same time I got my first set of walkie-talkies for Christmas." Alan pointed to the sheet of paper with the code index he'd provided Lauren. "They had a table similar to this one written on them in raised lettering that felt almost like braille, and I was fascinated by it. Ever since, I've always wanted to learn more."

Lauren cocked her head to the side. "So why did you wait until now?"

"Learning a different language isn't exactly the easiest thing in the world, L...at least for some of us mentally challenged folks, anyway. Initially, I tried learning it like you see it now—as a series of dots and dashes on a sheet of paper. After getting my ham radio license, I was told I'd been doing it wrong the whole time. The best way to learn it was audibly, and instead of looking at the code as dots and dashes, it was far better to learn by thinking of them instead as sounds...*dits* and *dahs*."

"That's kind of what they sound like, more or less."

Alan nodded. "Yeah, more or less. Granted, I'm still learning, and I've managed to learn a lot more since I changed tactics, but I still have a long way to go. I suppose I'm lucky in a way, at one time if you wanted to upgrade your license and use the longer distance HF bands, you had to prove proficiency with CW. But the FCC removed the requirement a while back, and I was able to snag my *general* without passing a Morse code test. A long time ago, anyone who wanted to transmit on the lower frequencies had to learn CW, and by learning it, that meant being able to send and receive it at twenty words per minute. They lowered that number from twenty to five not long before you were born and then eventually did away with it altogether, which is unfortunate."

"What makes it unfortunate? If they got rid of something that was difficult, it made taking the test easier."

"It's unfortunate because Morse code is much more than just a mode of communication over the airwaves. It's a universal language." Alan turned to her. "Think about it, L. We're talking about a simple series of dots and dashes, dits and dahs, that can be encoded and decoded using a number of methods, audibly and visually. You could use a flashlight or a signal mirror to send Morse code if it's all you had. And that makes it not only a universal language, but a powerful asset...the ability to communicate without having to make any noise."

"Do people still use it?"

Alan nodded his head. "A lot of people do, especially the older generations. For some of them, it's their preferred method of communication, the only mode they utilize, and believe you me, there are hundreds of different modes you can use on the ham bands."

Lauren hesitated, her youthful expression displaying her fascination. "Is it something I can learn?"

Alan laughed heartily. "Lauren Jane Russell, it has always been my contention that the mind the Lord blessed you with is capable of pretty much anything, up to and including becoming proficient with interrupted continuous wave."

"But I don't know anything about your radios."

"You don't have to," Alan said. "Universal means universal. It's like learning and knowing any other language. You can use it anywhere, and it becomes an advantage to you and to anyone else like you."

Lauren's face brightened. "Just like sign language."

"Exactly like sign language. You know by personal experience there are folks out there who can't communicate any other way…so think about it. Put yourself in their shoes for a minute. What if *you* only had one way to communicate? What if using your voice wasn't possible because you'd lost it somehow, or it was too loud? What if you didn't want to make any noise? It would come in handy then, wouldn't it?"

Lauren nodded her head.

"A similar phenomenon happens often in the radio world. A lot of times, band conditions prevent me from maintaining voice contact on certain bands due to atmospheric or environmental conditions. Sometimes, it's a simpler explanation, like time of day or weather activity, but there's been times where I've had to break from a conversation because I could no longer hear the station I was talking to, or the other way around. For some reason though, CW seems to always get through, and that's why a lot of hams simply refuse the notion that it's outdated, and I agree with them."

Lauren pointed to the computer screen and watched as the audible dits and dahs became letters, and the letters themselves formed words and sentences along with intermixed punctuation. "So you're using a computer and an app to decipher it for now until you learn it," she surmised.

"Pretty much. I come home some days and listen to it and try to tune in on it, but when I'm not at home, I use this." He held up a small black plastic box with an LCD screen.

"What's that?"

"It's a Morse code reader," Alan said. "You can set it up to read or send the code to you at different speeds. It has different modes, too. You can choose to learn the alphabet in sequence or out of sequence, or you can have it read words or full sentences to you, and you can either write them down or copy along in your head. I've been doing a little bit of both."

Lauren reached for the code reader and studied it. "Do I need one of these?"

Alan smiled at her. "You can have that one if you want. Something tells me you'll pick up on it a lot faster than me and I'll get that reader back before I even know it."

Lauren looked to him, uncertain. "Are you sure?"

"Of course," Alan said. "It'll give us another way to talk to each other in case we ever need it. And you never know, L, with the way the world is going, someday it just might benefit you somehow. And me."

CHAPTER 1

Kristen Perry's residence
Trout Run Valley
Saturday, November 30th

MARK MASON'S THOUGHTS WOULDN'T ALLOW him solace. He was restless and agitated, sitting in an unsteady wooden chair perched before a two-person dining table. The chair across from him, visually identical to and just as rickety as the one he was using, sat lonely and empty.

Beside him, on the dust-covered hardwood floor, lay scattered pieces of the shredded garment that made up his homemade ghillie suit. It was the camouflage he typically wore while assuming his duties with his brother, Chad, or any one of the Brady boys at the Wolf Gap barricade.

The table had been placed beside a window in a diminutive kitchen area during Kristen's move, and through the cloudy, cobweb-covered panes, it provided Mark with a view of an unkempt backyard, which hadn't been visited by a lawnmower or a weed trimmer in a while. In fact, the grass was so tall now, it nearly obstructed the view of the forest on the other side of it.

Seized by a moment of deep contemplation, he glanced over the yard's feathery tops and beyond, high into the leaf-barren trees, and sorted through his thoughts. But as rampant as they were, he just couldn't make sense of them. It was much easier to simply stir, hum tunes from memory, and fidget.

Mark used his fingers to twirl around a glass of homemade sweet tea—but it wasn't just any sweet tea. It was a special formula to him, one that his mother, Kim, had perfected over the years and, in recent months, had been obliged to reinvent.

Before the collapse, the Mason family had normally consumed a gallon of the most sugar-replete tea imaginable each and every day. Sugar had been easy to come by then, but it wasn't anymore. Still, Mark's mother had done what she could to replicate the formula without the use of popular store-bought sweeteners, using natural honey from her apiary as a substitute.

Even without the extravagance of ice cubes and deprived of sugary sweetness, Mark found it enjoyable. It was a familiar and soothing taste to him, one that reminded him of family, his youth, home, and the way things had once been.

On the table beneath Mark's hand lay an unfolded, faded, and somewhat tattered map displaying most of Shenandoah County, with locations indicated in a specific area not far outside the town limits of Edinburg. It had been given to him by the same person who had also provided information of an incoming attack the previous month. The information had turned out to be valid and had likely been the key reason for their victory against an invading force of enraged, psychopathic killers.

A set of footsteps descending the cabin's staircase broke his attention away from his daydream, and Mark turned to see his brother, Chad, entering the kitchen across the threshold with his chin lowered, looking a bit distraught.

"So? What's the verdict?" Mark asked, his brow raised. "Is she going to live or what?"

Chad didn't answer him directly. He took a quick stroll around the kitchen, studying the manner in which Kristen had begun unboxing and arranging her belongings; then he walked to the rear window and squinted out into the backyard.

"Well?"

"Dude, seriously. You need to calm down," his brother replied. "Getting information out of Kristen isn't exactly easy right now. She's been a zombie lately, and with everything we've got going on now, that lady friend of yours upstairs is the least of her worries."

"Whatever."

"Whatever nothing," Chad snapped back. "She's running late for that meeting at the church. She also said something about needing to go check on Peter...and Liam."

"Their little boy is sick too now?"

"Looks that way."

"Damn. Everyone is getting sick," Mark said, looking away. "This isn't good."

"No, it's not."

"Chad...look, I'm sorry for being...wound up. It's just that it's been over a month now, and...nothing. And I'm really bothered by how it all went down."

"I know you're bothered," replied Chad. "Hell, I'm bothered, too, I'm pretty sure we all are. But you've been all over the place ever since—and like it or not, you're going to need to stow that shit and get focused, and I mean soon. You and I need to get back to work."

"Yeah..."

Chad paused a moment and shrugged. "Dude, look. That woman—I know you care for her. I have no idea why, but it's pretty obvious. I haven't seen you this preoccupied since you dated that Jennie girl back when you were a freshman. But the chick is in a coma and has been for over a month now. She's breathing, but other than that, she's been totally unresponsive. There's just no way to know how this is going to pan out."

Mark exhaled a labored, drawn-out sigh. "Why can't we have a doctor living nearby?" He took a drink of his tea, set the glass down gently, and licked the sweetness from his lips. "That would fix *everything* right now. A doctor would know how to handle her coma...*and* this poisoning thing that Lauren figured out—which I still can't believe is actually happening."

"But it is."

"Yeah, I know it is, Chad."

"And we have to keep moving forward, bro."

"I know that, too."

"Then stop living in the past."

Mark glared at his brother. "I can't help it. I'm not exactly over the *past*."

"Here we go again…"

Mark sighed. "I seriously can't believe one of you guys shot her."

"Mark, we've been through this. I didn't shoot her…I've told you that a hundred times."

"I know. And I believe you. One of those Bradys probably did it and will never own up to it. None of those idgits can shoot worth a damn."

"No, they didn't, either," Chad disagreed. "I was there. I saw her go down when she got hit in the chest. The shot had to have come from one of her own people."

"That doesn't make any sense."

"No, it does. Just not to *you*. She was running away from them, Mark. I could see it in her eyes—the woman was scared shitless. My guess is they somehow found out what she did, and when she tried to get away, they followed her for no other reason than to permanently cancel her membership." He paused. "Bottom line is we killed them, every last one of them. We just couldn't stop them from shooting her first. And I am sorry for that."

"Maybe you're right about all that, but saying you're sorry doesn't make it right, and sorry will never make her okay," said Mark. "She helped us. Without her, we'd all probably be dead right now. If it weren't for her, we'd—"

"Mark, I get it. Believe me, bro, I get it. I've ran what happened through my head a bunch of times, and I'm telling you, it couldn't have gone any other way." Chad peered down to the map underneath his brother's hand. "I see you still got that map."

Mark let out a breath while trying to calm himself down. "Yeah."

"If you don't put it away, your sweaty palms are going to ruin it."

"My palms aren't sweaty." Mark turned his hands over to examine them, realizing his brother was right. "Whatever. It doesn't matter anyway. I've memorized it."

"Are you serious?"

Mark huffed. "Of course I'm serious. I haven't let go of it since she gave it to me."

His brother nodded, pursing his lips. "Then it's pretty obvious you haven't let go of something else, either."

"She asked me to make her a promise—and wound up sacrificing herself for what she believed in. Some of the things she said hit me pretty hard. It was like she knew she had nothing else to live for…and knew she was going to die…like she knew she *had* to die. And she was okay with it. I've never seen someone be so resigned—and gutsy at the same time, before. Sorry, Chad. I can't just let that go."

"Dude…did you fall for this chick or something?" Chad asked, a shrewd grin etched on his face.

"No! Seriously? What the hell?"

"I'm just sayin'."

"Shut up, Chad. Really."

Chad took a couple of steps closer to the table. "Okay, maybe I misread. But you're still thinking about doing what she asked you to do." He paused. "Am I right about that?"

After a moment's hesitation, Mark nodded as his features hardened.

"Mark, bro, listen to me. It's been a month."

"I don't care," Mark snapped. "I don't care if it's been three months. I still have to know. If what Sasha told me was true, then those girls are still there, locked up in some basement. No one else knows about them but us, because everyone who did know is dead now—besides her; and *she* obviously can't do anything to help them."

"And *you* have to be the one who does something about it?"

Mark paused to contemplate, his expression falling flat. "Who else can it be?"

Chad nodded, folding his arms across his chest. He sighed and hesitated a moment. "You know, if Dad heard any of this, he'd crack you upside the head with a boot heel. And he'd make me run twenty miles just for listening to you."

Mark nodded, his eyebrows setting sail.

"And there's no way he'd consider letting us go."

"What did you say?"

"I just said there's no way Dad—"

"No. I heard that part. You said *us*…as in letting *us* go."

Chad smiled and shrugged apathetically. "Come on, Mark. You're my brother. The only one I got in the world. I can't just let you go and do something stupid…all by yourself."

"Wait—so let me get this straight. You actually *want* to go with?"

"Now, don't get all sentimental on me," Chad replied, holding a palm outward. "I don't like the idea of leaving the valley. With FEMA crawling around and lurking behind every corner, it's dangerous over there. But, yes. I'll go, so long as we find a way to keep from getting caught by the feds *and* by Dad. I don't need another family court-martial. I've been through enough of those already."

Mark pulled his tea glass close to his lips. "I've already thought through a plan. It's close to being foolproof, just gotta work out some of the minor details. Edinburg isn't far from here, and we can leave at first light and use back roads—we'd be in and out and back home in no time."

Chad laughed slightly and stepped over to the table. "Sounds way too easy. Oh—before you finish that glass, is there any more tea where that came from? Or did you drink it all again like you usually do?"

Mark set his glass down. "No, I drank it all again," he jested straight-faced, awaiting his brother's response to his lie. When Chad reached for Mark's glass, he pulled it abruptly away. "I'm joshing you. Mom made a batch for Kristen, and I brought some for us in a thermos. There's some in there you can have—not much, but some."

Chad smirked and nodded. "Let's take what's left up to the barricade." He turned, looking over his shoulder as he advanced into the adjacent room. "It might help our Brady compatriots be a little more sympathetic to your cause. If you're serious about this plan of yours, we're going to need their help to make it happen."

"Good idea. Thank you."

"You can thank me later—if we survive."

Another set of footsteps descending the cabin's staircase startled the siblings, and after spotting two slender legs wrapped in a pair of rolled-up sweatpants through the entryway, Mark jumped up from his chair and anxiously backed away while reaching for the pistol holstered on his belt. "Jesus Christ! What in the hell?"

Chad responded immediately to his brother's reaction, moving to intercept whatever awaited them.

As Chad and Mark went shoulder to shoulder with one another, both their jaws fell to the floor at the sight of the woman emerging from the stairway. A very pale, very emaciated Sasha Ledo limped her way barefoot into the kitchen. She had not only resisted death, but had somehow beaten it, having recently arisen from her coma without so much as a warning.

Sasha rubbed her eyes and pulled at the bandages clinging to her chest, then scratched at the sutures that had been sewed into her skin to close her wounds. "Fuck me running up the stairs—I feel like death warmed over," she said, her voice raw and abrasive, her tongue sticking to the desiccated roof of her mouth. "You two were being so loud down here, I had to come see what all the uproar was about."

She glanced upward, taking turns scrutinizing the mystified looks she was getting from them. "Seriously? What the hell are you two staring at, for God's sake?" Annoyed, she turned away, catching sight of Mark's tea glass. She pointed to it with a bent finger. "Mmm, that looks good. I'm as dry as a dustbowl," she said, shadowed by a raspy cough. "What is it? Bourbon?"

Mark hesitated. "No. It's…uh, tea."

"Of course it is." Sasha frowned, breathed a vexed sigh, and sat at the table, feeling her bones scrape and her unused muscles throb. "Well? Are you dudes just gonna stand there? Or offer a lady a drink?"

CHAPTER 2

The cabin
Trout Run Valley
Wednesday, December 1st

GRACE PEERED OUT THE LIVING room window, a sheen of mild trepidation coating her youthful face. Her mood was somber, but she felt hopeful despite the circumstances weighing on everyone she knew and cared about. Like most other things affecting her moods, attitude, and her overall outlook on life, the lull was brief, and Grace was quick to dismiss it.

Letting out a loud sigh, Grace slid her arms across her chest, enfolded them, and squeezed into a mild shiver while she watched the vehicle convoy careen out of the driveway and head north along Trout Run Road, disappearing shortly thereafter.

For several minutes after they had departed, Grace couldn't help but be idle. With nothing else demanding her attention for the moment, she gazed affably out the window at the dust settling back onto the driveway at the road's edge. She wanted to take all the time in the world right now. It was her way of wishing Lauren, Christian, Norman, and those accompanying them safe travels.

Grace eventually turned away and plopped down on the couch, only to listlessly stare up at the ceiling. "I just sent the love of my life away on a sterile endeavor to save my sister, of all things," she deliberated, smirking in amusement at her thoughts while she toyed with her hair and flicked at her fingernails. "Grace, my dear? I hope you understand, despite your attempts to prove otherwise, there's a good chance you might *actually* be a little schizophrenic."

The cabin had never been this quiet before, devoid of life's activities, daily commotion, and mixed conversation. Ordinarily, John would be sleeping his day away after another graveyard shift on the porch, but his brother's condition had diverted him to the Masons' home. Lee had been experiencing a fever nearing one hundred four degrees, the symptom of the late stages of the severe illness befalling him having begun to rear its ugly head.

Norman and Christian had both gone along on the expedition to find desperately needed medical assistance, food, and sundries, leaving Grace to *grace* the cabin with her presence, accompanied only by John and her stepmother, Michelle.

Prior to his departure, Fred Mason had left strict instructions for those lingering at home in the valley to remain vigilant and on constant alert. Despite the circumstances and overwhelming stress, which could very easily take their minds off their most recent threat, the evidence that Lauren and Grace had uncovered on the mountain was still in play. It was a trail of bread crumbs, and whoever had left it was certain to return. The situation therefore required awareness and anticipatory action.

Vehicle patrols were to continue twenty-four hours a day, and foot patrols had been made into a requirement. No one was to be outside their residence without a loaded weapon within reach at all times. Everyone was instructed to watch for anything suspicious, keeping their eyes to the trees—especially to the east. If a hostile force was encountered, they were to engage it and terminate it by any means necessary. If the force was overwhelming, they were to gather and fall back to the Mason home and defend the position until it became no longer feasible.

As a last resort, they were to bug out and utilize Fred's remaining Humvee and his M35 deuce and a half as transportation, since it was among the few remaining vehicles left in the valley capable of transporting the sick without the need to remove them from their beds.

There was no doubt in anyone's mind, the situation had become desperate. Lives were hanging in the balance, and now, due to the division of human assets, the overall defensive state of the valley was at an all-time minimum. As a result, Fred's instructions were heeded to the letter, even by those who had a habit of taking matters too lightly and questioning most things, like Grace typically did.

In addition to Fred's explicit directives, Christian had also provided Grace with a set of policies to abide by while he was away. He had told her, "Fred might not be certain about who's responsible for all this, but I am. I know who it is, Grace, and I'm telling you, you and everyone else need to be ready when they decide to pop their heads out. Trust me—they are coming."

Grace squinted, and her lips pursed as her expression settled. She recalled the tone in Christian's voice.

"I know you don't want to hear this. But you need to be ready to take them out," he had said.

She had peered at him scornfully. "Take them out? You mean kill them, correct? Is that right?"

"That is precisely what I mean. You can't hesitate, Grace, and I mean not for a single second. Because they won't. If they get a clear shot, they'll kill you because that's what they've been trained and ordered to do. And I know this because it's what I was trained and ordered to do. We are their enemy now, and we must acknowledge the same about them. We know more about the layout of the land here than they do, and that's an advantage. We can outmaneuver them, but that won't be the be-all and end-all. We have to kill them, and that means *you* might have to kill them. So don't hesitate, because I can guarantee they won't give you the same chance you give them."

Grace shuddered while her thoughts raced back to the present. "Don't hesitate, Grace," she said aloud to herself. "You heard the man. Getting yourself killed will not be tolerated."

Grace knew she was capable of pulling the trigger and taking a life, having done so before already in several instances. She had fought alongside Christian and the others during the battle with the bikers and had killed a handful of human targets, and had also, mere days ago, shot a young man several times in his chest while defending Lauren's welfare on Mill Mountain.

Her thoughts glided by, soon bringing her back to another conversation she'd had just before the expedition had departed the valley, one she'd had with her younger sister.

Both Grace and Lauren had spent the time they shared before the departure divulging much more than they'd intended. Just before stepping out the door on her way to leave, Lauren had turned to Grace, her eyes denoting her undying inquisitiveness, her body language displaying unease. She'd said, "Grace, I need to ask you something."

"Okay. Why the warning, then? Today is just like any other day, kind of. Just ask me."

"Warning? No…it's just that something's been bugging me, and I need you to answer a question that won't stop incessantly pounding my brain."

"Want me to get you some ibuprofen? There's some in the med—"

"Grace…"

"I'm joking. Sister, my life is an open book—it is for you, anyway. I just exposed all the gory details about Christian and me. Whatever you need to know probably pales in comparison."

"Oh—it's nothing like that at all," Lauren had said through a sheepish smirk. "It's about the other day—on our hike to Big Schloss—when you said you thought I'd gotten used to killing and that it didn't bother me anymore."

"Yeah? So? Do you think I overspoke or something?"

"No, never. It's just that…the thought occurred to me that you've been pulling the trigger quite a bit lately yourself," Lauren had explained. "Lord knows, I haven't had the time to do a body count, but odds are it was your gun that took out some of those bikers. And if it had, doing so didn't faze you one bit, at least from what I can see. You even shot that boy so I could get away from him without shedding a tear."

"What's your point?" Grace had asked.

Lauren had given her a cross stare. "My point is, you pointing out to me that killing doesn't faze me anymore even though at one time it had. But looking back, you've pulled the trigger, too. You've killed, same as me. And I don't see one single bit of hurt or regret on the surface."

"And?"

"And I know you're a heck of an actress…but some things are impossible to hide—yet you're hiding them or not allowing them to affect you somehow."

"And?"

"*And* I want to know why."

"I'm not sure I want to tell you why," Grace had said.

Lauren had cast an indignant stare. "Why wouldn't you?"

"Because. It'll probably sound stupid, and you'll make fun of me about it, like you usually do."

"No, I won't."

"I'm quite sure that you will."

"Try me."

After an extended moment of hesitation, Grace had said, "Fine. If you must know, I'll tell you. But I swear to God, I'll shoot you too if you tell anyone."

"Okay, fine, whatever."

Grace had wavered slightly. "I…I close my eyes."

"What?"

"That's it. I close my eyes."

"You close your eyes?"

"Yeah. Like—before I shoot the guy. I aim, and right before I pull the trigger, I close my eyes."

Lauren had cocked her head in disbelief. "And that's it?"

"Yeah, that's it. I always thought if I did it that way, I can't see myself shooting them, and I can't see them die when I pull the trigger. It's, like, plausible deniability or something."

Lauren had giggled and used her hand to conceal a smile. "Jesus. That's, like, the most ridiculous thing I've ever heard or something."

"Hey, like, shut the hell up or something, like. Not everyone is a born-again, hard, ruthless, friggin' cutthroat assassin like you are, twisted sister. Some of us find ways to preemptively cope before coping becomes requisite. Closing my eyes is my way, and it works for me, and so far, I like it. So you can just kiss it."

As the fire crackled happily within the black iron Timberline, tempering the air nearby, Grace's look of worry returned as she scanned the uninhabited cabin. She'd grown fond of seeing Christian lounging in the recliner. Now it sat upright and empty, deficient of the warm body that had once made it whole.

"Just like me," said Grace, leaning her head to point to the chair. "You and I got something in common now, mister La-Z-Boy."

After a few minutes, Grace rose and shimmied to the kitchen table, where she'd begun to arrange her gear. She picked up what she now considered her own personal AR-15, a Palmetto State Armory build her father had put together several years before the collapse. Grace had never paid close attention to the mechanics or the finer details of the weapon until recently. Now she was beginning to become accustomed to it, and she liked the way it felt in her hands. But even more than that, she liked how it made her feel safe and powerful.

"Well, Lauren, since you're not around, I suppose it's my turn to do this stuff now," Grace said to herself, her voice echoing against the walls of the vacant cabin.

She peeked at the table, where she had previously arranged the items she intended to carry with her for the next several days, weeks, or for however long it took for her sister, Christian, and the others to return home. There were extra magazines for each of her firearms, a SOG folding knife, and the Baofeng radio she normally carried with her.

Grace patted her side with her right hand, verifying the Glock 27 she normally kept holstered on her hip was there. Then she pushed her hand into the front pocket of her pants and felt something she didn't normally keep in her front pocket, remembering that before Lauren had left, they had decided to exchange gifts.

Grace had given Lauren the plate carrier she'd been holding onto since the fight with the Marauders, and Lauren had given Grace their father's custom Ruger LCP, the same weapon Lauren had used to dispatch the club's leader. At first, Grace didn't want it, but her sister's insistence was as stout as her own, and Grace acquiesced.

Grace had always considered the Glock 27 to be a small pistol, as far as pistols go, even though it fit perfectly in her hands. The Ruger, on the other hand, was even smaller than the Glock. It worried her that she'd never shot it before, and she made a mental note to put holes in some paper with it before the need arose to put holes in something else.

"Thanks, Lauren. I love you, sister," Grace said, feeling the inseam of the tactical pants her sister had also given her. They were a little long in the legs, but fit her well, and Grace was finding all the extra pockets to her liking. There seemed to be a pocket for just about everything she could think of and, as well, for things she couldn't.

Grace set her rifle on the table. She picked up one of the matching thirty-round composite magazines and slid it into a thigh pocket while discovering two other pockets existed inside it.

"Well, isn't that special. Pocket pockets. I wonder who thought of that? The genius is probably a millionaire by now." Grace giggled to herself. "Or I guess, maybe he was, anyway."

Grace soon realized these *pocket pockets* were perfectly sized for an AR-15's magazine and slid one into each of them. She grabbed the remaining items from the table and placed them on and around her person, then slung her rifle over her neck and arm in a comparable manner to how her sister did, so it would drape in a ready position across her chest.

Afterward, she turned and looked down the hallway into a mirror mounted on the wall. "Grace? What in the hell have you gotten yourself into?" She turned sideways. "You're not exactly *Red Dawn*. Lauren was chosen to play that part. Maybe…no, I guess not really a *Charlie's Angel* or *Sarah Connor*, either." She turned again and sashayed. "You look better suited for a role as an extra in *Kill Bill*." She paused, sighing. "Oh well…fake it till you make it, Gracey Lou. A clever act has gotten you through most predicaments…why should this be any different?"

Fake it till you make it.

Grace had always been a phenomenal actress. Her career as a thespian had begun in junior high and continued throughout the remainder of her life pre-apocalypse. She had won awards and trophies and had even been accepted into schools of higher learning based solely on her skills and performance abilities. But Grace had also learned how to exploit her talents to get whatever she wanted. If a particular angle wasn't working for her, she'd put on a different face and eventually find a suitable character to act her way through a situation. Any situation.

Grace walked outside the cabin, and in the relative silence, she thought she could hear a faint buzzing noise, seeming to originate from above her somewhere in the sky. She glanced skyward in search of the source, an aircraft of some type, since it was the only contraption she could compare the noise to.

"Watching the birds fly south?" John called to her teasingly as he approached, Mossberg shotgun cradled in his arms and a small pack dangling from his shoulders.

"What?"

John laughed, knowing he'd caught her off guard. "What are you looking at?"

"Oh…I don't know. I thought I heard buzzing. Like an airplane or maybe a helicopter or…something like that."

"I haven't seen or heard anything artificial in the sky since we've been here," John said, taking a second to have a look for himself. "I can't hear a thing. You sure you heard something?"

"Yeah...I mean, who knows? I can't hear it now. It's probably nothing." Grace fidgeted. "Could be my brain playing tricks on me. I get that from time to time." She noticed John's face appearing sullener the closer he got to her. "How's Lee doing?"

John didn't respond immediately, and his sluggish pace soon slowed to a stop. "He's still got a hell of a fever. Kristen is trying to invent ways to get his temperature down. I was going to suggest rocks from the creek, but I guess that's out of the question now. I sure wish we had about fifty bags of ice."

Grace nodded in recognition but didn't say anything. She, too, was worried about Lee, but she knew her level of preoccupation paled in comparison to John's.

John moved to stand shoulder to shoulder with her, pushing out a despondent sigh. "Aside from that, I have nothing of note to report. The valley looks good, I suppose. Everybody seems to be doing like Fred asked them to." He pointed through the trees in the direction of the Taylor residence. "Bryan is on foot, walking the road between his house and the barricade with an HK-91 Fred must've given him. I haven't seen Sarah, so I'm guessing she's inside keeping Emily occupied. I'm not certain if *she's* armed, but I hope she is." He paused. "Everybody else is at the Masons', obviously."

Grace checked her AR's safety and let it drape to her side. Folding her arms, she shifted her weight to her left heel. "I think Sarah has been coming around... if you know what I mean. At least that's what I've been hearing."

John nodded, still staring off into the distance through the trees. "That's good. Lord knows, if something does pop off with us divided like we are, we'll need everyone on the same page. We won't stand a chance any other way."

"No worries," Grace said lightheartedly with a shrug. "I'm sure we'll handle it."

"How do you know that?"

"Easy. Because if we can't, we're all dead anyway."

"That's awfully apathetic, don't you think?"

"Creative use of apathy is the only technique I have in my repertoire that keeps me positive." Grace paused while John snickered. "So what's your plan for the day? Isn't it about time for your nap?"

John nearly snorted. "I don't have time. With everything going on right now, I don't think I'll get a wink of sleep until it's over."

"That's if it's *ever* over."

John laughed slightly. "You've never had a problem being realistic, either, have you?"

"Nope." Grace cocked her head to the side. "It's served me well too. Realism and I have had a pretty good relationship. It's an immaculate symbiosis."

John pointed to the line of Honda Rancher ATVs, two of which were left still parked. "We're missing a machine," he said. "I take that to mean Michelle left already?"

Grace nodded. "She went to Alex's house right after the others left, and not a moment after. She was in a hurry, but she knew Fred would've lit her up if he saw her go alone."

"There's no doubt about that," said John. "Being honest, I'm not completely comfortable with her going by herself, either."

"I don't think either one of us could have stopped her had we tried."

"Still—I would have liked to have had the option of going along."

Grace shook her head. "No way. Right now, you're needed here, John. You're one of the only capable men left in the valley who isn't bedridden. And I, for one, am glad you're here. Thanks for staying."

John turned to her and smiled. "Wow. Positivity disguised as apathy, realism, and now sincerity. I'm impressed, Grace. I didn't know you were capable of the latter. I don't know what's gotten into you lately, but I'm digging it."

Grace fidgeted a moment before a sharp cramp churned in her abdomen. It lasted about a minute before slowly subsiding. It was a familiar pain, something she had experienced several times before over the span of the past several days. "Nothing has gotten *into me* per se. I guess I'm just starting to acclimatize, finally."

John patted her back gently. "I was wondering if that was ever going to happen," he jeered, then paused a moment to scan the tree lines both in front and behind them. "By the way, I know you had something to do with Christian going on the expedition, but I don't want to accuse you of anything. I just want to say thank you."

Grace cut her eyes at him. "Thank me? John, believe it or not, I love my sister just as much if not more than you do. I know when she needs someone to watch her back, and I also knew the someone couldn't have been you. At least, not now. Definitely not now."

John's face began turning pale. "It should have been, though. I worry about Lauren all the time. And I mean *all* the time. And that's now. Back before all this crap ever started, I never gave her welfare much thought. But the situation's changed drastically, and now I just can't help myself. And I know that probably sounds crazy, especially considering what she's capable of."

Grace nodded her recognition but didn't say anything.

After a moment, John asked, "Do you have any idea what her backstory is?"

"Her backstory?"

"Yeah. Like where she learned all this…I don't know. The shooting skills. The fighting skills. The full-on badassery."

Grace twiddled, knowing she was privy, but feeling discretion was in order. "I don't know…I've always just accepted Lauren for who she is."

John nodded. "Me too. But recently, I've considered going the other route with her. I think I should start demanding answers. I think I deserve them." He paused, turning his head away. "I shouldn't have let her go. Dammit. I want her back here right now."

"She'll be back soon with bells on," said Grace just as another row of cramps edged their way through her abdomen, causing her to keel over. She tried to continue her response, but found herself unable to speak. The pain was taking her breath away.

John noticed immediately. "Grace? Are you all right?"

Grace held her breath and moaned, "I don't know. My stomach feels like it's being twisted in knots—like a muscle cramp or something." She wrapped both arms around her belly, trying to squeeze away the pain. "Oh boy, oh man. Holy hell, this isn't good. This is really not good."

John reached for her and knelt beside her, his face coated with distress. "I'll go fetch Kristen."

"Yeah, you'd better go do that," Grace said, her teeth clenched. "And you might want to hurry."

As John took off in a sprint in the direction of the Masons' home, where Kristen Perry was tending to the others, Grace vomited the food she had eaten this morning. She wiped her mouth with her sleeve, slid her pack off, and reached for her water bottle, rinsing out her mouth and taking a few sips.

John raced away, hopped the gate at the end of the driveway, and disappeared across the road.

After losing sight of him, Grace started hearing the buzzing sounds in the sky again. She began feeling weak and light-headed. Her skin tingled and her vision went blurry, and seconds later, she blacked out.

CHAPTER 3

Thorny Bottom
Hardy County, West Virginia
Wednesday, December 1st

JESSECA HAD A VINTAGE KOREAN War-era M1 carbine propped against her knee. While leaning inward to the conversation, a considerable amount of cleavage protruded from the top of her button-down insulated flannel shirt.

She rested her chin in her palm and perched her elbow on a knee nearest the carbine, which bore indecipherable East Asian inscriptions on both its wooden stock and well-worn leather sling.

Just above her steely gaze, one of Jesseca's eyebrows sat an inch higher than its twin, and the look she was giving off was difficult to interpret. She looked interested, but her interest was mired under multiple layers of skepticism. "So, let me get this straight…let's see if I'm following you correctly." The index finger of her free hand danced in random order. "Basically, you're telling me that the Department of Homeland Security or FEMA…one or the other, or both, has it out for you for some reason, is that right?"

Michelle held up a finger, only to be interrupted before she could offer a reply.

"Hold on—wait a sec…I'm not finished yet," said Jesseca. "And these two federal agencies have sent agents into the mountains specifically to hunt you and your neighbors down. You also believe at one time, they hired a gang of mercenaries on motorcycles to kill all of you. And since that didn't work, they've decided to bait and poison the wildlife you hunt, and poison your sole water source?" Jesseca rolled her eyes and leaned back into the sofa, taking the M1 carbine into her lap. "I gotta tell you, Michelle, that's the best story I've heard in a long time. We may live in the boonies and suffer from a lack of entertainment, but you needn't conjure a story like that just to have an excuse to swing by for a visit."

"I know it sounds far-fetched," Michelle said, "but it's not a made-up story at all, and we have the sick to prove it. Truth is, I didn't want to believe it, either. In fact, I was probably among the hardest to convince. But it's true. It's as true as I'm sitting here with you now."

Jesseca lowered her gaze to the firearm on her lap. "This M1 carbine belonged to my dad. He was probably the last good man…hell, who am I kidding—the *only* good man I've ever known. I loved him to death—still do, and my girls share the feeling. When I told him I was moving to the middle of nowhere with the girls, he about lost his mind. He wouldn't hear of it. He told me he wouldn't let us go unless we had a way to protect ourselves. To this day, it's the only gun we own. In fact, I don't even know how much ammunition we have for it."

"Have you ever needed to use it?"

Jesseca shook her head. "No. Living so far away from people has done a superb job of keeping us from trouble. We have yet to make any enemies—apart from the occasional vagrant racoon, pesky coyote, or hungry black bear." She stared hard at Michelle. "Just so you know, your story isn't difficult for me to believe. Being honest, I've often wondered just how long it was going to be before the sugar and spice fairy tale changed its tune forever."

Michelle furrowed her brow. "I think…I mean, I believe we've already seen it happen. And I would love to sit here and relish every factoid and estimation, but I'm sorry, I didn't come here for that. Time is of the essence. I came here to solicit your help."

Jesseca nodded and half smiled. "I know. I was just giving you shit for taking so long to visit."

Michelle exhaled. "It would have been sooner…but we've had our hands full."

"Alex hasn't stopped talking about you and the others since she's been home. I'm not what you'd call a trusting person, Michelle, but the things Alex has told us about you and Grace and Christian and Lauren, Norman, and all the other names she's brought up, have given me little choice other than to consider all of you my friends, as if I didn't have a reason to before." She paused, leaning back on the sofa again. "So what exactly do you need from me?"

"The last time I was here, you told me you grow practically all of your medicine."

"That we do," Jesseca said proudly. "Analgesics, antibiotics, antihistamines, decongestants…"

"What about antidotes?"

"Hmm…I see what you're proposing. I'll be the first to say I'm no expert, but there's not much that can't be learned by reading." Jesseca gestured with her head to the bookshelf behind her. "I can think of about five books off the top of my head that might have what we're looking for." She paused a moment while concern filled her expression. "How many were poisoned?"

"Quite a few."

"Any idea what it was?"

Michelle reached into her backpack for her husband's only self-published book, opening it to a bookmarked page. She handed the book to Jesseca. "We think it's one of these listed here. Something my husband referred to as weaponized biological agents."

Jesseca probed at the book a moment, then eyeballed Michelle curiously. "Something *your husband* referred to?" She thumbed through the pages, then flipped it over to read through the blurb on the back cover. "Are you saying this is your husband's book?"

Michelle nodded without hesitation. "Yes. He published it a few years ago."

Jesseca smiled. "Holy crap. The girls are going to be thrilled! They know someone who knows someone who's an author! It looks super-interesting, and the blurb genuinely speaks to me. I bet there's a lot of informative subject matter inside." She set the M1 down on the floor, taking care to point the muzzle safely toward the wall. "Would you mind if I kept it for a while so all of us can have a chance to read it? It's been a long time since we've had anything new to read around here."

"Sure, I don't see why not. Just, if you would, please be very careful with it. It's the only one we have."

"You needn't worry about that," Jesseca assured her. "We take good care of books around these parts. They're…well, irreplaceable, if you catch my drift."

Michelle nodded. "I believe I do." Looking up, she saw a sparkling set of eyes peering at her from around the corner of the hallway.

While Jess thumbed through the pages of her husband's book, Michelle waved a finger at Alex—who waved back in kind.

In that instant, Alex emerged and launched herself into Michelle's lap, hugging her around the neck. "Where have you been? It's been a month of days. I never thought it would take this long for you to come visit us…I've been worried about you."

Michelle returned Alex's affection with an embrace of her own. "Don't take it personally. I've been meaning to visit you and your mom for a while now. We've just been busy. Recently though, circumstances have made coming here a priority."

Alex pulled away from Michelle and stared at her with concern, noting the momentousness of Michelle's features. "Has something happened?" Alex pointed at her. "Remember, I can sense worry a mile away."

Michelle nodded. "I haven't forgotten, nor will I. And yes, something *has* happened…something very harmful to us, and I've come here looking for some help."

Alex whipped her head to her mother, her ponytail inadvertently smacking Michelle in the cheek. "Mom? We're going to help them, right?"

Jesseca remained transfixed on the book's pages as she thumbed through them. She hesitated before glancing up at her daughter. "You know how we do things, Alex. At least, I hope you do by now."

Alex furrowed her brow, lowering her head slightly. "I do, Mom. Of course I do."

"These people saved your life and brought you back to me," Jesseca continued, a stern look in her eye. "I thought I'd lost you, and when you showed up with Michelle that day, my world was complete again. Somehow, they were in the right place at the right time—right when you needed them most. Things like that don't *just happen*." She paused. "And now they need *our* help, and there's no way I can tell them no. Of course we're going to help them."

Alex hopped down from Michelle's lap and pranced over, enclosing her mother's neck with her arms.

Jesseca kissed Alex on the temple and, with her eyes closed, nuzzled her like a dam with newborn puppies. "So, listen…we'll be leaving soon. Gather your things…go-bags with extended overnight gear, extra food, and weapons. Pass the word along and have your sisters do the same."

Alex's look of excitement dissipated and was replaced with one of dire importance. She glanced at Michelle momentarily before looking back at her mother and darting away. "Yes, ma'am."

Michelle couldn't help but be amazed at what she was witnessing. The willingness to help pleased her, and the overall reverence and mindfulness of the family structure in Jesseca's home was impressive.

She could remember how rare it had been, especially before the collapse, to see children—particularly teenagers—be this obedient and respectful of their parents. Single-parent households had often seemed the most affected. But it was clear Jesseca had been able to persevere despite society's decaying moral standards.

Jesseca finished perusing Alan Russell's book and carefully folded it closed. Bringing it to her chest, she stood and set it on the table beside her and then made her way to the hallway, turning her head over her shoulder seconds before disappearing. "We'll just be a few minutes. It's been a while since we ventured out, so we need to gather up all our things…that is, if we can find them all." Jesseca held out her hand and smiled. "Make yourself at home while you wait. *Mi casa es su casa.*"

CHAPTER 4

"Every action has equal and opposite reaction. This is law of the universe and spares none. Wrong done and injustice inflicted is paid back in the same coin. No one has escaped justice of the universe. It is only a matter of time."

—Anil Sinha

Exact location unknown
Allegany County, Maryland
Saturday, December 4th. Early morning. Present day

"AND THE ROCKET'S RED GLARE," Lauren said, her voice nearly cooing with joy. Her expression was eager, her eyes skittish and wide, her concentration hinged on the transposing early morning sky.

After a half-dozen or more muffled thumps, beckoning like shotgun blasts going off in the distance, the first in an ensemble of pyrotechnic flares soared into the sky overhead and burst into ignition—the turbulent mixing of gasses letting go a boiling rumble. Subsequent bursts flashed to life seconds later, illuminating the heavens above and draping the landscape beneath in a vivid, flickering, rubescent glow.

The startling light show in the lower troposphere quieted the celebratory squeals and laughter of the crowds outside the crude stockade holding Lauren and the others captive. The overall disposition of their imprisoners had also taken a drastic turn for the worse, and it seemed as though their evening of festivities was coming to an end. The dancing, chanting, and horseplay had ceased to be, and the gathering now stood pale-faced and expressionless, jaws clenched, and brows drawn together in worry, their eyes practically glued to the sky.

Lauren reasoned from their reactions that something similar, or perhaps identical to this had happened to these thugs before. What Christian had shared regarding previous attacks by a militia or paramilitary group, serving as reasoning for their captors' being so brutally hostile toward Fred Mason, was starting to make sense. That correlation aside, she knew positively nothing could serve as justification for their actions, and retribution had become requisite.

Lauren took hold of two wooden supports in front of her and squeezed them while gritting her teeth. "It's time for all of you to get what you deserve." She glanced skyward, feeling a fluttering in her stomach while her heart pounded away in anticipation. "Come on, guys. Make things right. Do what you do best. Send it."

Christian stood like a sentry at Lauren's side, his lips parted, his eyes convex and dreamy, his expression exhibiting childlike wonder at the fiery scene unfolding above them. He was nearly shoulder to shoulder with her, a mere inch of space keeping them apart.

Zero Dark Armageddon, Christian thought. What in the hell did that mean, anyway? Surely the phrase wasn't something Lauren had come up with on her own. But where did she hear it? Who had she heard it from?

Lauren's behavior since he'd met her had never made much sense to him. In fact, it had bowled him over at times, especially in the span of recent weeks while he'd observed her becoming progressively more deliberate and lethal.

Christian didn't know what Zero Dark Armageddon meant, but he got the feeling after the most recent turn of events, coupled with what he was now witnessing, that it was going to be something extraordinary.

Extraordinary. Like the overall mystery of the uncommonly bold, mesmerizing young woman perched so steadfastly inert to his left.

Christian's mind continued to wander as several audible thumps sounded off in the distance, perceptible at first by feel as they vibrated the ground underfoot. *This must be it*, he thought, turning his head to regard Lauren again. He wanted to say something to her—something encouraging, something uplifting, or maybe even offer up a quick joke to further lighten the mood, but he just couldn't find the words. His impulses had abandoned him.

Admittedly, his head was spinning. He had so many questions, dozens more now than he'd ever had before, but Christian made the choice to place them all on hiatus. This was neither the time nor the place. It was time to sit back, watch, and wait. Things were about to get interesting.

Then a thought occurred to him. "You know, I think those are M126 Red Star signal flares," he said, his finger pointing at them. "A guy I knew—a collaborator in the Legionnaires—brought a few to an FTX. Everyone at camp got pretty shitfaced on white lightning that night, and he set them off not long before we all turned in." Christian chuckled. "It freaked people out—especially the old warhorses with PTSD. I'll never forget the looks on their faces. Hard to forget the way the sky looked too."

After a couple of seconds' hesitation, Lauren shrugged with mild disregard. "Did your friend make it through the night?"

"Well, yeah. We trained together the entire day following, sweating out alcohol in the sun, hungover as hell. Why?"

Lauren set a grim smile. "Then he should count himself lucky."

"Lucky?"

"Lucky one of the vets suffering from post-traumatic stress didn't cut his throat or light his tent on fire," Lauren said, her eyes transfixed on the sky. "Their supply catalog designation aside, I think those flares are beautiful. They remind me of an Independence Day fireworks display. Definitely a sight for sore eyes."

Christian gazed upon Lauren thoughtfully, his eyes focusing on the upturned corners of her mouth, a simple yet radiant closed-lipped smile that had been etched on her face in one form or another since the moment she had seen someone she recognized. A person she had referred to only as a friend.

Lauren's so-called friend was an enigmatic, alert, agile man dressed in black military fatigues, wearing body armor and night-vision goggles, armed with a suppressed carbine and a strangely unique sword he had slung across his back.

Since the point of making contact with him, the clouds that normally hung over Lauren's temperament had lifted. She had been practically overjoyed and remained so even now, beyond her efforts to visually suppress her excitement.

Christian counted the number of times he had seen a true, radiant smile from Lauren since they'd been introduced, and it didn't take long to arrive at an answer. The sum was a single-digit integer.

He pondered for a moment what she'd been like before the two crossed paths. What kind of person had she been before the EMP and the blackout, before the day she'd last seen her father—before the end of her world as she'd known it to be. Christian guessed it a good chance that Lauren had been a generally happy person then. Contented and normal. Adventurous to a fault. Kind. Conventional. Popular and full of life. The type of person everyone always wanted to be around and have near them. Just like he had been.

Then he contemplated the other things he had seen. Her unbridled instinct for self-preservation. The willingness to do whatever was needed to survive. Lauren's inner warrior.

Christian had seen her wrath manifest on more than several occasions, directly witnessing the inferno that had oftentimes existed within her eyes. Now the only flame he could detect between her delicate eyelids was one of unpolluted passion and raw courage—attributes of a fierce, young woman who had lost everything, only to keenly stare death in the face and instruct it to fuck off.

As the last few flares ruptured to life, others launched in advance ejected their parachutes one by one, a commencement of their floating descent amidst plumes of dense, twirling, crimson and white smoke.

Confusion was starting to overtake the crowd of wildlings and ruffians gathered outside. They scurried about indiscriminately while gawking at the sky in trepidation and awe.

Several shots rang out as a team of expletive-shouting men took aim on the hovering fireballs, attempting to shoot them down. The men whooped and hollered upon finding their efforts ineffective, only to reload and continue firing their weapons in vain anyway, stopping only at the point when they had exhausted their ammunition supply.

The group's collective rage grew and festered, and the unnerving silence that had overtaken the expanse outside the cage melted away into panic. Infuriated, maniacal cries flared out from the crowds milling about the bonfire, and from that point forward, the commotion began a hasty transformation into chaos and all-out bedlam.

Men began pushing and shoving each other while yelling obscenities in multiple dialects and languages. Heated arguments and fights broke out, many quickly escalating into full-on, no-holds-barred brawls. The social fabric holding the group together had frayed beyond repair.

Two bearded men in tattered clothing, their builds broad and husky enough to challenge a professional football linebacker, tackled each other to the ground and began beating one another senseless. As they wrestled, growled, and shouted incoherent curses, the fight came to an abrupt halt when a third man wearing a dark gray trench coat emerged from the shadows. He pulled a satin-finish .357 Magnum revolver from his waistband and shot both combatants, one point-blank in the face, the other execution-style in the back of the head. Directly following the savage deed, he nonchalantly knelt and rifled through their pockets, gathered whatever possessions he thought valuable, then took his leave of them as if nothing were amiss.

Christian pointed to the men and mused, "Did you see that? They really are a bunch of cornflakes. One minute, they're all buddies, ready to cook us on that fire over there. Now their plans are busted…and they're shooting each other." He sniggered. "This is insane!"

Lauren shook her head, diverting her attention away from the fireworks show to take a knee. "No honor among thieves," she said, motioning for Christian to do the same while she eyeballed the man holding the revolver with caution. "I suppose it shouldn't surprise me that you find this entertaining."

"What? You don't?"

"No," Lauren blurted. "But to be clear…it is strangely gratifying."

Christian moved to one knee as directed. "You're developing a taste for vengeance. Nothing wrong with that, considering what almost happened to us. Look at it this way—what if it escalated? They might have a little civil war over this debacle and wind up shooting each other dead. Would that at least be visually stimulating for you?"

Lauren nodded slightly, flicking a pebble on the ground between the wooden posts. "Visually, mentally, and spiritually. They could kill each other off—wipe themselves out, for all I care."

"Well, my dear, the night is young." Christian nudged her. "Keep your chin up. I have a feeling good things are coming."

"You have no idea," said Lauren, elevating her brow. She turned away, leaning closer to the stockade wall, her smile gradually returning while her adversaries' movements became more and more frantic. They started to disband, heading off alone and in groups to find darker regions in which to lurk or conceal themselves. "They can run, but they can't hide."

A whistling sound caught the attention of everyone within earshot just as the bonfire in the distance became engulfed in a blinding flash of light. A split second after, it detonated into a massive, towering firestorm, showering the area with sparks, blazing hot embers, and burning debris.

Those standing close by, including the man in the trench coat, were obliterated by the blast, not having had the time to react or find refuge. Scores of others within the blast radius were blighted by the concussion, some having their clothes ripped free from their bodies, others being literally cut to pieces by sprays of flying shrapnel.

At the onset of the explosion, Christian reacted, instinctively grabbing Lauren by her arm and pulling her down to the ground with him.

With sharp eyes, Lauren fought against him, but Christian overpowered her. He took hold of her head and wrapped his arms around her, effectively shielding her from the blast's shockwave and superheated drafts as they jolted past, causing the ground and everything around them to shudder ferociously.

Christian spoke softly with his mouth next to Lauren's ear as he eased his grip on her. "Hey—don't punch me, okay? I'm sorry about that—I should've warned you. I think your friend gave us some good advice. We should heed it from here on out."

Her senses overloaded from the blast, Lauren pulled away from him, coughing and brushing dirt and debris from her hair, arms, and chest. She tossed the entwined strands of her hair over her shoulder and grinned nervously, doing her best to convey an expression of gratitude. "I'm going to have to agree with you," she said, barely able to hear her own voice over the ringing in her ears. "Thanks."

Christian shrugged. "No sweat." He meekly gestured behind them. "We should probably get everyone else on board again…before another one goes off."

Lauren glanced over her shoulder and nodded her recognition. She knew who had arrived and was mindful of what was happening. She even had some semblance of an idea of what to expect, and it had become her responsibility to offer direction to the group of terrified faces huddled nearby.

Wetting her lips, she took advantage of a brief intermission in the assault. "Everyone listen to me, please. Like we told you before, stay as low as you can and keep your heads down. Cover your head with your hands and shield your eyes and ears, and try to stay that way until it's over. This is only the beginning."

While Christian echoed her remarks, an agitated man's voice asked, "The beginning? The beginning of what?"

"Yeah—seriously. What the hell is this?" another voice, panic-stricken, called out. "Are we being attacked?"

Lauren shrugged, turning her gaze to Christian momentarily as a set of faint blasts echoed off in the distance. "Just please do as I say. We're not being attacked…we're being rescued."

"Excuse me, miss? How exactly do you know that?" another voice, one carrying a faint British accent, questioned her. "We've seen this happen before, yet we all still remain enslaved here."

Lauren didn't have time to answer him. More explosions, some far away and others close by, silenced the group as the ground trembled beneath them and wafts of heated air passed by.

Christian placed his hand on the dirt. "I suppose that would be 'the bombs bursting in air'." His facial features tensed in urgency. "I think they're getting closer."

Lauren cocked her head to the side just as the detonations intensified. Seconds later, the intensity persisting, they started going off in rapid succession. She plugged her ears with her fingers and tucked her head into her arms to safeguard herself from the blinding flashes of light and concussive jolts emanating from the blasts. The area around the stockade quickly became saturated with thick, billowing dust, smoke, and ash, making it difficult to see and nearly impossible to breathe. Lauren pulled her shirt collar up and over her mouth and nose and waved her hand at the others behind her, attempting to get them to do the same.

The explosions continued relentlessly in an abrupt, reverberating cadence as mortars, rocket-propelled grenades, and other munitions rained overwhelming power and a spectacular display of force upon the encampment. They annihilated every target, personnel or otherwise, leaving behind nearly incomprehensible levels of destruction, and the leftover hostile forces were left paralyzed and in complete disarray, unwilling to put up a fight.

Lauren couldn't help but be curious. It was in her nature. A battle was being fought tens of yards away, and she wanted to see what was happening as the attack transpired. At one point, she wiped her eyes and peered out into the smoky, glowing darkness, hued burgundy by a multitude of burning fires, only to regret her decision mere seconds after making it.

A severed arm, bloodied and still wrapped in a torn shirtsleeve modestly singed by fire, smacked into the wooden poles of the cage, landing on the ground outside directly in front of Lauren and Christian.

"Oh…oh God," Lauren groaned. She turned away and lurched, her hand moving to cover her mouth while fighting her body's sudden urge to regurgitate.

Christian tried to make light of it. He patted her on the back and jested, "That's not something you see every day." He slid his hand through the poles and did his best to move the appendage aside and away from view.

After an assault lasting nearly two minutes, as quickly as they had begun, the outbreak of booming detonations ceased to be. The lingering smoke wafted, swirled, and cleared away, aided by the breeze, and the last of the parachuting luminous flares completed its descent, making a final touchdown with Earth as the dust settled.

Several figures, mere silhouettes, could be seen moving to investigate the flares still burning while others stood by scratching their heads, static and dumbfounded. Some used the respite to tend to their fallen or injured comrades, but nearly all who remained alive were back on their feet, milling about aimlessly.

"Jesus H Christ! Now *that* was somethin' else!" a thin man said while thumbing a Fu Manchu mustache. "A hell of a lot worse than some of the other attacks we've had."

His cohort, a black man wearing a cowboy hat, his face covered in dust and ash, rubbed his eyes before replying. "You think so?" he barked, his voice shuddering. "How'd you come to that conclusion, genius?"

"Do y'all think it's over?" a man in a torn denim jacket standing nearby asked while surveying the devastation, nearly tripping over several dead bodies piled up near his feet. "Think it's the same jerks as last time?"

Fu Manchu huffed, palming a Colt 1911 variant. "Hard to say. Sure looks like it, though."

The black man pulled off his hat and wiped his forehead with his sleeve. "Both of you shut the hell up and get ready to shoot! If it's the same folks as last time, then you both should know by now. Shit's not over yet!"

As the words escaped his mouth, a fusillade of heavy gunfire kicked off. And not unlike the alleged first shot taken in the American Revolution, as portrayed in Emerson's 'Concord Hymn', it was 'the shot heard round the world' that started it all.

A rifle bullet left the muzzle and went instantly supersonic, its organic tracer fuel alight, marking its trajectory. It struck the man in the cowboy hat just below his left eye, splitting his head in half and nearly decapitating him. As he fell in a lifeless heap, what could only be described as a pandemonium of high-cyclic-rate machine-gun fire commenced, rattling off in a turbulent, errant discord. The second wave of the assault had begun.

Fu Manchu turned to run, but was eviscerated by a burst of shots just after taking his first step. Denim Jacket was cut in half at the abdomen only seconds later after watching his comrade drop in a thick mist of blood spatter.

What was transpiring now was unlike anything Lauren had ever seen before and bordered on anything she'd even imagined coming to pass. Her ears felt like they were stuffed full of cotton, and they were starting to ring worse than the first time she'd heard a pistol go off from an adjacent lane at an indoor range years ago. A time when she had been remiss enough to slip off her earmuffs to remove a set of earrings.

The gunfire was devastating and persistent, and there was no escape from it. It emanated from almost every direction from the encompassing boundaries of the encampment. Tracer bullets streaked across the visible landscape like a laser light show at a rock concert, and sparks jumped and sprang to life from friction when the rounds struck concrete or metal objects.

The cage holding Lauren, Christian, Norman, Fred and the others seemed to be the only sanctuary remaining, the only place yet to be fired upon or otherwise struck by one of the previously hurled incendiaries. Outside, the once carousing, chanting, dancing rabble of wicked hooligans never stood a chance. They were being crushed. Their faction's populace appeared to have already been cut in half, and they were losing tens more by the second. The barrage of suppressive heavy-weapons fire continued at the same pitiless rate with no regard for the dwindling numbers, mowing them down like a bush hog through a field of unruly, dense weeds.

Lauren peered just above her forearm to see if she could spot anyone still alive she recognized. The men who had brazenly taken part in Fred's beating were nowhere to be found. Their bizarre bald-headed Shakespeare-spouting leader and Gus, the giant grunting mute who had spat in her face, were also both long gone. She hoped to find them lying amongst the dead. One could only be so lucky.

The type of evil those men possessed, the wickedness inside them that made them tick, had no purpose, no right to remain existent anymore. It was a by-product of the collapse, and they were nothing more than the superfluous afterbirth of humanity, dregs of a society gone astray.

Lauren continued to visually scour the area, searching for anyone or anything related to Dave Graham's unit, but her visibility was severely limited. She couldn't even see where Woo Tang had gone off to. He had disappeared into the darkness not long before the first flare had been sent into the air to light ablaze and set sail.

The only thing observable now was the aftermath of a well-planned, well-executed assault. Only, it looked more like a massacre or a bloodbath—an ethnic cleansing of evil men sent to their graves by a bombardment of precision explosive ordnance and a lethal volley of tracer rounds.

Nearly catching him off guard, Christian turned his head in time to see a man who had crawled over to them on his knees and elbows. When the man extended his arm in Lauren's direction, Christian intervened, kicking the man's hand away with his boot. "Whoa—slow the hell down there, hero. Hands off the lady. Is there something I can help you with?" Christian moved closer to him, his fist poised to strike.

The man drew back, half-covering his face with his hand in anticipation of another hit. "Well, being completely honest, I'm not sure if you can or if you can't," he rebuked, a mild British accent coating his words. "That all depends on if you can tell me what the devil is going on. I think the rest of us here, myself included, have a right to know."

Christian mocked his accent with some added extravagance. "Well, chum...I think it's pretty obvious what the devil is going on. We're getting the hell out of here. So hail a hackney carriage, gather yourself some Hobnobs, and be patient."

Lauren turned to have a look at the man who had decided to join them. He wore a soiled gray sweater with a collared shirt underneath and had on a well-worn designer-brand down jacket that was missing most of its loft. He even had on a necktie, which while slackened and not pulled in tightly, was still threaded through his button-down shirt collar.

There was something about this man—a certain aura perhaps, and for a moment, Lauren thought she recognized him. She had seen his face somewhere before, but couldn't place him. She didn't say anything to him, and the man didn't say anything to her. In fact, he didn't even look her way. He was too busy steaming and cutting his eyes angrily at Christian while he rubbed the pain away from his recently booted hand.

After a period of time had elapsed, the flurry of weapons fire began to die down and eventually terminated altogether. Shouts of men bellowing orders could be overheard, along with the occasional report of a single gunshot. Groups of up to six individuals could be seen entering the boundaries of the camp, most carrying flashlights with smoke-penetrating beams shining through red filters.

Lauren rose when she noticed a group of men heading her way. Six men in black fatigues marched over, and while three of them put their backs to the exterior wall, their rifles covering separate fields of fire, two others removed tools from their packs and worked to unfasten and permanently disable the primitive locking mechanism on the entry gate.

"So, Lauren," Christian said while minding the armed men in black, "before things start to get even more...crazy around here, I have a few questions."

Lauren sniffled and tried brushing her fingers through her hair. "I sort of figured you would. I'm surprised it's taken you this long to start probing."

"Yeah, well, it's been...rather loud. And I didn't think my voice could compete with all the gunfire." Christian gestured to the men outside while lackadaisically rising to his feet. "You said that guy, the one with the sword who was here earlier on, was a friend." He paused long enough for Lauren to gesture her response, then pointed outside to the men in black. "Would that make all these guys…your friends, too?"

"I don't know," Lauren replied, her attention switching beyond those nearby to others in similar uniforms farther away, in what had become a much larger assembly than she had anticipated. "It's hard to say, really." She paused. "The last time I saw them, there was only about a dozen or so."

"The last time you saw…them."

"Mm-hmm."

"Okay. I guess," Christian said, looking befuddled. "You know—I've never been the best at math, but by my count, there's at least a hundred men out there now."

"And I would agree with you. That's an accurate estimate…maybe your math skills are improving."

Christian hesitated. "So…I guess, maybe, whatever…team you used to train with has done some recruiting, then. You know, since the last time you saw them, that is." He glanced away, giving her time to respond, but kept her in the corner of his eye. "Wouldn't you say?"

Lauren quickly turned to him, smiling coyly. "That took you a lot longer to put together than I thought it would."

Christian shrugged. "Yeah, well, you haven't exactly been forthcoming with information."

"You're right," Lauren said, hanging her head a bit. "I haven't been."

"That's okay…I'm used to it. I just did the best I could with what I had," Christian said. "The clues I had to go on—what few there were, have always been rather vague, but it's coming together nicely now."

After the men in black forced the gate open, they removed the door completely from the frame, placed it on the ground, and destroyed it. They moved inside, announced their presence as friendlies without giving their names, then stood by while ushering out the former captives, using their flashlights' red-filtered beams to illuminate the path. Another group of armed men in black had gathered together outside to hand out basic comfort items in the form of bottled water and blankets.

Lauren waited patiently for everyone to exit the stockade, except herself, Christian, Norman, Fred, and Ricky and Austin Brady. When she went to take her first step outside, Woo Tang treaded out from the shadows and moved into her avenue of travel. His mask was pulled under his chin now, and his NVDs were locked in the upward position. She could clearly make out his scar, a feature that had caught her attention upon meeting him years ago and had been key to helping her recognize him again today after he'd practically materialized out of the darkness.

Overcome by everything that had transpired, Lauren didn't know how to act. She found herself speechless. She stood stationary, frozen in time, her memories and wistfulness getting the best of her. *What are you doing? Say something, stupid.*

Woo Tang spoke first, his disposition forthcoming, his face and tone bearing little to no emotion. "Good morning, Lauren Russell. Fancy seeing you here, in a place such as this. Do you...come here often?"

Lauren tried to pull together a smile. Her body trembled while shaking her head in the negative. "No. This is my first time here," she said hesitantly. "And I'm really hoping it's going to be my last."

Woo Tang shifted his stance while one of his eyes focused tighter than the other. "I am glad to hear you say that. I very much hope it is your last visit, too. Places like this should not exist and are certainly not meant for bright young women such as yourself." He took a step closer. "I am in a quandary. It troubles me to see you here, locked inside a corral—a place far better suited for animals like swine or bovine." He paused, looking her over, paying special attention to her torn, ragged clothing, remnants of which were dangling beneath the fleece jacket liner Christian had given her. "As you probably can imagine, seeing you here has spawned many questions. For the moment, I will spare you them and will only concern myself with your physical and psychological well-being." He inched closer and studied her as his expression slackened. "Are you...squared away?"

Lauren hesitated. A potent emotional state in combination with her physical exhaustion was becoming too much to bear. "I've been better," she whimpered, her voice cracking. "It's been a really rough year, and my friends and I have had an even rougher past couple of days. I'm weak, tired, my hair is a mess, and I can't remember the last time I had anything to eat or drink." She sighed, on the verge of tears. "Apart from that, right now...this is the happiest I've been in a really, really long time."

Woo Tang's features softened even more. He nodded and cracked a sheepish grin. "Okay. Fine business. Am I to take it that you are...glad to see me?"

Lauren's body quivered beyond her ability to control it. She closed her eyes and covered her mouth, and then her emotions broke loose from their bonds and overcame her. She dashed to Woo Tang in a burst of tears and latched on to him, her body trembling, wrapping her arms tightly around his neck. She nodded her answer at first, unable to get the words out. "Yes, I'm glad to see you. You…have no idea…how glad I am to see you here."

Woo Tang barely had the time to move his rifle out of the way. "Whoa—easy there, Lauren Russell. I cannot remain on alert with all of that hair of yours blocking my view," he said lightheartedly. "By the way, I know it has been a while since we last saw each other, and I do not want to come across as rude, but have you showered recently?"

Lauren smiled and squeezed him. "Just shut up and hug me back, Jae," she said through tears of pure delight.

Woo Tang relented. "Okay, I give. I suppose…there is no harm in it." He snapped his fingers, sending two of the armed men to stand on either side of them. Only then did he allow himself a moment to close his eyes and respond to the embrace.

"I missed you," Lauren purred. "I missed you so much."

"I can tell. And I…missed you, too."

Lauren pulled away and began wiping her tears. She wanted nothing more than to continue the reunion with her old friend, but she knew there were far more pressing items in need of attention. "Jae, we have a problem—a serious one. Fred is here…and he's hurt really bad. He needs help."

Woo Tang drew back, displaying his surprise at yet another bombshell. His hand moved to his rifle. "Fred? Are you referring to Fred Mason?" He peered over Lauren's shoulder through the entrance into the dark recesses of the cage. "He is here with you?"

"Yeah, he's here. Him and a few others."

The former Navy SEAL's brows knitted. "Take me to him."

As Ricky and Austin Brady passed by on their way out without so much as even glancing at her, Lauren ushered Woo Tang farther into the cage to where Fred lay with Norman tending to him.

Woo Tang took a knee and sent a brief, supportive nod Norman's way while removing a flashlight from a pocket on his plate carrier and bringing it to life with a button click. He studied Fred's condition with a stringent, yet deeply concerned gaze before placing his fingers to a button located next to a microphone strapped to his neck. "Net, this is yellow one actual. I have wounded—category immediate...single male patient at the corral with severe facial fractures, multiple penetrating wounds and lacerations. Patient is unconscious and breathing at this time. Request immediate evac. Watch for my lasso. Over." Woo Tang turned and motioned to his men, instantly seizing their combined attention. "I need an IR lasso in the clouds, gentlemen."

"You guys have radios?" Lauren asked, her eyes studying the device, following a single wire to a covert earpiece. Another set of wires snaked to a short rubber antenna mounted to the back of his plate carrier. "I thought Dave hated those things."

"He still hates them and always will. But we use them on assaults such as these because they are available, and it is the prudent thing to do."

"Was that Stewie who responded, then?" Lauren asked, her voice slurring. "Please tell me he's here with you guys."

"No, Stewie is not here with us. Not today, anyway. He is with Staff Sergeant Reese, preparing for another operation near the town of New Creek."

Lauren looked confused. "What do you mean another operation?"

"It is one of many. Do not worry, we have several other highly skilled medics, all of whom are capable of helping Fred."

"Jae, Fred needs a hospital...and a doctor," Lauren urged. "Those men...they beat him so badly. I watched it happen right in front of me. It was awful."

Woo Tang rose. "Lauren Russell, as you may have already noticed, you are standing on a battlefield. This is a war, and bad things happen in wars and on battlefields. This battle is over now, and what is done is done. We will do everything in our power to help Fred. He is a brother, and we have a medical treatment facility not far from here, where he can be taken to be patched up." He went to place his hands on her shoulders, causing Lauren to wince when one hand got too close to the back of her head. Woo Tang furrowed his brow. "Have you sustained injuries yourself as well?"

"No. I mean...yes," she stammered. "Yeah...a little."

While steadying her with a solid grip on her shoulder, Woo Tang pointed the beam of his flashlight intermittently into Lauren's eyes, sweeping back and forth across each one several times. "Your speech is slurred. And one of your pupils is dilated more so than the other. You look concussed."

"If she looks that way, that's because she is," Norman said from his spot on the ground, no longer able to keep his silence.

Lauren sighed irritably. "Thanks, Norm."

"Sorry, sweetums, but I know how proud you are. You never would've admitted it yourself."

Without another word, Woo Tang advanced behind her and shined his flashlight on her head while moving her hair up and out of the way. "Holy Moses. What happened to you? Get in a fight with a Buick or something?"

Lauren gritted her teeth from the pain of having her hair repositioned. "I got blindsided."

"You most certainly did. I take it you have a hellish headache to accompany the swelling I am seeing?"

Lauren nodded.

"Did you lose consciousness?"

"Yeah. I was in the woods when it happened. When I woke up, I was here."

"Do you feel shaky? Numb? And have you vomited recently?"

"Yes, yes, and…almost, but it wasn't because of the headache."

Woo Tang returned to his spot in front of her, dousing his light. "I believe we should have our medics take a look at you as well."

"Fine, fine. Just tend to Fred first, okay?" Lauren insisted.

"It is already done." Woo Tang gestured to the headlights of an approaching vehicle.

As the vehicle came to a stop, several men in black fatigues jumped out and, after procuring a canvas stretcher from the rear of the vehicle, made their way promptly into the cage. They placed Fred on the stretcher, strapped him down, and hoisted him away.

Christian finally made his way over as Fred was being carried out. When Woo Tang saw him, he stared at Christian fiercely, his hand moving to the backstrap of a holstered Sig Sauer.

Lauren saw immediately and moved to intercept. She put a hand on Woo Tang's tensing forearm, preventing him from drawing his weapon. "Jae…he's a friend. It's okay. This is Christian." She then pointed to

Norman. "And that's Norman. He's one of Dad's best friends. He used to come with us to Point Blank, but I don't think you've met him before."

"That is accurate, we have not met," Woo Tang said, his hand moving away from his sidearm. He regarded Norman and Christian for a moment and said, "Gentlemen, I apologize for the unapproachability. I assure you there is no animosity here. But while I do know Lauren Russell and have for years, I am not familiar with either of you."

"I'm not offended," Norman said, just now getting to his feet. "Everything being equal, I'm just enthused with the thought of not dying today. Thanks for getting us out of this mess."

Christian turned his head, noticing two of the men in black now had their rifles trained on him. "Are you sure about that no-animosity thing?"

Woo Tang smiled uncomfortably and motioned for the men to lower their weapons. "All parties are confirmed friendlies. Set up a perimeter," he ordered, and the men hurriedly dispersed. He turned to Lauren, and while angling his M4 carbine back to a ready position, he slowly ushered her away from Christian and Norman. "We must speak alone. I am sorry we cannot spend more time catching up, but the op is not yet complete, and my team must get back to business. Before we go, I would like to brief you. Would you prefer now or later?"

"Brief me?"

"To bring you up to speed. It will only take a moment."

"Okay," Lauren said shyly. "I guess now, then."

"First order of business is the neutralization of all remaining hostiles, which includes those who may have gotten away during the assault. Once the remainder of the unit arrives, we will strip the encampment of food, fuel, weapons, and supplies, then make camp for the night. We are set to rendezvous with Staff Sergeant Reese and Unit Delta tomorrow at a rally point sixty klicks due west, where we will rearm, regroup, and make ready for the next op."

Lauren began shaking her head. She held up a hand. "Jae, hold up, just wait a minute. Neutralize all the hostiles you want…but I don't know anything about a Unit Delta or some rally point or any op. We aren't even supposed to be here right now. Before we got ambushed, captured, and brought here, we had a mission of our own. Things aren't exactly squared away at home…we have sick people there, and we need to find a doctor somehow and get back as soon as we can with help."

Woo Tang exhaled through his nostrils. "I am sorry to hear of your difficulties at home, Lauren Russell. I can only imagine how upside down things must be for you. Finding you here can only serve as a preface for me, and for us. It was not something we expected."

"Tell me about it."

Woo Tang removed a glove and compassionately rubbed a spot of grime from Lauren's cheek with his thumb. "You know I am a man of honor. I would very much like to help you, and I would if I were able to. I would gladly join you on your mission and help you find the assistance you need and even accompany you back to your home. But as the situation stands, I cannot. Those decisions are ones I am not at liberty to make on my own." Woo Tang squared his shoulders. "If you need to do something other than accompany us, something which deviates from our current objectives, you will need to discuss it with you-know-who."

Lauren folded her arms and nodded. "Okay, fine. I'll do that. And where is you-know-who?"

"You-know-who is en route," Woo Tang said, looking down at his watch. "ETA…approximately ten to fifteen mikes. You can wait here for him if you prefer. It should not be much longer."

"He knows I'm here?" Lauren asked, taking a quick glance at Woo Tang's watch, an item she had done away with long ago.

"Affirmative."

"You told him?"

"Affirmative."

Lauren hesitated, slipping her hands into her pockets. "What did he say?"

Woo Tang strolled off and outside the stockade, gesturing for Lauren and the others to follow him. While glancing at one of his men, he pointed and said, "Burn it. Make certain the materials can never be used for this purpose again."

"Jae? Are you going to answer me?" Lauren reiterated, her tone elevated, sounding slightly perturbed. "What did he say?"

Woo Tang grabbed some blankets and several bottles of water from the soldiers handing them out and brought them to Christian and Norman. He took the remaining blanket to Lauren and, after handing her a bottle of water, wrapped it around her shoulders, looking to her only a second before turning away. "He did not say anything."

CHAPTER 5

Allegany County, Maryland
Saturday, December 4th. Present day

CHRISTIAN MOVED IN CLOSER BY Lauren's side. He didn't say anything at first and, after a moment, nudged her softly with his elbow.

Lauren stood in place with her jaw set and her expression stone-faced, looking as though she had just seen a ghost. She seemed ostensibly immersed in thought, fully absorbed in her current state of mind, but that didn't hinder Christian from mouthing off.

"Thanks for the brief introduction back there," he said. "After that rather flamboyant rescue, I was really looking forward to meeting that guy."

Still no reply came from Lauren in return. With lips slightly parted, she grimaced while her mind ran through the likelihood of what it would be like seeing Dave Graham and other familiar faces again for the first time after so much had ensued.

Warming up inside the wool blanket Woo Tang had provided her moments before, her heart raced, and her skin was tingly, like she had just awoken from a dream. Things almost didn't seem real to her, she felt excited, yet unsettled.

"Your friend seems like a real treat," said Christian, feeling the need to persist. He took several deep gulps from the bottle of water he'd been given. "Speaks pretty good English through that accent of his. Decent personality, too. And that sword…I got a good look at it. That is one fine piece of weaponry. Not exactly what I'd call a *commonplace* weapon, but hey, I have a thing for kukris—and we're all entitled to our tools of the trade. Hell, going by appearances alone, looks to me like we're right smack-dab in the middle of a war now. Rapid gunfire, explosions, death around every corner. A real-life hell on earth."

Lauren sulked as she watched Woo Tang move farther away, bounded by his squad of heavily armed, ACU-clad men she'd never seen or met until today. She tightened the fold in her arms and shifted her weight to one side. "You talk too much sometimes."

Christian pursed his lips, then rubbed his chin. "I do? Sorry, I—"

"Yes, you do. And you choose to do so on the worst possible occasions." Lauren huffed bitterly and walked off, but Christian reached for her elbow, pulling her to a stop before she got too far.

Lauren turned to him, forcing his hand away. "Do you remember what happened the last time you tried your luck with me?"

Christian backed off in surrender. "Hey, what the hell? I was just messing around. Relax."

"I'm not in the mood."

"Damn. You were fine just a minute ago. In fact, dare I say, it's probably the happiest I've ever seen you before."

"Christian, you might want to take note of this and heed it well. A woman's moods are like the weather, only worse. They can change at any given moment without warning," Lauren asserted. "And it can happen either by chance or by decision. You should keep that close to heart—especially if you want this thing to work out between you and my sister."

Christian inadvertently took a few steps backward. "Okay. I'll do that. But for your information, this thing between me and your sister means a hell of a lot to me. It's not just a *thing*." He paused for a moment. "Look, I'm sorry…I guess I felt the need to rejoice a little. A few hours ago, I thought we were all headed to a meeting with the grim reaper, until your friend with the sword showed up, that is."

"Rejoice all you like," Lauren hissed. "We haven't achieved one damn thing we left the valley for yet. Fred is hurt, I've been officially diagnosed with a concussion, and there's still *a lot more* to be concerned about. Or have you forgotten?"

"I haven't forgotten anything," Christian replied. "I know we still have a crisis back home, and I'm worried, same as you are. But I'm also excited. It's good to still be alive and see the sun coming up over the horizon. It could have very easily gone the other way."

"I realize that."

Christian paused a moment to casually adjust his posture. He stretched and crossed his arms. "So, what's shorty's deal, anyway?"

Lauren cocked her head, cutting her eyes at him, determining he was referring to Woo Tang. "His *deal*?"

"Yeah. What makes him tick? Where did he get all that—I don't know...machismo from? I mean, he looks buff. Definitely looks like he's spent some time in the gym, but the man is barely five and a half feet tall. That bigheaded persona he's exuding has to stem from something."

Lauren seethed. "Damn you. You can be such an asshole. Bigheaded? Jesus, Christian, you don't know anything about him. Woo Tang is the furthest thing from bigheaded."

"*Woo Tang*?" Christian repeated, attempting to sort out the familiarity of the nickname. "I take it that's not his *real* name."

"Don't sidebar. In the few minutes you've been around him, I haven't the vaguest clue how you've managed to get the wrong impression. That man is the epitome of honor, integrity, discipline, and courage."

"That sounds like rhetoric from one of Fred's speeches coming from your mouth." Christian took a few hesitant steps closer to her, but remained far enough away to gauge Lauren's increasingly agitated mood without endangering himself. "So what is he? Or I guess I should say *was* he? Government contractor? Bounty hunter? Military?"

Lauren hesitated and turned away, her lips pressing together. She bit the inside of her cheek. "He was an operator."

"What kind?"

"The latter...of the ternary of dogmatic choices you gave."

"Really?" Christian droned, jerking his head back. "What branch?"

"The Navy."

"Heh. No shit. Short stuff is a squid, huh?"

"No, short stuff is a combatant swimmer," Lauren blurted out while still looking away, her expression floored. "At least he used to be."

Christian perked up, his brow elevating. "And now we're getting somewhere." He pointed his finger beyond into the hustle and bustle of black-clothed, armed men moving with regulation amidst the surrounding grounds. "So that would make all these other guys one and the same."

"Like I told you before, I don't know all of them," replied Lauren. "But the ones I trained with, all of Dave's original unit, were either veterans or actively serving before hell broke loose."

"Dave?" Christian asked, turning to her with a smirk. "Hey, Lauren, let's pretend for a second I don't know who that is."

Lauren simpered uncomfortably, her calm only just beginning to return. "Sorry. Dave Graham. The unit commander. He's a former Green Beret. I met him when my dad took me to learn basic tactical shooting on my sixteenth birthday."

"The unit commander," Christian repeated, taking another drink. "All right. I'm going to go out on a limb here. Seeing as how you're on a first-name basis with the leader of the group of badasses who just turned our most recently acquired enemies into dust." He paused. "Is this *Dave* also…a friend?"

Lauren smiled and soon nodded with confidence. "Yes. He most definitely is a friend. And if anyone can help us get what we need *and* find a way back home, it's going to be him." She tilted her head and spoke in a placated tone. "So please don't screw it up, okay? Don't do something stupid or run off at the mouth like you ordinarily do and torque him off. Doing so wouldn't be wise. Trust me."

Christian nodded, looking puzzled. "You sound like you speak from experience."

"And to help you put together the full connection, Dave happens to be Kim Mason's brother, making him—"

"Fred's brother-in-law," Christian cut in, his brows elevating. "I see." He paused, turning away, his face displaying mild astonishment. "Small world."

Lauren rolled her lips between her teeth. "In some cases, too small. I have no idea how he's going to react to seeing Fred in the condition he's in."

"Or how he's going to react to seeing you in the condition you're in."

"Yeah," Lauren agreed. "I don't know what I'm going to tell him, or what I'm supposed to say about that…or anything else he asks about."

Christian huffed. "Come on, Lauren. I know you just got your bell rung, but that should be a gimme for you."

"Huh?"

"It's obvious you have a history with this man," said Christian. "If he knows you, he probably cares about you." He paused. "Just tell him the truth."

Several minutes later, amidst the parade of bodies moving in and around the camp, Lauren saw several men in black ACUs on the approach, none of whom she recognized, failing one. The squad marched toward her and Christian vigorously, their rifles held at low-ready, their grime-covered faces beneath battle helmets displaying looks that could only be described as intimidating.

"You might want to make yourself scarce for a little while," Lauren told Christian while eyeballing the face of the man in the middle, who could be none other than Dave Graham. "I'm not exactly sure how this is going to go down."

"I thought this guy was your friend."

"He is. But we haven't seen each other since…since before. He doesn't know everything that's happened to us, or to me…or anything else. And he doesn't know you." Lauren turned to him. "I promise I'll acquaint you when the time is right. But I need to reintroduce myself first."

Christian hesitated, then finally nodded while giving off an air of reluctance. "So with your old friends back in play, I guess I'm not needed anymore, is that it?"

Lauren sighed. "Christian, come on—"

"Hey, it's okay. I'm fine. I'll just take a casual stroll around the remnants of the prison camp that nearly killed us. You know, just like any other day." He pointed to the line of railcars in the distance. "Guess maybe I'll go over there, check out the cute little choo-choo train or something. Maybe I'll find a box of Cheerios to munch on."

CHAPTER 6

Wolf Gap
Hardy County, West Virginia
Wednesday, December 1st

CHAD MASON FINISHED STRAPPING DOWN a backpack loaded with several days' worth of gear to the backside of a custom motorcycle he'd recently acquired. Several feet away, his brother, Mark, was busy doing the same with a similar-looking bike, another that had been salvaged following the battle with the Marauders.

In the light of daybreak, the two sent infrequent looks each other's way and quietly critiqued one another's actions. Mark's look was one of determination, while Chad's expression displayed the gravity of the decisions they were making, and of the journey they were about to embark on.

Several yards behind them, an engine came to life, its muffler burping and sputtering abruptly in a loud, audacious chorus while the smell of exhaust fumes wafted through and permeated the air. Sasha jerked forward on her bike and squeezed the clutch while ramping the throttle, increasing the engine's volume level dramatically. She then casually leaned the bike on its kickstand, tilted the handlebars, and glided her body from the seat in a noticeably suggestive manner.

She pranced over to join the brothers and gave Chad's ride a curious glance before looking in Mark's direction. "Goddamn," she breathed, sliding her fingers into her front pockets. "I could really use a cigarette.

I'm guessing neither of you boys smoke, do you? You two look a little too demure for that."

"Nope, sorry," Chad answered her. "Even if we did, cigarettes wouldn't be easy to come by these days. You'd be shit out of luck."

"Yeah, there is that." Sasha leered, looking somewhat annoyed. "Swell. Maybe I can roll up some dry pine needles. Got any notebook paper?"

Chad shook his head, smirking. "Fresh out."

Mark reached into an interior pocket of his jacket and pulled out a pack of unopened cigarettes, offering them to Sasha, much to her surprise. "I snagged these from a pile of garbage we gathered after the fight. There was all sorts of stuff in there, cigarettes included. Figured they might be worth something someday."

The tension released in Sasha's expression as her eyes grew wide. "Thanks, kid. You just saved my life…again," she said, taking the pack from him. She pulled a cigarette from it and placed the filter between her lips, taking a moment to study the pack. "It's not my brand, but I really couldn't care less right now." She ignited it with a Zippo Mark provided, and took a few puffs, then pulled it away to swallow over an impending hack. "Still got that map I gave you?"

Mark nodded while reaching into his pocket.

"I take it you still plan on going with us?" Chad quizzed, his steely gaze transfixed on the woman with streaked hair.

Sasha nodded. She blew a plume into the air while unfolding the map. "You see me standing here, don't you?"

"Yeah, I do—you're kinda hard to miss," Chad heckled. "But do you really think it's such a good idea after all you've been through?"

"I feel fine, stud. Thanks for asking."

Chad nodded, showing off a sardonic grin. "Fine. But if you get hurt out there, you're on your own." He adjusted the H&K MP5 hanging by a sling over his shoulder, the same close-quarters weapon his brother had slung across his chest. He gestured to Sasha's idling motorcycle. "Are you sure you can ride?"

Sasha gave Chad the stink eye and took an immensely long drag from her cigarette, exhaling smoke from her nose. "Look, stud. This flawless keister of mine has been riding on two wheels since it was old enough to go commando. Now, if you don't mind, I'd appreciate it if you'd stop troubling yourself over my welfare and start concerning yourself with what we're getting ready to do." She glanced at Mark and then ogled Chad sheepishly. "Speaking of which, and I might've had a brain fart, because I can't remember if I asked already, but I'm going to need a gun." She pointed at Mark's MP5. "One of those will do."

Chad let out a chuckle. "Yeah, I knew that was coming."

"You knew what was coming?" Sasha probed.

"I'm not giving you a gun," Chad declared, pointing at his brother. "And don't you even think about it, Mark. I'm serious, bro."

"Seriously? Why not?" Mark inquired. "If something bad happens, three people with guns are a lot better than two with guns and one without."

Chad stood at attention. "She's gained your trust already? You barely even met her, had about three full conversations with her, and you're already sure she won't shoot you in the back if given the chance? How do you know this whole thing isn't a trap? What if there aren't any girls locked up in some basement? Have you given any thought to how many ways this can go wrong?"

Sasha took one last drag and dropped her cigarette to the ground, stomping it out with her boot. She pointed a finger at Chad, looking perturbed. "Easy there, stud. You're being a little douche right now, and you don't have to be. Tell you what, for the sake of argument, forget I asked. If something bad does happen and you feel I need one, fine, gimme one then. But until then, I won't give a shit." She paused. "I'd rather gain your trust and be looked upon for doing the right thing than be judged for the color of my hair, the clothes I'm wearing, or the assholes I used to spend most of my time with. I get it, you know…my past isn't all sunshine and rainbows, but I've had about all I can take of that judgmental crap."

"Sorry, Chad, but I agree with her," said Mark. "I think she deserves a little leeway after what she helped prevent happen. We could've been slaughtered if she hadn't taken a stand. She risked her life for us."

"You want to give her leeway, fine. Give her leeway," Chad said. "But we're not giving her a gun." He turned his back to them and walked off towards the hide they had built in the woods near the barricade. "I'm going to have a final chat with the Brady boys before we go. Mark, if you give her a gun…when I get back, I'm shooting her myself."

Sasha and Mark stood there and watched him leave.

"Well, isn't he a treat," Sasha purred. "It takes a lot of practice to be that much of an ass-bandit."

"That's just Chad," Mark explained. "It's in his genes...he's a lot like our dad, just not as crusty. Lucky for me, I ended up a lot more like Mom, but I think Meg got half and half."

"Meg?"

"Megan. Our sister."

Sasha nodded and lit up another cigarette. "What made your dad into such a curmudgeon? Did he have a hard life or something? Abusive parents? Drug addiction?"

"No," Mark said, shaking his head. "He's a Ranger."

Sasha lifted a brow. "Park ranger? Forest ranger?"

Mark chuckled. "*Army* Ranger. The ones who carry bigger guns."

Sasha laughed at herself. "Oh," she said. "My next guess would've been Texas Ranger, but now I'm glad I didn't say anything." She took a few puffs from her cigarette. "So I guess the two of you had an interesting childhood, being brought up in a military household and all."

"Interesting isn't the word I would use, more like trying. My brother and I had to toe the line all the time for everything, even when it came down to something simple like brushing our teeth or making our beds. Dad was the sergeant major, making him the sourpuss, while Mom always played the mediator. I don't know if you can tell, but my brother is more disciplined. He's always been better at conforming than me."

Sasha nodded as smoke drifted from her teeth. "Oh, that's as clear as Waterford crystal." Reaching out, she put her fingers to Mark's wind-chilled cheek. "For what it's worth, kid, so far as looks are concerned, you won that battle with your brother. Keep your head up."

Mark studied the woman awkwardly while his cheeks filled with color. "Um, thank you," he said with a shiver as goosebumps rose on portions of his skin. They dissipated upon seeing his brother making his way back to them, and Mark's focus slowly drifted away from Sasha. "How did that go?"

Chad shrugged, his hands held outward. "Actually, not as bad as I thought. The sweet tea went a long way. Tommy and Wayne both said their mom hasn't had sugar to make sweet tea with in years, and then they asked me for more. They said we're covered for twenty-four hours...so as long as we can get this done in a day, mum's the word."

Sasha turned away, heading for her ride. "Okay, no time to lose, then. Let's blow this joint." She straddled her bike and zipped up her jacket, reaching for a pair of leather gloves buried in the outside pockets, then pulled them on one finger at a time. Sasha then removed a black wool beanie from one of the saddlebags and pulled it on, down over her head, covering her ears.

Chad and Mark both jumped on their motorcycles and took a moment to put on helmets before starting them up.

Chad waved to Sasha. "Sure you don't want a helmet? There's an extra low-cut open-face one in my right saddlebag."

Sasha chuckled. "I think I'll do without this time around, if you don't mind."

Chad gave her a look of indifference. "Oh, I don't mind at all. It's your brain hanging in the balance, not mine."

"Listen, stud," Sasha barked. "In the span of my life, I've been abducted, beaten, tortured, stabbed, gang raped, and passed around like a communal Fleshlight through the germ-infested ranks of an outlaw motorcycle club. I've recently been shot three times, once in the head, only to somehow be parked here having to explain myself to you for some appalling reason. I've also been a two-pack-a-day smoker since the day I turned fourteen. If not even one of those things managed to kill me, not wearing a helmet today isn't either. I'll take my chances."

Chad nodded. "Funny—you bringing up getting shot in the head. I was there that day. And that helmet you were wearing then? Probably saved your life."

After the brothers started their bikes, the group departed Wolf Gap and headed into the Shenandoah County, Virginia, side of the National Forest along Wolf Gap Road. With Chad taking the lead, they motored down the narrow turns, soon leaving the forest boundaries and arriving at state Route 42.

Looking both ways along the abandoned highway, the group turned and headed east along the route Sasha had indicated, passing by neighborhoods of dilapidated homes and farms, and inactive power and telephone lines cascading between poles, long since forgotten.

Occasionally, along the way they would pass a car or truck that had been left in place by its owner for reasons unknown. Sometimes they'd be in the way, and the trio was forced to veer around. Sporadic skeletal structures, left over from livestock and other farm animals, could be seen lying about in the fields, haphazardly slaughtered long ago for food after that very luxury had become scarce.

At the intersection with Stoney Creek Road, Chad motioned for Mark and Sasha to pull forward in parallel with him. He asked for the map, and Sasha handed it over just as Mark turned and spotted two human corpses not far away in a drainage ditch. Both were beyond the point of being decomposed, their clothing barely clinging to what was left of their frames, acting as the only leftover indicator of who they had once been.

Mark hung his head to the side. He covered his mouth with a hand as his stomach churned. "Oh…my God," he said, barely over his breath. "That's…wretched."

Sasha lit another cigarette and casually leaned over to examine the gruesome scene. "That one looks like he had his head smashed in with something big. His skull's completely flattened."

Chad glanced over while minding the map. "Bludgeoned? Or did somebody run him over?"

Sasha shrugged. "Could be either-or. The other body looks female, but it's tough to tell. Not sure what happened to her…but there's a few holes in her shirt. Probably shot to death."

At that point, Mark emptied his guts onto the pavement near his feet.

"Look at it this way, kid," Sasha said to Mark. "At least they've rotted past the point of smelling god-awful."

Mark choked. "How can you say that? How can you be so passive?"

"That's just the world we live in, kid, and I'm used to it. It's natural selection, only the strong survive. It's the way things were in the beginning, before we all got coddled and became soft. Nature's cruelty is starting to take over again. I'm surprised you haven't figured that out by now."

Mark wiped his mouth on his sleeve and reached for a bottle of water strapped to his pack. "I've learned plenty already, but it doesn't change the fact that it's difficult to look at."

Chad handed Sasha back the map. "My brother used to have a hard time watching those National Geographic shows. You know, the ones in the Serengeti when the cheetahs would chase down the gazelles and claw out their entrails, or when a lion would go to town on an antelope's ass while it screamed the whole time from being eaten alive." He chuckled. "Mother Nature can be a real bitch sometimes, right, bro?"

Mark gave Chad the finger. "You can shut the hell up anytime, *bro*."

The trio pulled away from the intersection with the corpses and followed the road until eventually passing through the town limits of Edinburg and, not long after, finding their way to the road leading into the last neighborhood ever to be ransacked by the Marauders MC.

Sasha leaned in and turned onto the road, only to pull to a stop a few yards in, waving both hands down towards the pavement. She promptly shut off her engine.

Hopping off her bike, she instructed both Chad and Mark to do the same while pushing hers off the road and over into the drainage ditch with urgency. "We gotta find something to cover these up with. Trees, bushes, trash, I don't know…something."

"What did you see?" Chad asked. "What's over there?"

Sasha whipped her head around and several long blond-streaked strips of hair slipped from the confines of her beanie onto her shoulder. "You didn't see the trucks?"

Chad glanced at his brother. "We've been seeing cars and trucks and whatnot the whole way here, but no one's been around. What's the difference?"

Sasha pointed down the road to the cul-de-sac. "There's a whole convoy of them…and they're not supposed to be there! That's the difference, stud."

Chad's eyes grew wide. "I knew it! See, Mark? This is exactly what I was worried about."

Mark had begun shoveling piles of leaves from the ditch and areas surrounding, attempting to camouflage his motorcycle. "Just shut up and help me, okay?"

Chad sighed and sped to his brother's aid. He began removing gear and weapons from the cycles while Sasha attempted to get a better look without being noticed.

"Do either of you have a pair of binoculars?"

Mark uncovered his pack and unzipped a pocket, removing a set of armored binoculars, then tossed them to Sasha.

Sasha spent a moment studying the scene at the end of the road through the magnified lenses. Parked in a semicircular fashion, lined up one behind the other, was a collection of vehicles, mostly SUVs and at least one school bus that had been repainted black to match the others.

Then she saw someone she recognized. "Well, look who it is," Sasha hissed. "Seth Bates. And he's giving orders now. I never knew that *beiber* was good for anything, other than being somebody's bitch."

"Who's Seth Bates?" Chad asked, glancing over his shoulder. "Friend of yours?"

Sasha sighed and removed the binoculars from her eyes. "Ha! Hardly. He's a light-in-the-loafers DHS dweeb."

"I'm sorry...did you just say he's DHS?" Chad inquired.

"That's what I said."

"How do you know that?" Mark asked, looking unsettled.

Sasha pranced over, her boot heels sinking into the soft grass alongside the road. "Well, my MC *did* work for them," she said, moving to get down on one knee. "And even if I didn't know him, all those blacked-out vehicles and tinted windows would be a dead giveaway."

Chad huffed and grabbed his water bottle while falling back into the tall grass on his rear. "Great. That's just great. Now what do we do, bro? This was your foolproof plan. Hope you got a plan B hidden up your ass somewhere, since this one appears to be FUBAR."

"What if I told you I did have a plan B and it didn't involve you?"

Chad spit out his water. "And what if I told you to go to hell?"

"Oh, please," Sasha griped, scooting herself in between Chad and Mark while unzipping her jacket to reach for her smokes. "The two of you are brothers, I get that, but this pantywaist bickering has got to stop." She pulled out a cigarette from the pack, lit it, and pulled on it merrily. "Now, I've never been an expert on strategy or tactics, and I've never once pretended to be the smartest person in the bunch, but seems to me, regardless of what our plans are, the first thing we need to do now is find a place to hide. And I mean *vanish*."

Chad nodded, the outline of his face becoming stern. "You're right. If these guys see us here, we're screwed. Next question is, what do we do after that?"

Sasha noticed Mark's anxiety and handed her cigarette to him after taking a long drag. "Take a puff, kid. It soothes the nerves."

Mark looked at her strangely before taking a drag and coughing out the exhaled smoke from his lungs.

Sasha patted him on the back to coax the gagging away, then took the cigarette from him before he dropped it. "Hang in there. It passes." She smiled and rolled her eyes. "I remember my first time...well, barely." She turned to Chad, offering him a toke, but he refused. "How far away do you think we are from where we...I mean, where you guys live?"

Chad shrugged. "Ten, maybe fifteen miles," he replied. It's a long way to go on foot." He pointed to Sasha's black leather riding boots, which carried a one-and-a-half-inch heel. "Especially for you and those shit kickers."

Sasha put the cigarette between her lips and tucked her hair back under her hat. "These aren't shit kickers—they're ass stompers. And they're not as bad as they look...actually pretty comfortable, and they provide great ankle protection. But it's the Dr. Scholl's insoles that do the trick...feels like walking on air." She cocked her head to the side, lifting her brow. "I remember wearing sneakers when I was a little girl, nice ones, you know? I think they were Reeboks or something else my parents could barely afford. Ever since the MC took me in, it's been nothing but black leather boots on these footsies. They kinda grow on you, you know?"

A smirk grew across Chad's face and he shook his head, attempting not to laugh. "No, I don't know."

"It's about time you loosened up."

CHAPTER 7

Mason residence
Trout Run Valley
Wednesday, December 1st

HER SENSES GRADUALLY RETURNING TO her, Grace took in a breath, exhaled, and opened her eyes.

Grace knew she wasn't at home, and for the moment, she didn't know exactly where she was. She was lying horizontally on her back, and there was a cobweb-covered, stippled ceiling above her. The flickering of nearby candlelight was casting a mixture of shadows on a wall covered in faux-wood paneling to her right.

She rolled herself over in the other direction and found a familiar face, that of her neighbor from across the road. "Kim?"

Kim Mason smiled at her, but it wasn't one of her normal, calm, hospitable smiles.

"Where am I?"

"In the basement," Kim replied in a whisper.

"Um...how long was I out?"

"Just a few hours. Not long. Not too long at all."

Fighting away the mental fuzz, Grace tried to recollect what had happened. "The last thing I remember was feeling like my insides were being twisted up something fierce. It was some of the worst cramps I've ever felt...and I get the regular ones pretty bad anyway, you know? Then John ran off for help. Where is he? Is he still here?"

Kim didn't answer.

Grace brought the back of her hand to her forehead. "Shoot me straight…what's wrong with me, Kim? I feel sweaty and sticky, and my stomach feels like there's a gerbil making a nest in it. Am I sick? Like Lee and the others? I have a fever, don't I?"

Kim shook her head leisurely and, not long after, glanced for a brief second over her shoulder. "You might have a slight temperature, but that's not uncommon for anyone dealing with stress. It's nothing to be worried about."

"What do you mean? Something's wrong with me, right?" Grace's voice grew panicky. "I know there is…that's why I threw up. That's why I passed out. I'm sick, aren't I? It's just my luck for something like that to happen."

Kim didn't respond, her attention too absorbed on the goings-on behind her. As she reached over to place a hand on Grace in an effort to quiet her down, a man whom Grace didn't recognize emerged from the candlelit shadows.

In one hand, he grasped a bolt-action hunting rifle with a wooden stock, while his other hand was busily feeding a length of jerky into his mouth. He gnawed on the meat from the side of his lips, gripping it with his molars while moving his hand away and closer to a revolver he had holstered in a cross draw.

He inspected Kim, then heeded Grace. "You two need ta keep it down over here. Yins all know those be the rules. And rules is 'sposed ta be followed, not broken like yins all be doing right this very minute."

"I'm sorry," Kim said, "it's just that the young lady here woke up only moments ago. She passed out earlier, you see…it happened a little while before you all arrived. She's not privy to the rules just yet…but I'll do my best to keep her quiet."

"That be the right thing ta do, ma'am," the man said, his voice coated in a drawl Kim had no problem comprehending, but Grace couldn't distinguish. "Yins all don't wants ta know the consequences for breakin' rules. There be consequences for rule breakin' and folks doing the rule breakin'." The man nodded to both of them and cradled the rifle in his arms before wandering away.

Grace jutted herself up onto her elbows, encountering a dizzy spell. She tapped her index finger on Kim's arm. "Okay, who the hell was that? Did I wake up in the *Twilight Zone* or a rerun of *Duck Dynasty*?"

Kim placed a finger over her lips. "Shhh. Grace, we should do as he says. I think he's serious about the consequences he's talking about."

Grace began to look perturbed. "Consequences? Kim, what is going on here? What happened after I passed out?"

"We got ourselves some visitors. They just sort of dropped in on us."

"Yeah, I can see that," Grace said, careful to mind the volume of her voice. "But who the hell are they?"

"We don't know."

"Okay…how many of them are there?"

"I'm afraid we don't know the answer to that either. All I can tell you is there's enough of them."

Grace squinted. "Enough of them? You mean more of them than us."

Kim only nodded and looked on.

Grace sat up a bit more and took a look around the confines of Kim's basement. Beds had been brought in for those who had fallen ill, including Lee, Scott Schmidt, Peter Saunders, and Peter's son Liam.

Amy Saunders was sitting at her husband's bedside, their son Jacob mere inches from her, a terrified look on his face. Whitney Schmidt and her daughter, Brooke, were tending to Scott, each taking turns placing cool, damp washcloths on his forehead and shoulders.

But the basement now contained other faces that, as far as Grace knew, weren't technically supposed to be there. Sarah and Emily Taylor sat nervously in the Masons' chair and a half, not far from the door safeguarding the secured confines of Fred's gun cave. And every female member of the Brady family, sans George Brady's wife, Elisabeth, were huddled together in the middle of the floor, their husbands and sons nowhere to be found.

"One minute, this place looks like the intensive care unit at Walter Reed. And the next minute, it reminds me of some strange underground redneck feminists' rally," Grace whispered. "By my estimation, we're being held captive down here…but where is everybody else, Kim? Where's John? Bryan? And the other…I don't know, menfolk?"

Kim shook her head slowly. "We don't know. They divided us up not long after they got here." She paused. "They're keeping the men elsewhere."

"Where? And why?"

"I don't know, Grace."

"Do we know what they want?"

Kim pursed her lips. "Well, they haven't exactly told us, but I have a pretty damn good idea what it is."

Grace took another long look around the room. "Where's Megan? I don't see her anywhere, either."

Kim hesitated, her body beginning to tremble. "I don't know. Like I said, they separated us, and they…they took her, too."

CHAPTER 8

Thorny Bottom
Hardy County, West Virginia
Wednesday, December 1st

ARRANGING THE SHORT-BARRELED AR-15 FRED Mason had given her into a secure position, Michelle mounted her Honda Rancher ATV and prepared for departure.

Jesseca and her three daughters paraded around from the rear of their house, each seated on a bicycle. Modern, multispeed mountain bikes for the teenagers, and a somewhat outmoded, one-sprocket beach cruiser for Jess. Jesseca's bike had broader tires and a much wider seat, and while it lacked the bells and whistles of the newer bikes, it did appear to provide a more comfortable ride.

Jesseca threw out her hand, aiming a finger downhill as she lined up her bike in parallel with Michelle's ATV. "Lead the way. Only, watch your speed and take lots of breaks. My knees aren't in the best shape. And these bikes won't win any races against that quad cycle."

Michelle nodded and started her engine, allowing it to warm up while she regarded the mass of gear Jesseca's girls had strapped to them. Mack, Alex, and Desirée each had bulky, military-surplus style backpacks hanging from their shoulders, olive drab in color, crammed to their brims with an assortment of items. Each also had a knife of some type attached to or otherwise hanging from their belt.

Mack's knife was a full-tang Bowie, complete with wooden handle and leather sheath, while both Alex and Desirée sported daggers, Alex with a duo, one on each hip. None of the handles matched and no blade was the same length, but they were all double-edged and just as deadly as their companions. A handmade slingshot hung just outside Mack's hip pocket, and a recurve bow enfolded Alex's backpack, along with several twisted, wavy arrows lashed alongside, appearing themselves to have been handcrafted.

Michelle was fascinated, and she allowed her curiosity to get the best of her. When she turned her attention to Desirée, the youngest of the three, to scan for more improvised weapons, Jesseca pulled up and intersected her gaze.

"See something you like?" Jesseca asked with a smirk. "Or maybe something you don't like?"

Michelle smiled uncomfortably, feeling caught in the act. "Sorry—I wasn't gawking. I was just getting familiar with the girls' choices of weaponry."

"I see," Jesseca said. "We're fond of primitive weapons. They never run out of ammunition. We like knives the most, they can be used for just about anything, up to and including constructing other weapons." The proud mom motioned to Mack and then Alex. "Mack made her slingshot herself. Carved it from hickory, same as Alex did with her bow. They're not perfect, but they don't have to be perfect to be functional."

Michelle nodded her agreeance. "Or lethal."

The group departed the house and continued downhill over grooves and potholes along the narrow washed-out path back to the road. With Michelle maintaining a leisurely pace the others could sustain, they eventually returned to the confines of the valley and the undermaintained asphalt surface of Trout Run Road.

Continuing south for several miles, the northern barricade soon came into view. George Brady and one of his sons or grandsons were normally found guarding it on the opposite side of two rusted-out cars, which had been parked bumper to bumper, effectually blocking the road.

But as they drew closer, Michelle let off the throttle upon coming to the realization that not only was the barricade undefended, an opening had somehow formed between the two vehicles. One wide enough for an automobile to breach. For reasons unknown in her time away, both antique cars had been moved.

Michelle turned the wheel hard, pulling her ATV to the side of the road. She cut off the engine, then motioned for Jesseca and the girls to fall in behind her.

"What is it?" Jesseca asked, leaning her bike over. She struggled to gauge Michelle's demeanor. "Is something amiss?"

Michelle hesitated, her anxiety mounting. She didn't know what to make of the scene at the barricade and didn't know what to say to begin with. It had been practically drilled into her that something such as this was entirely possible and could occur without warning. Still, it was unexpected and was taking her completely by surprise. "Amiss? Yeah. Something definitely looks amiss. I...I think there might be a problem."

Jesseca sighed, almost chuckling under her breath. "A problem? You mean another one?" She chuckled aloud this time. "You do make a habit out of this sort of thing, don't you? Finding or otherwise running into problems, that is."

"Look—I'm sorry, Jess. But I'm not joking. I wish I were, but I'm not." Michelle dismounted her ATV and leaned out to study the scene as she grew more nervous. "That's our southern border," she said, pointing. "We barricaded the road a while back, and there's usually at least two people standing guard over there."

"Usually?"

Effortlessly tossing a leg over the frame of her bike, Alex hopped down and pushed it forward to join Michelle and her mother, urgency on display in her body language. "She's right, Mom, I've seen them. And those rusty cars are usually so close together you couldn't get this bike between them."

Jesseca unslung the M1 carbine from her shoulder and pulled the bolt back to verify a chambered thirty-caliber round. She glanced at Alex, considered the zest in her eyes, then shook her head disgustedly and frowned. "I was really hoping I wasn't going to have to use this thing anytime soon. I suppose we do have ourselves a problem though, don't we?"

Michelle cocked her head. "We?"

Jesseca glared. "Yes, we. We, Michelle. The five of us. *We* have a problem." Turning away, she took turns regarding each of her daughters, all three of whom returned her glance with undivided attention. "Girls, mouths shut, ears and eyes open." Jess pointed to the woods. "Go. Into the forest. Make yourselves scarce. Stay hidden from sight until I call for you."

Almost simultaneously, and without protest, all three of Jesseca's daughters uttered the words, "Yes, ma'am."

Mack was the first to grab her things and disappear.

Desirée started to follow, but stopped shortly thereafter, rerouting to her mother. "I'm scared, Mom," she said, reaching for Jess.

"Don't be. Stay close to your sisters. Do what they do. You will be fine." Jesseca placed her hands to Desirée's soiled yet unblemished cheeks. "Evil is nothing to be afraid of. You're better than that…you've survived worse. Remember, you're strong now. Stronger than ever."

Desirée ran off to rejoin Mack after a moment of reassurance.

Alex remained. Unlike her sisters, she dragged her feet, gathering her things together slowly while she stared at the barricade. "Hey, Mom? Don't be mad…but I have an idea."

"What is it?"

Alex looked unsure. "I think maybe I should…I mean, should I… reconnoiter?"

Jesseca exhaled through her nostrils, wavered a moment, then nodded hesitantly. "Yes. Yes, you probably should. That's good thinking, Alex. I can't be mad at you for that. Get over there and get back as fast as you can."

"Yes, ma'am," Alex said, her eyes enlivened with exuberance. "I will."

Several minutes passed before the two women remaining behind said anything.

Jesseca took a seat on the road's edge and laid her M1 across her lap. She glanced at Michelle for a second before returning her attention to the barricade. "You look troubled, Michelle."

Michelle nodded while she took a moment to study the short-barreled AR-15 in her hands, realizing only now just how unfamiliar it was to her. "That's because I am troubled." She gestured ahead. "We shouldn't be the ones sitting here, waiting behind. I feel as though your girls should be here, and we should be the ones doing the investigating."

"Don't be so quick to discount them," Jesseca said, a sharpness in her eyes and tone. "My girls have had a lot of practice in similar matters."

"Similar matters? What do you mean by that?"

Jess sighed. "Do you recall my rather forthcoming commentary concerning the former fifth unit in our household?"

Michelle nodded.

"Well, there were times...times when the ex made the decision to make me his primary target. That so, the girls were never far from his aggression when he got mad enough to...well, when he got mad enough. And that scared me. So we practiced these little maneuvers." Jesseca paused, peering left into the forest and then right. "Needless to say, my girls have become very adept at staying hidden if the need arises."

"Staying hidden is one thing, but you just gave Alex permission to go up there and investigate a potentially dangerous situation...and I don't know if I—"

"I know what I told my daughter, Michelle," Jesseca cut in. "Alex is a capable young woman. If she wasn't, she wouldn't have offered, and I wouldn't have allowed her to go."

Michelle hung her head slightly. "I'm sorry, I didn't mean to interfere."

"It's okay...you're stressing," Jess said, doing her best to console her. "And there's a lot you don't know about us. The girls' grandfather, my dad, for all his faults, was a decent man. He always impressed upon us how crucial it was to feed our inborn human will to survive. But he capitalized on the notion by sharing a lot of his knowledge with me and the girls." She paused a moment, glancing down at the inscriptions on the sling of the carbine her father had given her. "My dad was in the Army, First Air Cavalry to be precise, something he used to call a 'highly unconventional infantry unit'. He used to tell us his unit's only objective was to engage the enemy and never be seen, rarely be heard, and only be felt. He did several covert tours in southeast Asia—the kind no one talks about." She paused a moment to recollect while pointing ahead to where Alex was emerging from the woods near the barricade. "There she is. Watch her now. I swear, she moves like a cat."

After checking twice to verify her weapon was safe, Michelle brought the SBR's optic to her eye and watched Alex tiptoe around the cars at the unguarded barricade, a dagger in each hand. "She definitely looks like she knows what she's doing. But it still makes me nervous." She hesitated. "Gosh. She reminds me so much of Lauren."

"Hmm...and where is Lauren?" asked Jess. "It just dawned on me, the rest of us still haven't had the pleasure of meeting her." She squinted her eyes. "And it also just now dawned on me that you came alone today." She paused a moment to give Michelle time to fill in the blanks, not getting a response. "Where is she, Michelle?"

Michelle lowered her weapon's muzzle, turning her head shamefacedly away. "I let her go. I let her go on that goddamn expedition. Like some idiot."

"What do you mean, you let her go? She's old enough to make her own decisions, isn't she?"

Michelle cast a scornful gaze in Jesseca's direction. "That isn't the point. I didn't stop being Lauren's mother on the day she turned eighteen."

"I didn't mean it like that."

"Look, I know it's wishful thinking, but I still like to believe I have some level of influence with her," Michelle said, her tone dreary. "I guess I should know better than that…definitely by now. I'm just worried to death about her. I've had a bad feeling in my gut ever since she left."

Jesseca reached over and rubbed Michelle's lower back. "I didn't mean to dredge up negative feelings." She suddenly perked up upon noticing Alex motioning to her with hand signals in the distance. The two conversed back and forth before Jesseca concluded the exchange with an index finger being pulled across her throat.

"What's that mean?"

"I told Alex her little recon mission is over and to hightail her booty back here," said Jesseca. "She says there's two dead bodies up there. Any idea who they could be?"

What little confidence Michelle had managed to piece together within herself started to dismantle in short order. Her lips set into a grim line, and her shoulders slumped. She looked heartbroken. "Two? Oh, Jesus." She shuddered. "Can she describe them?"

Jesseca shook her head. "I'm afraid our hand-signal vocabulary hasn't progressed too far beyond the basics. She'll be back in a few minutes to fill us in." She leaned in closer. "You see? I told you Alex was capable. My father might not have been the best dad in the world, but he was an exceptional granddad. My girls learned an awful lot from him."

After a few minutes, Alex returned. She pounced out of the woods and, after looking both ways, crossed the road to rejoin Michelle and her mother.

Wiping her forehead, Alex pushed back her long curly bangs from her face. Her forehead puckered, and she hung her head slightly while looking to Michelle. "I think it's Mr. Brady and his wife. But I'm only going by what you've told me, since I've never actually met them. I don't know who else it could be."

Michelle put a hand over her mouth. "You're certain they're dead?"

Alex secured her water bottle after taking a sip and nodded solemnly. "Yeah. Both of them."

Jesseca reached for Alex and brushed some of her hair over her shoulder lovingly. "How did you verify the deceased?"

"I checked the old man first. He didn't have a pulse, but I didn't expect him to. It looks like he got shot with a cannon." Alex retrieved two spent shotgun shell casings from a jacket pocket and handed one to her mother. "The lady didn't have a pulse, either. Her head was mashed up and had lots of cuts on it." She paused. "Their blood was still warm, Mom."

Jesseca handed the shotgun casing to Michelle. "It happened recently, then. Possibly within the last hour or so."

"They shot him with his own gun," Michelle lamented, her voice stricken with grief. She admired the expended shell, taking note of its overall length and the unmistakable stamping on the brass indicating '10 gauge'.

There had been a time when she wasn't aware what that meant, back when calibers, gauges, and millimeters weren't spoken of every day with regard to firearms. But now, Michelle knew beyond a shadow of a doubt there was only one person in the valley, and perhaps only one person she had ever known in her lifetime, who'd been the owner of a shotgun chambered in 10 gauge.

Michelle limply handed the casing back to Alex. With a sorrowful voice, she said, "Rest in peace, George and Elizabeth. May the Lord have mercy on your—"

Jesseca snapped her fingers and got in Michelle's face. "Enough! Snap out of it, Michelle. We don't have time for this…do you have any idea what's happening here?"

"No. I—"

"Two people were murdered. Two friends of yours are dead, and their blood is still warm. Do you have any clue who might have done it?"

Michelle cut her eyes at Jesseca, disturbed by her impulsiveness. "What are you asking me?"

"You said they, as in *they* shot him with his own gun," said Jess. "Who, pray tell, are they, Michelle? The only 'they' I can think of is the ones you've told me about…but what Alex found doesn't exactly scream DHS involvement, if you ask me."

Michelle sighed, now coming to the slow realization that sentimentalities required deferment for now. "Look, I know what I told you earlier sounded far-fetched. But I assure you, anything else I tell you from here on out isn't going to fall far below that threshold."

Jesseca repositioned herself to get comfortable. She took in a breath and released it and wriggled her fingers. "Okay. I'm primed and ready now. Go on, fire away."

Michelle searched the sky. "We've done everything in our power to keep to ourselves since living here. Not once have we gone looking for trouble, but that hasn't stopped us from making enemies. There's a group…a small society of people living nearby. We don't know much about them, and we don't know who they are or where they came from, we just know they're violent. We call them 'takers' because that's what they do. It's all they do. They've attacked us several times, and they've been nothing but hostile to us ever since last summer." Michelle paused. "To me, this looks like their doing. Their attacks have been sporadic and inconsistent at best, but we've always had the upper hand. We've always won. I guess they must've been waiting for this. They must've known we divided ourselves up…and were vulnerable."

Jesseca sighed and lowered her head, then beheld Alex. "Are these the same people who snatched my Alex from me?"

Alex stared at Michelle anticipatively, the sparkles in her eyes diminishing.

"We believe so," Michelle said. "They've tried to steal from us, attacked us in our homes twice, burned a family's house to the ground, and they tried to kill Lauren and her friend on the day we found Alex. I wouldn't put anything past them."

Jess nodded, her brows knitting. "Fine. So be it. I'm a simple person, Michelle. I'm not fond of overcomplicating things, as things generally don't require complication. Black and white, good and evil, alive or dead, kill or be killed, make a move or sit still…that's the simplicity I'm talking about."

"I don't understand."

"I've told you before—there's nothing to understand," Jess said. "You've been attacked. Your people are dead. That much is obvious. Question is now, do we do something about it, or do we run away and pretend it didn't happen?" She paused, taking hold of her M1. "What say you, Michelle? It's your call."

CHAPTER 9

Allegany County, Maryland
Saturday, December 4th. Present day

LAUREN FELT LIKE PINCHING HERSELF. Was this a dream? With so many unexpected events coming to pass in a matter of hours, nothing seemed real to her. Seeing Dave Graham again for the first time after a year's worth of misfortune was no different.

The esteemed soldier carried himself in the same manner he always had, with charisma and poise, and the intensity of a war veteran with a lifetime of combat experiences under his belt. But today, even at a distance, Lauren could sense there was something different about him, and in the dimness of the early morning sky, she was beginning to see it, as well.

Dave was in full combat uniform, and his sleeves were pulled all the way down to a pair of faded black hard-knuckle gloves, shrouding his tattoo-covered forearms. He had grown a full beard since the last time Lauren had seen him. It was unruly and coarse, extended nearly to his collar, and it didn't appear he spent much time grooming it, if at all. A look existed in his eyes, way more momentous and powerful than Lauren could ever remember it before. Dave looked focused, determined, and remarkably intense, as though he was undergoing the foulest portions of another tour of duty, one with an end nowhere in sight.

After barking orders to several men standing nearby with the same raspy, foreboding voice he'd used to grasp Lauren's attention so well in the past, Dave trudged over to her.

He slung a mud-caked M4 over his shoulder, rubbed his chin, and hesitated, taking a lengthy moment to look her over. "Well, I gotta admit. Right about now, I'm at a real loss for words." Dave's brows raised into sharp, narrow angles as creases emerged on his dirt-, sweat-, and grease-covered forehead.

"That makes two of us," Lauren said, her voice broken, a grin barely noticeable.

Dave squinted while he eyeballed her like a drill instructor performing an inspection during basic training. "I'm glad you're alive...but you really look like shit, Janey."

Lauren examined herself clumsily. "I know I do."

"What in God's name happened to you?" Dave asked, a distasteful look befalling him. "The last time I saw you, you smelled like a daffodil. Your hair was a little more...salon-styled, and your wardrobe was fresh out of the summer REI catalog. Now you look like you've been sifting through a dumpster for the past month."

"It's been more like a year."

"What?" Dave asked, squinting his eyes tighter.

"Dave, please...can we just start over? Stop pretending you're not glad to see me," she said, trying hard to gauge his temperament. "You don't always have to play the hard-ass Point Blank instructor with me. It's not necessary, especially now."

"I'm neither pretending nor playing," Dave said. "You know me, Janey, I don't subscribe to either of those notions. Truth is, yes, I'm very glad to see you...glad to see you aboveground, that is. Admittedly though, I'm more *surprised* to see you than anything else. Add to that, virtually goddamn stupefied...finding you in some derelict, godforsaken shithole like this. I'm sure you can imag—"

"Please don't lecture me, okay?" Lauren interrupted, rubbing her temple. "Please? My head is killing me, and I've been put through the wringer enough lately."

Dave sighed. "Fine. I'll save it for later, then."

Lauren's eyes softened with gratitude. She pointed beyond. "I see you've found some new recruits. Looks like well over a hundred men, give or take, but I haven't seen anyone I know besides you and Jae." She hesitated. "Is the original team still around?"

Dave exhaled to release some tension. Lowering his hands to his waist, he removed his gloves and hooked his thumbs behind his belt, nodding a response.

"Jae said that Stewie was on another mission with Tim."

Dave Graham only nodded again.

"What about Neo? Is he here?"

His lower lip protruding, Dave nodded yet again, jutting a thumb over his shoulder. "He's where he's happy, where he belongs. Setting up temporary midrange comms in the northern sector, close to the highway."

"Santa?"

"He's here too, somewhere. I tasked his squad with demo."

"Demo of what?"

"Weapons caches," Dave growled. "We've been finding all sorts of shit…these pricks and others like them have taken custody of entirely too much firepower for their own damn good."

Lauren nodded her understanding. "What about Sanchez?"

Dave gestured his head to the west. "My favorite jarhead? I never leave home without him. He's probably got eyes on us both as we speak. He's perched five hundred meters out on the M82, right where he's happy…right where he belongs." He paused, taking a few slow, careful steps closer to her. "While we're on the topic, would you mind conveying to me verbally why you aren't where *you* belong? And how in the name of good initiative and bad judgment I happened to find you, of all people, in a hellhole like this so far from home?"

Lauren didn't respond immediately. Thoughts of all the days that had passed since the last time she'd been addressed in this manner began to burden her. She turned away at first. "It's a really long story."

"I have no doubt. Lucky for you, we got a little downtime before we mosey out of here." Dave shuffle stepped, adjusting his stance. "So spill it."

Lauren sighed. "No—I mean it's a *really* long story, long enough to write a novel about. There's too many details to cover in one conversation. Besides, I have some pressing items I need to talk to you about."

Dave's eyes danced. "We're doing everything we can for Fred. Fortunately for us, and at the same time regrettably for his adversaries, I've been advised he's already stabilizing. The man's a damn enigma. I'm sure he's going to pull through in due course."

Lauren nodded, smiling at the thought of Fred recovering. "Thanks for telling me that. I'm glad he's in good hands. But—"

"Tang says you have a concussion," Dave interjected, switching gears. "What happened? You get hit with something?"

"Yeah. Something."

"Turn around. Let me get a visual."

Lauren rolled her eyes and sighed, but did as instructed. Reaching back, she lifted her hair so he could get a better look.

Dave clicked on a flashlight beam. "I got a medic en route with orders to assess your injury. And, Janey, you're going to allow him to assess it. Is that understood?"

Lauren nodded slightly. "Okay."

"This doesn't look good. I'm surprised you're able to stay upright."

"I don't have a choice in the matter—I have to stay upright. There's no time for anything else."

Dave grimaced. "What do you mean by that?"

"We have a few dilemmas we're dealing with at home, Dave. Big ones."

"Dilemmas, huh? I suppose those dilemmas were what caused you and Fred and the other folks to end up here?"

"In part, yes," Lauren began, turning around. "We're in urgent need of food, and some of our friends have gotten sick, perhaps terminally. I think they've all been poisoned somehow."

Dave furrowed his brow. "Poisoned?"

Lauren nodded. "Yeah, and that's another story entirely."

He minded her gravely, urging her to go on.

"We were running out of time and options. Fred devised a plan and we went to look for a doctor, but our first attempt came up short. I found some clues that he might've relocated to Keyser. So we decided to head out farther, and—"

"You got ambushed along the way," Dave said, a repugnant, disgusted tone marking his words.

Lauren nodded her response.

Dave huffed. "Christ Almighty, Janey. I know information hasn't exactly been easy to come by since the world went to hell, but I would've expected a fellow former grunt like Fred to do a little recon before taking untrained civilians into a combat zone."

"Not all of us are untrained."

"You know what I mean."

"And we didn't exactly have a lot of time to plan the trip," Lauren added. "Fred wasn't enthused at the thought of leaving the valley, either. As far as things go, it's been relatively safe there."

Dave held up a hand. "Wait one. You're living there now?"

"Mm-hmm."

"Near Perry? Where Fred and Kim live?"

"Yeah."

"Well, color me conscious. When did that happen? And why?"

"Yet *another* story," said Lauren, trying her best to stay on topic. "We couldn't just sit there. Fred knew it—we all did. Not with lives at stake. And thanks to this little hiccup, it's probably too late for some of them."

Dave folded his arms over his chest once again while he put together the fragmented puzzle of Lauren's story in his head, and the medic he had summoned appeared to begin diagnosis and treatment. "You can advise me of the details later. I'm guessing there's something you want from me."

"Just a little help."

"Specifically?"

"Jae told me about the mission...and he assumed after today, we could just accompany all of you. But we can't do that. We have to get back home—as soon as we can...preferably with the help we were looking for."

Dave primed his lips. "And by help, you're referring to the medical persuasion."

Lauren nodded affirmation.

"I can't spare any of my men, Janey. Especially medical personnel, I'm sorry," said Dave, his nostrils flaring. "I need every able body I can get right now and then some. I can probably spare a ride to get you back, but even that requires me to utilize personnel I can barely do without." He paused. "Obviously, I'll do what I can. But sending away one of my medically trained personnel is out of the question."

Lauren hung her head and fretted, paying no mind to the medic tending to her.

"You really don't have a clue what's been going on outside your bubble since the feces hit the fan, do you?"

"I suppose not." Lauren frowned, taking a sip from her water bottle. "Like you said, information hasn't been easy to come by, but after what happened to us, I can wager a guess."

Dave rotated away while his medic continued to work. Closing a nostril with a finger, he blew his nose onto the ground. "Our original plans have been placed on an indefinite back burner. We've been finding camps like this one peppered all over the Allegheny Highlands and surrounding valleys." He paused. "Most of the ones we've already hit sat within a thirty-mile radius of Cumberland. They're all basically identical, same type of weirdos running them, and for the most part, utilized for the same purpose."

"What? What purpose?"

"Imprisonment," replied Dave. "And dehumanization. We've come across some forced-labor camps and even some death camps, believe it or not, complete with gallows, guillotines, etcetera. Most of the camps were set up where large stores of food had been discovered nearby, like this one. And usually where there's trouble-free access to clean or treatable water sources." Dave took a brief pause. "We're finding the same ole situation in pretty much all of them. Large groups of well-armed hostiles who've taken families from their homes and either killed them or brutalized them and made them prisoners.

"They're putting them to work as slave labor, using them for entertainment, and carrying out other inhumanities far worse than that. Consequently, we've spent the better part of the past year dealing with them. It's done a decent job of deferring our original plans. These folks are abominable, the walking, talking embodiment of vile, as you've already ascertained. And there's one god-awful thing they're doing, something downright demented...even I can't find the words to describe it."

Lauren turned to look Dave in his eyes. "What are you getting at?"

He sighed exhaustively. "Look around, Janey. You see men and women here, mostly adults. The cage we found you in was full of them." A pause. "Take a good look. What is it you don't see?"

Lauren took a couple of steps away from Dave and his medic, her brow lowering. She dropped her blanket and scanned the scene, the light of daybreak aiding her view. Her eyes met with Dave's again. "Children."

"Yahtzee."

The medic instructed Lauren on the symptoms to be wary of after receiving a mild concussion, while Dave listened attentively. After handing her a handful of ibuprofen, he took his leave, passing by a pair of others who approached cautiously.

While Dave cycled into defensive mode, Lauren recognized one of their visitors as the man who'd become acquainted with Christian's boot during the assault, the one she could've sworn she'd seen somewhere before. He gracefully sauntered over, accompanied by dainty, fair-complected woman with short hair. She held tightly to his hand, an uncertain smile stretched across her face.

"May I help you?" Dave asked, his hand looming near his sidearm.

"Pardon me, sir," the man began in the same mild British accent he'd exposed before. "So sorry to interrupt...but I'd like to offer my sincere gratitude for what you and your men have done for us here today. You've saved us, you see. And my wife and I...well, we're both eternally grateful."

"No thanks is required," said Dave, holding up his free hand while providing about half his attention. "All in a day's work."

"Don't be so modest! Jolly good show, I might add. Splendid show...just splendid. Never seen anything quite like that before in my life. Beats any New Year's Eve celebration I've experienced before."

"Well, we aim to please," Dave murmured, sounding annoyed. He hesitated, assuming the couple would venture off after a moment of reticence, but they only stood there. "Was there something else?"

"Yes, sir, actually, there is. Thank you for asking," the man said awkwardly. "I'm not usually this...abrupt, but we were wondering...if there would be any way we could bother you for...well..."

"A ride," the woman beside him said in a soft voice, carrying a similar accent. "What my husband is attempting to request is means of transportation."

Dave pursed his lips, glancing to Lauren. "Must be contagious," he said, becoming more exasperated. "Where to, exactly?"

"Keyser," the man said, a look of excitement overtaking him. "Potomac Valley Hospital, to be more specific. We're both employed there, you see."

"I didn't know there were any hospitals still in operation," said Dave.

"Oh well, perhaps *employed* isn't the suitable word. The hospital itself as a whole is far from operational, so I suppose that would make you correct. We do indeed work there, though, and have actually managed to maintain a small clinic, though it hasn't been easy," the man explained. "We've been doing so with what you might call a skeleton crew, and if it weren't for the photovoltaics we salvaged to run our wing, we'd be sorely lost."

"Wait a second, you're a doctor?" Lauren probed, unable to keep her silence.

"Well," the man said in a chuckle, "we certainly aren't janitors."

Dave muttered under his breath. "That remains to be seen."

"Sorry, dear. Only pulling your leg." The man held out a hand, presenting his wife with a smile. "Actually, we both are. And I do apologize for our disarray. Allow me to introduce my wife, Dr. Pamela Vincent, the only practicing obstetrician for perhaps hundreds of miles."

The woman stepped hesitantly forward to shake Dave Graham's stubborn hand.

Lauren pushed impulsively past the man's wife and up to him. "Wait...Vincent? As in James Vincent?"

"Why, yes. I'm sorry, do we know one another?"

"Are you Dr. James Vincent of Wardensville?"

The husband and wife physicians glanced at one another and shared a laugh. "Bizarre...I don't look that old, do I?" He turned to Lauren. "No, no, my dear. Not quite. I'm afraid you're referring to my father, James *Wilson* Vincent, the general practitioner. We are not one and the same, but we do, however, bear the same name." He held out his hand to her. "It's a pleasure to make your acquaintance. I am James Vincent the second. But please, call me Jim."

Lauren shook his hand while trying to find the right words to express her conclusions. "You both were in the cage with us, weren't you?"

Dr. Vincent nodded. "Why yes, as a matter of fact we were. And before you say anything else, my dear, let me intercede by expressing my deepest apologies. We are both very sorry about your friend and for what happened to him. It was taxing for us to stand by and watch it ensue. We would have done something to help, but I'm sorry to say we were afraid to act. We've witnessed nightmarish things happening to doctors as of late, you see. Several of our friends and colleagues were captured from the clinic not long before we were...and some ghastly things happened to them. My wife made me swear not to say or do anything that might give up our true identities." Dr. Vincent turned to his wife as she urged him on with her eyes. "Alas, that was then, and this is now. We saw the men take your friend with them...where is he now? If it wouldn't be imposing, we would like to offer our professional assistance."

While Dave gave the doctor and his wife the information needed to find the temporary field hospital, Lauren recalled why the doctor had seemed so familiar to her before. She had seen the couple's faces in a photo frame mounted to a wall in Dr. Vincent's home only days before.

The letter.

While watching Dr. Vincent and his wife caper away, she was reminded of the letter left behind by his father and what she had done with it. Initially, Lauren had returned it to the table. Then, for some reason, she had decided to keep it, folding it up and placing it in her back pocket just before vacating the residence.

She unsnapped her back pocket and felt for it. It was still there.

Letter in her grasp, Lauren intercepted Dr. Vincent. She handed it to him while his wife closed in, gazing upon both Lauren and the letter with curiosity and concern. "Dr. Vincent, a few days ago we stopped by your father's home in Wardensville, and I found this letter," she said. "I decided to take it with me for some reason. Strangely enough, I think I know why now."

Stunned by Lauren's admission at first, Dr. Vincent scanned the letter as his brows drew together and his form started showing signs of grief. Moments later, after finishing the note, he handed it to his wife while he wiped his tears away, looking to Lauren. "Have you read this?"

She nodded, her lips pressed together.

"Father always told me if anything bad ever happened and we didn't make it to his estate, he would try to rendezvous with us in Keyser at some point," Dr. Vincent said, wiping his nose with the blanket provided to him by Dave's men. "He had plans for us all, you see. Long-term provisions and the means to protect ourselves from harm. He was one of those survivalist types like you've probably seen on television. Suppose I'll never know what happened to him now, after all this time. At least I know poor Mother has been laid to rest and her pain is finally over." He paused. "God rest her."

"I'm sorry," said Lauren. "And I'm even more sorry you had to find out this way."

"Oh, dear…it's not your fault. Mother had been sick for some time, and I'm certain Father did everything he could, in light of the circumstances. I do wish to thank you for providing me with this letter. Believe it or not, right now it means the world to me." He paused. "But I feel as though I should ask…exactly what were you doing inside my parents' home?"

Lauren looked away at first. "We were looking for a doctor, and your father's name was first on our list." She spent the next few minutes explaining the predicament in the valley to Dr. Vincent and his wife as they keenly listened to her heartfelt story. Then Lauren posed a rather straightforward request, one she hadn't found time to rehearse.

The doctors both drew back, offering her puzzled looks.

"I imagine my parents' home was in quite a state of disarray," Jim Vincent said, "being vacant and uncared for so long after a disaster like this one."

"Actually, it wasn't. Everything looked in place, as far as I could see."

"Really…"

Lauren shrugged. "Mm-hmm. The floors, walls, even the windows were all nearly spotless. I think the front door might need replacing, or at least some new hinges, but other than that…"

"Interesting. I take it the intolerant jackass who decided to kick it in didn't take a few moments to look for the hide-a-key under the porch?"

Lauren felt embarrassed. The time when Christian had been so adamant in searching for the key to Sugar Knob Cabin months ago came to mind. She didn't respond.

Dr. Vincent smiled as his wife whispered something into his ear. "Young lady, I'm only pulling your leg again. Your friends here just rescued us from this hellhole and those appalling ingrates. God only knows what they would've had in store for us. Simply put, my wife and I both feel as though we are in your debt. I assume, if we join you, there will be accommodations for us?"

Elated, Lauren nearly jumped for joy. "Sure…I'll let you have my room if need be. Thank you. Thank you both so much."

Both doctors continued on, waving as they walked off.

"Well, wasn't that altogether serendipitous," Dave said wryly with an irreverent smirk. "You might wanna find some wood and rap your knuckles on it, Janey. Things typically don't come to pass in that fashion without divine intervention or some added luck."

"Yeah," Lauren said, shrugging. "I'm...blown away, actually. I can't believe any of this is happening." She peeked at her forearm. "It's giving me goose bumps."

"Well, it may be giving you goose bumps, but it's making my stomach growl. I'm so hungry right now, I could eat a Clydesdale." Dave glanced downward and tapped Lauren on the belly. "I think I heard an echo in there, kid. I know you haven't exactly been taking the best care of yourself, by the looks of you. When's the last time you put any food in that diminutive stomach of yours?"

"I honestly can't remember."

"Then it's been too long." Gently, Dave put his arm around Lauren and pulled her in tightly to him. "Come on. The men are setting up a DFAC not too far from here. Let's go find you some chow."

CHAPTER 10

Allegany County, Maryland
Saturday, December 4th. Present day

LAUREN PACED THROUGH THE CAMP, making her way through hordes of lifeless bodies and piles of rubble, searching for a comfortable place to sit down and eat. As she strolled, the savory aroma of a freshly cooked freeze-dried entrée tugged at her nose from the confines of a mylar bag she held in her grasp.

She found an older 4x4 wagon parked among several others and took a stroll around it, giving it a good once-over, noticing a set of keys still dangled from the ignition. Moving to the rear, she opened the tailgate, then propped open the windowed rear upper door and slid herself in to take a seat with her feet dangling inches off the ground. With each oversized spoonful of beef stroganoff she placed in her mouth, she swung her legs back and forth merrily with youthful eagerness, in a way reminiscent of her childhood, suspended in a swing set.

The spot Lauren had chosen sat up higher than most of the camp and provided her with a good vantage point. The truck was an antique, painted in a nearly flawless baby blue, and it stood out to her from the other vehicles in proximity.

Lauren inspected the insides of the mylar bag, regarding the nearly purged contents of her meal and scraped free one last spoonful. Then, from the far corner of her outlying vision, she caught sight of a slender man in MultiCam ACUs approaching from the passenger side of the truck to her rear. She turned to see who it was, recognizing him instantly as the youngest member of Dave's original unit, someone she remembered well and, for reasons only she knew, had long ago tried her best to forget.

Upon realizing he'd been spotted, Richie strolled up to Lauren casually without pause. "LT told me to bring you another one of these. Told me you might want more," he said, reaching out to hand Lauren another mylar bag of beef stroganoff, and steam wafted from the top while his eyes probed her. "You must be special. The troops only get one serving of chow per sitting. It's not entirely clear to me why you're entitled to two, but here you go."

Lauren squinted her eyes at him before reaching for the food, managing to take possession of it only after a pedantic game of cat and mouse. She gestured her thanks. "Not special. Just hungry." Dismissing him, she started shoveling portions into her mouth with little affection.

"Hello to you, too. Still a woman of very few words, I see." Richie took a few steps forward while arranging his rifle to his side and out of the way. He moved closer and widened his stance in front of her, puffed his chest out and obstructed her view. "I guess some things never change."

Lauren continued to nourish herself while doing what she could to ignore Richie, but she knew from prior experience if she didn't give him even the slightest bit of recognition, he would never leave her be. "Can you move out of the way, please?" she asked. "You're blocking my view."

"What view? There's nothing to look at down there anyway except a bunch of men working." Richie jutted his chin. "Is it too much to ask for some undivided attention from you?"

"At the moment, yes."

He rolled his eyes. "If you say so."

Lauren shot her eyes at him, her mouth half-full of food. "You know something, Richie? You're right. Some things never change. Like you, for instance. It's been over a year since I've seen you. And you're still a dick."

Richie guffawed. "And boom! Like a grenade...there she is. It never has taken much effort to crack that shell."

"Well, maybe if you hadn't pulled the pin..."

He knelt on one knee after noticing a boot lace had gotten loose. While re-tying it, he looked Lauren up and down. "So, seriously. How've you been? I know it's been a while. You look...I don't know...good, by the way. All things considered."

Lauren coughed, gagged, and nearly spit out her food. Recovering, she glared at him coldly. "What the hell did you just say to me?"

Richie shrugged. "I just said you look good. It's been like what...a year? You just look like...I don't know...like you've matured. Like you've turned into a woman or something."

"Richie, do yourself a favor. Stop fishing. This isn't the time or the place, and I can assure you, right now I'm really *not* in the mood."

"Oh Jesus, stop it. Come on. Why do you have to act like that? Just let the past die already."

"The feedback you're getting from me in this moment has nothing whatsoever to do with the past," Lauren barked.

"Oh, really?"

"Yes. For some reason, here you are again, somehow trying to insinuate that I'm not over you. Same as always."

"Why deny it?" Richie poked. "It's obvious you're not."

"Don't flatter yourself. Like I've told you countless times before, there's nothing for me to get over."

"Well, I beg to differ."

"Beg all you want," Lauren jeered. "You can even grovel and genuflect...like you did when you wanted that second date we never had."

Richie rose and stood over her after he finished arranging himself. "Ha, very funny. Fine, explain the hostility, then. What reason do you have to be so combative with me?"

"You've never seen me be combative."

"Whatever. We planned this assault for an objective unrelated to you...and wound up rescuing you and your friends in the process. We've quartered you, and now, we're feeding you—hint, we're taking care of you."

Lauren tilted her head, pursing her lips. "Do you intend to arrive at a point?"

Richie tried his best to appear irritated. "My point is, in view of your position, I expect some gratitude. I even decided to offer you a compliment just now, in spite of the fact that you really...*don't* look good. What you really look like is hell warmed over, and you could definitely use a bath. Maybe even two."

Lauren set her food to the side and jumped down from the tailgate. She pushed her chest into Richie, cutting her eyes at him and forcing him to back away. "You know, Richie, it has been a long time since we've seen each other. And while some things never change, the declaration isn't universal. I'm not the same person I used to be. Watch what you say to me."

Richie held up his hands and backed several feet away as his expression contorted and turned. "Okay, okay. Obviously, somebody is down in the dumps today. I'll give you what you want, as usual. It worked then, so maybe it will work now. I'll leave you alone. Maybe when you're not so bitchy, we can talk again."

"Or maybe not."

"Have it your way," Richie shot back. "I'm out of here, but I'm going to leave you with some words of advice. When people go out of their way to be nice to you—and, well, save your life, you should be thankful for it—you know, show some appreciation. Someone who doesn't know you as well as I do might not find your behavior this amusing. You really never have known how to take a compliment."

Lauren shook her head and laughed herself into hysterics as she scooted back onto the truck's tailgate and reached for her food. She placed a spoonful of stroganoff into her mouth and spoke mannerlessly as she chewed. "You might find this amusing, Richie...but, there's a chance you and I might be even now."

"Even? How in the hell are we even?"

"Because the last person who implied that I didn't know how to take a compliment died suddenly."

Richie laughed. "And let me guess. You killed him, right?"

Lauren hopped down again and strolled nonchalantly over to him. She contemplated him, then pursed her lips and nodded. "I pushed a blade through his throat and shoved it into his brain stem...after I dumped a magazine of eight rounds in his chest."

Richie scoffed, his expression denoting he was unsure whether to believe her. "And that somehow makes us even, huh?"

Lauren gritted her teeth as her gaze turned virulent. She nodded. "It does. Because twenty seconds ago, I just saved *your* life."

CHAPTER 11

WITH RICHIE DECIDING TO TAKE his leave of her, Lauren enjoyed a few minutes to herself to eat alone and undisturbed. It wasn't long, though, before Dave Graham joined her, bringing along with him a meal of his own, along with several bottles of water and a stainless-steel thermos.

He handed a bottle to Lauren, motioning to the truck bed. "You good and comfortable, young lady?"

"About as good and comfortable as my fourth point of contact can be."

He grimaced, then smirked. "Cute. Mind if I cop a squat?"

Lauren shrugged and tossed her tousled hair over a shoulder. "It's a free country."

Dave grinned and slid himself onto the truck's tailgate about a foot away, and it creaked under his weight. "I think calling it a free-for-all is more accurate." He took a bite of his meal with a long plastic spoon similar to the one Lauren was using. "So. You wanna start giving me the scoop on how you all wound up here? I think I can theorize the gist, but you know me, Janey, I'm recklessly meticulous. I prefer to hear the nitty-gritty when and if I'm able."

Lauren swallowed a mouthful and nodded, then took a drink of water to wash it down, only now beginning to feel even slightly reenergized. "Dr. Vincent's house was in Wardensville, not far away from the valley. We were just going to head straight back if we found him there and worry about everything else later. Since that didn't work out, the next stop was Moorefield using Corridor H the whole way. We wouldn't encounter many overpasses on that route, and Fred seemed to appreciate that aspect...he said that overpasses were predisposed for ambushes... and ambushes get people killed."

She paused a moment, wiping her mouth on her sleeve while recalling the point in time when she'd seen Bo Brady fall. "As it turned out, his concerns were justified. Moorefield was just a part of our itinerary. One of the guys in our group had access to an underground bunker he claimed was full of food and rations—something we needed desperately. So, before continuing our search for the doctor, we went there first...and he wasn't exaggerating. There must've been enough food to feed a city of people for years down there. But we didn't have the means to transport it all, so we planned to return on our way back home and make additional trips as needed."

Dave turned his head to her. "You know, Janey, forgive me if I'm wrong, but I was under the impression at least two people involved behind the scenes, namely Fred and your father, had both prepared long in advance for this sort of...disaster."

"Both of them did, but there have been a lot of...extenuating circumstances since then. Many of the variables changed—just as variables tend to do," said Lauren. "Sometimes they exceed your expectations, no matter what you plan for. And in our case, they got a lot more arduous."

Dave bobbed his head. "I get that," he said, digging into his food. "And I'm sorry for interrupting your story. Please continue."

Lauren smiled grimly and leaned forward. "We took Route 220 north out of Moorefield. Fred took the lead in his Humvee, and we followed in Norman's truck. Fred was nervous about the trip, and he had every right to be. I remember driving on that road years ago with Dad. It has tight turns, hills, switchbacks...you name it. In addition to overpasses, there's about a hundred places to get ambushed in the thirty miles between Moorefield and Keyser."

Lauren paused, taking another drink of water. She twisted the top back on and set the bottle down, a fretful look settling in as she recounted the fateful day. Had it not been for the man sitting beside her, it surely could have signified the end for her and those closest to her. Those thoughts weighed on her immensely, and she would be certain never to forget them.

She continued. "About ten or twelve miles north of Moorefield, Fred radioed back to us when we came to the first overpass. He said to drive under in one lane and change lanes underneath, so we'd be in the right lane going in and the left lane coming out. I took that to mean he was worried someone could toss something at us from above."

"Generally," Dave inserted. "Not always, though. It's still a judicious practice."

"The first overpass made us all jumpy. Me, Austin, and Bo were in the back of Norman's truck. I had my rifle trained on the bridge the entire time. If I saw somebody pop their head out, I was going to shoot it off. But I didn't, and it was an amazing feeling to get out of there unscathed. Then, about a mile later, the next one came, and once again, we went under and did our lane change. And then, it felt amazing again—for about forty-five seconds until we got to the next overpass. After that, the mood went to hell in a handbasket."

Lauren paused again as she put the pieces of the story back together in her mind. "Fred swerved to the left, and Norman swerved right, and everyone jumped out of their vehicles to find cover. Fred went weapons hot on the bridge in a microsecond—yelled at the rest of us to do the same. There were so many men up there, I couldn't count them all at first glance, and all I saw were muzzle blasts. I ducked behind Norman's truck and pushed myself against the rear wheel. They unloaded on us for several minutes before any of us could even return fire."

"They were disabling the vehicles," said Dave. "Fire was concentrated on the engine blocks, radiators, tires, and so on."

"Yeah. No human targets at first. They just peppered the living shit out of the vehicles. The Humvee took it well—guess it was made for that sort of thing. But they turned Norman's truck into Swiss cheese…as if his poor Dodge hadn't seen enough abuse already. It died on the road that day in about five minutes…before Bo did."

"Was he the boy's father?"

Lauren nodded. "Yeah. When we were finally able to return fire, it was mostly in panic. We were shooting back just to keep them from pinning us down, even though they'd already accomplished that. I couldn't get any clear shots. They were hiding behind the concrete barriers and angling their guns over top, shooting wildly. In fact, most of their shots were wild, except for the one that hit Bo in his head. That one was well placed. It happened right beside me."

Lauren paused, closing her eyes a moment. "At first, I thought it was me who got hit. All I saw was blood on my shoulder. I thought I died and I was looking at myself…after…from some other perspective. But when I heard Austin's cries, I knew it wasn't, and for a moment, I was thankful it wasn't me. Then I saw Bo's body. Things kinda went into a blur from there on out. I really don't recollect much of anything until Fred started screaming my name."

Dave turned directly to her. "What was he saying to you?"

Lauren's eyes met with his. "He was telling me to leave…but not in those words."

Dave almost cracked a smile. "Yeah. That sounds about par for the course." Dave patted Lauren on her thigh. "You didn't have any business being there, Janey, and Fred knew that."

"None of us had any business being there," Lauren corrected. "I couldn't believe he was telling me to leave; in fact, I refused. I told him, hell no, there was no way I was leaving, and that only made him angrier. Then Norman yelled at me, telling me the same thing. About ten seconds later, Christian did too. They all wanted me to leave."

"So you had three men hollering at you, telling you to get the hell out of Dodge, and you just stood there?" pondered Dave. "Tell me, Janey, what made you finally decide to abort?"

"I don't know. I can't answer that. But when I did, I grabbed everything I could, and I ran like hell. I didn't even know where to go. And it wasn't easy under the weight of all the gear I had. Between all the stuff I was lugging and the plate carrier I had on, there had to be ninety extra pounds attached to me."

Dave pursed his lips and nodded slightly, casting his stare to the prison camp and the men milling about. "It's a shitty situation, no doubt. Completely FUBAR. But you did the right thing, Janey. And it's not easy doing what you did. Not everyone is built for situations like that."

"You think so, huh?"

"I know so," Dave asserted. "My dear, I've been in uber butt-pucker situations and have had to make those kinds of judgment calls more times than I care to compute. And I'm sitting here beside you—alive still today, and I'm telling you, if you don't have to be there, then you don't need to be there. And you don't want to be there, either."

"If only I'd had the choice," Lauren said. "The fight chose me this time—same as always."

"You made the decision to put yourself in harm's way," Dave said. "But you made it out alive, and that makes it a life lesson you can learn and build from. Overall, the injuries were minor and the casualties minimal. At the end of the day, things turned out for the better. It was a good battle."

Lauren turned her head to him, casting him a cold glare. "A good battle? Did you just really say that?"

"Indeed. You're still alive, Janey. Your unit lost a man, yet everyone else remains alive and unharmed, for the most part, still able to breathe, pick up a weapon and fight again someday if that day ever comes. In any battle, during any war, if you and your men don't get dead, it's a good thing." Dave softened his tone, not wanting to push Lauren too far. "There's no denying the boy losing his father was a tragedy. I know Fred's hurt, but he'll pull through. Some of your friends got beat up, and I know you incurred some trauma of your own. But injuries heal, and so does pain, and watching our friends fall has an inexplicable way of making us stronger. I know it's dim, but there's always a bright side. The experience is invaluable, as is the trigger time. It hardens you—renders you into a better warrior."

Lauren turned away, reaching for what remained of her food. "If you only knew."

Dave Graham's tone sharpened. "If I only knew what?"

Lauren didn't respond.

"Details, Janey. Remember my preference for such things."

Still, Lauren restrained herself. She sat there stoically, searching for the correct way to tell her old friend about everything that had happened to her and to her family in the days since the collapse.

Dave was a man of poise, but his patience was waning. Feeling concerned, he set down his food and slid himself from the tailgate, then reached for her gently, putting a calloused index finger under Lauren's chin. "Hey, talk to me. You've never been this cryptic before. What's going on inside the memory banks of that intricate mainframe of yours?" he asked. "Did something happen?"

"A lot of *things* have happened."

"Okay. Look...there's a reason we're both standing here talking right now. And there's a reason we showed up when we did. In my experience, there's *always* a reason for the way everything goes down.

That's just the way it is; there's nothing to be ashamed about." Dave held his hands aloft, touching the tips of his index fingers and thumbs together, forming a circle. "Did you know that a blue whale is the largest animal in the world…but its throat is only this big?"

Lauren scrutinized him. "No…"

"It is. Those blue bastards are as big as a locomotive, but they can't even swallow a beach ball. You know why?"

She shrugged.

"Because that's the way it is, Janey."

"Clever."

"I was trying to lighten the mood a little," Dave lamented. "So much for that. Look, you have my undivided attention…but that's subject to change before long. So talk to me. Tell me everything if you want. And if you don't, that's okay too."

Lauren had never planned on having this conversation. Up until this point, she never dreamed she'd have to. There was no way she could've predicted a future encounter with Dave Graham or anyone else she'd been separated from since the latest timeline in her life had begun.

Still, she felt obligated—she owed him some sort of explanation. "There's a lot you don't know. The only way to explain everything to you is to just go back to the beginning." Lauren paused. "Back to the day when everything went to shit. Back to when my dad never came home."

"Say again?" Dave bellowed. "Hold the phone…what do you mean he never came home? What are you talking about?"

Lauren shrugged and shyly peered over, her hair falling over her eyes. "The last time I saw him was the night before the EMP struck. He went to work Saturday morning, same as me. He had some overtime work scheduled in the city that day. Everything seemed so normal until the lights went out in our building, and I saw all the cars stalled in the road. That's when my heart sank. I knew what it was. My friend Maddie and I rode home on a couple of bikes we stole from work about an hour later. My sister, Grace, was there, Mom came home soon after, but Dad…well, he never did. We waited for him and worried about him. Days went by, and those days turned into weeks. And we…never saw him again."

Dave sighed loudly and gritted his teeth, his arms falling lifelessly to his sides. He turned his head away. "Goddammit."

"We were fine at first, actually, for a while. Dad planned things out for us really well. We had everything we needed and then some. We kept to ourselves and stuck to the plan we had. But one of our neighbors wouldn't leave us alone." A pause. "One day...a few months after, he became way more persistent; then he got violent. Things...got physical, and he attacked my mom, and..." Lauren trailed off.

After a moment, Dave, who had grown disturbed upon hearing the news of Alan Russell's fate, rotated back to her. His voice was stern, but forgiving. "And you acted on instinct. Like you were trained to."

Lauren nodded, her eyes welling up from remorse and nostalgia. "Yeah. I shot him," she said, her chin in her palms. "We bugged out the next day—loaded up everything we had and drove to my grandparents' house in Woodstock. But it wasn't long before things got really hairy there. The FEMA presence was strong—they were all over the place, dressed up like the Los Angeles SWAT team. Orange notices about martial law were stapled everywhere, and we were told if we didn't comply and relinquish all luxuries like stored food, they were going to come and take it, and our guns along with it. Then they were going to take us." She paused. "My grandfather practically ordered us to leave after that. We moved to the cabin that night, and we've been living in Trout Run Valley ever since."

"So no FEMA presence there?"

Lauren shrugged apathetically. "Not yet. But there's little doubt in my mind that's subject to change."

Dave Graham put his hands on his hips and stared off into the distance. Hanging his head, he let out a deep sigh. "Jesus, kid. You have been through some shit, haven't you? I'm sorry, Janey. I really am very sorry to hear all this. Now I feel like a true asshole. I had no idea."

"It's okay. You're right, you didn't know. There's no way you could have."

"Yeah, but finding out now...like this, really makes me feel like shit," Dave said. "God only knows how the hell you've been getting along since then, but it couldn't've been easy."

Lauren cracked a grim smile. "It hasn't been easy at all, but we've managed. For a time, it was the worst thing in the world to me." She paused, taking in a breath. "We've been attacked a few times, but we stuck together and fought back. Fred has done a great job leading us.

And up until recently, everything's been...okay, until people started getting sick."

Dave nodded. "The scene of the world has definitely changed—if it's not one thing, it's another," he said. "You mentioned something about poisoning?"

Lauren told Dave about the piles of apples and deceased wildlife she and Grace had found that had led to her suspicion. Then she went on about what Norman had showed them, and her conclusion that Trout Run had ostensibly been contaminated with a biological agent of some kind.

"And it's your contention the feds are somehow involved in this?" Dave asked.

"It's them," Lauren declared. "It has to be." She hesitated, watching his expression closely. "Why? Do you disagree?"

Dave curled his lips. He began pacing back and forth while looking away. "Let's just say I wouldn't put it past them. Damn—I can't imagine how much of a toll all this has taken on you, Janey. I can't even conceive it. I've been fond of your dad for a long time. I always knew him to be a stand-up guy. Never heard anyone speak so warmly of his daughter or his family before. He earned my respect not long after we first met, and that's not something easily accomplished by most folks I cross paths with."

"I think he liked you, too," Lauren said, trying to smile and push away the negativity conjured up by recounting the past. "Seemed to, anyway. He always had the funniest things to say about you, but he trusted you, too. And Dad didn't trust anyone."

"I'm flattered, Janey. I am truly flattered. And I'm glad he kept bringing you around. I always liked seeing the Russells show up for training, especially after we turned things up a notch and got the unit involved. It was good for both of you. I hope you learned something in your time spent there."

"I learned a couple of things," Lauren said, her eyes glistening.

"That's good. Real good. And have those *things* served you well?"

Lauren nodded, her expression hardening. "I'm still breathing," she said. "A lot of people who've tried to harm us can't say the same."

Dave smiled and almost chuckled. "Janey, there's not a single, solitary doubt in my mind that whoever they were, justice was levied appropriately. I'm confident they had it coming to them." He paused, taking a close look at her. "But since we're on the topic, let me ask you this. How are you taking it?"

Lauren lifted a brow. "How am I taking what?"

"Let me rephrase," said Dave. "How are you dealing with the fact that you've taken a life?"

Lauren paused for long moment. *Lives would be a more appropriate term,* she thought. "I don't think I know how to answer that."

"Give it a shot."

"I am. And I just don't have an answer for you."

Displaying concern for her, Dave put both his hands on Lauren's shoulders. "Look at me for a second. How...many?"

Lauren hesitated, then shrugged, looking somewhat ashamed. "I stopped counting."

"You stopped counting? Or you lost count?"

"I don't know. Maybe it's both. But it's the only way I know how to cope with it," Lauren spouted off. She hopped down from the tailgate and stepped away. "I know I probably didn't turn out the way you expected, and I'm sorry if what I'm saying disappoints you."

"Hey, watch yourself," Dave ordered. "If anyone knows about life's tendency to throw curveballs, it's me, young lady. Believe me. It's up to each of us to adapt individually...the only way we know how. And this has diddly-squat to do with my expectations. So let's just nip that in the bud right here and right now. This is me you're talking to, David R. Graham, former first sergeant, United States Army Special Forces, and I am exhibiting the magnitude of my concern for you. I'm worried about you, Janey."

"Well, don't be," Lauren said firmly. "I am doing just fine."

"Yeah. I can see that. How's your head feeling, by the way?"

Lauren tracked him, detecting a playful smirk emerging on his face. She tried displaying one of her own. "It hurts. And that ibuprofen your guy gave me doesn't seem to be helping much." She took several steps closer to him. "I'm sorry. Truth is, I missed you. I missed all of you. And I'm really glad you guys decided to show up when you did."

"It's good to be missed," Dave said. "And, baby girl, if something ever happened to you, there's no way I could live with myself. That being said, I'm glad we happened upon you when we did, too." He reached for her, and Lauren stepped in, wrapping her arms around his torso. The embrace was brief. Dave cautiously put his hand on top of her head, placing an affable kiss on her forehead. "I want you to know that I'm sorry about what you've had to go through, and I'm extremely sorry to hear about your dad. Good-natured, genuine people like the two of you shouldn't have to be forced to deal with the nastiness in this world. I've never met your mom or your sister or anyone else in your family, but I'm certain they deserve the same consideration." Dave paused, kicking the ground with the tip of his boot. "Be that as it may, I've changed my mind regarding your predicament. Whatever help you need back home, including getting there, I'm going to make happen for you."

"Why?"

"Oh hell, I don't know, Janey," Dave retorted playfully. "Maybe it's because I met this teenage girl a few years back with this…vastly large chip on her shoulder. She used to piss me off like the dickens, and I was ready to give her the boot there at first. I thought she was the same as all the rest, but she proved me wrong. She was intelligent, dedicated, and sincere—willing to work hard to get what she wanted. She strived to be better than average. She was a fast learner, and while she was my student, she even managed to teach me some things along the way. Up until the point of meeting her, I had all but lost faith in the youth in this country, but she turned me into a believer and showed me there were things out there still worth fighting for."

A smile slowly emerged on Lauren's face. "That doesn't sound like you changed your mind to me. It sounds more like you had a change of heart."

"Yeah, well, maybe I did," Dave said, grinning. "So here's the deal…I'll arrange some decent means of transport back home, along with the good doctor and the good doctor's consort. I'll even look into what kind of meds we can spare so we can ship them along with you. I can't guarantee anything, but as you're aware, there aren't many guarantees in life."

Lauren smiled. "I'll take what I can get."

Dave walked back to the truck and reached for the stainless thermos he had brought along with him, then handed it to her.

"What's this?" Lauren asked.

Dave winked at her. "Liquid sunshine. Just a little something to make you feel better for the time being. It might calm your nerves a bit after all the shit you've been through."

"Okay. If you say so."

"I do say so. Look, I know things look really bad right now, Janey. But believe it or not, we're on the upswing of this mess. Lord knows it's far from being over, but the good guys are well on their way to pulling out a win."

Lauren twisted the top off the thermos, and steam rose from the upper orifice into the brisk morning air. While watching Dave closely, she took a whiff. "Holy shit," she said, her eyes widening. "What is this?"

"It's a present. From your secret Santa."

"You're kidding."

"Nope. He told me to tell you happy belated birthday, and he's sorry that he hasn't had time to come see you," said Dave. "He's off on a foxhunt, looking for any stray rabid dogs that might have gotten away during the assault." He paused. "It's not a typical birthday gift, but then again, you're not a typical eighteen-year-old, either."

Lauren sniffed the thermos once more. "It smells incendiary. Is it going to blow up in my face?"

Dave snorted. "No, but it'll work better than that ibuprofen, just might make your vision a little blurry, so go slow."

Lauren giggled and hesitated before trying it. "Great, that's all I need." She turned the bottle up, pouring a portion of the warm distilled concoction onto her tongue, wincing at the point of contact. "Dear Lord…that is wicked strong. Is this what I think it is?"

"Santa called it a hot toddy, but it's not the typical recipe," Dave said. "I think he makes his with moonshine instead of bourbon. Now, don't drink all of it. It's probably not the best idea after a concussion. But for someone who's been through the hell you have…and definitely looks it, I doubt it could hurt. You look like you could use a little tranquility."

"Dad wouldn't disagree." Lauren took another sip, gasping over the sting when she swallowed. "I appreciate it. And I'll make sure to tell Santa if I ever get a chance to see him. I guess these missions are keeping you guys really busy."

Dave nodded. "Yeah, that they are."

"It's been so long since I've seen you," Lauren lamented. "I'm already dreading the point where we say goodbye again."

"All things being equal, I'm not looking forward to it either, Janey. Thing is, I don't think I can allow our paths to remain separate anymore. After what I learned today, it just wouldn't be the right."

"What do you mean by that?"

"I guess what I mean is, if I'm going to provide you and your friends with transport and a security detail to go along with it, eventually I'm going to need those things back. Meaning I may plan on dropping by for a visit every so often."

Lauren squinted, her lips parting. "What?"

Dave folded his arms and rocked back and forth on his heels. "I'm going to send you home with a force substantial enough to ward off *problems*. And believe you me, Janey, the Allegheny Highlands and surrounding valleys are practically replete with problems. I'll send two, maybe three squads of men along—well-qualified men—and a few armored transport vehicles in a convoy. They'll be under orders to remain there with you, and the rest of the unit will rendezvous with them at a later date. At that point, we'll put our heads together and come up with a plan. Something that works out for all of us for the future. As uncertain as it is, I don't need, nor do I desire, any more uncertainties."

Lauren felt her heartbeat flutter. She put her hand on her chest to assess. "Do you mean that? Are you serious right now?"

Dave swallowed hard, pursing his lips. "Yeah, I believe I am."

"I don't know what to say."

"I'm going to send Neo. That'll guarantee we'll be able to maintain comms between your valley and the rest of us, no matter where we go. He'll have a squad with him, but those guys aren't the best at grunt work, so Richie's going too. He's got a team of advanced light infantryman who are well trained and adept at guaranteeing safe passage."

Excited as she was, Lauren sighed loudly. "Richie? Look, I'm not trying to sound unappreciative, Dave, but does it really have to be him?"

Dave squinted at her. "I know Richie's a pain in the ass…trust me, I've worked with him for years. But one thing's for certain, in a firefight, he is an absolute menace to the enemy, a force to be reckoned with. Kinda like you."

"Fine. I don't exactly treasure the comparison, but you're right about him being a menace. I guess I'll find a way to deal with him somehow." Lauren smiled slightly. "Thank you so much for everything."

"You're welcome. Dividing my team up puts me at a disadvantage. But I can't leave you hanging after everything you've told me today." He paused. "For now though, I gotta make myself scarce for a while to get some shit done. You and your friends are welcome to move about freely. The men know who you are now, so make yourselves at home as best you can until it's time to move."

"Can you answer a question for me before you go?"

"That depends on the question."

"Earlier on, you hinted at something...I haven't been able to get it out of my head since you said it."

Dave turned on his heels, adjusted his rifle's sling, and spit into the dirt. "I have a feeling I might know what you're getting at...but, shoot."

"The children," Lauren said, "where are they?"

The former Green Beret hesitated. "They're keeping them in separate camps."

"Why?"

The slits in Dave's eyes opened wide enough that Lauren could see his stone-cold gray irises yards away. "It doesn't matter why. They're children, Janey. One of our most prized commodities, though you'd never know it by the way they were mistreated, molded, brainwashed, and practically thrown to the wolves by the state over the years. Let's just say not much has changed."

Lauren looked away, her expression contorting. "Indoctrination..." she whispered, trailing off.

"What was that?"

"Just something Dad used to say all the time." She hesitated. "I don't like the thoughts that are swirling in my head right now, Dave. Not in the least."

"All things being equal, I'm far from getting the warm and fuzzies, too." He paused. "Edmund Burke was right. All it takes for evil to triumph is for good men to do nothing. Well, the men you see here playing slap-ass are just that. Good men—handpicked by yours truly. And no one is standing around idle while evil runs rampant through these hills. We're doing something about it." He adjusted his rifle again and placed his weight on his right heel. "It's kinda funny, you know...we always knew a day would come where a war would be fought here, but the face of our intended enemy sure has changed. As it stands, Zero Dark Armageddon has been placed on semipermanent standby. There's more precious items requiring our direct attention."

Dave turned and started away. "Our enemy may have changed, but the rules haven't. There are no rules of engagement for any war fought on American soil. I don't care who the enemy is. If their intentions are evil, tyrannical, or malicious in any way, as God as my witness, we will put them down once and for all, or die trying."

Lauren watched the venerable former Special Forces soldier march away, his shoulders squared and his posture formidable, same as it had been on the day she had first met him.

No rules of engagement, she thought. After what she had witnessed and personally experienced, it was a notion Lauren could not disagree with.

"We'll pop smoke sometime tomorrow morning, so if you need anything in the interim, don't hesitate to ask," Dave hollered back. "Within reason, of course, don't let your mind wander too far."

"How do I find you in a sea of other black uniforms? And why black, by the way?"

Dave stopped and quarter-turned. "Because good guys wear black." He pulled his collar down, exposing a throat mic identical to the one Lauren had seen Woo Tang wearing on his neck. "Just grab somebody wearing one of these and tell him or her to holler for me on the radio. I usually answer after the third or fourth time. Usually."

As Dave walked on, Lauren began to recount their whole conversation. "Radios," she said under her breath. "How ironic." She shook her head and leaned against the truck's tailgate. "For a man who detested them as much as you, Dave."

Lauren sat there for a moment, running her spoon through what remained of the beef stroganoff she hadn't yet finished, noticing that it had abated from hot to lukewarm. After a moment, a thought occurred to her.

Radios. Dave hated them, said never to rely on them, and preferred training without them while leaning on alternative means of communication.

Neo was here. And Dave was now sending him to the valley with them.

Dad.

"Oh, shit," she said, her brow furrowing. "Dad's radios. Dammit, I totally forgot…"

There had been a reason Alan Russell had packed away a spare set of ham radios inside an EMP-resistant container, and there had been a reason Lauren was the only other person who knew the combination to the lock securing it. It had occurred to her the day she had opened it, but she hadn't given it so much as a thought since that day.

Had their purpose been specifically for her father to make contact with her and her family? She had no way of knowing—they could have just as easily been for his own use had he made it home. But what if it had been the other way around? What if he had specifically placed the devices there, believing that Lauren would figure them out and assemble a station so that he could communicate with his family?

And what if he had been trying to contact them—this whole time?

"Oh Jesus," Lauren whispered to herself as her stomach turned. She recalled the titles of the chapters she had skimmed through in the black three-ring binder accompanying the radios. Solar power. Antennas and direction finding. Propagation. What was propagation? Had there been enough information in the notebook to put together an operable radio station?

Lauren tried desperately not to dwell on the past and the things she had failed to follow up on, but she couldn't help but wonder.

Then she remembered what Dave had said to her only moments before.

There's always a reason for the way everything goes down.

By some means, a perilous situation had concluded with a fortunate ending. Lauren and the others would be returning home soon, bringing along with them what they had left the valley in search of.

And now Dave Graham's RTO, his number one communications expert, was coming along with them. And there was a reason for that too.

Lauren needed to find him.

CHAPTER 12

Allegany County, Maryland
Saturday, December 4th. Present day

R TO THEODORE PARSONS, BETTER KNOWN by his chosen moniker 'Neo' to those closest to him, had been one of the original cast members inducted into Dave Graham's unit. Of those usual suspects, he had also been the most challenging for Lauren to get to know, due to a characteristic incapacity to socialize or carry on typical, everyday conversations. Although no positive confirmation had ever been provided to her concerning his behavioral irregularities, it had been rumored that Neo was autistic, and if Lauren were to wager a guess, she would presume he fell somewhere in the higher functioning portion of the known autism spectrum.

Although plagued by repetitive mannerisms and lacking the common skills that came natural to most, Neo possessed a finely honed set of unique strengths all his own and an aptitude considered by many of his fellow servicemen to be extraordinary. While most sufferers of autism were typically affected with communicative difficulties, both verbal and nonverbal, so long as some type of radio equipment was involved, Neo remained unaffected, and his skills and knowledge had earned him a permanent and well-respected slot within the ranks.

Lauren had spent the better part of an hour exploring the grounds, but it hadn't taken her long to find where Neo had set up his temporary communications outpost. All she had to do was look for the masts, angled guy ropes, and wire antennas she had seen him erect many times before during extended field training exercises at Point Blank Range.

Neo was seated atop a five-gallon bucket in front of a folding table with several metal cases appearing to be radio equipment sitting atop it. Each case was either black or green in color and had a profusion of switches, knobs, and glowing meters on the front, along with an accompaniment of assorted wires hanging from the rear. One of Neo's hands was busily spinning a large knob while the other was gripping a microphone.

Spotting the headphones covering his ears, Lauren decided that orally beckoning for him was out of the question. She decided to move in closer and try to steal his attention with visual cues.

Once she got within ten feet of Neo's table, he peeked up at her and abruptly snapped his fingers, pointing to the rope supports and guylines being used to hold his antenna masts upright. "Don't trip over those. It took me forever to get them up."

"Don't worry, I won't," Lauren replied. She started to say something else, but noticed that Neo was paying her no mind.

"I can't talk right now," he said, his voice rattling off at a high rate of speed. "I'm checked in to a net." He glanced up at her awkwardly before turning away and resuming his activities.

"Will you be done soon? I really need to talk—"

Neo waved her off midsentence.

"Okay, I suppose I'll just stand here and wait until you're done... with whatever you're doing." Lauren drew closer, watching Neo's eyes glance up at her with scrutiny and dart away with every step she took. Finally, she got within reach of the table and took a knee beside him. She waited, watching him work the radios and occasionally utter something into the microphone she didn't understand.

Several minutes later, Neo keyed the mic and said, "Roger that, net. This is foxtrot-alpha-nineteen going secure. Foxtrot-alpha-nineteen out." Neo slid the headphones just above his right ear and adjusted the volume on a different radio set to his far left. After fidgeting with a few other knobs, he eventually looked Lauren's way and gave her a crooked smile. His pupils shifted horizontally behind the thick lenses of his eyeglasses. "LT said you were here. But I didn't believe him." He pushed the frames of his glasses over the bridge of his nose. "Long time no see."

Lauren grinned. "It's good to see you. I see you're still doing your thing."

"My thing?"

Lauren pointed to the radio equipment, and Neo's attention shifted to her finger. "Yeah...your *thing*."

"Oh. Yeah."

Smiling, she looked beyond to Neo's antenna array. "I sometimes wish I understood more about this stuff. I still have no idea what I'm looking at."

Neo continued to fidget with his radios. "That's funny. I never knew you were interested."

"I agree, it is funny," Lauren said. "Because I never knew I was either." She pointed to a device Neo was tapping on with the index finger and thumb of his left hand. "Is that a Morse code key? I think my dad used to have a few of them."

"Actually, it's an iambic keyer, sometimes called a two-lever paddle. I used to use a straight key, but I can send faster with these. One paddle sends dits and the other sends dahs." Neo turned to her momentarily. "Your dad's a ham, right?"

Lauren nodded a yes. "I'm surprised you remember that."

"My mind was built to remember things. Did he teach you the code?"

"He introduced me to it, but I learned it myself. Granted, there's no way I could read it as fast as you're sending it right now, but I know it well enough to know it."

"It takes lots of practice."

Lauren smiled at him. "I bet it does. But it takes even more practice to carry on two conversations at the same time."

Neo let a grin slip out, and a hint of color filled his cheeks. "It's good you know the code," he said. "We sometimes use it to supplement hand signals and other unspoken comms."

Lauren raised a brow. "I'll make sure to keep that in mind."

"You do that. And I'll make sure the unit knows you're proficient." Neo scratched an ear. "You know...maybe someday, if there's time, I can teach you more about radios. It's not that hard, really. Just simple math, electricity, and basic electronics. Beyond that, it helps to know how the sun affects the atmosphere and propagation. Then you have other things like reflection, diffraction, refraction, absorption, polarization, and scattering…but it's not complicated." He eyeballed her from the corner of his eye, then looked away.

"Okay…one of the words you just said…*propagation*. I used to hear my dad say it all the time. What does it mean?"

Neo turned to Lauren, his face lighting up upon hearing her interest. "You really want to know?"

Lauren nodded her head.

Neo spoke with gusto. "Propagation is just a fancy word for travel," he began. "The way a radio wave travels varies depending on its size or frequency. Radio waves in the VHF range—which are anywhere from around ten to a hundred meters in length, mostly travel by line of sight. Radio waves in the HF range are much, much longer and utilize environmental factors such as ionospheric refraction to propagate from one location to the other. The higher the frequency, the shorter the wave, and the more directional and the more line of sight the propagation characteristics become. The lower the frequency, the longer the wave is, and the more dependent propagation becomes on environmental and atmospheric conditions. And lower frequencies tend to travel greater distances." He paused. "There's a lot more to it, but that's the basic premise. Have I lost you yet?"

"Kind of," Lauren said, grinning.

"Want me to start over?"

"No, that's okay. It's a lot to digest, but I think I understand. My dad used to tell me about his walkie-talkies and how he used to talk to other people for hundreds of miles when he was on top of a mountain."

Neo nodded with exuberance. "Right. It's called hill-topping…it's like a cheat mode. It extends your overall line of sight. That's why VHF, UHF, and microwave radio transmitters are placed on mountaintops. Depending on elevation, it can extend their range for hundreds of miles, even with low-power transmitters. But you don't need elevation or strategies like hill-topping when you're using HF."

"HF?"

"It's the abbreviation for high frequency…the term used for frequencies under thirty megahertz and down to around three thousand kilohertz." Neo peered at Lauren clumsily, unaware of the proper way to look at her. "Did you stop by for a quick primer on radios? We'll be departing soon to take you home, and it's going to take me at least twenty-one or twenty-two minutes to dismantle the station and pack up all this gear."

"No, I didn't come here for a lesson, but I would love to learn more, though. Maybe someday you can show me when we have more time."

Neo nodded awkwardly and stood. "Maybe."

Lauren hesitated, watching him fret over dismantling his station. "Neo? I have a favor to ask of you."

"Like what?"

"Something that's right up your alley. I wanted to see if you could look into it for me when you get back to the valley."

Now in the process of unplugging and rolling up cables, Neo stopped in his tracks. He peeked Lauren's way, but only for a second. "You're not going with us?"

Lauren understood that Neo was just as analytical as she was. There was no point in her hiding anything from him. "No, I'm not. I've decided to stay. And, oddly enough, you're the first one I've told."

Neo nodded and resumed his activities. He opened the five-gallon bucket he'd been using as a stool and began to stow rolled-up cables inside it. "LT told you about the kids, didn't he?"

Lauren hesitated, watching Neo closely. "Yeah. He did."

The look on Neo's face was indiscernible, as if a thought occurred to him and had taken him to a place he didn't want to be. He stopped all activity and stood dormant, a resigned look befalling him. "Did he tell you what those people are doing to them?"

"He said they were being kept separate in other camps, but he didn't elaborate much beyond tha—"

"I remember when my dad used to *hit me,*" Neo blurted out, almost angrily. He squinted his eyes and forced his words through clenched teeth. "He used to ask me…questions. Tough questions. Inane questions. And when I didn't give him the answers he wanted, he would hit me—sometimes with his hands, sometimes with other things. He didn't understand my…impediment." Neo studied Lauren fleetingly. "It's not that I didn't want to answer him…it was because I couldn't. I don't suppose you've noticed, but I am a trifle socially and emotionally inept. Far from what most people consider normal."

Lauren stood and moved closer, looking upon him thoughtfully. "I don't think you're any less normal than anyone else I've met before."

Neo smiled self-consciously at the remark, but it vanished quickly. "My mom understood me, but no matter what my mom told my dad, it didn't matter. He'd hit me. And if he couldn't reach me, he'd hit me with whatever he could. Pens, books, rulers, cell phones...I think he threw a briefcase at me once. When he didn't get what he wanted in the time he wanted it, that was how he acted." He glanced at Lauren again, suppressed discomfort from long ago evident in his eyes. "Abuse is bad. It's one of the worst things. It's damaging, and it shouldn't be allowed. Those kids...are being abused, Lauren." He paused for a long moment. "It needs to stop—the abuse needs to stop."

Lauren began registering the look in Neo's eyes, and she could feel the fire inside her soul rekindling again. She didn't fully understand the situation, but it had become evident that something evil was going on—something directly related to the wickedness that had taken advantage of a country brought to its knees by a societal collapse.

Lauren reached for him, but Neo pulled away. "Neo, I—"

"Abuse is bad," he said. "Even after it's over, it's not over. It's never over. The memories remain, and try as one might to ignore them or flush them out, they never stop haunting you." He glanced at her again, vacantly. "Is that why you decided to stay?"

Lauren shrugged. "I don't know, Neo. I honestly don't know. I just haven't been able to stop thinking about it."

"If you can't stop thinking about it, there's a reason why," Neo said. "I think it's both good and bad that you decided to stay. I think it's good because you are a *force multiplier*, and we can use someone like you. But I think it's bad because this is a war. And not everyone is ready to fight in a war." Neo began packing his radio equipment into large mil-spec containers. "So what was the favor you needed?"

Lauren tried snapping herself to attention to match Neo's tempo. "My dad left a set of ham radios in an EMP-shielded container. It's sitting in the shed behind our cabin and—"

"Ham radios?" Neo rubbernecked, his interest piqued. "Are you sure? What kind? What brand names?"

"Easy there, killer. I don't know much about them. I don't even know if they work or not. I just know where they're at and that he put them there."

Neo half-smiled. "And you want someone to figure them out for you."

"Not just anyone."

"I'll look into it the moment we arrive. No problem."

"I knew I could count on you," Lauren said. "There's a lock on the case. The only two people in the world who knew the combination were my dad and me." She handed him a folded napkin with a scribbled sequence of numbers. "Now there are three of us who know it."

Neo took the napkin, read the numbers aloud, and handed it back to Lauren a few seconds later. "Got it."

"Are you sure you don't want to keep this?" Lauren asked, looking confused.

"No need. Radios might be my thing, but numbers are my everything."

CHAPTER 13

Allegany County, Maryland
Saturday, December 4th. Present day

AS LAUREN EXPLORED THE RAILYARD GROUNDS, a setting malformed into a post-collapse prison camp, she started to notice the human elements of Dave Graham's unit were no longer paying her little to no mind. Instead of peeking at her and turning away, they were now looking upon her with kind regard and smiling at her. Several of them had even sent along informal salutes. Lauren took their gestures to indicate the cat was officially out of the bag, and her identity was no longer a question mark.

The unit had set fire to all of the remaining buildings and improvised structures, and the arid smell of burning wood and plastic cascaded through the air, mixed with the rotten-egg smell of sulphur and the occasional garlicy odor of phosphorus.

All weapons caches had been emptied of their contents and destroyed. Utilizable supplies were now in the process of being requisitioned. Fuel was retrieved, and vehicles were checked for their operational status. If their engines turned over, they were added to the slapdash collection of civilian and military vehicles already in the unit's motor pool.

Amongst the thirty or so military vehicles Lauren had spotted parked in and around the camp, she recognized modern-day ones she'd seen before, such as Cougar MRAPs and even the new Joint Light Tactical Vehicle, or JLTV. Some were painted olive drab, others in beige or sand,

and there were even a few appearing to have been spray-painted on the fly. However Dave and his men had managed to attain them, Lauren guessed there to be a colorful story attached.

As she continued her stroll amongst the river of vehicles, debris, piles of bodies, and talking heads, Lauren spotted Christian walking towards her, having emerged from the middle of a crowd of black-clothed troops, and he was eating something. Something half-exposed in a shiny, thin, foil wrapper, and it was sparkling in the early-morning sun like a ten-karat diamond ring.

As she got closer to him, Lauren pointed at it. "Christian, what is that? Is that what I think it is?" She paused, squinting. "Is that a Pop-Tart?"

Christian nodded, crumbs coating his smiling lips. "Yup," he said, his speech garbled through a mouth full of half-chewed pastry. "*Cherry* Pop-Tart. Frosted, too."

Lauren narrowed her eyes even further. "Are you seriously just going to stand there and eat it right in front of me?" She could feel her stomach begin to twinge at the sight of something so rare. It was practically a culinary delight.

Christian shrugged. "I don't know, you want me to break off a piece of it for you?"

"You inconsiderate ass. You didn't really just find one solitary Pop-Tart and walk unswervingly over here to eat it in front of me, did you?"

Christian took another bite, then smiled deviously. "Come on, Lauren. I know we've been on the down and outs…but at least give me a *little* credit." He reached into his jacket pocket and presented another, then handed it to her.

Lauren grabbed it and ripped it open in a rush. Within seconds, she had the entire pastry stuffed in her mouth and was chomping down on it merrily. "Holy crap. It's insanely delicious. I can't remember how long it's been since I've had one of these."

"You're welcome," Christian said, licking some crumbs from his fingers.

"I take back everything bad anyone's ever said about you."

"Cool beans." Christian shot his thumb over his shoulder, gesturing to the railcars in the distance. "There's an entire container of these things back there, in assorted flavors. But frosted cherry has always been my favorite."

"Mine too, oddly enough."

"We must've been separated at birth," he joked. "This is nothing, though...just an appetizer. You'll never guess what else I found over there."

"I'll believe anything you tell me right now," Lauren said. "Breakfast junk food has always been my kryptonite, and this sugar high I'm feeling right now is ruthless. This filling might as well be sodium pentothal."

"Hmm...Lauren Russell has a weakness. That's good to know... I'll file that one away," Christian remarked, turning to gesture to his aft. "There's another container back there...and it's full, top to bottom, with...candy bars."

Lauren's eyes boggled. "You're joking."

Christian grinned and shook his head ever so slowly in the negative.

"Okay, you're not joking."

"Nope. Afraid not. Snickers, Three Musketeers, Milky Way, Twix, you name it."

Lauren's expression was covetous. "Enough said. I'll be raiding that one in approximately thirty seconds, then."

"Same. You know, a few hours ago, I thought we were screwed... like we had somehow fallen into some bottomless pit, right into the depths of a living hell. Now, after what I just saw, I'm pretty sure we might've just died and gone to heaven."

Lauren finished her Pop-Tart and stuffed the wrapper in her pocket. "Speaking of heaven...I have some news."

"What kind? Good, bad, or meh?"

She thought a moment. "Somewhere in between, only, way better than what we're used to. Have you seen Norman? It would be good for him to know what's going on too."

Christian nodded. "Last time I saw him, he was with Fred, over in that little MASH tent your buddies set up near the highway. You don't seem distant or let down...did things work out?"

"And then some. Dave is going to provide transportation for us, the well-armed, not-to-be-messed-with kind."

"Well, damn. That's nice of him."

"And Fred is coming around. He's going to pull through. They have him on pain meds now, but he's conscious, and he hasn't stopped bitching about wanting to go home. They're working to get him stable so he can go along for the ride."

Christian's eyes lit up. "That's amazing. Way better than I expected. But what about the doctor thing? Is he sending a medic with us too?"

"Not exactly."

"Not exactly?"

Lauren smiled at him. "You're never going to believe this, but I found Dr. Vincent…just not the same Dr. Vincent we were looking for."

"I'm not following you."

"There are two, father and son, and I ran into his son here…or rather, he ran into me." She paused, offering him a sheepish grin. "Remember the guy you kicked?"

Christian looked puzzled. "Yeah, the one who tried to grab you…the fanny tosser, right? I don't know, Lauren. That's bizarre. It's fortuitous, ironic, and kind of irritating all at the same time. Why the hell didn't he do something to help Fred while we were locked up?"

"Calm down, I already got to the bottom of it. He was keeping their identities a secret. Apparently, our captors haven't been treating affiliates of the medical society very well."

"Fine, whatever," Christian said indifferently. "I guess it's neither here nor there now. So what type of crew is your buddy Dave sending back home with us?"

Lauren turned her head away. "At least three squads. And I know two of the guys going along. I used to train with them."

Christian sighed as his brows elevated. "Well, that solves a portion of *one* of our problems, I guess." He shuffled up to Lauren's side and folded his arms. "I take it, once Fred is ready to go, we'll be taking our leave of this place, then. Shame. I was just starting to like it around here."

Lauren hesitated, knowing what she was about to divulge wasn't going to be nearly as easy for Christian to swallow as the Pop-Tart he had just inhaled. "There's something else I need to tell you. And since I don't exactly know how else to say it, I'm just going to spit it out." She hesitated again, long enough for Christian to stare her down. "I won't be going home with you."

Christian's arms fell to his sides as a look of disgust formed on his face. "Come again? You're kidding, right?"

Lauren didn't respond.

"Jesus. You're not kidding."

"No," said Lauren, shaking her head slightly. "I'm sorry, but I'm not."

"Okay, if you're not going home with us, then where the hell are you going?" He paused, pointing to the group of men gathered in the distance. "With them?"

Lauren didn't offer a response again, but Christian didn't need her to fill in the blanks for him.

"Oh, come on! You've got to be kidding me! After everything we've been through so far? Lauren, I'm sorry, but I don't agree with this at all. Jesus…talk about selfish and careless."

"You're free to think what you want, but it's my decision. And for what it's worth, I'm sorry, Christian."

"Yeah. Yeah, I bet you are. You know, forget me for a second…but you might want to consider how the people who care about you the most are going to take the news."

"I already have," Lauren said. "I haven't stopped thinking about it since I made the decision."

"Can you at least tell me why? Can you explain to me why you're doing this? I mean, seriously, Lauren, your behavior lately has been off the charts, and this…is just absurd. Read my lips—we've already divided ourselves to the point of risking everything, and now you want to split us up and add yet another fragment and make the rift even bigger than it already is?"

"That's not what this is about. And that's not what I'm trying to do. There's something keeping me here, and I have to figure it out."

"Your mom is going to go apeshit when we pull up and you don't get out of the truck," said Christian. "And that's nothing. Grace will do worse…she'll probably skin me alive or cut out one of my kidneys in my sleep over this."

Lauren closed her eyes and turned away.

"And what about John? How's he going to react? Have you given any thought to how devastated he's going to be?"

"Of course I have."

"And? Christ, Lauren! All that man does all day, every day is think about you…like you're the center of his universe, the only thing he lives for. You can see it in his eyes. He worships the ground you walk on, and all you do is shit on him every chance you get."

Lauren shot Christian a torrid look, forewarning him not to expound. "All right. You can bring this lecture to a standstill, right there," she hissed, her tone blistering. "I mean it, don't tread further along that course with me. Listen, Dave told me some things…about some of the camps they've found. Then I talked to Neo, and what he said *more* than corroborated what Dave told me. It's been weighing on me ever since, and I can't explain it. I just—"

"Lauren, you're babbling," Christian interrupted. "What exactly is going on?"

Lauren hesitated, sliding her hands into her front pockets. "There's children out there involved in this mess. Kids. Little fucking kids… being held in cages like the one we were just in, or worse."

"Kids? Lauren, they're not your responsibility. You don't even know who they are. They're not your family or your friends…they're virtually nothing to you. It's not up to you to save them, and it's not up to us to save this country or the entire world, either. We have to stay focused on what directly affects us."

Lauren bristled. "Those are probably the most selfish words I've ever heard you say. How can you possibly think for one second that the future of this country and the entire world doesn't somehow directly affect people like you and me? The children are the future, Christian. Newer generations fade in and bloom while older ones wither away and die off eventually…that's the way of the world. No one can escape that. And whatever these people are doing, whatever diabolical plan they have, it has Dave's full attention, and it merits mine." Lauren paused. "And that's why I have to go. I'm needed here, and for the time being, my place is here with them."

"No," Christian barked. "Your place is at home with us. With your family. That's where you're needed, Lauren. I seriously cannot believe I'm having this conversation with you right now." He paused. "You know, your sister put me up to this charade. She told me to go on this expedition to protect you, because you supposedly needed me. Looking back, I don't think that's the case at all. Maybe you did at one time, but certainly not now. I don't have the foggiest idea what you need, other than some sedatives, a decent psychiatrist, and a boot in the ass."

"I've made my decision," Lauren said resolutely. "And amazingly enough, I've somehow managed to cover all the other bases too. So no need to thank me. Everyone gets a ride back home—safely, I might add—along with a doctor and medical supplies and some much-needed food, seeing as how every railcar in this place is practically chock-full of it. You'll all be back soon with everything we left home for. And I'll be home in a few weeks or so. I won't be gone forever."

"Stop making light of this. You know this is wrong—dead wrong. You know this is going to hurt people, Lauren. People you and I both care about."

"Please!" Lauren snapped. "Don't you even dare go there with me! Don't you fucking dare start in on me about hurting people. Let us not overlook my grandparents and their current whereabouts, and who among us was integral in having them placed there, because I pledge to you, Christian Hartman, former FPS officer, former DHS security agent, I won't forget any of it." Lauren paused, giving him time to consider her arguments while her demeanor allayed. "I swear to you, if I could do this any other way, I would. But this has to happen, just like you and the others getting back home has to happen. We left the valley practically defenseless, and for all we know, DHS is still stalking us, just waiting for the right moment to strike. Unless you've somehow managed to overlook that too."

"I haven't forgotten," replied Christian. "I'll never forget that. And I know when we get back, there's still plenty to do. It would just be preferable to have your...skills along for the ride instead of leaving them behind."

"I promise you, the skills of the men Dave is sending along with you will be more than adequate."

"I'd still rather have you with us than them—regardless."

Lauren shook her head in refusal. "And I've already told you that's not going to happen."

"Fine," Christian spat. "I give. I mean, truly...I give up. There's no point to this. There's just no resolving this...no matter what, no matter what I try, I can't fix this. And I sure as hell can't fix you."

Lauren scowled at Christian. With an enraged look in her eyes, she flipped her hair over her shoulder, squaring off with him. "That's good. I'm glad. Because I'm not broken."

She pulled her arms from the sleeves of the fleece liner Christian had given her the night before and handed it to him. "Go home, Christian. And when you get there, make sure to tell my sister that."

Lauren spent an uncomfortable portion of the final hour before his departure explaining everything to Norman. Although pleased to know they had managed to procure a doctor and medical supplies, and with that, the chances of his son Lee surviving his illness had improved, he wasn't fond of leaving Lauren behind. He made his opinion clear to her, told her he loved her like the daughter he never had, and promised he would pass her sentiments on to his son John, knowing John wouldn't be thrilled.

Later that evening, after taking some time to contemplate her decision, Lauren made her way through the camp to where Dave Graham, Woo Tang, Sanchez, and Santa had gathered together. They stood in a huddle, bent over the hood of a brown, 1970s-era Land Rover, and each man had a bottle of beer in his hand.

Woo Tang caught sight of her immediately and, seeing her approach, broke from the group and moved over to her with a perplexed look on his face. "Lauren Russell, your ride home was set to depart hours ago. But something tells me you are mindful of that detail."

While she half smiled, Lauren nodded affirmation. "I am. I'm fully mindful of that detail, Jae."

One of Woo Tang's eyebrows rose while the other remained in place. "I see," he said, tipping up his beer. "Is something wrong or out of place?"

Lauren pursed her lips dismissively. "Hmm, no."

"Then I take it you have decided to accompany us on the next op?"

"Yeah. Yeah, I think I might've done just that."

Woo Tang paused a moment and gazed at her with a keen, attentive eye. "Are you certain you know what you are getting yourself into?"

Lauren reached for his free hand while grinning shamefully. After a moment, she grinned, blinked a few times and shook her head no.

"Then I will stand by your side until you become certain," he said, and took her by the hand, leading her back to the others, who were all now cognizant of and surprised by her presence.

Sanchez tapped the brim of his boonie hat and smiled broadly. "*Oye! Que bonita!* Attention on deck! There's a pretty face I haven't seen in a metric shit ton of days. Come here, *chica*! Give your homeboy a hug."

Lauren smiled and ran to him, finding herself wrapped in his beefy arms. "As you were. It's good to see you too, homeboy."

Sanchez tilted his head down, his nose coming within inches of Lauren's soiled, matted hair. "Damn, girl. What happened? Run out of shampoo at home?"

Lauren giggled. "No running water. Sorry about that." She slowly pulled away from him and looked up. "Showers haven't exactly been easy to come by."

"It's cool, it's cool. It's not that you smell bad or anything…you just don't smell as sweet as you used to," he jested, tilting his bottle up. "We're supposed to head back to Rocket Center at some point next week. Maybe we can get you all dolled up and back to normal there."

"Rocket Center?"

Sanchez started to respond, but was silenced by the harsh snap of Dave's fingers. "I'll…let LT explain it to you…when it's apropos."

Lauren backed away from Sanchez and something pudgy bumped into her right elbow. She turned her head to see Santa, the husky demolitions expert with the naturally painted white beard, standing within inches of her. She assumed he was smiling by the squint of his eyes, but couldn't see his mouth or teeth through the furriness of his facial hair.

"Did you get my present? The one I sent you?" he asked. "Or did douchebag Dave drink it all?"

"Watch it there, Gandalf," Dave chided, "or you'll be cleaning out piss tubes all day tomorrow with your tongue."

"I got your present. Thank you," Lauren said.

Santa lifted her off the ground into a hug. "I got plenty more where that came from…in assorted flavors."

Lauren tried to squeeze him back but couldn't, the length of her arms unable to match his circumference. "I've been given more presents in the past twenty-four hours than I know what to do with…and I appreciate all of them…and all of you, too."

"Aww," Santa said. "Isn't that darlin'? Tell you what, as long as you keep smiling and saying sweet little nothings like that, we'll just keep bringing them to ya. This Santa knows you deserve them."

After Santa let her down, Lauren turned to face Dave, somewhat dreading his reaction to her remaining behind after the convoy he'd put together as a favor to her had departed.

Instead of the vicious scowl she expected to see, Dave only smirked at her, one of his eyes squinting a little more than the other. "So, how do we explain this one, Janey? Change your mind? Or change of heart?"

Lauren shrugged. "More like a change of plans. You did say you needed every able body you can get."

"Is that what I said?"

"You did," she replied, inching her way over to him. "But it's mainly my heart that's keeping me here. Dad used to say it would always lead me in the right direction." She paused. "I hope you don't mind me deciding to hang around."

Dave huffed. "Seriously? Like I could do anything about it, even if I did mind." He winked at her.

Lauren smiled. "Permission to come aboard, then, Lieutenant? Or LT, or whatever they call you now?"

"Permission granted."

Sanchez and Santa offered slow claps and wolf whistles, and Lauren took a bow. She had always considered these men family and felt tremendously fortunate to be reunited with them. "Um, Dave?"

"Yeah, Janey."

"There's something I need."

Dave held up his bottle. "There's more of these in the back of the Rover. Help yourself. Unless you're referring to some other requirement of yours."

Lauren laughed. "No…it's something else."

"Here we go again. What is it this time?"

She gestured to herself. "I need a gun."

"Is that a fact?" Dave griped rhetorically, a slight edge in his voice.

"Yeah. I sort of…misplaced mine."

Dave eyeballed Sanchez, who had only now begun to stifle his goofing off. Then he cast a stare in Lauren's direction. "You did, did you? I seem to recall a lesson or two I taught…hell, it might've been three of them…concerning the magnitude of doing the opposite. Guess you weren't paying attention."

Lauren shrugged. "No, I remember your lessons—and a lot of the things you used to say all the time, too. In fact, I was hoping one of them in particular might afford me an alibi."

"And what might that be?"

Lauren shrugged. "Shit happens."

Dave groaned, rolled his eyes, and took a long drink. "Sounds like a crock of shit."

Santa presented his beer and tilted it. "Come on, LT...we both know how a crock of shit can undoubtedly become Army policy," he said, laughing. "And if our young Janey here needs a gun, by God, I say let's give her one."

"I second the motion," Sanchez said.

Santa smacked his hand down on the hood of Dave's ride. "Motion carried. Hell...looks to me like she could use two or three of them. And some fresh rags, too. Those civvies you got on look pretty ate up." He paused to look at the sky. "I'll take care of it. I know just the place."

"I will locate a suitable location for you to rack out for the night," said Woo Tang, moving to Lauren's side from behind. "Somewhere accommodations will far exceed those you have experienced in recent days."

Lauren twinkled at the thought of not having to sleep on the cold, rigid ground. "That would be divine."

"Outstanding," Santa said. "Miss Jane, get yourself some quality shut-eye. Tomorrow...Santa takes you shopping."

CHAPTER 14

Town of Edinburg
Shenandoah County, Virginia
Wednesday, December 1st

WHILE MARK SAT ON THE floor, he twiddled his thumbs. The living room of the home they had broken into to use as a temporary hideout was dusty and smelled of mold and mildew and other foul things he couldn't distinguish. He didn't much care to, either. The worst of the odors seemed to emanate from one of the home's bathrooms, and he'd already gotten queasy one too many times today.

Mark's plan wasn't turning out as he had expected, and he felt dissatisfied and anxious and was growing more frustrated by the minute. With a DHS team congregated not far away from their position, they were stuck here. And their refuge had to have been the filthiest home in the neighborhood.

Every so often, Mark's dissatisfaction with his predicament would find a distraction. His eyes would dart off to his right, only to clumsily look away and then repeat the process soon after.

Using the binoculars Mark had given her earlier on, Sasha was situated on all fours on her knees so she could watch from the corner of the bay window without being noticed. Using her free hand for support, both of her slender legs were pulled tightly together, effectively propping her curvy, denim-covered posterior into the air.

Sitting directly across from and facing his brother, Chad eyeballed Mark sternly, and after seeing him covet Sasha's backside for the umpteenth time, he hauled off and thumped Mark's shoulder with a glancing punch.

"Ouch!" Mark yelped. "What the hell was that for?"

"You know what it was for. You're all over the place right now, rubberneck. Square that shit away."

Sasha pulled back from the window, turned and moved in closer, plopping her butt on the floor. "I could've sworn I asked the two of you to stifle that crap." She sighed and, once again, reached into her jacket for her cigarettes.

"Sorry, Sasha, but my brother seems to be a bit distracted today, for some *reason*...or another," Chad explained. "I'm simply trying to keep him on point."

Sasha shook her head and lit up while examining the limited quantity of smokes remaining in the pack with a woeful gaze.

Mark sat up straight to catch a glimpse. "I can't believe you smoked that many already. You're like a chimney."

"Well, I kinda did go about a month without. I guess my body's playing catch-up." She looked to Mark sheepishly. "I don't suppose you have another pack of these beauties stuffed inside that backpack of yours, do you?"

Mark shook his head at first, then halted while a smile slowly spread across his face. "I might." He paused and awkwardly stirred while trying not to make eye contact with Sasha. "Suppose I did have some. What would you...give for them?"

Sasha snickered and removed the beanie from her head, allowing her streaked, graying locks to fall onto her shoulders. She coughed a couple of times, and her facial muscles tensed, allowing the crow's feet and subtle wrinkles in her skin to come forth and denote her age. "That's cute, kid. I like being buttered up, and I'm flattered, I am. And if I had anything to give, I would. How about I just smile and ask you nicely?"

Mark's smile dissipated as his cheeks blushed. "Sure," he said. "That'll...work just fine."

Chad sighed and rubbed his head. "Jesus. Enough. Either find a room or a bucket of cold water, Mark. If the carnal tension in this room gets any thicker, I'm leaving you both and turning myself in to DHS."

Sasha snickered and crawled back to her spot at the window, pulling the binoculars back to her eyes. She positioned her body in a manner slightly more modest than before. "The two of you are fine, upstanding young men. And while a little flirting never hurt anybody, let's be real with ourselves, shall we?" She paused and chuckled. "You boys would fall in love, and Sasha would fall asleep."

Several minutes of uncomfortable silence passed by before Mark felt obliged to say anything. "Any ideas what DHS is doing here?"

Chad nodded while pointing his index finger at his brother. "Damn good question, bro. I've been sitting here wondering the same thing."

"I've been watching agents going in and out of the Anderson house, with boxes and plastic bins in their arms. And some of them have been going around back with empty dollies and coming back loaded with buckets and all sorts of crud strapped to them." Sasha took a drag. "My club used to hole up there. It's not the first time I've seen a black DHS SUV entourage parked in the cul-de-sac, but it is the first time I've seen them on a shopping spree like this." She paused. "That was one of the reasons why Damien wanted to stay here as long as we did. Evidently, the owner was one of those doomsday preppers—he had enough supplies locked up in his basement to feed his family for a couple of years, maybe more. No guns though, oddly enough."

Mark leaned in. "What happened to the family who lived there?"

"Don't be naïve, kid. What do you think happened to them?" She let out a remorseful breath. "An unarmed family against a small army of heartless, drunk madmen with guns. They were easy pickin's. And it wasn't exactly a painless ending, either...for any of them."

Mark turned his head away contritely and rolled his lips between his teeth.

"So they're here to confiscate supplies, then?" Chad asked, his head cocked to the side.

"That's what it looks like," Sasha breathed.

"Weird."

"What's weird is how clean it is down there. The last time I saw this street, it was in complete shambles, and now it looks like somebody dropped a dime and called in the Merry Maids." Sasha snickered. "I could've sworn I even saw one of the spooks outside with a broom and dustpan a minute ago."

"Too bad they never made it to this place," Chad joked.

Mark hesitated. "But...no signs of the girls, though..."

Sasha closed her eyes and let out a sigh of despair. "No, I'm sorry, Mark. No sign of them at all. And I was hoping I would too, after seeing that creepy school bus sitting there. I thought it was a transport. But they got it filled to the brim with all the stuff they've been taking from the house." She paused. "I'm hoping maybe they came and got them weeks ago."

"Why would you say that?" Chad quizzed. "They'd be locked in the FEMA camp, then, wouldn't they?"

"Mm-hmm."

"And how could you hope for something like that?"

Sasha took a seat on the floor again and crossed her legs. Finishing her cigarette off, she doused it on the toe of her boot. "Hon, listen. Anywhere is better than here. No one wants to be forced to fend for themselves, especially those girls. You two, and a lot of fellas like you, were blessed to have skills that can keep you alive out here. Those chickadees, and so many others like them...since the moment they were plucked from their families, were lambs to the slaughter running scared in an open field bounded by starving wolves. I don't know who's caring for them now, and it doesn't matter...I guarantee it's way better than being stuck here alone, and galaxies better than how the brotherhood was treating them. I know what I'm talking about—I saw it with my own eyes, and I'm telling you, if DHS came here and took those girls to that camp, then there's a damn good chance they're all still alive and well. And that's something I can live with."

"Still seems shitty," Mark added.

Chad nodded his agreeance. "Very shitty."

"Oh, there's no doubt the camp's a sty. It's ran by turd burglars, too. And no one wants to be kept in a sty ran by turd burglars. But there's electricity there...food and shelter and heat. Plus, they've got doctors, nurses, and medicine." Sasha paused, glancing down between her legs at the floor. "Out here, in the wild blue yonder, they had nothing. Here, all you got is nature...and nature, as we've seen already today, can be a cruel bitch."

Chad hesitated before asking, "Have you been inside?"

Sasha nodded. "The camp? Sure. A bunch of times. That's where we came to know ole Dougie Bronson. He's the regional DHS commander, by the way. *El jefe*. Mr. King Shit himself." She gestured out the window to the cul-de-sac with her thumb. "That maggot weasel Bates over there is his number one."

"What's it like?" Mark inquired, his curiosity aroused.

Sasha rested her head in her hand and combed through her hair with her fingers. "Oh, as you might imagine. Lots of people, all ages, shapes and sizes, either hard at work or on their way to being hard at work. When they're not working or eating, they walk around aimlessly, looking sad and dejected with no clue what the future has in store for them. Then there's the agents. Lots of them. Black suits, security guards, and people with guns." Her brows elevated. "Lots of guns."

Mark nodded, turning his head away. "I've dreamt about it, but I don't think my imagination could do it justice."

"It's really not that big a deal, Mark, honestly," Sasha said. "After the collapse, or whatever everybody's calling it, FEMA rolled in heavy to put down mobs and rioting and shit. They were given an inch and took a mile; then a few months later, they took a few hundred of them." She paused. "You know that saying about absolute power corrupting absolutely? Well, I'm thinking that's exactly what happened, especially after I had the pleasure of meeting that Bronson dude. He's full of himself—an egomaniac on a power trip. Thinks he's God's gift to women too, and he's not even that good-looking, but he tries to make up for it by being smarmy."

Chad's eyes perked up. "Did you say smarmy?"

"Yeah, skeevy. Like when a man goes out of his way to be overly nice to a woman…but he's full of it. And his words basically drip out of his mouth like slime." Sasha rolled her lips between her teeth. "He's a monster, a sleazeball of the highest degree, and he doesn't care who knows it, either. People follow him because they're scared of him…and being a former club officer's former old lady, I know what that's like. But the shit he's doing…I think it's way beyond anything he was ever given permission to do by his superiors. Hell, I don't think he even has superiors anymore. I think he's acting on his own."

Mark looked confused. "Okay, but why, then? There has to be a reason why."

"Not always, kid. People don't need a reason to breathe, it just happens. Same goes for being an asshole, some of us are just born that way. I mean, look at me. I've only recently decided to part with my old errant ways. Aside from this recent transformation, I'm no different than any of them."

"I don't believe that," said Mark. "I don't believe that at all. And you're proving it to us right now."

Sasha smiled and reached for Mark's chin, cupping it with her thumb and index finger. "That's sweet, kid, it is. But if you knew the real me, the person I was before you met me on the mountain, you might think otherwise."

A sudden rumble from outside the house brought the conversation to a close. Whipping his head around instinctively, Chad crawled to the window and rested his chin on the sill. "Shit. We got more company."

"What kind?" his brother asked.

"The kind that drives around in two black MRAPs." Chad motioned for Sasha and Mark to keep their heads down and away from the window. "Looks like they're headed to join their friends."

"This is a popular place," said Mark. "What the hell are they doing bringing MRAPs to a deserted neighborhood?"

Sasha went to light up another cigarette, but after catching sight of the mine-resistant vehicles with gun turrets parading past through the window, she thought better of it. "It's a show of force. Normal for the times. They mosey those things up and down the roads all over the place, all day, every day," she said passively. "Don't forget where you are right now, kid. This is occupied territory…FEMA region three. That right there is the same show of force they used to scare everyone into handing over their guns and turning themselves in."

"Not everyone," Chad said.

Sasha nodded slightly. "You're right, stud. *Most* everyone. The ones who refused or played tough guy were either taken by force or took two to the chest."

Chad shook his head in disbelief. "I'm still amazed every time I hear something like that. Dad even used to say there was no way Americans would just bend over and give up their guns, especially to a corrupt government. Consequences be damned."

"Cold dead hands," Sasha huffed in a contemptuous tone. "Spoken like a true *'Merican*."

"What?"

"Sorry, hon. That's ill-begotten patriot logic," Sasha quipped. "It's easy being tough when a gun's not pointed at you or someone you love.

What if the consequences involved some clown federal agent with an attitude in full riot regalia, all hopped up on barbiturates and Red Bull, screaming demands at you while holding an MP5 like the one you've got to your mother's head? Or maybe your brother's? Or your sister's? Because that's what they did, and it worked wonders." She paused. "All they had to do was scare the living shit out of people, one house at a time, one loving family at a time, gestapo style. Did you really think their plan was to come after everyone at the same time? Or wait until everyone in the country found a way to unite and be strong enough to actually put up a fight against them?" Sasha chuckled. "Please…you don't fight your enemy at their strongest point, hon. You split them up, divide them as much as possible, and attack their weak spots. That strategy has been working like a charm for years."

Chad's expression contorted into a frown as he contemplated what he was hearing. "I guess I can see your point. It's not easy to swallow, but it makes sense."

"Back to my question," Mark interjected. "*Why* are they doing it?"

Sasha shrugged and searched the scene beyond the window once more. "Who the hell knows? It's a business of haves and have-nots like it's always been, except now the haves are snuffing out the have-nots in grand fashion so they can have even more." She sighed, shaking her head, then finally lit her cigarette. "Taking a look around, though, there doesn't seem to be much left. They've wiped out so many. I suppose the goal could be to rule over one big damn graveyard."

"A graveyard," Mark repeated timidly. He paused, then asked, "Do you know if they're…killing people in the camp?"

Sasha didn't respond immediately. She sucked in a deep drag and let the smoke roll from her mouth in a slow fashion; then she made a smoke ring and broke it with her finger. "I've only heard rumors," she said. "Supposedly, policies exist under martial law that authorize corporal punishment, which in their eyes, I'm sure means good old holocaust-style euthanasia. There's a little-known building in the camp's southern annex they call Area E. I remember Dan—my ex-husband—talking about it with some of the club elders over scotch and cigars one night. It's where they 'humanely terminate' people, whatever that means."

"Jesus," Mark reacted. "I never thought—"

"Me neither, kid," Sasha said. "People can be sick sonsabitches.

Sure would be nice to see whoever's responsible get what they deserve someday. A little karma goes a long way, and it's coming to them. Of course, karma affects all of us equally. It'll come knocking at my door one of these days, too."

"But you haven't always been...a criminal," said Mark. "You said it yourself. You were abducted when you were young. You didn't choose to be influenced by those bikers."

"No, kid, you're right. I didn't choose to, initially. But I made plenty, and I mean plenty of decisions on my own that resulted in a lot of people getting hurt, and just as many, if not more, getting killed." Sasha paused, smiling a little. "Before I was coerced into a life of semi-organized crime, I was a skinny, bowlegged farm girl from West by God Virginia. I know, to look at me now you'd never know it. I grew up in Pendleton County, right along the river, and while my memories have faded over the years, there's lots of things I see around these parts that remind me of home. Sometimes...I can still see my mom's and dad's faces in my mind."

"Maybe you'll make it back there someday."

Sasha grinned. "Yeah, kid, why not? That's some serious wishful thinking, but I suppose crazier things have happened."

"Like us sneaking out of here," Chad said, glancing out the window. "Look, I'm not trying to kill the conversation, as lovely as it is, but I don't want to be here any more than either of you do. I think we should take our chances and get out of here now while we still can."

"Yeah, maybe he's right. This is getting a little too hairy for me," Mark said. "As much as I like the conversation...and the company, I think we should consider heading back. Even if we have to walk it."

Sasha sighed. "Okay, boys. Fine. I suppose we can come back later for the bikes. I really hate to lea—"

The sound of multiple barking dogs halted Sasha midsentence. She sat there, pale-faced, hesitating to even release the inhaled smoke from her lungs. Both Chad and Mark went into full-on alert.

Chad crawled to the window yet again, looking to his right, then left toward the intersection where they'd hid the motorcycles. "I swear—must be a party at that house today. It's a damn DHS K-9 unit," he whispered urgently. "They're pulling past...I don't think they saw the bikes."

"Yeah, but did they *smell* them?" added Mark.

"Dammit," Sasha hissed. "I hate dogs, especially those furry Marmadukes the feds always have with them. They're always shedding all over the place and slobbering everywhere—and that's when they're not chomping a hole in your ass."

CHAPTER 15

Trout Run Valley
Wednesday, December 1st

ALEX GOT DOWN ON HER knees near Michelle and Jesseca and explained what she had seen. She pointed to the woods on the left narrowly past the bridge. "Looks like there's a group of houses tucked in the woods down there. They're really close together and look kind of run-down."

Michelle nodded. "That's where the Bradys live. The late Mr. and Mrs. Brady's house is the first one you come across. The other three houses belong to their sons."

"All four families on the same lot?" Jess asked. "That close to each other?" She lifted a brow. "Strange folks."

Alex heeded her mother. "I didn't have the best point of view from where I was standing. Should we check the houses out next?"

Jesseca pursed her lips, looking a bit unsettled. "I don't know. Can you do it without being seen?"

"It looks pretty open, but I can try."

"I don't like this," Michelle said. "Did you see signs of anyone around or hear anything when you were up there, Alex?"

Alex shook her head. "No, it was way quiet. I was worried at first too because I didn't see the houses until I was in the middle of the road. If someone had been there, they would've seen me." She looked to her mother. "Should I go now, Mom?"

Jesseca hesitated.

"No," Michelle blurted out. "Sweetie, you've done enough. I think it's high time the adults stepped up to the plate. I'll go check it out."

Michelle went to stand, but Jesseca reached for her shoulder. "Not without us watching your back, you won't."

"Fine," Michelle said, "suit yourself."

Michelle cleared the barricade and used every bit of her willpower to disregard the slain bodies of George and Elizabeth Brady, peering over only for a second to verify their identities.

She turned the corner, passing the stack of corroded mailboxes, and trudged along the hard-packed dirt driveway leading into the Bradys' property. In seeing the first house on her left, Michelle reminisced about the initial time she had visited just a few months ago. She imagined seeing crazy-eyed, wild-haired George Brady dash out of his doorway, mammoth double-barrel shotgun in hand, shouting threats in her direction while being just as obtuse and irrational as he'd always been. Though she reminded herself he'd never so much as spoken a foul word to her.

The front door was sitting wide open, appearing to have been kicked in, and the tattered screen door hung at an awkward angle to the side, ripped free from most of its hinges. The homes belonging to his sons and their families showed similar damage.

With the SBR held tight to her shoulder, Michelle moved cautiously onto the front porch of the home belonging to Bo and Amber Brady. She examined the doorway for a second, then stepped inside, feeling her heart pound away furiously.

The interior of the home was trashed, appearing to have been completely ransacked, although Michelle didn't have any basis for comparison. She'd never actually been invited to tour the interior of any of the Bradys' homes before. For all she knew, this was how they lived, in utter disarray.

The farther she walked into the rickety shack of a home, the more the scene gave off a different air. Broken photo frames, mirrors, and other glass items, along with torn-apart furniture and smashed children's toys, were strewn about amongst piles of garbage and soiled clothing.

Michelle knelt upon finding a decapitated stuffed animal, its lining scattered from place to place all over the splintered hardwood flooring.

Rodent feces peppered the floor, as though small animals had already started to take possession of the material to use for bedding in their dens.

A sudden noise creaked behind her, and Michelle rotated quickly to see Jesseca entering the home, the muzzle of her M1 carbine leading the way.

Jesseca lowered her weapon and exhaled loudly to the point of sounding repulsed. "Ugh. What a mess!" She moved farther inside, and the floor creaked underfoot. "I take it the place is empty?"

Michelle dropped the headless doll on the floor and stood. "Looks that way. But something happened here. I'm just not sure what."

Jess reached up, finding the ceiling low enough for her to touch with her fingers. "And here all along, I thought my place was small. How many people lived here?"

"This is Bo's home. He and his wife have a son and three girls, two of them younger than ten...all of them with hair as blond as Goldilocks," Michelle said. "Bo and Austin are with the others on the expedition, so that leaves a headcount of four. All female."

"And no sign of them," Jesseca expounded. "Four females in a house this tiny, we would've definitely heard something by now."

Michelle headed back outside. "This is bad, Jess. Really bad. Where's Alex?"

"Checking out the hovel behind this one."

Jesseca followed Michelle out the front door and around back toward the house belonging to Ricky, the youngest of the three brothers, who had also joined the expedition, leaving his wife, Nicole, to look after the house. His sons, Tommy and Wayne, had stayed behind to continue their guard duties at Wolf Gap.

As they approached, Alex exited the home and sheathed both daggers she had been holding in her hands, then shrugged her narrow shoulders. "This house is empty, and everything inside is all broken and busted up, like they were robbed. I don't think there's anyone here anywhere."

Michelle let out a sigh of despair. "Ricky has a wife and two teenage sons." She pointed to the remaining house. "That's Junior's house. He's the only one of Mr. Brady's sons who didn't go on the road trip."

"I checked that house, too," Alex said. "It's as empty as this one."

Jesseca exhaled through her nostrils. "Well, shit. This day just keeps getting better and better, doesn't it?"

"I'm sorry, Jesseca, I don't know what to say," Michelle said. "Something terrible is happening here, and I didn't mean to get you and the girls mixed up in this."

"Oh, come on, Michelle," Jesseca quipped. "You didn't know you were gonna leave your house today and come back home to a damn invasion. If I didn't want to be here, my girls and me would simply head home and leave you to it." She hesitated a moment. "Now, I do have to admit, while there are many things I consider myself good at, frontal assault isn't one of them. My dad, on the other hand, would love to be here right now, but I didn't inherit his knack for making moves." She sighed. "That being said, any idea where we go from here?"

Michelle looked at Jesseca, then Alex, realizing she had indeed been inadvertently placed into a position of leadership. "Dammit," she huffed. "I can't believe it. Lauren said this was going to happen. I swear to God, that kid…"

Alex grew inquisitive. "Lauren said what was going to happen? That the valley was going to be attacked?"

Michelle nearly chuckled. "No, not exactly. She said with Fred gone and our group divided, I might have to take the lead. I guess I never gave any thought to it actually happening."

"Interesting, this daughter of yours," said Jess. "The one whom I've yet to meet. Michelle, if we make it out of this alive, I really would like for that to happen someday."

"Jess, I promise you, if we figure this one out, once she gets home, that meeting is next on my list."

"I'll hold you to it," Jesseca said, looking around. "I suppose there's no point in staying here any longer. I vote we make ourselves scarce, but I'll defer to our newly crowned, reluctant leader. What's our first order of business?"

Michelle let out a long, worried sigh, then shrugged. "I don't know. But I'll think of something."

Not having worn a watch on her wrist since well before the collapse, Michelle had no way of knowing precisely how long it had been since Jesseca's girls had departed. The sky was beginning to get darker, and she sat nervously beside her buxom new friend in the woods just off the road, keeping her eyes peeled for signs of their return.

"I swear," Michelle said, breaking the silence. "It's been at least two hours."

"No, I think it's been more like one." Jesseca tweaked the M1 carbine's position, finding a more comfortable spot against her shoulder. "You act like they're *your* kids. You're more worried about them than me."

"I *am* worried about them. And the only reason I even suggested sending them on the errand was per your confidence in them."

"They'll be back soon, Michelle. You needn't worry. And once they get back, we'll know everything there is to know. And hopefully, that'll be enough."

"Yeah, hopefully. After witnessing what's happened today, I'm really scared for everyone else." Michelle paused to fret. "I'm frightened for Grace especially."

"Grace?"

"My stepdaughter. She's like a second child to me."

Jesseca shook her head, ostensibly taken aback. "Stepson, stepdaughter, stepchild, step-whatever…that's just the socially correct term. It's far and away from representing how you feel."

"What are you saying?"

"I'm saying that stepdaughter or not, if you love her, and it's pretty clear you do, then she's your daughter. Period. And that makes her Lauren's sister. Period. End of sentence."

Michelle sighed, hanging her head a bit. "I pray nothing's happened to her…or anyone else. Fred called it…he even told us that dividing us up like this was going to put a damper on our defenses. As if our friends getting sick wasn't bad enough. Sometimes…I feel like we're running out of options here."

Jesseca pointed into the trees on the other side of the road, diverting Michelle's attention. "There they are. See them? I count three pretty heads of hair."

Michelle let out a breath of relief. "Thank God."

Jesseca smiled and patted Michelle on the back as her daughters made their way, one at a time, across the road and into the hide.

Desirée, the youngest, darted over first and settled in Jesseca's arms. Mack followed her, and Alex brought up the rear, strolling across the road with poise and in no apparent rush.

Jesseca regarded her girls in loving fashion. "Okay, talk to us. Don't keep us in suspense. What did you guys see?"

Mack worked to catch her breath while watching for Alex. "As best we can tell, there's about thirty men walking around outside, mostly between Michelle's house and another house Alex says is the Masons'. And they're all men, Mom, not a single woman anywhere to speak of."

"She's right," Desirée added, feeling comfortable enough now to rattle her vibrant voice off. "All shapes and sizes of men. Fat, skinny, short, tall…even ones with beards and ones without beards. But like Kenzie said, not a single woman anywhere. It was weird, Mom. It was like they left all their wives, girlfriends, sisters, and female chums at home so they could go out and do guy things."

Jesseca lifted a brow. "What's that all about?"

"I haven't the faintest," Michelle replied. "But it definitely sounds like *takers* to me. From what we've seen of them, the entire faction is predominated by males."

Rejoining them, Alex took a seat in a lotus position between her mother and Michelle. "They're bringing loads of stuff from everyone's houses to the Masons'," she said. "Food and everything. But they're moving everyone's guns and ammunition to the cabin for some reason."

"There's people in my house?" Michelle asked.

Alex nodded her head. "Several."

Michelle started to look and feel ill upon hearing the news of strange men in her home. She had spent the majority of her life being a clean freak and could only imagine what the inside of her home away from home looked and probably smelled like.

Alex glanced at her sisters. "There was something else though, something weird. Something that made us wonder."

"Made you wonder about what?" Jesseca pondered.

Mack adjusted her posture. "Everyone was eating."

Jesseca's forehead crinkled as she grew puzzled. "Okay, got it. They were eating…that's very astute." She rubbed her hands together. "Can you explain why that was of note?"

"It was *how* they were eating, Mom," added Alex. "They were stuffing their faces. Like they hadn't eaten anything decent in years. Almost like they were starving to death."

Mack jumped in again. "Yeah, and they were eating stuff uncooked, too…even the rice and pasta and dehydrated stuff—like it was a gourmet dinner at a five-star restaurant." With a giggle, she glanced to Michelle, who was sending her a peculiar stare. "Oh…I've never been to one, but I've read about them…in books."

"They were drinking too," Alex continued. "Some of them were walking around with those airplane bottles of liquor you showed me, Michelle."

"Fantastic," Michelle groaned, rolling her eyes. "That's just marvelous. The private stash has now become public. I guess water is too lowbrow for them."

Alex shook her head. "No, some of them were drinking water, too. Just not all of them."

Jesseca sniggered. "Well, maybe that'll solve the problem for you, Michelle. If they drink poisoned water from the creek or cook food with it—boom. Dead."

"Not likely. We disposed of all the questionable water the day we declared it poisoned. All the reservoirs in the valley were refilled with rain-barrel water and treated with a purifying solution we made with pool shock. The only way they'll poison themselves is if they drink straight from Trout Run, and even that won't kill them overnight, and we don't have time to wait." Michelle sighed, glancing at the sky's waning daylight. "We have to do something about this now."

Jesseca put her hand to her chin and fell into a state of deep consideration. She gently rubbed heads with Desirée while taking turns casting thoughtful looks at her other two most prized possessions. "Girls, you said the men you saw looked really hungry…"

All three young women nodded their heads with ebullience.

Jess smiled at them. "Okay. But exactly *how* hungry?" She paused, holding up a finger. "Let's pretend we're in school for a minute," she began. "This evening, we're in English class and I handed each of you a pop quiz about adjectives. Which adjective best describes their hunger?"

Mack lunged forward with bright eyes and a cheeky grin. "Voracious! On the verge of being gluttonous!"

Jess's smile grew larger. "Superb. Both great adjectives, Mack." Jess tapped Desirée's head. "Dizzy?"

"They looked famished to me," Desirée said, giggling her answer. "At least to me. My adjective is famished."

"Another fantastic modifier," Jess said, giving her a squeeze, then turned to cye Alex.

Alex hesitated before speaking, fidgeting with her hair. "Insatiable. Like hungry enough to eat the crotch out of a low-flying duck."

Alex's sisters doubled over laughing, both with palms covering their mouths. Alex, Jess and Michelle joined in with heartwarming laughs of their own, and the gravity of the dilemma dissipated for the moment.

"I don't know where she gets these things," Jess said, her face awash with color from her laughing spell. "So, Michelle, in your previous run-ins with these…takers, did they come just to steal food? Or has it been other things?"

"We never gave much thought to it," Michelle replied, her joyous tone returning to normal. "And we never asked them, either. When people show up in your backyard with guns attempting to kill you, details don't matter much, do they?"

"No, they sure don't," Jess agreed. "But if these kinsmen are this desperate for a bite to eat, maybe we can use it against them."

Jesseca ran her fingers through the plants growing on the ground nearby amidst the scrub and sporadic grass. "It's funny, you know. Hardly anyone pays much attention to the edibles we walk past and step on every day. Right here, right beneath my fingertips, there's plantain. Not the fruit you can fry up or make pancakes with, but the herb that grows almost everywhere like a common weed. The one with incredible medicinal properties, the one that, if cooked right, tastes like spinach and pairs perfectly with a portion of well-cooked meat."

Jesseca separated one of the plant's broad leaves and held it aloft for Michelle to see. "How long do you think it's been since these chaps have enjoyed a healthy salad fresh from the garden…or maybe some freshly dried homegrown seasoning?"

"Seasoning?" Michelle asked, her interest piqued.

Jesseca nodded with a sly grin. "Sure. Adds the right amount of flavor to any dish. But the seasoning we're going to need to solve this problem is of a particularly toxic variety, and as I've already shown you, it's a variety I happen to cultivate…in droves."

CHAPTER 16

Mason residence
Trout Run Valley
Thursday, December 2nd

WHEN GRACE AWOKE AGAIN, SHE sat up rapidly in a panic, unable to discern if she was dreaming, while not remembering having fallen asleep.

She studied her surroundings again, only to find that nothing had changed. The sick were still lying in their cots and were still being tended to. Kim Mason had been joined by Kristen Perry, and the two women were busily administering medications and distributing portions of food and water to them and others nearby.

Another man whom Grace didn't recognize had joined them, along with the burly strange-talking one, and he was similarly armed. He paced slowly behind Kim and Kristen while they made their rounds, watching them and closely scrutinizing their movements.

Grace lifted an arm and touched her forehead with the back side of her hand. She couldn't tell if she still had a fever, but her stomach still hurt, and she was beyond the point of being incredibly thirsty.

As Grace went to slide herself from her cot, Kim noticed her and excused herself to dash over. "Hey there, pretty girl. I see you finally decided to join us again. How are you feeling?"

Grace steadied herself, looking a bit woozy. "I don't know... nauseated, I guess. Just sick to my stomach, but not really sick, if that makes any sense. Did I pass out again?"

A faint smile spread across Kim's face as she took a seat. "No. You just fell asleep rather suddenly." She placed the back of her hand to Grace's head, followed by her temples. "Your fever's gone, though. Looks like you're in the clear."

Grace smiled. Ever since the point of getting sick, she'd been worried she'd somehow been poisoned. She guessed she must've drank or eaten something that had given her the same symptoms as the others who had fallen ill. Knowing that the initial symptoms were flulike and she didn't appear to have them was reassuring.

Kim placed her hands in her lap. "I think it's safe to say that whatever's ailing you is nothing like what the others have."

Grace pointed to a glass of water sitting on a bedside table, and Kim handed it to her. She then took several large gulps. "Are they getting any better?"

Kim let out a faint sigh. "I wish I knew the answer to that. I wish I knew the answer to a lot of things right about now. We've been doing all we can for them, but our hands are tied. At first, they were getting all the antibiotics we had, but due to recent events…it hasn't exactly been that easy."

"What are you talking about?"

Kim lowered her voice to a whisper. "They aren't allowing us to use the medicine we had. These gentlemen have taken possession of just about everything—food, medicine, weapons—and haven't exactly been allowing us any freedom of movement."

"I'm confused, Kim…what does that mean?" Grace asked, cocking her head to the side angrily. "What exactly do these pricks want from us? We're giving them everything else…are they really taking what little medication we need to help the sick, too? If that's the case…I'm sorry…that's freakin' bullshit."

Kim tapped her finger on Grace's thigh with enough force to get her attention. "Keep your voice down. These men, whoever they are, are still letting us have some of the meds, but not all of them. They've just taken the pick of the litter." Kim turned away, hesitating. "And like you…I just wish I knew why."

"Has Michelle come back yet?"

"I don't know."

Grace put her hand on Kim's shoulder. "Do they still have Megan?"

Kim didn't respond.

"Jesus. I guess so," said Grace. She began gritting her teeth and found herself in a stare down with the man who had been inspecting everything Kristen had been doing, no matter how innocuous. Grace rolled her eyes and huffed. "You know, Kim, we can't just sit here and take this shit. Somebody has to take the lead and try talking to these people. Maybe we can negotiate with them, who knows…but we'll never know unless one of us takes a stand."

As Kim reached out and pled with her not to do anything rash or stupid, Grace rose and strolled directly to the man guarding Kristen.

Kim reluctantly followed.

The man's brows angled inward as he looked upon Grace curiously. His skin was unclean and even in the dimness of candlelight, it was easy to distinguish that one of his eyes was a different shade of brown than the other.

At the point his lips parted to crack a sardonic grin, he displayed a single front tooth broken in half beside another nearly blackened with rot. "What the blue fuck is this?" his voice thundered. "Is somebody feelin' better?"

The nausea Grace was experiencing was instantly exacerbated after catching a whiff of the man's putrid breath. She hesitated long enough to will away her urge to upchuck, assuming doing so would serve as an ill-advised method of making a first impression. "I am feeling better, thanks for asking. But I would be feeling incredible if I knew exactly what was going on around here. Namely, who you people are and what exactly it is you want so badly."

The man chuckled. "First off, I don't give a two-headed frog's shit how you feel. And it's not my job to pass along information for you, to or from anyone else. I'm not a mailman, and I'm not no liaison. I'm here to guard you and keep you girls from getting yourselves in trouble. That's all, nothing else. So get your skinny, loudmouthed ass back over there on that cot where you came from and sit there until I tell you it's okay to get back up."

Grace took a step back, folding her arms. "Sheesh, you're bossy. How am I supposed to respond? How about…'your wish is my command, sir'. How's that?"

"Exactly like that—'cept it ain't no wish."

Grace pointed her finger at the man, nearly making contact with his slightly crooked nose. She spoke with added bitterness etched in her tone. "Well, let me tell you something, you foul-mouthed, shit-breathed, Ted Nugent-looking son of a destitute whore, nobody comes into our valley and treats us like this. I won't allow it. And I don't give a damn who you are, I want you to take me to whoever oversees this swarm of merry men. Right now."

One of the man's eyebrows lifted to its apex. He sucked his teeth while taking a step backward from Grace, and then pulled out a weighted-knuckle leather glove from his jacket pocket and began sliding it onto his fingers. "You know...I'm a patient man, but the last time some little bitch spoke to me in that tone of voice, I broke her fucking jaw," he said. "You know how hard it is to fix a broken jaw these days? Let me tell you, it's damn near impossible."

He wiggled his gloved fingers and licked his lips while staring at Grace so angrily his eyes watered. "Needless to say, that bitch don't say much anymore. And you're about to find out what that's like."

As the man drew back and Grace ducked for cover, Kim Mason jumped in between them, expecting to be struck. "Please don't! Please don't hit her! She's...she's with child."

The man released the tension in his arm and lowered it slightly. "Shit, you say?"

"No, it's true. She's still in her first trimester, and any stress or injury she endures can harm the baby." Kim looked up and, noticing the man was no longer in a position to strike, started to back away.

Grace was completely blown away. Her eyes were as wide as a twenty-lane highway.

"This true?" the man inquired. "You gotta baby in your belly, girl?"

Grace's eyes darted back and forth between the man and Kim, finally finding the man's gruesome stare. Maybe Kim was trying to tell her something without telling her something. Maybe it was time to put some of her acting skills to effective use. "Yes, that's correct. Woe is me, my...fiancé and I are indeed expecting a little tot, our first." She hesitated, not knowing exactly where to go with this. "I am indeed with child, and I'm sorry, but I guess that explains why I'm so...forward. I didn't mean to anger you."

The man gulped. "Anger me? You were about a second away from losin' more than half your teeth." He paused, removing the glove from his hand. "I honestly don't know what you women are thinkin' these days. Acting so damn independent, thinkin' you can say whatever the hell you want to whoever you want. Birthin' kids, raising kids and shit. Personally, I think it's a good thing for y'all to get a good smack every so often. Helps remind you where your place is." He paused again, producing a wicked grin. "So, which one of these old boys 'round here is daddy? Maybe I'll go smack him around instead."

"Well, none of them."

"Oh? Where is he, then?"

"He's...not here..." Grace grieved, trailing off.

"Not here? Where'd he run off to?"

Grace turned her head away and quickly drudged up some tears. "He left. The bastard...left me. I told him not to go, but he went anyway. Told me I had no right to tell him what to do. He just up and left me with the others. Left me here all by my lonesome to fend for myself and *our* child."

Kim began to back away even farther now, seeing that Grace's surprise act appeared capable of managing the situation.

The man stuffed the weighted glove back in his pocket and wiped his greasy hair with the same hand before returning it to the rifle. "Ain't that a bitch. Guess that makes you a statistic now, doesn't it, single mom?" He rubbed his chin a moment. "Well, since it wouldn't be right to beat on you, maybe I can find somethin' else you need." He reached out and grabbed hold of Grace's arm in a not so gentle fashion. "Come on, single mom. You wanted to see the man in charge. Let's go see the man."

CHAPTER 17

Allegany County, Maryland
Sunday, December 5th. Present day

SANTA LED LAUREN ALONGSIDE A succession of military-style cargo vehicles until they came upon one painted in dull desert camouflage, bearing a 6x6 wheel configuration with tires nearly as tall as she was.

Lauren reached out to get a feel for the tread's ruggedness. "Where did you guys get all these trucks?"

"The M1083s? Some of them were handouts from local armories. Others, we tactically acquired."

"Tactically acquired?" Lauren queried through a giggle.

"Yeah, don't ask. And don't lose sleep over it, either," Santa said jovially. "Nobody died—no one important anyway. Wait here." He held up a finger and pulled himself up and into the back of the vehicle through an opening in the cargo tarp.

Lauren listened while Santa rustled around inside the truck bed, trying to pick up on the tune he was whistling. For a moment, it almost sounded like 'Jingle Bells'.

"There we go! I think I found just what you need."

Lauren's eyes met with Santa's where his head had jutted outside the tarp. He tossed her a wadded, mixed bundle of clothing. She untangled the bundle and pulled a pair of ACU fatigue pants up to her waist, noticing the inseam fell way beyond the length of her legs.

"Yeah…yeah! That's the ticket," Santa said. "Try them on for size. Let's see how good they fit."

"I think they might be a little long."

Santa pulled his cover off and scratched at his head. "There's some drawstrings in there along the waistband, and some Velcro, hook-and-loop-type stuff, too. You should be able to tighten it up a bit to make it work."

Lauren dropped the pants to the ground and examined the matching ACU blouse that accompanied them, also finding it to be several sizes too large for her person. "Santa, look. I appreciate this, I really do. The clothes I'm wearing could probably walk all by themselves by now, but—"

"Wanna give it a go? Go ahead. Rip 'em off and throw 'em against the truck. It'll be like an experiment. Like some of that shit Mr. Wizard used to do."

"Who's Mr. Wizard?"

"Eh, never mind. Probably a bit before your time."

Lauren giggled shyly. "Do you think you might be able to find something a little more, I don't know…petite?"

Santa scratched his head again, then thumbed his beard a moment. He stuck a finger in the air as if to indicate an idea had come to him. "Hold that thought," he said with crazy eyes. "I'm going in for a closer look. Cover me."

He disappeared back into the truck. Lauren could hear him rummaging around while he cursed occasionally in between bumps and sounds of boxes being torn apart.

Moments later, he emerged with another armload of clothing. Santa slid himself from the truck and presented it to Lauren, then stuck a thumb into his mouth. "We have wounded! Call it in! Damn cardboard cuts hurt like hell. Oh well, I think I got a tourniquet stashed around here somewhere." He pulled out his thumb and wiped it on his pants. "Wanna hear a story? Sure you do. So get this shit. About a month ago, we raided a camp and fragged these pussies who stole a bunch of camping, hunting and fishing stuff—clothes, too. It was like they went on a shopping spree at a Cabela's or a Bass Pro before they started hunting down and killin' folks. Damnedest thing I ever seen. We found lots of name-brand designer shit and whatnot, like some of them real nice Blackhawk and

5.11 Tactical getups." He tilted his head, and one of his brows shot into the air. "Even found some of the ever so lovely...*female* kind." He dropped the pile of clothing at Lauren's feet and pointed to it before plopping down. "Let's see what we got."

Watching Santa's hands as he separated the articles of clothing in the pile, Lauren sat opposite him. "There's actually a lot of nice stuff in here," she said, holding up a pair of khaki pants with the retail tags still attached. She glanced at the size on the tag—a near perfect fit for her. "Looks like my spell of modest luck hasn't changed yet. These will fit me just fine."

"Those are nice," Santa said, then presented a pair of women's tactical range tights. His eyebrows danced and bounced up and down while he tugged at the waistband. "What do you think about these puppies?" he joked while continuing to prod, pull, and stretch the material.

Lauren smirked embarrassingly and nearly chuckled. "They're nice...but not really my style."

"Oh, come on!" He held the leggings to his chest and stretched the fabric to its limit. "That's some skin-tight durable shit, right there. But, kinda sexy though, am I right?"

Lauren blushed. "It's not that I don't like them, I just don't think they'd be suitable for our...environment right now. And if my dad saw me wearing them, he'd threaten to cut off my hair."

"He would, huh?"

"Mm-hmm."

Santa huffed and nodded, then tossed the tights over his shoulder, where they landed under a truck tire. "Damn overprotective fathers. Well, I gave it my best shot. Back to the drawing board."

Lauren snickered. "What did you say?"

Santa resumed rummaging through the pile. "I'm just messing with you, Miss Jane. Thought it would be fun to poke at you a bit." He made eye contact with her, bearing a rare look of sincerity. "It's good to have you back, by the way. We missed you, and we're all glad to know you're doing okay."

Once Lauren had successfully completed finding a cleaner, less raggedy set of apparel, she followed Santa farther along the vehicle train to another military truck very similar in size and color to the previous one.

"Now for the fun part," Santa announced. "What kind of battle rifle do you want? I can't promise we're going to have unlimited options for you, and a lot of what we have isn't exactly unblemished, but trust me… all the bang-bangs inside this truck are fully functional."

"Did you check them all yourself?"

"Yep. Guilty. I…get bored sometimes."

Lauren shrugged and cocked her head to the side playfully. "I've heard beggars can't be choosers. I'm partial to ARs, and my last rifle was an M4, but I guess anything will do. Any gun is better than no gun at all."

Santa laughed. "Okay. I'll see if I can find you a nice Ruger 10/22, seeing as how *any gun is better than no gun at all*." He then hopped into the truck, under the tarp, disappearing from sight.

Lauren went after him at first, but soon stopped. She had a feeling he was only kidding, at least, she hoped he was. If there was anyone in Dave Graham's unit who met with the definition of unpredictable, it was Santa.

Santa mumbled and chuckled and chatted with himself while he rummaged through what Lauren could only assume to be an arsenal of confiscated firearms and other ordnance. Several minutes passed before the tone in his voice began indicating success.

While still inside the truck, Santa said, "Now, I know this isn't what you might've chosen for yourself, but if you'll allow me a few minutes of your time and indulge me a little, while I am a man of certain madness, there is a method to some of it."

Santa emerged and hopped down with what could only be described as a nearly immaculate AK-47. He held it aloft in both hands like a priceless trophy and gazed upon it as a father would while holding his firstborn minutes out of the womb. "My lady, allow me to present to you the most stunning *Avtomát Kaláshnikova* I have ever laid eyes on." He pulled it in close to his chest and considered it while his arms cradled it, his tone becoming subdued. "What do you think we should name her?"

"It's a nice-looking gun, Santa, there's no denying it," Lauren said, allowing a chuckle to escape. "And I think it will do just fine." She reached for it, but Santa tucked it away and took a step back.

"Hey, easy there, vise-grip," he scolded, giving her his version of the stink eye. "The fuck are you doing? You can't just be all reckless and manhandle her like that. You have to work your way into it, move slow, speak softly and romance her a little. I know you kids have all heard how robust and indestructible these rifles are, but that doesn't mean they don't deserve respect and love."

"Okay, I'm sorry," Lauren said, looking coyly at him. "And you're right. Do you want me to leave so the two of you can have some time alone?"

"That's not funny," Santa growled, making it nearly impossible to gauge his level of seriousness. He presented the rifle to Lauren again so she could see the inscriptions on the block. "You see that? See that Cyrillic shit right there? This ain't your ordinary Kalashnikov. It's no chopper or cheap-ass Western clone, neither. This darling is a Zastava M70. It's Serbian, former Yugoslav…and that makes it not only an endangered species, but a goddamn pièce de résistance." He pointed to the foregrip. "You can tell these apart from any other AK ever made by these three cooling slots. The wood used for the stock is typically elm; it's a lighter color than most other variants. This one even has a grenade sight on it, and you could fire twenty-two-millimeter shells right off the barrel if we had some. Just gotta replace the slant-brake with an adapter and, boom, rifle grenades. Talk about fun."

Lauren nodded, and Santa finally allowed her to take possession of the weapon. She couldn't tell if he was being overly facetious or not, but it didn't matter. He spoke with expertise as well as passion, and she would never look at this rifle the same way ever again.

Santa lowered his head slightly while sliding his index finger along the receiver. "These used to be milled from one solid block of steel, not stamped together like this one. For a time, folks looked down on stamped receivers because they weren't as strong. But the most widely produced M70s were made like this one, with the same thickness of steel as their milled ancestors—about one and a half millimeters, thicker than Soviet AKMs. They were the most commonly used rifle during the Yugoslavian wars twenty or so years ago."

Santa paused, watching Lauren study the weapon. "I seem to remember you being a southpaw," he continued on through his whiskers. "I think that might mean you and Dragana here will get along well."

"Dragana?"

"Yeah, means precious. Valuable. And she looks like a Dragana to me."

"Okay, then henceforth shall she be christened."

"That's the spirit." Santa combed his beard with his fingers. "Have you ever run an AK?"

"A couple of times. Norman has two of them, and Dad bought one a while back, but I don't think it's ever left the gun safe." Lauren pulled back on the bolt and released it, then repeated the motion, feeling the snappy newness of the weapon.

"Dragana looks hungry to me," Santa said. "We need to find her some chow most ricky-tick. I think her previous owner tried starving her to death."

Lauren nodded, then opened the bolt and held the chamber to her nose. "I don't think this thing—sorry, *she* has ever been fired before."

"Indeed. Realize, young miss, that this *thing* isn't your everyday AK, either. It's selective fire. You know, what you kids like to call full auto." Santa pointed to the fire selector. "On the AKs you're used to, there's two positions—fire and safe, bang and no bang. On this one, there's three. In the middle position you can still see the R marking. That stands for *rafalna* or *burst fire*. That's over six hundred rounds per minute cyclical rate of fire. Slap the selector all the way down to the J, that's semiauto, one bang for every trigger press. Don't forget that."

"Okay. I won't. Not sure how you haven't, though," Lauren said, her eyes following his finger. "What about magazines?"

"Magazines?" Santa reached back into the truck and extricated a small canvas shoulder bag. He flipped the top open to display a half-dozen standard thirty-round magazines. "What about 'em?"

Lauren smiled. "Okay, you seem to have that covered. Would you also happen to have a sidearm hidden inside one of these trucks?"

"Damn, you're needy. I was getting to that. You think I'd send you off to battle without some means of retrieving your rifle? Especially one as regal as Dragana?" Santa chuckled. "What do you prefer, young lady? Glock? Sig? Beretta? I think there might be a few Hi-Points lying around somewhere. In a pinch, they're useful for a good flinging."

"A Glock, preferably."

"Roger that. I'll find you one. We got all the other stuff you'll be needing, too…I just gotta find it and dig it up. Be patient, young one. Christmas is right around the corner. And this year…for you, it comes early."

CHAPTER 18

Town of New Creek
Mineral County, West Virginia
Sunday, December 5th. Present day

EVEN THROUGH THE DUST-COVERED GLASS of the JLTV she was riding passenger in, Lauren could see the wooden poles, wire fencing, and other fortifications belonging to the prison camp from a long way off.

It appeared gruesomely artificial and looked as though it had been painstakingly pieced together with a blend of leftover, randomly mismatched components. It was strikingly similar to the camp from which she and the others had recently been rescued, and it seemed to jut out from the surrounding rural landscape like nothing she'd seen before.

The convoy slowed its pace and soon pulled off to the side of the road, coming to a stop not long after. Engines began to shut off, and doors were overheard as they creaked open. Unit personnel were soon seen filing out of the vehicles, but Lauren couldn't tell if anyone from Tim Reese's Unit Delta was present to greet them.

Then suddenly, as if they had all been drawn to the same commotion, several of the men furthest from the convoy darted toward the camp's entrance while motioning and yelling for others to follow.

"What the hell was that all about?" Lauren asked, her head snapping left as her hand grabbed the door handle. "Did you see that?"

Woo Tang tranquilly removed his hand from the steering wheel and reached for her arm, pulling Lauren's hand away from the door. "I did see. And while I am not certain what caused it, I am surely going to find out." He glanced at her with a cautious eye. "Lauren Russell, you wait here until I return. Copy?"

"Yeah, I copy…I guess, but—"

"Please, just do as I have requested of you." He then exited the JLTV and jetted off in the direction the other men had gone, leaving Lauren to remain with the influence of her inborn curiosity gaining ground at an exponential rate.

Lauren sat quietly for several minutes, but it was all she could do to remain that way. She stared out the window, her heart beating rapidly, unable to see anything apart from the makeshift, artificial structures within the camp and the primitive fencing surrounding them. "Dammit. This sucks. Am I a part of this campaign now or not?" she pondered aloud, but no one was present to provide her an answer.

She allowed a few more minutes to pass before taking one final look around and making the decision to exit the vehicle.

With the Zastava M70 pulled close at low ready, Lauren stepped cautiously away from the JLTV and the convoy, meandering off the gravel road and into the tall unkempt grass. The closer she got to the camp's exterior walls, the more she could hear the source of the commotion.

Peering down the hill into a small valley and through the fence, she was able to see a large group of men, some of them members of the unit, others appearing as prisoners having recently been released from captivity, and they were engaged in a raging hand-to-hand brawl against one another. "Oh my," Lauren said, her eyes opening wide while they skimmed the faces for participants she recognized.

When Lauren saw Sanchez's face in the dead center of the scuffle, she broke from her position and hurried along the fence line, soon coming upon an entrance to the camp. It was instinctive, as if she had seen a member of her family being attacked.

Dave's unit, mostly dressed in black and MultiCam ACUs, were fighting a number of men wearing similar getups. At first glance, they appeared to be members of a militia or even some form of paramilitary group. The clash was chaotic and hair-raising. Punches, kicks, and even head butts were being exchanged amidst infuriated screams and constant yelling, and there were just as many men involved in breaking things up as there were inciting the battle to continue.

Lauren had seen fights before and had even been involved in a few of her own, but had never quite seen anything like this, and bearing that in mind, she didn't know what to do. She stood there stoically, her eyes wide in amazement, taking in the scene as the testosterone- and anger-fueled melee reached a crescendo, moving about like ocean waves during a coastal thunderstorm.

Soon the ratio of peacemakers began to overrun the agitators, and members of Dave's unit started to pull each other away from the fight, eventually leaving one noncomplying devil dog to remain in the middle of a small sea of men to fight on his own.

Sanchez was bruised and beaten. His clothing was torn, and his face was bloodied, but he showed no signs that he had any intention of giving notice.

While one man grabbed Sanchez around his waist, attempting to throw him to the ground, Sanchez throttled a second man with a devastating roundhouse punch, the impact creating a sound lurid enough to echo between nearby buildings. While he smiled and cursed them, Sanchez rocketed his elbow into the man holding him in a bear hug, striking him square in the nose and dropping him.

After pummeling two others into submission with a tantalizing smile on his face, Sanchez watched a final combatant looming toward him. The man seethed with anger, his jaw agape and saliva dripping from his lips. Froth slipped between the gaps in his teeth as he exhaled. He stood there a moment, hands held up in a guard, livid enough to fight a war all on his own, only unwilling to make a move.

"What's up now? Did you forget your *cojones* at home like the rest of the *chaputos* in your crew?" Sanchez jeered. "Just like Tupac said— you ain't shit without your homeboys." He grinned and wiped the open cut on his lower lip.

His opponent screamed expletives at him and growled, one of his eyes tapering. Spotting a steel spike on the ground, he snatched it and held it aloft, aiming it in Sanchez's direction. "I'm gonna ram this so far up your ass, you're gonna taste your own waste—straight from the tap. After that, I'm going to send you swimming back across the Rio Grande."

Sanchez laughed hysterically, almost to the point of tearing up. "Whatever. Another racist bitch. All that mouthing is foreplay to me…

and I'm already getting blue balls." He stomped on the ground like a raging bull. "Let's do this already! Come at me!"

The man cried out and lunged at Sanchez, who effortlessly dodged him and sent his boot into the back of the man's knee, sending him to the dirt. The Marine then moved in from behind and pulled his attacker into a textbook choke hold while steadily increasing constriction. "Yeah, that's it. Don't fight it…just let it happen. Time for your nap, *puto!*"

With Sanchez in control of his tussle, and most other fights seemingly over, Lauren studied the crowd of onlookers and found a set of errant eyes that gave her a particularly bad feeling. A mere ten seconds later, she learned why. The shifty-eyed man in the horde took two quick looks around before dashing for Sanchez, and the time left for second-guessing went to zero.

Lauren could see something in his hand, but he moved with such speed that she didn't have time to discern what it was. She could only guess the worst—that it was a weapon of some kind and his intention was to harm Sanchez in some way.

In a streak, Lauren intersected the man's path. Flipping the M70 around in her hands, she swung it at him and viciously smashed the buttstock into his chin.

WHAM!

The aggressor didn't even see her coming, and as the unyielding wooden stock thundered into him, his legs went limp. He lost his footing and his eyes rolled into his forehead; then he fell backwards and lifeless to the ground over a pair of buckled knees.

Lauren didn't see anyone else she knew, and she didn't know if this man was the only remaining agitator in the crowd. But she could sense after what she had done, she had a red bull's-eye painted on her, and anyone choosing to side with him who had seen him fall would be next to strike.

She wasted no time in preparing herself. Lauren returned the M70 to a firing position while scouring the angered faces within the mob, gauging them with scrutiny. Soon, she was relieved to see several of Dave's men approach with weapons at the ready, providing her friendly nods and confident looks.

Lauren placed her boot on the man's right wrist, now finally having the chance to see what his choice of weapon had been. She shuddered at the sight of a large-diameter hypodermic needle in his grasp. She could only guess what the contents inside the cylinder were, and there was no telling what would've happened had the needle made contact with her friend.

The man lay there writhing in pain, using his free hand to survey the damage levied on his face.

"I suggest you play nice from here on out," Lauren hissed, pointing the barrel of her AK mere inches from him. "What's in the needle?"

The man started struggling under the weight of her boot, and Lauren didn't think she'd be able to subdue him much longer. As she pushed down hard, ready to repeat her question, Woo Tang approached from behind and relocated her, motioning in earnest for her to back away.

Pushing his carbine to the side, he knelt and removed the syringe from the man's hand. "You are not one for following orders, are you?" Woo Tang asked, reaching for a set of zip cuffs. "I could have sworn I told you to remain with the convoy."

Lauren backed away a few steps. "Orders? I didn't know you were pulling rank on me. I didn't even know I had a rank."

"One does not need to possess a rank for one to behave sensibly." He rose after securing the man's wrists, adjusted his gear, then ogled the syringe. "It would please me greatly if you guided yourself at a snail's pace into this. It truly should not be rushed. Do you understand?"

Lauren hesitated, remembering her recent injury and reaching for the soreness in the back of her head. "Yes. I'm sorry, Jae. I do understand."

"Very well." He dropped the syringe and smashed it with his boot, then eased through the crowd of former combatants to make them aware of his presence. Their eyes boggled at the sight of the sword on his back.

"Why are you fighting us?" a male voice from deep within bellowed, vexation marking his tone. "Aren't you guys the damn military? For crying out loud! One minute, you're here to rescue us, and the next minute, you're throwing punches? What kind of army are you?"

Sanchez brushed past Lauren and pushed through the crowd to the man. He puffed his chest out, squared off with him, then banged his fists on his rib cage. "Army? Listen, brah…you have us mixed up with another crew. The military takes orders from 'the man'. We don't. In case you haven't noticed, while you were busy being captured and shit, the country has fallen, homie. And if you want to know why we're fighting you, maybe you should ask some of your peckerhead, racist friends… because if you roll back the play-by-play, it was you mofos who started it. We saw our brothers getting pushed around, so we provided an appropriate response—and opened a can of whoop ass."

Another man hobbled out from the group, to all appearances unhurt and unscathed, as if he had never thrown or received a punch during the melee. He was shorter than most and overweight, looking as though he'd helped himself to a few more daily meals than others in present company. "But, daddy, he hit me first, he hurt my feelings, blah, blah, blah," the stocky man said, his tone scornful and emulating that of a younger, petulant child. "You two sound like a couple of bratty, whiney preschoolers." He paused, moving in closer. "Who cares who started the fight? The real question is what took you guys so long to get here? We've been stuck here for weeks. Ain't no reason why it should take this long for help to arrive…guess there were other pressing matters. You all really know how to take your good ole time."

Sanchez cocked his head and cracked his knuckles. "The hell you just say to me, fat man? I don't believe we've met."

The man skirted even closer. "You're correct. We haven't, until now." He adjusted his olive green tactical cap, on which a frayed Velcro patch was attached, displaying an oak leaf. "I'm Major Frank Gardner of the Potomac Trailblazer militia, acting CO of this regiment. I also happen to be the only remaining regional commander of the patriot movement around these parts."

Sanchez's dark eyes gleamed. He cackled loudly and sent along a derisive grin. "Really? Militia, huh? *Puta madre*—that's friggin' adorable. Well, Major…and forgive me for not saluting, I'm Sergeant Carlos Santiago Lorenzo Sanchez, former scout sniper…but still lean, still mean, and still very much a Marine. And while you sissy Carls were safe at home chugging PBR, bragging about how badass you were, pissing in fire pits, banging each other's old ladies, and playing footsies, I was in-country getting my hands dirty being the badass you always wanted to be…painting the sand with the blood of my enemies, vaporizing tangos from a thousand meters out and making it look easy."

Major Frank laughed, his belly jiggling along. "Well, I'll be damned. I appreciate your service, scout sniper. And don't worry yourself about the salute…I'll overlook it, for now."

"*Coño*...spoken like a true *pendejo*."

"And just so you know...while grunts and leathernecks like you were in-country, we stayed home for good reason...so we could take care of business, not to mention the old ladies you fellas left behind to go off and fight yet another stupid political war."

Sanchez's eyes narrowed into slits, and he looked away while pointing a finger. "I'm going to warn you, fat man. I will chop your male parts off in front of you and force-feed them to you while you scream... that is, if I can find them."

Lauren took turns watching Sanchez jaw back and forth with the militiamen, and looking around for indications of inbound threats. Woo Tang rejoined her a minute later, and the two were eventually joined by Dave Graham, and he wasn't the least bit pleased with what he was seeing.

"What in the name of Sam Hill is going on here?" Dave demanded, his tone abrupt.

"We encountered a substantial disagreement upon our arrival," replied Woo Tang.

"Disagreement? With each other?"

Woo Tang shook his head. "It was more of a rescuer versus rescuee type of thing."

Dave scoffed. "That's a new one. Ain't that something."

The Korean-American shrugged his shoulders. "I know, right? I do not yet know the full story, but it appears there were some choice words exchanged between some of Staff Sergeant Reese's unit and this group of irregulars. The scuffle broke out when we arrived."

"Not exactly what I'd call the attitude of gratitude, but whatever. Irregulars, huh? Militia?"

"They refer to themselves as the Potomac Trailblazers."

"I see," Dave deliberated, studying the crowd. "A lot of young faces over there. Looks like a damn Boy Scout troop meeting." He paused, letting out a sigh. "I finally located Tim...he's with the medics getting patched up. Had himself a close encounter with a thirty-caliber tracer."

Woo Tang peered over gravely. "What is his status?"

"Down for the count, for now. And he's not the only one. We lost a few on this one...places us in a bit of a pickle."

"I'm sorry about your men," Lauren said.

"Makes two of us, Janey."

Woo Tang pursed his lips. "Three."

"Is Tim going to be all right?"

"Wound's in his upper arm, near the shoulder blade," replied Dave. "He got lucky…problem is, he doesn't think a hostile shot him. Says it was one of these jokers. It apparently happened after the rescue."

"That might explain the exchange of words," Woo Tang said. "We will need to monitor these men closely, then. The fight was turbulent. Very close to getting out of hand."

Dave spit on the ground. "Message received. If it materializes again, shoot them, Tang. All of them."

"Hooyah."

Dave watched as the heated argument between Sanchez and Major Frank intensified and shared a glance with both Lauren and Woo Tang before finally breaking away. "Jesus. You know…I can't take you all anywhere."

He then made a beeline directly to Sanchez. Grabbing him by his ear, Dave pulled the Marine aside and away from the others. "Hey, Taco! Calm your tits for a hot minute! What's gotten into you? Whatever happened to respecting human dignity? Respect and concern for your fellow man? All that Semper Fi, jarhead-honor-code shit?"

Sanchez pulled away from Dave in protest. "Fuck human dignity, and he ain't my fellow man. If these guys want respect, they'd better *show* me some respect. These pretend go-to-war wannabes are nothing but a bunch of ingrates!" His voice bellowed loud enough for all to hear as his expression boiled. "The next camp we come to, if we find any more of these guys, I'm gonna let the tangos cook and eat them, because that's what they deserve. Why should I lift a finger to save these unappreciative sons of bitches again?"

Dave tried for several minutes to calm Sanchez down, but found his endeavors pointless. Sanchez ultimately stormed away, leaving all his gear behind save his rifle.

Dave sighed in disgust, then placed his fingers between his lips and whistled. "All right! Attention, company! If you prefer to remain in my good graces, listen up! We've been working our butts off lately, and I know we've all been on edge, myself included. Today, it looks as though we've reached a point where it's beginning to seriously influence our judgment. As such, some modifications are in order." He rotated on his heels. "Change of plans, ladies. As of right now, everyone under my command is hereby placed on standby for the next twenty-four hours at minimum. Sentries and night watch will be assigned by the squad leaders, and we will rotate in and out of those duties for the duration. But the rest of you, consider yourselves officially voluntold to relax and have mandatory fun." He paused. "There is one single proviso, so listen up, folks. Read me Lima Charlie, as I am unbendable on this. I have zero tolerance for infighting and rebellious behavior. There will not be any more of this shit."

Dave pointed to the group of militiamen, who had now all gathered together along and behind the rotund and seemingly foolhardy Major Frank. "And if I see any of you window lickers accosting my men, verbally, physically, or even carnally, especially after being decent enough to deliver you all from the jaws of Satan, I'll hang every single one of you upside down by your toenails with fishhooks. You'd be smart not to test me, because I do not bluff.

"Despite our apparent differences, we are all fighting for the same purpose, and unless I'm mistaken, or you fellas aren't actual members of the so-called patriot movement, whatever's left of it, that purpose is the restoration of our country to a condition not unlike our founding fathers intended. We have all spent entirely too much time in discord. A populous divided politically, racially, religiously, socially, financially—you name it…because we were all too stupid to prevent it from happening. I'm here to inform you, the time for that shit to end is here. And it ends tonight."

Dave took several steps forward into the group. "Make a hole," he directed. "I see a lot of unhappy faces, so allow me to attach some good news to this. To help alleviate some of the bitterness, tonight we'll have ourselves a little shindig, complete with fire and fellowship, and I'm providing refreshments. One of my trucks is crammed with an assortment of confiscated cans and bottles…and I'm not talking about tea, water, or Snapple, either. Maintain your virtuous behavior, show a little goodwill toward your fellow man, and you are all welcome to attend and partake. Does anyone present in the recently eradicated prison camp take issue with anything I have just said?"

A moment of silence passed before Dave finished with, "Nothing heard. Imagine that. You're dismissed."

CHAPTER 19

Town of New Creek
Mineral County, West Virginia
Sunday, December 5th. Late Evening. Present day

"I JUST DON'T KNOW WHAT I'M gonna do," a disheveled man repeated for the third time, his tone dispirited. He held his hands open, warming them against the fire as it crackled, sending embers soaring into the night sky overhead. "I mean…we're free now, I guess, but at what cost? What good is it? I don't know where to go from here. Those men…they burned my house to the ground, and they took my wife and son from me…and I have no idea where either of them is now." His body trembled, and he began sobbing. "They're probably dead…they were all I had, and now they're probably both dead. And I just don't know what I'm supposed to do."

Another man spoke after turning up a can of domestic-brand beer and slurping down a long frothy gulp. "Joe's got a good point. What the hell are any of us supposed to do? Where the hell do we go? Those of us that still have homes don't have much left to go home to. And most of us don't even know where our families are. What kind of life is that? I'll tell you what kind of life it is. Without our wives and children, we have no life."

Major Frank emerged from the group and stumbled in closer to the fire. He belched a few times and rubbed his belly before tossing an empty bottle of rye whiskey into the flames. "Well, maybe if our rescue party would've shown up a wee bit sooner, we wouldn't be having this discussion," he slurred. "And maybe Joe's house wouldn't be burned to the ground…and his family would still be there. Maybe everybody's families would still be here. Maybe nothing would've happened…we could've prevented all this mess if somebody would've just stepped up and stopped this shit when they should have."

"The government is to blame!" a voice shouted. "They're the ones that did it to us!"

"Damn right they did. They're always to blame," the major slurred. "Damn politicians never did anything to help us, much less protect the homeland."

"And the government runs the military! They get their orders from the president! That's why you can't trust either one!"

The crowd howled chants of agreement.

"Then you-know-what hits the fan, they declare martial law, and the National Guard and military take over everything!" another highly intoxicated man groaned. "And we don't stand a chance. Martial fuckin' law…"

"Sounds about right to me," a younger man said, his contorted face bursting with alcohol-induced grief and repugnance. "I'd always heard anyone with any respect for his oath would never take up arms against the citizens. But that's where the whole enemies foreign and domestic clause comes in. That's us. We're the enemies domestic. An' they treat us no better than terrorists."

"Right! And if the government wasn't involved with this EMP business somehow, why in the hell didn't they come out here and help us?"

"That's easy," another gruff, inebriated voice murmured. "Because they don't give a shit."

"Speaking of giving a shit…if the damn Army and Navy and Marine boys gave a shit about the oath they took, why didn't they do something about our government a long time ago, for heaven's sake? They could've gone straight to Washington a long damn time ago and arrested all them tyrant politicians. Hell—they should've hanged them at the steps of the Capitol—just like Tom Jefferson would've!"

"What happened to all the veterans we always heard about?"

Major Frank spoke again. "That's a good point, Walter. How many times did veterans, both inside and outside our ranks, brag about how they were all sitting back and waiting for the day when the shit hit the fan so they could take up arms and fight for their country again? Buuullshit! Now where are they? Because I don't see a damn one of them. Bunch of worthless has-beens."

A younger man with bruises on his face stepped forward so his voice could be heard. "They're probably all holed up in the same place together," he said. "Probably in some bunker underground like the one they got underneath Mount Weather or Cheyenne Mountain like *WarGames*, or one of those other underground places they used to talk about on TV a lot. Somewhere, they're all hanging out, having a good time, watching all of us suffer."

"The government? Or our blessed military?"

"Or the veterans?"

"All of them!" a voice heckled. "One's just as worthless as the other."

A man in the middle of the crowd shouted amongst assorted laughter, "Hey, where's that Mexican tough guy at? Anyone seen him?"

"Probably tryin' to find his green card!"

"Bring his ass back here so we can ask him some of these questions. He said he was a Marine…maybe he's got some answers for us."

"Or maybe he'll be up for round two."

While sitting next to Lauren several yards away from the fire and the crowd of exasperated militiamen, Dave Graham tossed a stick at the ground, his stare locked on target as the group's verbal desecrations perpetuated. After a moment, he exhaled and rose to his feet. "I've had about all I can take of this crap for the night."

"You're not seriously going over there, are you?" Lauren asked, still seated with her legs crossed.

"I reckon I am."

"By yourself?"

"Ordinarily, I'd think better of it. Damn liquid courage has me feeling bulletproof."

Lauren gave him a look of concern. "But you're not, though."

"Think so, huh?" Dave handed her his beer. "Let's find out. Keep that warm for me. I'll be back for it in a bit."

Lauren nodded reluctantly, watching him stroll away. "Don't do anything I wouldn't do."

"That doesn't exactly leave me with a lot of choices, Janey."

Dave approached the group and pushed out his chest, his right hand falling perilously close to his sidearm. The crowd's volume decreased to a murmur. "Gents, I understand you're a trifle riled up, and it looks like the drinks I endowed you with haven't exactly served to enhance your sense of calm. That's all right, I suppose. All of us need room to vent every now and then. But you can all forget about round two. There isn't going to be one. Unless, of course, we're talking about a round of drinks. I'd serve them up myself if that were the case. But seeing as it's not, the only way round two is going to happen is if I'm involved. And I mean right here, at this very moment."

"Shut uuup! You're out of your league, old man!" the gruff voice shouted.

Dave hung his head in laughter. "Now, which one of you peckerwoods said that?" he asked, his hands not having moved from his hips. "Go on now, speak up." A pause for reply, though none was heard. "Okay. Remain anonymous then, pussycat. You might want to beware this old man, though, or any old man who works in a profession where men tend to die young."

No one said anything for a moment until the leader spoke. "Not meaning to insult your uniform," Major Frank droned, "but do you honestly think any of us is stupid enough to tangle with you while you got a gun on your hip?"

"Thanks for pointing that out, Major pain. How silly of me." He unbuckled his belt and removed it, along with his holstered Sig Sauer, spare magazines, Gerber LMF fighting knife, and IFAK. Snapping the Cobra buckle back together, he tossed it, where it landed safely in Lauren's hands yards behind. "It's pretty irresponsible of me to be carrying a weapon after I've consumed a few adult beverages." He held out two open palms. "See? Now I'm naked. You boys feel any better?"

Dave used his index finger to count heads while he scanned the cluster of faces. "Let's see...eeny, meeny, miney, moe, catcha, tango, by his, toe. Looks like six or seven brave souls with the eye of the tiger... along with one or two bigmouths still hiding in the middle, who may or may not jump in later on, leaving the rest of you to stand by as cowards. I'm just one man. I say that makes us even."

Dave squinted and stood erect, offering cocky winks to accompany his confident grin and sly brow. He did so without saying anything, anticipating an attack all the while, though none came his way. "So that's it? All of you against me and no one wants to kick off the crusade?" He spit on the ground. "No one wants to be the first? What do you think about that, Major? Kind of funny, don't you think?"

"What's so funny about it?" asked Frank, his mouth twisting into a scowl.

"Wasn't it you guys—the patriot militia and three percenters who came up with the saying about everyone wanting to be a patriot until the time comes to do patriot shit?" Dave badgered. "Gentlemen...wake the hell up! Time is of the essence! Here I am! A veteran! Right here in the flesh! From what I've overheard tonight, you're pissed with me and others like me. Made us all objects of your hostility. I've just given you an opportunity to clean the slate and make things right, and not a single damn one of you stepped forward. Now, take one guess what that tells me about you."

Dave turned away after another moment of silence, motioning for Lauren to return his sidearm. She hopped over hastily with his gear and stood by him a moment before walking away, but not before taking several sips of his beer, making sure he saw her do it.

"Now that I have everyone's attention, I'm going to address some of the things I heard tonight," Dave said, lecturing the crowd as a whole, the bitterness of his tone finding some calm. "I am a man who simply cannot allow things to slide by without delivering an adequate response. It's my personal belief that continued lack of that very thing was the foremost reason this country transformed into a full-on idiocratic shitshow. And I'm talking long before the lights went out."

Dave broke off as one of his men approached with a fresh bottle of German lager. "I have a question for you fellas," he began, cracking it open with his Gerber. "What did you really think was going to happen? I mean, it's no secret. Your group and most others like yours have always represented the embodiment of government distrust. Did you really believe FEMA was going to come way the hell out here and save you when the world turned upside down? That the Red Cross, National Guard, and all the other federal, state, and privately run agencies were sitting around, waiting for something like this to happen, so they could respond in kind and make your lives better again? Tell me—when has that *ever* happened before? During which disaster? The countless wildfires and earthquakes in California? Tornado outbreaks in Kansas, Nebraska, and Oklahoma? The Mississippi River flooding? All the blizzards in New England? Hurricane Andrew or Katrina? When was the last time you ever witnessed a performance by any disaster relief agency, particularly FEMA, that displayed anything other than widespread incompetence?"

Dave took a long drink. "News flash. It's not the Army's job to play rescue on the home front, and the National Guard is inclined to put down civil unrest before taking part in any recovery effort, if at all. Now, gentlemen, we can sit around here, argue, gripe, and complain. We can bitch about why this particular scenario happened and whether or not it was chosen for us, and why things didn't happen the way they should've, why it took so long for some level of response to take place, and why things got so bad as quickly as they did. We can do that, or we can all choose to direct our collective focus to the future and concentrate our efforts on what matters and what we're trying to achieve, because we can't go back and change what's already happened. It doesn't matter who did it or who's responsible. We could find out tomorrow, or we may never find out.

"Let me clue you in on something. The folks who really rule this world of ours, the ones you've heard called all sorts of things—the elite, the one percent, the establishment—they play people in our government like game pieces on a chessboard, and the moves they make trickle down and eventually affect all of us. Every move serves to elicit a reaction from another player. They're patient, and they think things through, and they've been at this business for a long damn time. They make a move, sit back and thumb their beards, and sip brandy, watch, and wait. If they don't get what they want, they try something else. Changes come in increments. Not fast or in chunks, because the working class would take notice, and that's not what they want. Consequently, for the past century or longer, they've been slowly planting the seeds of hate. Pitting us against each other and doing everything in their power to divide us as a people and as a country, to serve as a means to an end. And sorry as I am to admit it, they succeeded."

"So what are you saying?" the young man with the bruised face asked. "That the government and the elite did this to us? Or they didn't?"

"Neither," Dave replied sternly. "I'm saying I don't know. I'm saying nobody knows for certain. But I'm also telling you it doesn't matter."

"It matters to me. What if they really are sitting in a bunker somewhere, watching all this go down?"

Dave took a long drink, grinned, and wiped his lips with his sleeve. "Do you know how stupid you sound right now? You actually ever been to Mount Weather, son?"

"No..."

"Do you know what's really underneath that escarpment of limestone and granite? Nothing. Not one damn thing worth getting riled up about. I know because I've been there. Because I'm former SF—United States Army Special Forces, which is a subtle way of saying I know more than you do. During my stint in the military and my prior career as a civilian, I garnered one of the highest clearances attainable by *Homo sapiens*. I've been all over Area B. But I've also been to the sections that've never been declassified, to places so deep underground you can feel the effects of geothermal flux.

"There's a self-contained power plant, water and sewer, and even a desalinization plant, so they can utilize the saltwater aquifers the Corps of Engineers dug up by accident during Operation High Point in 1954. There are hundreds of offices, sleeping quarters, a hospital, a crematorium, and they even got Wi-Fi. But there's no city, no shopping mall, and no ultranationalist, all-knowing, all-powerful, new world order collective down there in some marble Noah's Ark trimmed in gold and diamonds. You can believe that if you want, but it just isn't so."

The young man hung his head and shuffle-stepped away, unwilling to say anything else.

"What the facility is set up for is disaster mitigation and continuity of government. And for all we know, it could be in operation today," Dave continued. "If so, fine. Whatever. Doesn't change a damn thing for me, my men, or any of you. The government does not have our best interests in mind, and never did. And the greater good isn't about us, and never was. They're not coming to help us. All the government ever served to do was violate our rights and remove our freedoms systematically, replacing them with permission slips and illusions of security. Then they surveilled us and spied on us and turned our nation into a fascist police state. No. Our true enemy is an ethereal leviathan that's never once shown its face, probably never will, and at least for now, remains untouchable. If this was their doing, well, I guess they got what they wanted. But they found their Zion a long time ago, and this ain't it."

Major Frank inched closer to Dave, seemingly unimpressed with his speech thus far. "You know a lot," he garbled, a newly opened bottle of liquor in his grasp. "Explain to all of us what happened, then…why the military, in all its might, didn't get called in to help clean up the mess? Riddle me that with your la-di-da, 'I know more than you' security clearance."

Dave began again with a shrug of indifference. "The whole point of clearances is compartmentalization, Frank. They're not set up for people to know things, its purpose is so they *don't* know things. It's echelons of information, treated as real, when most of it means nothing. It's disinformation—mostly bullshit, like most of the stuff you think you know."

He paused before continuing and started pacing around the fire. "When the power went off, so did our lights. Cell phones stopped working. Cars idled to a stop in the middle of the roads. All the familiar and comforting sounds people were used to hearing just went silent. It was like time ended. And it didn't take long for panic to set in and for people to lose their sense of normalcy, and their damn minds soon after. They tried to make calls, and they couldn't. Tried to revive their cars, and couldn't. They asked questions, and no one had any answers. They went to get money and found their credit and debit cards were useless. Most everyone depended on imaginary currency, and no shop owner was stupid enough to accept anything but cash, so people couldn't buy the things they needed or wanted.

"People found themselves miles from home with no way to get back, no means to buy anything or call anyone. Kids were stuck at school with no one coming to pick them up…and that's just a smidgeon of what happened in the small towns and rural areas, Major. How do you think it went down in the big cities and outlying suburban areas? We're talking millions upon millions of people stacked one on top of each other—crammed together like pigs in a slaughterhouse. Boston, Philly, New York, DC, Baltimore, Charlotte, Chicago, Miami. Need I go on? Those cities were turned upside down—transformed into war zones in a matter of days, some in the span of hours. And the National Guard, Army, and eventually even the Marines were called in. And that's why they didn't have time to show up to your doorstep in BFE to deliver food, offer protection, and wipe your ass for you. We sent our bravest men and women, our country's finest, into metropolitan America to protect the cities and fight against our own people. Can you imagine what that would be like?"

Dave paused, taking a breath. He cast a frigid stare beyond the tens of eyes staring back at him. "You trained for years to become a soldier, an infantryman. Trained rigorously to defend your country, its people, and value democracy, the republic, and freedom more than you value anything, even your own life. And then, one day, you're being ordered to march in lockstep into one of your own cities and turn your rifle on the very people whose liberties you were trained to protect. That is the absolute quantification of a mindfuck. To make matters worse, you're vastly outnumbered, and men, women, and even children are now attacking you because you're supposed to be there to help, and you're not, because you can't.

"You're aiming a gun at them now, and you've been given strict orders to put them down. To save the cities. To save the country. To protect the so-called greater good. And I'm telling you, as God as my witness, it wore on them…in no time flat. I'd bet anything that the majority of them went unauthorized absence or AWOL, and I wouldn't blame them. Officers relinquished their commissions and went back to their families. And, I imagine like most wars, there were thousands of casualties. God only knows what happened to the rest. Probably spread out all over, searching for another way to survive. Like us."

Dave poked the juiced-up major in his chest. "As far as veterans go, you're looking at them," he continued, motioning beyond to his men gathered in the darkness, most of whom had moved in closer to hear what was being said. "Those are your worthless has-beens, Major pain. Approximately ninety percent of the men and women in my unit have prior military experience. I spent years training with them, but it took a hell of a long time finding people who wanted to train. Before the collapse, almost a million vets across the country, men and women both, came home to nothing after their tours and had to struggle to keep their heads above water. Deployed, their skills were viable, but at home, it just wasn't so. Most ended up on government programs, welfare, food stamps and the like, while the VA did its part in making them feel even more useless, diagnosing them with PTSD, manic depression, ADHD, sleep disorders, and mental health issues galore. Then they filled them up with painkillers, antidepressants or other psychotropics because they needed them.

"About two hundred thousand veterans found themselves barred from owning guns because of one cheesedick psychiatric evaluation." Dave continued, taking a look around. "Take a perfectly good man, a decorated serviceman who's valiantly served his country, seen his share of blood and guts, then bring him home and convince him something's wrong with him. Diagnose him with some bullshit psychosis and make him feel more alone than he already is, then drug him to the point he falls helplessly into depression or worse, and his only option is becoming a recluse no one wants to be around. Alone, he pops pills and drinks himself into oblivion every night and eventually turns a gun on himself, if he doesn't manage to take a hundred other people with him purely for the goddamn hell of it."

Dave regarded all the watchful eyes in proximity. He had their undivided attention now. "People, last thing I want to do is spend all night long harping on you folks. I promised everyone here some downtime, and I meant it. If you have questions you want answers to, ask them and I'll tell you what I know. Aside from that, I have no intention of allowing the division to continue between our groups, especially over something so petty. Before I started running off at the mouth tonight, everyone here was ready to rise up. Some of you probably for the first time in your lives. But it wasn't against a real enemy. It was over inconsequential differences with a fellow human being—a fellow American. And for what? Because he disagrees with your opinion? Because his skin is a different color? Because he wears a different uniform?

"Sun Tzu said that if an enemy's forces are united, to separate them. That if sovereign and subject are in accord, put division between them. Meaning an enemy divided is easily defeated. And that is exactly what's happened to us on the grand scale. Those in power found innumerable ways to divide us. They showed us how to hate one another, and even found ways to make us feel good about it. Then they propped their feet up and enjoyed the spoils while we were left to quibble over the scraps they spoon-fed us. Well, fellas, I gotta tell you all…I'm done quibbling. My preference is to move forward, rise above all this, and see us all get what we want, but the only way that's gonna happen is if we work together toward a common cause. There's simply no other option. If you have a better one, please speak up. I am all ears. But the men behind me feel the same way I do; if they didn't, they wouldn't be here."

"Can we leave?" a voice called out. "Can we just go home?"

"Of course you can," Dave said. "All of you are free men, free to go anywhere you like. But it's tough out there. That's why I'm indulged to allow you to stay and join us. But if you decide that's what you want, know now that I do not allow dissention within my ranks. Take a stand with us, we fight together. Go against us, or try to subvert us, and I'll kill each and every one of you and let God sort you out. There is entirely too much on the line, and I intend to get my country back with or without your help. I don't care what it takes."

Dave paused. "I don't have, nor do I offer a panacea, but I do possess the means to get this done. I just need some more bodies. Able bodies with the proper mindset. Men and women who want to see the republic restored and our Constitution reinstalled as the supreme law of the land. It doesn't matter what got us here. One-world government and the push for a totalitarian global system, population control, whatever. I'm telling you it doesn't matter. What's done is done, and this country's population has been decimated as a result. Those wanting to know how, use your imagination.

"The whole point of this rambling is to clue you all in on something probably not many of you have given any thought to. That this country, up until the point the EMP took us out, wasn't free. We were living under an illusion of freedom. You can scoff all you like, grumble and groan all you want, but it won't change the fact that we had a fascist government at best. One that spied on us, stole from us, scared us into submission every day, and did so with complete autonomy. We were slaves then, but we're not slaves anymore. If anything, that pulse installed some balance and allowed nature to take its course...while having done so at great cost." Dave shrugged. "But that's life. Such is history, folks. We cannot achieve the things we want without sacrifice. And if we want to continue getting what we want, we've got to build on that sacrifice and keep moving forward together despite our differences." He paused, turning to Major Frank. "That's all I got, Major. Mull it over in that melon of yours. I'll be over there with that pretty young lady, enjoying a few more of these Bavarian beers, if you decide you want to talk."

Dave left the crowd of men in their silence. He shook hands with several of his men before returning to his seat beside Lauren.

"Nice speech," she said. "I'm impressed…you didn't even have anything written down."

"Thanks. I've been saving that diatribe for a special occasion."

Lauren hesitated, toying with the dew-covered grass before her. "Think it did any good?"

"Who knows?" Dave said, tipping his bottle up. "If it did, great. If not, at least major pain and his throng got some much-needed tutelage. And they know exactly where they stand with me."

Lauren nodded. "Right. But that begs the question, *will* they stand with you?"

"Whether they do or don't changes nothing for us, Janey. We'll just pick up where we left off, putting back together the pieces of a country put asunder." Dave paused, looking into the mouth of his bottle contemplatively. "We'll be heading back to base for a few days after a while. The unit's been humping for months on end, and we urgently need to resupply, refuel, and regroup. I think I've been pushing the men too hard lately. And men under that kind of pressure have a tendency to snap. I don't want them to forget what they're fighting for." He sighed. "That…and we could all use the rest, I suspect. Myself included."

Lauren cocked her head to the side. "Where is base?"

"No one's told you yet?"

"No one's told me anything…"

"Roger that. It's a place called Rocket Center, not far from here. I think you might like it. It has some…redeeming qualities." Dave paused for a long moment, staring off into the distance. He took a final sip and set the empty bottle aside. "Janey, you remember that phrase 'united we stand, divided we fall'?"

"Of course I do," she replied, grinning. "It was pretty common."

"Indeed, it was. You know its origin?"

"History was never my forte," Lauren said, shrugging. "But I did spend a few Sundays of my youth in children's church. There was a verse printed on a banner in the front of the room. It said, 'If a house is divided against itself, that house cannot stand'."

Dave chuckled. "You never cease to amaze me with that wit. The phrase was Kentucky's state motto. Patrick Henry used it verbatim in the last speech he made, two months before he died. I always loved hearing it, whether spoken or in song, and I used to think it was timeless. But I don't anymore."

Lauren ran her fingers through her hair. "Why not anymore?"

"Because the United States fell, and everything that once was has changed. We've all been through our share of trials and tribulations, even you, Janey, yet we're still here, still alive to sit by the fire under a moonlit night and chat about it. We've all fallen and been torn apart, as a people and as a country, but I can see us slowly coming together again and finding a way back to our feet. And I think the phrase merits some rewording to compensate. Because from what I've seen, whether united or divided, we stand."

CHAPTER 20

Trout Run Valley
Thursday, December 2nd

GRACE'S LATEST COMPANION TUGGED ON her arm with such vigor that she could feel her shoulder ready to slip out of its socket. It was an injury she had initially endured while participating in a dance competition many years before, and had become one of the primary reasons she had stopped competing in dance altogether. Today, she was certain it was close to becoming reinjured.

The man led her out the front door of the Masons' home and down the front porch steps into the driveway. Grace didn't say anything until she noticed he was pulling her toward the cabin.

"Where exactly are you taking me?" she asked, the pain in her arm and her perturbation both palpable in her voice. "And would you mind easing up with your grip? This nutcracker-crusher thing you're doing isn't necessary—and it really hurts." She resisted, only to have him pull harder on her.

"You wanted to see the man, didn't you? The head honcho?" He pointed ahead to the cabin. "Well, he's in that house over there. So that's where we're going, to see the man. So far as my grip is concerned, I think I've given in to your nonsense enough already today."

"Is that...a fact?"

The man continued to tug on her while reaching to open the gate leading to the Russells' driveway. "Goddamn right, that's a fact. It's been years since

I've come across someone, correction, a skank near as flippant as you." He paused, licking his teeth. "If it wasn't for the fact you got a potato growin' in your garden, I'd smack the tar out of you for the simple fact I don't like the way you're looking at me. And the shit your mouth's been talkin' would get you a full-on ass beating."

"Well, I'm sorry that my gestational condition is interfering with your ability to get in a proper workout," Grace quipped, gesturing to the man's belly. "Looks like you could use a few. Maybe we can find you an inanimate, nonhuman punching bag somewhere. The kind that doesn't hit back."

"Keep that shit up, and your gestational anything won't matter. I'll hang you by your ankles and make you my personal piñata. Maybe then you'll shut the hell up and show some respect."

"I doubt it."

As the words left her mouth, the man yanked on her, pulling her nose-to-nose with him. "You got sand. Can't wait to see you try that shit with Max. He's not nearly as patient."

"Is Max *the man*?"

"Yup."

"Can't wait to meet him," she purred.

The man loosened his grip only slightly while leading Grace through the cabin's front door. Once inside, she studied the floor, walls, and the furniture, attempting to discern how much, if anything, was out of place, relocated, or missing. At first glance, it didn't appear much had been altered.

Three men were seated at the table, two just as grimy and untidy as the slack-jawed yokel who had accompanied her. A third man, whom Grace assumed was the leader, was not only dressed differently than the others, but had a certain air about him. His stiff posture displayed gumption, and he reminded her of someone used to getting his way, used to being in a place of authority, like a corporate officer or a CEO of a business.

While the other men wore denim jeans, coveralls, or canvas work pants of some kind and had boots on their feet, he instead had on pleated khakis and a pair of incredibly clean penny loafers, of all things. His light blue button-up cotton twill shirt looked as if it had been recently ironed. His appearance seemed dreadfully out of place for the times, like he had just strolled into the post-apocalypse after staying the night at a fully operational Holiday Inn Express.

The man's presentation caught Grace napping. When he turned to her, she caught sight of an incredibly well-groomed, yet very seedy-looking mustache, a facial feature she'd often referred to as a 'pornstache'. She was so amused that she almost giggled aloud. "Okay, you most definitely have to be Max."

The man clasped his fingers together and placed his hands in his lap while leaning back casually in the chair. "Maybe I am, maybe I'm not. Depends who's asking. Who in the hell are you?" He turned to the cohort who had brought Grace along. "What's this about?"

Grace moved in closer as the other men at the table redirected their attention from the mounds of food they had on their plates. Setting their forks down, they eyeballed her, and one pointed a .45-caliber 1911 pistol in her direction.

While doing her best not to make sudden moves, Grace reached for a chair and slowly slid it away from the table, then took a seat.

The leader looked at his men with a grin, then turned his attention back to Grace while he thumbed the coarse hairs of his mustache. "Well, please. Take a seat. Make yourself at home."

"Thanks, but I really don't think I need your permission."

"Excuse me?"

Grace furrowed her brow and held up a finger. "Sorry…allow me to explain. This *is* my home." She downturned the same finger and tapped the table. "I live here. This is my table we're sitting at, and those are my chairs that your and your men's asses are planted in right now."

The man with the mustache lifted an eyebrow. "I see. Thanks for making me aware of this. Which room is yours?"

"My room is in the cellar, if you must know," Grace continued, her tone almost brazen. "This house and everything in it belongs to me and my family. My grandmother and grandfather bought the property as an investment years ago. I believe the original deed has twenty-five acres of land and includes this cabin, the bridge behind it, and two exterior buildings. I can show it to you if you like."

"There's no need for that," the man wearing the button-up shirt said, taking a more formal tone. "I'm fully cognizant that in normal times, such documentation had a strong legal standing." He scooted his butt to the edge of his chair and set his elbows on the table. "But my dear, all of our asses, including the one connected to that curvy, gaunt frame of yours, are planted right smack-dab in the middle of *abnormal*. And times…they are a-changin'. The only law present for miles around is present at this table, seated right in front of you, and you're looking at him right now."

"Oh."

"And this may have been your house at one time, but now it belongs to me. I've taken possession of it. In fact, everything that once belonged to anyone living in this valley is now also mine. Every house, every car, every road, every tree. Everything."

Grace could feel dryness begin to overtake her mouth. A sheet of warmth moved through her body, causing her to feel faint. She couldn't decide what act to take with this man. Maybe she needed more time.

She glanced into the kitchen and spotted Norman's two-bucket filter. "I'm sorry, I'm really parched. I didn't realize how thirsty I was. Could someone get me a glass of water?"

The man chuckled, as did his minions. He sat back and gestured to the filter. "Get it yourself. It *was* your house, after all. You should know where everything's at."

Grace smiled grimly and rose, making her way around the table and past the men to the filter. While pouring herself a glass, she could hear the man who had brought her saying something under his breath to the one with the perfect whiskers.

"Pregnant?" the leader barked. "Who in the hell would be dumb enough to bring another child into this Godforsaken world?"

Grace took a long sip of water and swished it around her mouth before swallowing. She turned and raised her hand. "That would be me."

All four men in the room only stared at her, no words escaping their mouths.

Taking another sip from the glass, Grace walked back to the table and took her seat. "It's my credo, my modus operandi. I've never been known for good decision-making skills. And my luck has never been very good either. This time around, I really screwed the pooch."

The leader's eyebrows danced while he toyed with his chin. "You can say that again. And to top it all off, your baby daddy left you. So what happened? Lovers' quarrel? Get into a big fight? Did you try and trap him?"

Grace could feel the nausea building in her stomach, and she tried reassuring herself about the water she was drinking. She knew it had come from the rain barrels and they had disposed of any water believed to be tainted, but in that moment, in her current situation, she wished it had been the other way around, and these men could get what was coming to them, simply by obeying their thirst. "No. No fight, and he didn't run out on me. I mean…don't get me wrong…he's a pain in the butt sometimes, but I'm no better. He's a good man, and I love him… even though I probably don't deserve him."

"Where did he go? And how long before he returns?"

Grace contemplated answering the leader's interrogation with lies, but she didn't see any point in hiding the truth. "Originally, we planned an expedition to search for food. We're well beyond running out, as you've probably already noticed. Then some of us got sick from some mystery illness, so they left in a rush to try to find a doctor."

The man laughed as his eyes rolled skyward. "A doctor? Jesus H Christ. Now that's some wishful thinking, if I ever heard it. Where in the name of the blessed Virgin Mary did you people think you'd find a doctor these days?"

Grace turned her head away and shrugged, trying her best to look shameful. "I don't know; it wasn't my idea. And I really have no idea where they went to look. So I guess I don't have a clue when they'll be back, either."

"That's a shame. And as sorry as I am to hear about your problems, these days, everybody has them. My men and I have been dealing with a slew of our own since this whole thing started."

Grace leaned in. "And are those problems what's brought you and your men here to hold us hostage and steal from us?"

The man rapped his knuckles on the table, looking derisive. "You know something, I like you. You're bold…feisty even. Were you always like this? Back before you got yourself inseminated?"

"I'm passionate," replied Grace, slightly taken aback at the man's jargon. "It just so happens, ever since I was…inseminated, I became a bit more sassy."

The man with the mustache chuckled. "I can respect that. I can definitely respect that. I admire your spirit." He turned to Grace's escort and ordered him back to the Masons' home, then pointed to Grace. "What's your name?"

"Grace."

"Grace what?"

Grace thought quickly about which character guise to adopt from her collection. "Grace Louise...after my mother."

The man exhaled through his nose, sat back in his seat, and crossed his legs. "As you already know, my name is Max. That's short for Maximilian, but I'd prefer it if you called me Mr. Armstrong, like my men do."

"Charmed."

"Yes, yes, I'm quite sure you are," said Max, not picking up on Grace's sardonic tone. "As you can probably guess, I've had women throw themselves at me practically all my life, but I've learned how to become oblivious to flirtatious advances. Relationships tend to interfere with business."

Grace snickered, finding herself transfixed by Max's pornstache. "Oh, I wasn't flirting with you. If it came across that way, I—"

"No need to renege, Grace. I know when a woman wants me. I am a man of many talents, and reading people is one of them."

"Oh, I see."

"I was a businessman...an affluent entrepreneur, desperate for some much-needed time away from work before all this shit came to pass," Max expounded. "I bet you didn't know that before winding up here, I ran one of the largest coal-mining companies in the eastern United States...well, the former eastern United States, I guess I should say."

"Which one?" Grace asked, pretending to sound sincere.

"The Strong Arm Energy Cooperative. I suppose you've heard of it."

Grace shook her head indifferently, her lower lip protruding. "Nope."

"Hmm, okay. Well, my father, you see, started the business forty-seven years ago and handed it over to me as an inheritance when he died. Been mine ever since. And I gave him quite the send-off. In my tenure, I managed to quadruple our production and revenue. Until this damn...blackout, or whatever, business was flourishing."

"I'm sorry, I blacked out for a second. Did you say strong arm or strong *armed*?" Grace pondered. "Is that like a play on words or something? Like strong-armed robbery?"

"Are you getting smart with me, Grace? Because I don't like that shit. I don't take to insults." Max gestured to his minion holding the pistol. "My nephew had a smart lip on him. Little bastard had to get it beaten out of him every day."

"No, no. Not smart. Sassy, remember?"

"Ah, yes. Her pregnancy hath made her sassy." Max pointed to Grace. "I got my eye on you. You are definitely one to watch." He paused to adjust his posture. "So what exactly can I help you with, Grace? You're pregnant, immersed in a rather bleak situation you can't get out of, surrounded by armed, ferocious-looking men. With a mouth like yours running out of control like it's been, whatever you wanted must've been pretty goddamn important."

Grace hesitated while gliding her index finger across the faded polish of the tabletop. "Well, I guess it is pretty goddamn important. It started as a single two-part question, the first being to find out who you were. Since you've already answered that part, I can move on to the next one…the one where I ask why you're here."

"I'm here because I choose to be…and let's get something straight," Max began, clinching his jaw. "You need to realize, Grace, first and foremost, that I am under no obligation to give you any information from this point forward. In fact, I'm under zero burden to give you or any of the folks still breathing here a goddamn thing. You're lucky that I'm letting the matrons over there give your sick people some of *my* antibiotics." He pointed to the glass of water in Grace's hand. "You're lucky that I'm allowing you to partake of *my* water right now while your sassy badonkadonk rides *my* antique fiddleback chair. You understand that, don't you, Grace? Because I can make things more clear for you if you don't."

Grace hung her head and provided a negative response as her stomach began to churn. "No, I don't need any additional…clarification. I'm fully aware who has the advantage right now. And I know you don't have to answer any of my questions."

"Good. Glad we've got that figured out."

"But," Grace pressed, "I also know you could have just as easily killed me the second I was pushed through that door. You could kill me right now, and for some reason, you haven't."

"He hasn't *yet*." One of the other, previously silent men slithered into the conversation.

Max shrugged apathetically after giving his underling a dirty look. "Maybe I'm keeping you around for my amusement." He tapped himself on the temple with his index finger. "Or maybe I'm trying to mess with your head, Grace. Ever think of that?"

"I would know it if you were," remarked Grace, her stare firm. "Over the years, my experience has made me sort of an expert on the deed."

"Very well," Max relented. "You know what? Screw it…what's the use? I'll level with you, Grace. There are about a half-dozen reasons why we're here right now, and the biggest one—the one that's been causing me the most headaches, is survival. Winter is fast approaching, and I don't have near enough food for my people to endure it…not to mention our shelter situation bites the big one."

"Having a roof over your head is one thing, but if you came here for food, I hope you're not too disappointed with what you found."

Max cleared his throat. "I can tell you all aren't exactly thriving," he said. "Not sure what happened to all of it; maybe you're hiding it. Maybe you buried it somewhere for safekeeping. If you did, we'll find it eventually. Fact remains, you're still doing a hell of a lot better than we ever did…I don't think the boys have ever had it this good." He glanced at his men. "Stomachs full?"

The other men at the table nodded in unison.

"See? It may be a little food to you, but a little food goes a long way when you've been living on scraps for months on end."

"So that's it?"

Max cocked his head inquisitively. "No, not quite," he replied. "I'm also interested in the vehicles you have here…as well as the fuel it takes to run them. And—"

"Women?"

"There's that sass again. Something on your mind you wanna divulge?"

Grace rolled her lips. "I couldn't help but notice that we've been separated by gender. And, aside from the sick at the Masons' across the road, I haven't seen any of the other men around. And a girl is missing. A blond girl about five years younger than me. Her name's—"

"I'll look into it," Max said with apathy, holding up a finger. "Certain behaviors are intolerable, but it's difficult to herd feral cats, Grace, especially when they're…hungry. And my men are hungry, feral cats." He paused. "Your men are being kept separate because they have a tendency to cause the most ruckus, while the fairer sex…well, let's just say your type tends to be more…submissive."

"Not all of us," Grace rasped.

"So I'm gathering," said Max, then paused. "I don't know if you realize it or not…maybe you've been absent, unconscious, or something. Who knows? But there's been a little war going on between your people and mine for about the past year or so, and it all started when some of my men came by looking for a bite to eat. They were told to leave by having guns pointed at them. Then they were shot without any further warning, and a few of them died from their injuries. And my brother was one of them."

Grace's forehead puckered. "Oh…I'm sorry to hear that."

"Are you, Grace? Are you? Because I had to become a husband as well as a father that day. My brother left a family behind," Max said, his tone gaining fervor. "With no one else left to watch over them, it had to be me. I did the best I could…not ever having been a family man. And his wife…boy, did she have issues. She was on medication for some mental illness—manic depression, paranoia, something along those lines. When the meds ran out, she started doing the strangest things… like taking walks by herself in the woods. Sometimes they were short little jaunts; other times she'd be gone for days."

Grace cocked her head to the side. "Why are you telling me this?"

"Because I want you to understand that you and your friends living here are not the only ones dealing with a set of problems," said Max, folding his arms. "Things escalated quite a bit between our groups a few months back when we had another little run-in, and even more of my people were killed. And since then…since that day…" He trailed off as if a thought had entered his mind that seemed to cause him a distinct level of discomfort. "Since that last little…incursion, some of our own remain missing, in particular…some of *my* own. Namely, my brother's crazy widow *and* her daughter. My niece, Isabel."

Grace's lips set in a grim line as the narrative began to pull on her heartstrings. "I…wouldn't know anything about that."

Max's brows knitted. "You were living here then, were you not?"

"Well, yes, but—"

"You didn't move here last week, did you?"

"No."

"Then how could you not?"

Grace hesitated. "We don't aim a gun at anyone unless it's called for. Unless we have to."

"Funny how that works," said Max, snapping his fingers. "We're not so different, you and I, your people and mine. We all…do what we have to do. All things being equal, if it weren't for our little error in judgement, going on vacation right when the shit hit the fan, we would've never been in this mess, and we probably would never have bothered any of you. As luck would have it, though, this valley of yours was right next door and has proven itself to be the land of plenty, at least up until recently, for some reason. Either way, we have come to claim what's rightfully ours after so much was taken from us. And now that we've claimed it, it belongs to us. It belongs to me. All of it."

CHAPTER 21

Town of Edinburg
Shenandoah County, Virginia
Thursday, December 2nd

SASHA'S HEAD WAS POUNDING. AFTER experiencing what it had been like to have a 9mm bullet strike her in the head, the pain was an alarmingly familiar feeling to her. It startled her at first until the point her eyes opened, and she was able to see where she was.

She was lying on a hardwood floor, and the rolled-up towel she'd found in the kitchen and used as a pillow had slipped out from under her head. It was old and smelled of dirty dishes, and she could detect that some of the stench had diffused into her hair.

Sasha rolled her head over, now able to distinguish her surroundings, recalling the decision had been made to stay overnight and try to wait out the lingering DHS agents. She stretched her aching back and arms and felt a sudden pressure on her leg, like something had grabbed her.

She sat up a bit and lifted the quilt she'd been using to cover herself while she slept, exposing a hand holding tightly to her thigh. Mark Mason was snoring with his back to her, still sound asleep, while his hand was busily exploring her upper leg.

Sasha shook her head and rubbed one of her eyes, then exhaled a puff of air against her bangs. "Hey! Hey, kid." She nudged him with the back of her hand. "Get up. You're dreaming."

Mark stirred in his sleep and made a few grunting noises.

Sasha nudged him again with added effort, this time reaching down and removing his errant hand from her leg. "Seriously. Come on, kid, get up. Rise and shine. It's time for Sasha's wine."

Mark's body jerked, and he slowly came to, rolling over and yawning. "What's going on? Did you say something?"

Sasha leaned forward and coughed a few times, then pulled one of the remaining cigarettes from her pack. "It's time to get up," she said, placing the cigarette between her lips. She pointed to the window at the growing daylight. "We gotta get out of here soon."

Mark yawned again and nodded his head, then reached over to wake his brother up.

The three sat on the floor together to get their bearings, then gathered their belongings in preparation for their departure.

"I was having the weirdest dream," Mark said. "I was being chased."

Chad elevated his arms above his head and stretched. "Who was chasing you? DHS?"

"A bunch of women," Mark replied, a sly grin appearing on his face. "It was a good dream."

Sasha blew out a large cloud of cigarette smoke into the air. "Could've fooled me." She sniggered.

Chad glanced out the window to the cul-de-sac.

"Are our friends still here?" his brother asked.

"You have got to be kidding me," Chad said, glowering. "Those motherf—"

"They're still here? They stayed all night?" Mark moved in to look for himself.

"Sure as hell did."

"Forget them," Sasha directed, pulling on her boots. "There's no sense in trying to figure them out. Let's just get going."

Watching in all directions for signs of danger, the trio exited the house from the rear door and traversed the backyard to a large field of thick, tall grass and sporadic trees.

Chad led the way, being the first to cross the transition between the yard and the field, though there wasn't much difference between the two. Sasha followed him, and Mark marched nearly in parallel. Then suddenly, a screech, just before a—

CLANK.

Someone, possibly the previous owner, had placed bear traps around the edges of the backyard, and not having seen them, Mark put his foot right into one.

As Mark tried hard not to cry out, Sasha and Chad pulled hard on the rusty jaws that had clamped their jagged teeth into his ankle. But even their combined efforts weren't enough to overcome the contraption's tensile strength.

The trap's teeth had embedded themselves into Mark's skin, and he was bleeding from the lacerations. He twisted and writhed in pain while he tugged with all his might on the mechanism, attempting to free himself.

Chad was growing increasingly frustrated. He yanked his hands away from the trap and pounded his fist on the ground. "There's got to be some way to break this piece of rusty shit free," he began, looking around the yard. "We need to find something to pry it open with... something we can use for leverage."

Sasha's eyes grew wide. "Like what?" she asked, looking around in the grass. "I left the Jaws of Life in my other purse."

Mark's jaw was clenched, and his facial muscles tensed as he spoke through the pain. "Look in my backpack. There's a...Bowie knife in there. Try to pry it open with that."

Sasha looked at Mark awkwardly, but didn't say anything as Chad rummaged through his brother's backpack, finally extricating a large Bowie-style knife. He removed it from its sheath and dug the blade's tip between the jaws.

Sasha recognized the knife immediately. She knew where it had come from and who its previous owner had been. In fact, she would recognize the blade and accompanying handle anywhere, even if she had come across it in a pawnshop surrounded by other similar blades. She furrowed her brow.

Chad focused his efforts and soon made progress, separating the jaws just enough for Mark to slide his foot from the trap's grasp while trying his best not to further tear the skin. Once his leg was free, he began unlacing his boot.

Sasha only stared at the knife. "Mark, where did you get that?"

"What?"

"That knife."

Mark spoke through his teeth, his hands moving to his leg, trying to rub away the pain. "I found it on the ground…when we were cleaning up. After we wiped your old buddies off the map. Why?"

Sasha shook her head while she gazed at the knife, helpless to take her eyes from it. "No reason. It's nothing."

Chad removed a triangular first-aid bandage from his medical kit and rolled Mark's sock down enough to expose the wound. "It doesn't look too bad, but some of the cuts are pretty deep. I think they got into the meat."

Sasha reached for the bandage. "Here, let me do it," she said, pointing to the med kit.

"Are you a nurse or something?" Chad asked.

"No. But I've had plenty of experience treating wounds," Sasha replied, peering up at him with her head downturned. She proceeded to clean the lacerations and applied a disinfectant, followed by an antibiotic ointment before using butterfly strips to close each wound. She finished with the triangle bandage, using tape to wrap Mark's ankle. "You have to watch this, kid. Keep it clean and make sure it doesn't get infected. Tetanus is one thing, but Lord only knows what other gross bacteria is living on that trap. I hope you guys have enough first-aid supplies with you."

Chad regarded their backpacks. "Both of us have IFAKs and a separate trauma kit, but they won't last forever."

Sasha nodded. "There's plenty of pine trees around here. We can use sap to disinfect and seal the cuts if we have to." She looked to Mark. "How about it, kid? Can you move?"

"I think I can," said Mark, and he stood while gingerly placing his weight on his injured leg. "It doesn't feel broken."

Sasha grabbed Mark by the arm and supported him while they proceeded farther and deeper into the thicket. Several feet in, they encountered a fence line compiled of ancient, rusted barbed wire, petrified wooden posts, and a long row of sporadically growing Osage orange trees.

Reaching for his belt, Chad extracted a multitool and used the wire cutters to cut away the fencing.

Sasha helped Mark down to his knees, then reached for a greenish, oddly-textured fruit lying amidst the sporadic grass. "I haven't seen one of these in years," she said. "I think my dad used to call them hedge apples. Farmers used to plant the trees where they wanted a fence line.

The branches are just as thorny as that barbed wire, but don't cost nearly as much. Probably don't rust as much, either."

Mark nodded. "We always called them brain fruit. There's a couple of trees growing in the woods behind the house. Chad and I used to bring the brains home and squish them in front of Megan to gross her out."

Chad snickered. "Yeah, those were the days. Try that shit with her now, Meg would probably shoot your ass."

Mark nodded. "No doubt."

The trio continued on after Chad finished separating the fencing. Mark tried walking under his own power several times and, although confident he could do so, decided to pretend he couldn't in order to remain in body contact with Sasha. While she was busy helping him along, occasionally he would turn his head to stare at her or catch a whiff of her hair. There was something about her he found irresistible, regardless of the point she had made clear to him earlier, and knowing she was probably twice his age or more. But to Mark, bearing those things in mind only made it even more intriguing.

Commotion from behind slowed their movements and eventually brought all three to a dead stop. They looked toward the cul-de-sac in time to see a handful of vehicles within the DHS convoy had started to move out while leaving several others to remain behind. Then what happened next scared them half to death.

Two of the blacked-out SUVs broke away and turned toward them, bouncing over a yard and crashing through a wobbly privacy fence seconds after. An armored MRAP left the road and followed, and the vehicles accelerated in the general direction of where Mark, Chad, and Sasha were hiding.

"Dammit! They made us!" Sasha gasped.

Mark looked to his brother frantically, then to Sasha. "How? How did they—"

Sasha grabbed Mark's face. "It doesn't matter. We have to go, now! Come on!"

Chad stood and reached for Mark's pack, swinging it over top of his own, then ran off as Sasha hoisted Mark to his feet, noticing it took less effort now than it had earlier.

The three darted from their position and made a break for it, but their foot speed was no match for the velocity of the vehicles in pursuit.

Harshly spouted demands to halt where they stood and drop their weapons blasted over the MRAP's loudspeaker, and several warning shots sounded off behind them.

"Stop! Or we will open fire!"

Out of breath and out of viable options, Chad hit the brakes and turned to face the incoming trucks. "Go! Keep going! I'll hold them off!"

"What? Are you insane?" Sasha questioned. "That's fucking suicide! You need to ru—"

At that moment, a single thundering gunshot went off. The bullet struck Chad's body, the force causing him to spiral nearly one hundred eighty degrees. His eyes went wide, and his arms fell to his sides as he slithered to the ground underneath the weight of the backpacks.

Hearing the shot and his brother's agonized screams, Mark dashed for him, diving to the ground where he fell.

Though still alive and breathing, the trauma to Chad's body was extensive. Blood poured from a large wound in his shoulder and through a sizable hole in his jacket.

"I think…my collarbone is…broken," Chad wheezed, barely loud enough to be heard. "I can't move my—"

"Shut up," Mark said. "Don't talk. Don't move. Just stay still."

Mark unsnapped the quick disconnects on the backpacks still clinging to his brother's arms and freed his body from them, then ripped Chad's jacket off to examine the wound.

Sasha fell to her knees and grabbed hold of him, reaching in and making an abrupt move for his MP5.

Mark reacted fiercely, elbowing her in the stomach. Then he turned and angrily grabbed Sasha by the throat. "What the hell are you doing?"

The MRAP's driver continued to bark orders, but Mark couldn't hear him.

Fear and misery mounted in Sasha's eyes, and she fought against Mark's grip on her throat until he let go. "Mark, they're right behind us," she said, anguish in her voice. "We've got to get rid of these guns befo—"

"No way." He pulled away from her and turned back to his brother, digging into his pack for the trauma kit.

Sasha quickly overcame the pain from the shot to her stomach.

She pulled on Mark yet again and fought the MP5 from him, using the quick-disconnects on the sling mounts to her advantage. Then, as he snapped his head to face her, she tossed the weapon as far as she could into the tall grass.

Mark dumped the contents of the trauma kit on the ground and immediately went for his brother's twin MP5, but Sasha dove for it at the same time, and the two wrestled for possession.

"Goddammit, Mark!" Sasha squealed. "They'll kill you...they'll kill us both! Don't you get it?"

"Let them. I don't care," Mark said furiously. "I don't care." His body tensed as he continued to fight against her. Then he started to sob. "Look what they did to him. Just look what they did to my brother. They shot him. I can't believe they shot him."

Sasha gritted her teeth as she pulled on the submachine gun with all her strength. "And he's going to bleed out if you don't stop fighting me! Let go!" she yelled, then punched him squarely in the nose.

Mark recoiled backward and let go of the MP5. "Why did you do that? Why?"

Nearly out of breath, Sasha rolled to her knees and tossed the gun into the brush. "Because I don't want to die any more than you do."

Within seconds, a group of armed DHS agents tackled them, placed their wrists into flex cuffs, and took them in to custody. Another lone agent manhandled Chad. As he writhed in pain, he was rolled over, cuffed, and forced to his feet.

"Bring them over here," a voice bellowed from the lead SUV's passenger-side window. "I want to see the three blind mice who fell into my trap."

The agents pushed Sasha along without much effort, but they had to shove and drag Mark, as he had chosen to fight them tooth and nail the entire way.

When they got to within several feet of the SUV, the tinted window rolled the full way down, and a face that Sasha recognized, but hadn't seen in a while, turned to look at her.

The man in the truck cocked his head, looking bewildered. "What the hell? You're that woman. That biker's wife, aren't you?" Seth Bates asked.

Sasha glowered. She rolled her lips between her teeth and jerked her head backward, knocking the hair from her eyes. "Widow."

"Oh, yeah, that's right. He is dead, isn't he? Yet you remain alive still. Funny, I could've sworn we watched every one of you get killed that day."

Sasha's eyes narrowed sharply. "You were watching?"

"Of course we were watching," Bates replied. "We have eyes on everything—we're the damn DHS, for crying out loud." He paused, looking her up and down. "You want to tell me what the hell you're doing here?"

Sasha hesitated, trying to decide what the best answer would be. She gestured her head in the direction of the other houses. "Food."

Seth looked indignant, and his tone quantified his appearance. "Food?"

"Yes, food. We're hungry. And that house over there had a ton of food in it, last time I checked."

Seth smirked. "Likely story. It doesn't matter anyway. It's all gone. We seized it all. It belongs to the government now."

Sasha nodded, turning her head guiltily away. "What about—"

Seth's face perked up. "What about?"

The former biker's wife turned her head away and hid her face.

"So you *were* here looking for something else, weren't you? Or was it *someone* else? Maybe even a few of them?"

Sasha looked to Seth, minor hope slipping through the desolation in her gaze. "Are they okay?"

Seth chuckled and turned to his driver, who shared a laugh with him. "Oh, yeah. They're doing fine. They did resist us, though…when we initially found them. So they were placed into custody, like you." He ogled Sasha. "Don't you worry, though. You'll be seeing them soon."

Seth bawled orders at his men. They pushed Mark and Sasha into the backseat of the lead SUV and shoved a bleeding Chad Mason into the rear compartment. They rejoined the convoy on the road and motored out of the neighborhood, never to return, bound for FEMA Camp Bravo.

CHAPTER 22

The cabin
Trout Run Valley
Friday, December 3rd

GRACE NERVOUSLY CONTEMPLATED HER PREDICAMENT while she perused the hand of cards she had been dealt, in more ways than one. Initially, she had requested to be returned to the Masons' home, but Max refused. He had instead propositioned her to keep him company and play a game of Spades with him, partnering her with one of his underlings, a thickheaded man by the name of Jeff.

Grace had played online as a teenager in a virtual reality with computerized players, and as a young adult, she had revisited it with an authentic deck and actual living, breathing, human players. It was a game her father, Alan, had been fond of playing at times when there had been enough family members around to support a match. Currently, Grace was counting herself lucky that she'd learned as much as she had from him.

Grace arranged her cards in order in the same manner she always did, where the higher-ranking cards stood out separately from the throwaways. Most importantly, she calculated the number of spades in her hand, carefully assigning rank to the definites and the definite maybes.

Of the four suits in a standard deck, spades contained all the trump cards, most of which were capable of taking any of the hands they were played on, provided the player utilizing the card had no other option than to play it, having exhausted all other possibilities beforehand.

It was ironic that Max had chosen to play cards to pass the time. He had done so in more ways than one, even metaphorically off the table, and he and his men were currently holding the highest trump card, while Grace was only concerning herself with playing the right card at the right time.

She glanced down to the sheet of paper that she'd been keeping score on, noticing she and her partner were only about five books away from winning the match, which was being played until either team reached five hundred points.

Grace scrutinized her hand casually and counted the cards that would dictate her bid before the hand was dealt, then waved a hand around to get her partner's attention. "Jeff. Oh, Jeeeff…" she called to him, drawing his name out in tune.

"Huh?"

"How many do you have?"

Jeff exhaled as his eyes nearly crossed. "Uh, hell, I don't know. Doesn't look like much to me. I don't think I can get any. I might can get one."

"Okay…so you might can get one, or you might can get none?" asked Grace scornfully. A hot flash moved through her, only to quickly subside. "Because typically, a person capable of playing the game would go nil and try to empty his hand without pulling books. But something tells me you'd find a way to fudge it up."

"That so? What in hell you want me to do, then?"

Grace sighed and waved him off. "Just bid one. I don't need your help. I've been playing most of this match on my own anyway."

Grace's partner made his bid and then stared her down as the bidding continued around the table. When the bidding reached Grace, she said, "We'll go six."

Max ended up with the closing bid this time. "Six? There's no way," he griped. "Bob and I barely have four between us, and Jeff went one. That's a bullshit bid, Grace. And you know it."

Grace shrugged. "Maybe it is, maybe it isn't, but it doesn't matter. Even if we end up with sandbags, we're still going to win the match with this hand."

"You think so?" Max pestered.

"I know so. You and Bob the bumpkin are going down."

"I think you're cheating. Counting cards or something."

Grace batted her lashes. "I'm not counting cards. I just know how to hustle the shit out of this game. I've been playing since I was a kid, and my dad taught me some tricks."

Max grunted. "What sort of tricks did he teach you? And where did *he* learn them?"

"He showed me how to bid, how to play off, and how to set my opponent," Grace said with a smirk. "He told me he learned how to play that way in prison, but he might've been stretching the truth. He was a damn good poker player, too."

Max let out a sigh. "Well, I suppose we may as well toss our hands down and let you win, seeing as how you already know you're going to. On second thought, screw that, let's play this out."

"Have it your way."

The game continued with players laying out their cards one at a time, following suit. Several minutes later, the final card was placed on the table, the final book was taken, and just as Grace predicted, her team achieved victory.

"Damn," Max said. "You are good, aren't you?"

Grace smiled as a feeling of sudden emotion overtook her. She didn't know where this influx of sentiment was coming from. She'd always been so adept at keeping her feelings hidden from view. But things had changed for her since falling for Christian, and for some reason since he'd left, she'd had more encounters with her emotional side than ever before.

Even now, Grace felt sick and uneasy, and it seemed to have gotten worse since the point Kim had uttered the words, thereby setting off this 'pregnant Grace Louise' performance. Still, there was something more to it than that, and even though Grace couldn't pinpoint the source, she couldn't push the thought from her mind. Had what Kim said to keep her from getting pummeled by a lead glove somehow become psychosomatic?

Grace knew deep inside, though, there was something else troubling her, something else entirely, and her newly developed moral sense of integrity was eating away at her core like acid on a new finish.

"Max, can we talk in private?"

"Mr. Armstrong."

"Sorry. Mr. Armstrong."

"About what?"

"There's something I need to talk to you about," said Grace, blurting out the words without so much as thinking them through. "Something's been…bugging me."

A frustrated look on his face, Max gathered the cards together on the table in a pile, ready to shuffle them. "Something's been bugging me, too. This blasted game, for instance. I'm ready for a rematch."

Grace leaned forward and batted her eyelashes at Max, having seen the gesture practically nullify him before. Her act was still working, but she was growing weary of holding a woeful secret inside, one that had risen to the surface since Max had so candidly provided the story of his family with her. "If it's possible, I'd like to talk to you about it alone."

While beginning to shuffle the cards in his hand, Max studied Grace's features a moment and then handed the deck to his partner while Jeff looked on. "We'll be back in a minute." He gestured to the front door. "After you."

Grace led Max outside and to the rear of the property, heading toward the bridge over Trout Run.

"Where are we going, Grace? On a hike?"

Grace rotated her head, looking back over her shoulder at Max's shoes. "Hardly. I detest hiking. And those kicks of yours wouldn't make it a mile in these mountains. There's something over here I need you to see."

"And what might that be?" Max asked, adjusting his khakis. "Something special? Just for me?"

"That depends on your definition of special," Grace replied. "If anything, it will clear my conscience a little. It might provide you with some answers, too."

Grace continued on with Max following in tow to the far rear of the property, until the point they reached the laurel grove, which had been chosen as a burial place months before.

Upon seeing the site, Max's expression changed from one of anticipation and curiosity to one of skepticism, followed by confusion. He glowered as he walked past Grace to where the crucifix had been placed over the little girl's grave. He pointed at it, his face contorting. "Why are we here, Grace? And who the hell is Angel?"

Grace hung her head. Her skin felt warm and flushed as a feeling of sadness swept through her while she remembered the last time she had stood here. Her feelings had haunted her until this very moment and were now in the process of clawing their way free. "I don't know. None of us knew who she was. I was hoping after what you told me, we might be able to piece the story together."

Max turned to Grace with a sullen look, rage building in his eyes. "Why would you think that?"

Grace hesitated, not knowing exactly where to go with this. She only knew there was no going back now. "What did Isabel look like?" she asked, her tone low and genuine.

Max cocked his head and took a couple of steps closer to her. "What?"

"Was she about four feet tall, skinny, with sandy blond hair?"

Max didn't answer and stepped even closer, his stare fixed on Grace's every movement, and every word.

"Was she wearing clothes that didn't fit her? Or maybe clothes that did at one time, but didn't anymore because she'd lost weight?"

His face turning crimson, Max rushed briskly to Grace and shoved a finger in her face. "You stop this. You stop this right now! You don't know what the hell you're talking about!"

Grace elevated her head, her lower eyelids welling up with thick tears. "She was wearing a pair of those shoes, wasn't she? The kind that light up when you take a step…"

Max drew his arm back and balled his hands into fists while his eyes grew wide and his jaw tensed. "No! This isn't right! This can't be!" A searing blend of anger and misery began to overtake him, and he turned away while he pounded the sides of his head with his fists.

"I think it is," Grace said softly. "I think the young girl we knew as Angel was your Isabel."

Max lumbered to the grave and fell to his knees, his hands finding their way to the crucifix. He sobbed, loudly at first, then tranquilly for a moment while clinging to it. "What happened to her? I want you to tell me what happened, Grace, and don't lie to me, either. I'll know if you do."

Grace closed her eyes and shook her head. "I have nothing to lie to you about. You're not exactly what I'd call a benevolent person, Max, but you've done nothing but be up front with me, and I think you deserve the same. That's why I brought you here."

"What…happened?" Max growled. "Tell me. Or you're going to see just how *malevolent* I can be."

"She was shot."

"By *whom*?"

Grace hesitated and bit her lower lip. "That's the tricky part about this whole sordid ordeal. It's…beyond comprehension, difficult to even bring up, much less put into words."

"Which one of your people did it? I want to know. You'd better come clean with me, or I'll beat the answer out of you."

"None of us did anything to her," Grace hissed, a slight bitterness in her voice. She hesitated. "It was her mother."

Max exploded into the air from his position on the ground. He ran to Grace and latched on to her shoulders, shaking her. "That's a lie and you know it! I told you not to lie to me!"

"It's not a lie!" Grace shrieked. "I swear on my unborn child, it isn't! It happened right over there. My sister found them in our shed, trying to take our food and supplies, and she told them to leave. But the woman had a gun, and my sister was forced to shoot her."

"Oh? And where is your sister now?"

"She isn't here! She thought it was over…the woman dropped the gun, but she'd told the girl to get it for her. When Angel gave it to her, the woman turned the gun on her…and shot her."

Max backed away from Grace and brought one of his hands to his mouth as tears rolled from his eyes, down his cheeks, and onto his clothing.

"You said she was on medicine," Grace said, trying desperately not to cry. "That could explain it…why she did what she did."

Max's face turned pale and he walked back to the crucifix. He hesitated a moment before yelling loudly into the woods and kicking it to the ground. "Isabel."

"What?"

"You called her Angel again, and that's not her name."

Without another word, Max stomped off, departing the cemetery and leaving Grace to stand alone.

She stood there stoically while drying her tears, watching him walk off and out of the woods, back toward the cabin, not able to believe he had left her by her lonesome. Without moving her feet, she scanned the trees in search of another one of his minions, perhaps two or even three of them. There was no way he had chosen to just leave her there, knowing she could choose to escape.

With Max completely out of sight, Grace finished scanning the woods, only to find that she was indeed truly alone. Her first instinct was to get the hell out of there, to leave and try to find help somewhere. But where would she go? She didn't know much about the outlying areas beyond the valley. She only knew it was dangerous.

After a few minutes of review, the idea of leaving was slowly becoming a moot point. She could run somewhere and hide, but Grace knew how much she despised running. With no supplies and the air getting colder by the day, there was simply no way for her to survive very long.

A breeze blew through the grove, and Grace picked up on it immediately when her body shivered in response to a sudden chill. It was then she realized she wasn't even wearing a jacket. "I guess I underestimated you, Max. You left me alone because you knew only an idiot would attempt to escape in these conditions." Grace threw her hair back, disgusted with herself for her lack of proper planning and inability to capitalize on an advantage. "Guess I'll be revising this act from the beginning."

She started off, making her way out of the laurel grove and into the short stint of forest between the grove and the cleared-out portions of the property. She stopped upon hearing a loud snap beside her, not far away.

Grace shuddered a bit, not knowing the source of the noise but fearing the worst. "Dammit. I swear, if that's a friggin' bear, I'm going to shit myself."

She stood motionless while attempting to remember the proper way of dealing with bears in the wild, but couldn't remember if black bears were the ones you were supposed to play dead with or climb a tree to escape. Just before her imagination and fear got the best of her, she heard a muffled voice call to her from the same direction she had heard the snap.

"Grace," the voice whispered. "Grace! Over here."

Realizing bears were incapable of speech, and even if one could talk, there was no way it could know her first name, Grace turned her head and soon found a set of eyes peering out from behind a large pine tree. She put a hand to her chest and took a step back, swallowing over the fear-induced dryness in her mouth and throat.

She gasped audibly when she realized who the sparkling eyes belonged to. "Alex? Alex, is that you?" Grace turned her head on a swivel to check for onlookers. "What the hell are you doing here?"

Alex gracefully exposed more of herself from behind the tree while remaining hidden from view. "I came here to help."

"You did? Alone? Are you nuts?"

"No, not alone, my sisters are with me. You just can't see them."

Grace's eyes darted around nervously in search of two more sets of eyeballs. "Okay...I guess. Tell them it's nice to meet them finally." She paused while continuing her hunt. "Look, Alex...I appreciate this, whatever you're doing, I really do. But you and your sisters can't be here right now. Takers are all over the place, and if they see you, they will take you...just like they took all of us."

"They won't take me or my sisters," said Alex. "They haven't even seen us, and they won't see us, either. We've been watching them for over a day now, and we've been taking lots of notes."

Grace took a deep breath and exhaled slowly, trying to regain some semblance of a normal heartbeat. "Fine. Suit yourself. But if one of these cavemen shows his face, you disappear and take your siblings with you, do you understand me?"

Alex nodded. "I do, but there's no one nearby. I would've never called for you if there was." She paused. "Can you come a little bit closer? I brought something I need to give you."

"Why does this remind me of the first time we met? Only...our roles have somehow been reversed. It's so anomalous." Grace shuffle-stepped gingerly over to the pine tree Alex was hiding behind, while trying her best to remain inconspicuous.

She wanted to believe what Alex was telling her, but experience had taught her otherwise. The woods had always felt alive to Grace, and she believed it to have several sets of eyes, keeping everything under constant surveillance. "Okay, fill me in. What exactly is this whole spy-style brush pass about?"

Alex stretched her arm around the tree, holding a small glass jar in her hand. "Here. Take this."

Grace reached for the bottle and held it at waist level while shaking its contents. "What the hell is this? Looks like oregano or parsley or something." She feasted her eyes on it. "This isn't weed, is it?"

Alex allowed a stern look to coat her young face. "No—it's not. So don't smoke it. And whatever you do, don't eat it. I wouldn't even touch it. My mom put it together; it's pretty potent shit."

Grace cocked her head. "Potent shit, huh?" She shook the bottle again. "Can you tell me what's in it?"

"I would if I knew. All I know is what Mom told me. She says it only takes a small dose to stop a man's heart. She even calls it 'Heartbreaker', like the Pat Benatar song."

"Okay, Alex. Look, I have to admit, my brain hasn't exactly been operating on all cylinders as of late," Grace remarked. "Things have been a wee bit fuzzy. Can you give me a little more to go on?"

"It's a mixture of dried leaves and crushed seeds from Mom's poison garden."

"Poison garden?"

Alex's face lit up to accompany her nod. "Yep."

"And I'm supposed to do what with it?"

"Use it on their food as seasoning or something. We've been watching. They're eating food like it's going out of style, and they might be hungry enough to not pay attention to how their food is being cooked."

"Oh," said Grace, her tone getting warmer. "*Oh.* I get it now. I totally get it."

Alex spent a moment divulging their side of the plan so Grace knew what to expect. Then she informed her how they had found George and Elizabeth Brady deceased and about the Bradys' homes being ransacked. "Michelle wanted me to ask you if anyone else was hurt or…well, you know."

Grace sighed, taking in the cheerless news of two more fallen neighbors. "I wish I knew. I've only seen about half of us. They divided us up, and they're holding most of the men somewhere else to keep us from fighting back. Unfortunately for us and quite the opposite for them, it's working. But insofar as casualties are concerned, tell her I don't really have an answer, but I'm glad she's okay."

Alex pursed her lips and nodded. "I'll pass on the message. Another thing, Michelle wanted me to remind you about the beef left over at the

Ackermanns' farm. She said Norman cured some of it and cold-smoked the rest."

"She knows me well. I almost forgot about that."

"Yeah." Alex giggled. "She said you probably would. Mom says it still should be okay to eat. They want you to find a way to suggest it to them…by way of a steak dinner or feast—something you can cook for them, like a meal they won't forget. Do you think you can do that?"

Grace thought a moment, fidgeting with her hair. She compiled everything, then smiled devilishly and nodded. The time had come for an entirely new act to begin. "Hmm. So it's up to Grace to plan a final meal before execution is carried out," she said softly. "Yeah, Alex. Yeah, I believe I *can* do that."

"Really?"

"Really."

"Okay. What should I tell my mom and Michelle?"

"Tell them I'm going to go with my usual, with what's always worked before," Grace said, displaying a set of piercing eyes and a matching sinister smirk. "I'm going to fake it till I make it."

CHAPTER 23

"When one door closes, another opens; but we often look so long and so regretfully upon the closed door that we do not see the one which has opened for us."

—Alexander Graham Bell

Trout Run Valley
Friday, December 3rd

MICHELLE WATCHED JESSECA RUMMAGE THROUGH a pile of items and materials she had recently dumped on the ground from a vintage US Army backpack. Jesseca had referred to it as an 'Alice' pack, explaining that it had once belonged to her father. She further described it as the style of pack issued to and typically worn by infantry combat soldiers during the Vietnam War. Jess said it was probably the most recognizable of all military backpacks in the world, though admittedly, Michelle had never seen one before.

Amongst the items in the pile were things Michelle was able to recognize, such as canteens, an angle-head flashlight, some canvas pouches, a webbed pistol belt, and a bayonet still seated comfortably in its scabbard. Everything was olive drab or a faded shade of green in color and appeared to be in decent, workable shape.

Jesseca smiled when she held up an ammo pouch and unbuckled the top, exposing ten full thirty-caliber magazines for her M1 carbine. She pulled one out to examine it, scratching at a rusty spot with a fingernail. "Hot damn. I thought I'd lost these forever. What a perfect time to find them."

Michelle peered over from where she stood. "I take it those fit your gun?"

Jesseca nodded with zeal. "Damn right they will. Ten magazines at twenty rounds a piece—that's two hundred rounds I can shoot in my enemy's direction. I mean *our* enemy's direction." She paused a moment, diverting her attention to Michelle's SBR. "Do you have any spares for yours?"

"That's a good question," Michelle replied, looking down at her rifle and then to the backpack strapped to the rear deck of her ATV. "The rifle belongs to Fred Mason, and I know he didn't give me any, but after Lauren saw me with it, she stuffed a few in my backpack. She probably thought I didn't see her do it, but I did." She sauntered over, unzipped her pack, and dug into it. "Lo and behold, my daughter, in her eternal vigilance, left me four of them."

"Smart kid. Every time you mention her name, I like her even more. That gives you what? About a hundred and fifty rounds?"

Michelle shrugged. "I think that's right," she replied, looking the mags over.

Jesseca unstrapped the cylinder of bedroll material from the bottom of the Alice pack and unfurled it onto the ground at her knees, separating a vinyl cloak from a heavy, rectangular wool blanket inside. She spread the blanket on the ground and pulled a knife from her back pocket, then began cutting the blanket into strips.

"I have to admit to you, Jess, I don't know much about the stuff we're planning to do," Michelle said. "I don't know much about guns… or tactics either."

"That makes two of us, if it makes you feel any better."

Michelle stammered and smiled grimly, her face turning pale. "No… not really."

"Guess I shouldn't have said anything, then."

"I guess not," Michelle agreed, watching Jess's actions with more focus. "Since moving here, I've been going with the flow, playing it by ear. This is still all so new to me. Lauren, on the other hand… well, let's just say if she were here, my guess is she'd probably know exactly what to do. She wasn't born with the skills she has, but it's become pretty damn obvious to me she's gathered them somehow, from someone, somewhere along the line, when I wasn't looking. And I have a distinct feeling my husband was involved. Those two were practically inseparable—always off on some adventure while I was busy doing my own thing. They asked me to come along a bunch of times…and I didn't, for whatever reason. Now I really wish I would've just sucked it up and gone with them. Maybe I'd be better prepared for all this."

"Hindsight has twenty-twenty vision, Michelle."

"Don't I know it."

"And I don't think anything can prepare anyone for something like this."

"You say that, but you seem to have *your* ducks in a row."

Jesseca peered up at Michelle, her head tilted downward at her work. "All the skills I have stem from what I've learned in books, along with the handful of things my parents taught me growing up. I was lucky to have a father who sometimes divulged information about his military past…it was like having my own personal black book of dirty tricks on the shelf. But he wasn't exactly an *open* book…anything I didn't know about and wanted to know about, I read about in field manuals he had lying around." She paused. "Listen, I know you're worried about this, but we'll work through it, one way or another."

"We don't have another option, do we?" Michelle said rhetorically. She wavered a moment, gathering her thoughts. "You know, in retrospect, it's just irritating that I didn't do what I should've—back when I had the time. Now we've run out of time, and I'm regretting being so idle back then. I know I probably sound like a broken record…but it brings me peace knowing my daughter is as capable as she is. It doesn't change the fact that Alan made plans concerning her without discussing them with me." She paused. "If I ever see him again, in this life or the next, I plan on riding his ass about it."

Jesseca laughed. "As well you should."

Michelle exhaled loud enough to clear her mind a little and moved in to observe. "I think it's high time you clued me in to your thought process, Jess." She pointed to Jess's project. "I've been able to follow along for the most part. But now I'm starting to feel lost."

Jesseca continued eyeballing the cuts she was making in the blanket, concentrating on their straightness. "I'm sorry, Michelle. I'm not usually this incommunicado. I'm not deviating from our plan, either, just adding to it a bit."

"I thought the plan was pretty well thought out already," Michelle said, scratching her head. "If Alex and the girls can get your poison-garden stuff to Grace, I can almost certify that she'll find a way of putting it into action."

"She's that good?"

Michelle sniggered, then jested, "She's imaginative. She'll probably have them eating from the palm of her hand. I'd love to find a way to help her along, but I don't know what else we can do other than stand by and wait."

Jesseca took the strips of wool blanket and begin rolling them into tight columns, laying them beside each other. She extricated a roll of duct tape from her backpack and began wrapping it loosely around the rolls, folding it over on top of itself at the end. Reaching for her M1, she arranged the muzzle perpendicular to her and rolled one of the remaining strips of blanket around the end of the barrel, using duct tape to secure it tightly. "That's exactly what we're going to do," Jess said with a devilish smirk. "We're just going to have guns aimed at our enemy while we wait."

"Oh."

"If your Grace can find a way to get an adequate dose on each plate, then there won't be a need for us to intervene," Jess explained. "But if she doesn't, and there's always that chance, it might take a while for them to…kick the bucket."

"How long is a while?"

"Oh, maybe a minute or two."

Michelle pursed her lips and nodded her understanding. "That's not very long."

"No, but it'll feel like an eternity," Jess went on. "Especially since they'll be aware of what's happening. The poisons attack the heart and central nervous system, but the brain goes manic, trying to process what's going on, and that means they'll be panicking. They might do something stupid."

"Hence the addition of guns to our plan."

Jess nodded with a shrug. "Just covering our bases. If we have to put them down, we will. You know…hemlock on its own can stop a heart in fifteen minutes, and hydrangea works like cyanide. But fuse them together and add foxglove, and we're talking seconds."

"In the right dose..."

"Right. But I even add a measure of belladonna berries. They have a semisweet flavor, similar to figs. If ingested, it causes swelling in the throat. It tends to shut them up. Quiets the screams."

Michelle tilted her head, a bit taken aback with Jess's statement as a notebook of ill-timed questions entered her mind. Her interest in Jess's project soon overrode her anxiety. "You know, when you showed me your gardens, especially the ones with all the poison plants in them, I didn't know what to think."

"I could tell by the look you gave me," said Jess. "The look of distrust...like the one you're giving me now."

"It's not deliberate."

"I know, no worries. We have a lot going on, and I know I'm not everyone's cup of tea. I'm sort of an acquired taste."

Michelle moved in closer. "Maybe so, but your sticking around shows character, and it means a lot to me. And I honestly can't thank you enough."

Jesseca gleamed. "It's not a problem. That's what friends are for." She pointed her knife at Michelle. "But I swear to God...if anything like this ever happens to me, I fully expect you and the rest of the folks here to come running to my aid."

Michelle held up her hands and backed away, completing the act. "Sure, anything you want. After this, I don't think anyone will disagree." She paused to watch Jess work as her interest grew. "You're making silencers, aren't you?"

"Very perceptive," said Jesseca. "For someone who doesn't know much about guns."

"Admittedly, I might've seen something similar done once or twice before."

"Oh?"

"Sure...in a movie my maverick husband coerced me into watching against my will."

"I see," Jess said, an inelegant smirk attached. "I remember Dad telling me a wool blanket would do the trick in a pinch...so do plastic water bottles and sometimes even a pillow, if you use them right. They're a great quick-and-dirty option...but I remember vaguely something else he said about them catching fire eventually. I suppose we'll find out here before long." Jesseca ran her hand along the other strips of wool. "At any rate, I'm planning ahead for that upshot. We'll have extras."

CHAPTER 24

Hardy County, West Virginia
Saturday, December 4th

CHRISTIAN MADE SURE HE WAS seated on the passenger side of the lead vehicle so he could give directions to the driver, a younger soldier he met by the name of Richie.

While Christian had tried to make conversation with him along the way, it had been difficult, even unbearable at times. Richie had come across to him as cocky, arrogant, and a bit of a prick. He was egotistical, self-absorbed, and aggressively argumentative, preferring only to talk about himself and what mattered to him, while ignoring most everything else. This made him nearly impossible for Christian to converse with without arriving at some sort of conflict, and he was more than trying Christian's patience.

Having reached the final stretch of the trip back to the valley, Christian looked over at Richie, deciding to try his luck with the conceited young soldier once again. "You know, I hate to be the one who beats a dead horse, but I still don't understand what the big deal is. You know I'm friends with Lauren, and your CO is obviously friends with her, too. I live in the valley we're headed to right now. So I don't understand why you can't let me have a gun."

Richie snickered. He sneered while gripping the steering wheel. "It isn't a big deal, it's just that I don't know you, never met you before until today, so your words don't mean jack shit. And right now, I'm in charge, and it's my call. I don't want anyone around me with a weapon in their hands unless I know who they are."

Christian rolled his eyes. "Look, man. I told you who I was hours ago at the beginning of the trip. I guess you forgot already. My name is Christian Hartman. I'm a member of the group you've been ordered to provide transport for. I'm a good guy, not the opposite, and I assure you I'm qualified to operate the weapons you guys carry."

"And, like I told you, I don't care who you are or where you live, you're not getting a gun. Like I said, I'm in command here, and what I say goes."

For the moment, Christian decided to concede. "That's fine for now. But know this…when we get back to the valley, you won't be in charge anymore. That's gonna change the second we get past the barricade. You'll be in my AO then, sport."

Richie licked his lips and nodded, looking at Christian from the corner of his eye. "Okay, we'll see. Just remember who was nice enough to provide you guys with this armed detail. I've always been told you should never bite the hand that feeds you."

Christian didn't say anything, but he could feel his temper rising into the extreme. He tried focusing on the fact he would be home soon and back in Grace's open arms. Then he remembered he was going to have to somehow explain everything that'd happened to everyone, and then find some way of telling Michelle why Lauren had not accompanied them back. He only hoped she would understand, and he prayed that Grace would.

Having reached the intersection of Corridor H and Trout Run Road, Christian pointed to the sign, informing Richie to hang a right. Richie turned the wheel and guided the truck onto the road with the other vehicles making the turn and following behind.

Home sweet home, Christian thought, realizing just how much he had missed it. He watched the parade of trees pass by, now downright leafless, awaiting winter to sink its teeth in. Along the way, everything seemed fine to him, and nothing was out of place until the point the barricade came into view.

Christian sat up in his seat, placing his hand to the truck's windshield. "Stop the truck!" he yelled, pointing ahead.

"Excuse me?"

Christian glared at him and angrily repeated his command.

With a confused look on his face, bordering on outrage, Richie pressed on the brakes, bringing the vehicle to a stop and causing those behind to slam on their brake pedals and lurch to a stop in the middle of the road.

Richie turned to Christian with his hands outstretched, begging to know what was going on, and in that moment, Christian removed his seat belt and lunged at him.

His left hand went for Richie's collar while his right deftly removed the mud-colored Sig P320 from the canvas holster on Richie's hip. "There's trouble up ahead. I'm taking this. I'll give it back to you when I'm done with it."

"And what do you expect me to do?" Richie sniveled, his expression puffed up, his tone snide.

"You can sit here and do nothing, or you can get your rifle and come with me—just don't shoot me with it."

A startled look on his face, Richie switched gears and said, "No problem, man, all you had to do was ask."

Christian pushed away from him and exited the vehicle. Taking a quick look towards the barricade, he turned to get the attention of the soldiers standing on the truck's cargo bed near the cab. "Guys, possibility of danger close at a hundred yards at the barricade up ahead. I'm moving in to get eyes on. Get ready to adjust your fire."

Christian started walking in the direction of the bridge. The Sig Sauer was an unfamiliar weapon to him, but it felt comfortable in his hand. He held it close to his chest while fear for the worst mounted inside him. Then he heard the all-too-familiar sound of an M4's bolt carrier group sending a live round into the chamber.

"Freeze, cowboy! Don't move a muscle," Richie's voice called from behind him.

Christian dug his feet into the asphalt. He turned on his heel to see that all the soldiers, including Richie, had him dead to rights. He held his hands up in the air slowly. "Oh, come on! You gotta be kidding me, right?"

Richie approached Christian, his M4 shouldered and his finger on the trigger. "Drop the weapon, pogue. Drop it right now, or I'll drill you."

Christian consented, realizing there was no way to control the situation as it stood. He slowly lowered the Sig to the pavement and backed away from it.

Richie lowered his rifle and gestured to the other soldiers. "If he moves, kill him." He knelt to retrieve his Sig Sauer. "You got a lot of nerve, douchebag. A lot of nerve."

"So do you. Why wasn't your rifle loaded?"

Richie ignored him.

"You're making a big mistake. We got a big problem right up there," said Christian, his head gesturing to his aft.

"It can wait, because now you got an even bigger problem," Richie spat. "Nobody threatens me. And nobody points my gun at me, either." He reached for a set of plastic zip cuffs nestled in the MOLLE webbing of his plate carrier. "I assume you know how to put these on? If I have to do it for you, you're not gonna like it."

Christian hung his head, shaking it with disgust. "We don't have time for this."

"I'm only gonna ask you once. If I have to ask a second time, you're not gonna hear me ask you. Because you'll be unconscious."

From the second vehicle in line, Norman hung his head from the open window. He jumped out of the truck cab and moved hastily to where Richie was holding Christian at gunpoint. "What in the name of all that's holy is going on here? And why in the hell aren't we investigating the barricade?"

"That's far enough," Richie said, still maintaining his focus on Christian. "My men will shoot you if you come any closer, Podunk."

Norman cocked his head, his eyes narrowing. "Just who the hell are you calling Podunk, greenhorn? Listen close, rifle or not, firing squad above me or not, I'll come over there, grab hold of you and twist you up. Then turn you over my knee and tan your damn hide."

A voice suddenly shouted from the bed of the second truck, grabbing everyone's attention. "Richie, goddammit, stop being an asshole." The voice was dry and raspy as if its owner was suffering from a bad case of cottonmouth. Even so, it was easy to discern who, in fact, the owner was.

"Fred?" inquired Richie.

"Yes, Fred, you blowhard CAB chaser. I may be ate up as hell and high as a kite on Vicodin, but I'm still the baddest motherfucker in this valley. And who the hell gave you permission to call me by my Christian name?"

Everyone in present company, failing Richie, watched as a bruised, battered, and bandaged Fred Mason turned the corner after extricating himself from the rear of the transport he'd been riding in.

Fred could barely walk, and one of his eyes was nearly swollen shut. He appeared weak and had a palpable limp in his step. His arm was in a sling, his head was bandaged, and most of his skin was riddled with stitches, butterfly tape, and remnants of gauze.

As he hobbled away from the truck, Dr. Vincent and his wife jumped out and gave chase while offering wide-eyed stares at each other. They pled with Fred to return, but he paid them no mind.

Fred continued along, his doctor escort in tow, past the lead vehicle, past Norman, and right up to Richie's side. "Lower that weapon, Private."

"It's corporal now. I was pro—"

"I don't give a departed rat's ass if it's captain now," Fred heckled. "Lower that weapon before it becomes a suppository."

Richie's posture gave in, and he slowly lowered the muzzle of his M4 while refraining from looking Fred in the eye.

Fred turned and gradually lifted his free arm to the other soldiers. "That goes for the rest of you boots and PX rangers," he ordered. "Lower them or I'll beat each of you to death with 'em—and don't let me ever see you pointing a weapon at any of these fine folks again."

A row of conflicted looks amassed as each troop obeyed the command.

Fred tottered lively to Richie and yanked the M4 from his grasp, then tossed it into Christian's waiting hands. "Consider yourself demoted. And you're lucky you don't have my steel toe in your ass right now, *Private*. Now get back in that truck and superglue your buttocks to the seat until I tell you to come out."

As Richie marched off with his head hung low, Fred hobbled to Christian, squinting his open eye. He was barely able to see the barricade from where he stood. "Now, what do you suppose is going on up there?"

Christian press checked the rifle with renewed vigor. "I'm about to find out."

Fred nodded. "Good man. I'd go with you, but I can't see a damn thing, and these pain meds got me feeling all kinds of fuzzy. I can shoot, but I doubt I'd hit anything. Plus, these doctors would never let me hear the end of it. Take Norm. You two take point, and we'll follow behind in the convoy." Fred looked up to the line of soldiers standing atop the lead vehicle and instructed one of them to hand his rifle to Norman.

Then, M4 in hand, Norman joined Christian in the middle of the road as the doctors quietly coaxed Fred back inside the transport.

Christian gave his M4 a once-over, press checked it, then slapped the selector all the way forward into full auto. He looked to Norman. "You know how to handle one of these?"

"I usually learn by doing," Norman said. "In this case, I'll take baby steps and follow your lead."

Just before turning away to leave, Christian and Norman caught sight of another soldier approaching. He wore MultiCam ACUs like the others and was carrying a rifle, but it wasn't Richie or any of the other men he'd seen pointing a gun at him today.

The young man approached them slowly and cautiously, and his eyes darted from side to side behind a pair of thick plastic-framed eyeglasses. "You guys look like you could use some help," he said, his voice moving rapidly.

Christian squinted at him, still a bit unsure. "Is it that obvious?"

The young soldier with glasses nodded his acknowledgment, then turned and shouted, "My squad, to the front with me. Double time."

A group of five other armed, ACU-clad troops filed out of the rearmost transport and sprinted to him. He then snapped his body around to face Christian. "I'm Neo. Richie can be a real jerk sometimes. But don't worry, we're the same rank. The men will listen to me."

"Especially now," said Norman with a smirk. "I think Fred cut him off at the knees." He reached out to shake Neo's hand.

Christian smiled at Neo, noticing he hadn't yet made eye contact with anyone. "Nice to meet you, Neo. I'm Christian; this is Norman." He gestured ahead towards the barricade. "We have a situation up ahead."

"I gathered," Neo said, nodding his head. "Kinetic?"

"Possibly."

Neo turned away again to instruct his men, both verbally and with a specific set of hand signals. Seconds after, four of them left the road, disappearing into the trees alongside. "They're going to scout ahead and cover the flanks. The squad on the lead FMTV will provide suppressive fire as needed. The rest of us have your six. Let me know if you need anything else…and you got it."

Christian offered him a lackluster smile. "Thank you, Neo. Just so you know, it gets a little tight up there."

"Copy that."

The group marched forward, keeping their eyes peeled for threats with no idea of what to expect, as the convoy of trucks followed them a short distance behind.

At the point of reaching the barricade, Christian charged forward and hurdled over one of the antique vehicle's hoods, landing on his feet on the other side, then pivoted in a circle searching for targets, finding none in sight.

Once he verified the perimeter was clear, Christian stood and scratched his head. George Brady's lawn chair lay folded up on the dull pavement like it had either been placed there purposefully or the wind had blown it down.

As Norman moved in to examine it, Christian trotted over to the Bradys' burn barrel and placed his hand inside. "There hasn't been a fire burning in this barrel for days. What do you got over there, Norm?"

Norman used his foot to push the lawn chair aside, exposing a portion of discoloration on the road. "I don't know, you think that's blood?"

Maintaining a high crawl, Neo glided in with his M4 pulled to his cheek, as did his partner. After a rapid scan for threats, both men lowered their weapons and stood back-to-back fully upright, keeping their attention to the unfamiliar tree lines on either side of the road.

Neo quickly picked up on what had garnered Norman's attention, and he marched over and knelt on the road for a closer look. "Did you just find this? It looks like blood," he said, his voice in rapid-fire, then he licked the tip of his index finger. He rubbed it on the road and placed his finger on his tongue. "Confirmed."

Ricky Brady suddenly appeared after hopping out of the truck he was riding in. Without a word, he ran past the barricade and up his family's driveway to his house.

Austin Brady followed him, stopping at the barricade to stare at both Norman and Christian. He spotted the folded-up lawn chair laying level on the pavement. "Where's Grandpa?"

Neither Norman nor Christian had the heart to answer him, both men assuming the worst. Knowing what Austin had recently been through in losing his father, the two men were decidedly silent.

After a moment, Austin ran off to join his uncle.

"You think they're gonna be all right?" Norman pondered.

"I don't know," Christian said. "We'll check on them later. Let's get going."

The convoy continued along Trout Run Road, soon entering the town of Perry and passing the old petting zoo. It wasn't long before they drove past the former Perry residence on the left, followed by Peter and Amy Saunders' home on the right. Seeing no activity of note at either location, they continued, passing St. James Church and then finally reaching the point where the driveway leading to the cabin meandered off to the left.

Christian looked through the driver-side window, past a much more humble and subservient Richie, and what he saw nearly caused his heart to skip a beat. "Stop here," he said, and leapt from the vehicle before its wheels stopped turning. He crossed the road in a flash and dashed toward the gate.

Grace and Megan Mason, each holding a man's leg in their hands by the ankle, were busily dragging a deceased body across the yard to a pile of other bodies, which lay strewn about haphazardly in a circle. A number of other neighbors were engaged in similarly unpleasant tasks, but Christian's only focus was on Grace.

He ran directly to her, and when Grace saw him, she let go of the leg and scurried to him, the two coming together in an embrace in the center of the driveway.

"You're home!" Grace shrieked. "Oh my God! I can't believe it! I'm so glad you're back." She began showering him with kisses. "I missed your face so much."

Christian held her tightly and accepted as much of her affection as he could stand before the question marks in his mind began hammering him for precedence. "Grace, wait…just wait a second. What the hell is going on around here? Who are all these…*dead* people? What happened?"

Grace pulled away while maintaining a grip on his hands, a hangdog look crisscrossing her face. "Oh, this?" She gestured behind her. "This is nothing," she said, shrugging innocently. "I mean, it *was* something, but now we're just cleaning up a slight problem we had while you were away. Nothing to get too excited over." Grace peered around Christian on one side, then looked around the other, catching a glimpse of the convoy. "Who are those guys? What's with the Army trucks?" She paused. "And where the hell is my sister?"

"I'll get to all that in a minute," said Christian. "First tell me what in God's name happened here."

Grace rolled her eyes and shrugged. "Damn, Christian, I swear. It's almost like you think we can't handle things without you or something."

Grace spent the next few minutes giving Christian a verbal recount of everything that had happened since the expedition had left the valley several days before. She told of the invasion and how the takers had separated them. Then she explained how their invaders had been so focused on their hunger, she had been able to propose a rare dinner to them and poison them to death the previous evening, in so many words.

"Once I told them about all the beef we had, it wasn't a struggle to convince them. Max had his men take me to the Ackermanns' to get it, and we cooked it all up in the Masons' kitchen, and that's where I ran into Meg. I was glad to see her, too. Kim told me they took her away, and I was worried something bad had happened to her. Strangely enough, they'd been keeping her upstairs the whole time just to cook food for them." Grace took a breath. "It took hours to fix all that meat. And it smelled friggin' good too, all sizzling and frying up in that cast iron...it took all the willpower I had not to indulge."

Christian looked at her askance, rubbing the bridge of his nose at the onset of a splitting headache brought about by the clutter of Grace's account. "Okay...so you poisoned them...but how, though?" He tripped over his tongue. "With the water?"

"Not with the water, silly pants. With the stuff Alex gave me," Grace said matter-of-factly, as if he knew what she was talking about. "And now we're just trying to get things back to normal again. You're looking at the cleanup crew."

Megan nodded and smiled brightly. "That's us, janitorial staff extraordinaire. Not like there's anything else better to do, but it sure beats KP."

"Does that answer all your questions?" Grace asked innocently, cocking her head.

"No. I mean, yes, I guess. For now," Christian said. He pointed to the path of the cabin where John could be seen holding a man at gunpoint. The man's arms were bound behind his back, and he had a gag stuffed in his mouth. "Who's that guy over there? He obviously wasn't poisoned."

"What guy?"

"That guy." Christian pointed again. "The one with the pornstache."

Grace giggled and whipped her head around momentarily. "Oh, him? That's Max."

"Max?"

"Mm-hmm. He was the one in charge."

"He's the leader? And you're on a first-name basis with him?" Christian interrogated. "Why is he still alive, Grace?"

"Because we chose not to kill him, that's why, Christian," Grace quipped. "Right, Meg?"

Megan looked away dismissively and walked off. "Don't involve me in this; that was your decision. If it were up to me, I would've shot him in his stupid face the first chance I got."

"Yeah, thanks for that." Grace turned back to Christian. "Whatever—ignore her. I found out some stuff about him. I couldn't just bunch him up with the rest."

"Such as?"

"Well, he's Isabel's uncle, for one thing."

"Okay, great…and who's Is—"

Grace put her fingers over his mouth. "Shh. Did you hear that?"

Christian was beyond the point of both looking and feeling extremely befuddled. On a normal day, keeping up with Grace was a chore for him. Today, maintaining her pace was becoming damn near insurmountable. "What noise?"

"I don't know, it's like a buzzing sound. I've been hearing it off and on the past few days. Sounds like it's coming from the sky, like from an airplane or something. No one else has been able to hear it, though, so it's probably just me. Anyway—back to what I was saying. Isabel is actually Angel, or rather, Angel is Isabel. Max is her uncle." She paused. "Are you following? You look like you're coming down with a headache."

Christian rubbed his head, his eyes squinting. "That's because I am. This is just…a lot to take in." A pause. "So you kept one alive, but the rest of them are dead. And you're certain none of them got away?"

Grace shrugged. "I don't know. I'm pretty sure we poisoned all of them. I thought keeping Max alive might help us in the future. If there's others out there yet to show their ugly faces, maybe they'll stay away or leave us alone if they know we've taken custody of their ringleader."

"Or maybe it'll really piss them off and they'll come at us full force to get him back."

Overlooking Christian's counterpoint, Grace motioned to the convoy and to the soldiers of Dave Graham's unit who had disembarked. "Looks like you brought along some company. A lot of company. Company with guns."

"Yeah. Those are your sister's friends. They were kind enough to give us a ride home. And it looks like they'll be hanging around for a while."

"More people and more guns. Just what the doctor ordered." Grace poked Christian in the chest. "Okay, I filled in all the blanks for you—or most of them, anyway. Let's make this an official tête-à-tête. Are you going to tell me where my sister is? Or do I have to get violent?"

CHAPTER 25

The cabin
Trout Run Valley
Saturday, December 4th. Late evening

CHRISTIAN PUSHED THE FRONT DOOR open with his foot and trudged inside with an armload of heavy boxes containing food and other supplies recently unloaded from the convoy.

Grace ran over from the kitchen to close the door behind him and seal off the frigid air outside. She jumped in to assist and slid the box stacked highest from the pile and muscled it over to the table, placing it haphazardly beside several others Christian had brought in on previous trips.

After Christian set his load down, he took a seat to take a breather while Grace unpacked. "I just had a chat with Kim Mason outside," he said, propping one of his feet on the chair across from him. "I was afraid she was going to ask me details about what happened to Fred."

"Mm-hmm."

"She didn't, though. It was kind of surprising. Didn't ask or mention anything. She didn't even seem mad. In fact, she was smiling a lot."

"Maybe she's happy her husband is home."

"Yeah." Christian nodded. "Maybe that was it."

"Mm-hmm."

Christian hesitated. "She told me about what happened to old man Brady and his wife."

Grace heard him, but pretended not to. She kept her attention focused on the items she was arranging in the kitchen cabinets.

"That took me by surprise," Christian continued. "I mean, I had a feeling something bad happened when we saw the stain on the road at the barricade. It's just that I hardly knew the guy, never even met his wife. And after losing Bo, I imagine it's going to be a lot harder to work together with the rest of them. I hope they don't find some weird backwoods way of holding ill will against us."

Grace held up a hand and shook her head back and forth a few times with her eyes closed, refusing to absorb what Christian was saying. "Okay—can we please just *not* talk about it right now?"

"I'm sorry. I just think that with all we stand to lose, it's a pretty serious situation, that's all. Worthy of a discussion."

"Well, I don't think it's serious," Grace shot back. "I think it's sad, really sad. Really, really sad, and I don't want to be sad, and I don't feel like crying about it. And I'm going to cry about it if you keep talking about it, so please do me a favor and don't talk about it anymore because I don't want to cry, okay?"

Christian was blown away at her reaction. He held up his hands in surrender. "Okay. Fine. I—"

"Sorry. I've been a little emotional lately," said Grace. "Actually, that's a dumb way of describing it. I've been more like on the verge of friggin' idiocy. I get sad at the drop of a freakin' dime, and I just don't want to be sad. Not right now. Especially after everything you've told me. I mean, you almost died. I almost lost you." Within ten seconds, she switched gears completely after uncovering a number ten can of steel-cut oats. "You guys really brought back a ton of loot. This is going to go a long way, Christian. It might even get us through winter."

Christian nodded and wiped the sweat from his forehead on his sleeve. "And that's not even a tenth of what we brought back. Everyone else is out there divvying up their share as we speak. They even packed extra, knowing we'd have a few more mouths to feed now that Lauren's soldier friends are going to be staying with us."

Grace smiled grimly. "I always knew my sister had friends in low places, I just never imagined the overall depth of the abyss." She paused a moment. "Christian...do you really think she's okay?"

"She's okay."

"You'd tell me, though, right? If she wasn't? Or even if you had the slightest inkling she wasn't?"

"If you're asking me if I think she'll find her way into trouble, I think you already know the answer to that," Christian replied. "But if you're asking me if I think those guys will watch out for her and treat her like she's priceless, then the answer is an unequivocal yes. Hell, there were times when they wouldn't even let *me* get within a foot of her."

"Probably because they hadn't yet had the chance to get to know you and see how truly debonair you can be," Grace jested. "Fair enough. I won't waste my time worrying about her. I'll let Michelle do the worrying for both of us."

Christian noticed John's bedroom door was propped open. "Any idea where John went? How is he taking the news?"

Grace hesitated. "He hasn't said anything, but that's normal for John, always has been. I don't know how he's feeling, but I can't imagine he's enthused, especially with Christmas right around the corner. I think he had something planned for her."

Christian looked intrigued. "Like what?"

Grace shook her head and held up a finger, rocking it back and forth like a metronome. "Sorry, lover. Privileged info. Certain matters must remain hush-hush."

Christian nodded his acceptance and shrugged, deciding to switch topics. "I gotta know something, Grace. Exactly how the hell were you able to figure your way out of that mess you were in? I've been trying to piece the puzzle together in my head. You all were screwed...they had you by the balls, and I just can't figure it out."

"But I don't have balls, Christian."

"You know what I mean."

Grace looked at him sheepishly. "You remember that time we were looking for Lauren in the woods, the day we found Alex, and you said that I was quite the actress?"

Christian cocked his head and narrowed his eyes. "Of course I do. Why?"

"Let's just say you ain't seen nothing yet," Grace said as she rolled her eyes and giggled. "It was Kim who planted the idea, actually. After that, it kind of snowballed. I took it and went with it, and it worked out better than I ever imagined it would. I never would've thought men with such hostile intentions would have such a soft spot for a depressed, emotional, pregnant girl who'd been deserted by her boo."

Christian cleared his throat. "Come again?"

"It's kinda strange, actually. Hell, it's been downright bizarre. Because I've actually been *feeling* really sick. My stomach's been twisting up, almost like contractions, and I've even thrown up a couple of times." Grace chuckled. "Oddly enough, there's even certain foods that gross me out now—ones I really used to love. It's like the whole act somehow became…I don't know…self-induced."

The door opened, and Michelle stepped in with an armload of supplies, kicking the door shut behind her. As she trudged forward, Christian hopped up from his chair to offer help.

"I got the doctors settled in," Michelle began. "Nice people, actually. A little eccentric, but nice. They seem very optimistic. And they've already started administering heavy antibiotics and antivirals. They want to start all of us on some supplemental multivitamins at some point to help our immune systems recharge from the lack of a proper diet. Of course, Jesseca argued with them…on that, as well as the use of pharmaceuticals. She insists the full-on natural approach is all we need." She paused to catch her breath. "Suppose we'll have to thank Lauren. That is, if she ever decides to come home."

Christian raised his hand. "Who's Jesseca?"

"Alex's mom," Michelle and Grace said in unison, then shared a laugh.

Christian turned away a moment after and continued his conversation with Grace. "Okay, let's backtrack. You said Kim planted the idea…meaning she told them you were pregnant for some reason?"

Grace nodded, her brow elevated.

"Then you started going along with it—pretending you were. And then, you started to *feel* like you were?"

Grace wobbled her head. "No. I mean…I don't know. I was feeling sick before."

"You were feeling sick before what?"

"Before Kim said what she said."

"Okay, what kind of sick?" posed Christian. "Expectant sick?"

"That depends."

"Depends on what?"

"On what the freak 'expectant sick' means," Grace quipped. "Is that some sort of code? Is it your intention to bamboozle me today?"

"It means *pregnant* sick."

Grace laughed. "Oh, okay. Then, no. I was just feeling sick. Like sick sick. The throw-your-guts-up kind. Like a stomach bug or something. I thought I was sick like Lee was…like I got poisoned."

"So you felt sick before, then Kim told them, and then—"

"Christian, chill. Enough of this." Grace said, leering at him. "You're making my head hurt. Besides, everything's fine now. You're home, we have food, and I'm not sick. You don't need to worry about me."

"Of course I do."

"Why?"

"Because I love you, dammit."

Grace dropped the box she was holding to the table as a burst of tears flooded her eyes in an instant. "Oh, gosh. That is so sweet." She sniffled and tried wiping them away. "I love you too, dammit."

Christian passed Grace a peculiar look in witnessing her touching, yet highly uncharacteristic spurt of emotion. "Grace, are you sure that you're not *actually* pregnant?"

The *P* word caught Michelle's attention long before she could reach for the door handle and exit the cabin. Gradually, she turned her body around and inched her way back to where Christian and Grace were standing.

"What? What kind of question is that? Of course I'm sure!" Grace exclaimed, looking appalled. She swiftly dried her eyes. "I mean, I'm pretty sure. How could I be? It's not even possible."

Christian lowered his head, his eyes fixed on Grace. His expression softened, as did his approach. "Grace, honey. Yes, it is."

"No." Grace shook her head. "No, it isn't. I mean, it can't be, right?" She fidgeted. "I mean…*it* happened. I *know* it happened. I was there, same as you. But it was just that one time."

Christian nodded slowly, giving her his best puppy-dog eyes. "Grace," he said, reaching for her hand, "it only takes one time."

Grace began to look worried, and her face turned pale. "Shit. I think I'm going to pass out. Again."

Michelle strolled up, reaching out to grab hold of her. "Nope. No passing out. You're coming with me. You too, Christian. No more crosstalk and no more guessing games. Let's get this figured out right now."

"Where are we going?" Grace asked.
"To the Masons'."
"For what?"
"Hopefully, to find you a pregnancy test."

An hour later, Christian and Michelle gathered around the table back at the cabin, staring down at the only remaining pregnancy test to be found in Trout Run Valley that had yet to reach its expiration date. Michelle waited patiently while Christian nervously tapped his foot on the floor and toyed with his beard.

Grace had chosen to pass the time a different way, using some of the newly acquired food items to whip up a batch of pancakes for dinner, something the family hadn't had to eat in a while. She pranced around the kitchen, singing showtunes under her breath while she worked the batter with a steel whisk.

At one point, Michelle lifted the test from the table and researched it with squinted eyes, only to exhale a sigh and place it gently back where it was. A second later, she suddenly reached for it again, taking another glance. Her eyes went wide before carelessly dropping it and making a prompt exit out the front door.

"What's her problem?" Grace asked, watching her leave.

Christian flipped the test over and stared down at it for a long, contemplative moment, then admired Grace with a notably humble gaze. He gradually pointed to it, his lower lip trembling.

Grace groaned. "What?" She set the bowl of pancake batter down, wiped her hands on a towel, then placidly skipped over.

Christian didn't say anything. He took a few steps back, allowing Grace the room he felt she might need.

Grace shook her head indifferently, then turned away from him, making her approach to the table. She busily tapped her fingernails before reaching for the test. "This is dumb. I know my body. I told you, there's no way I'm pr—" Grace stopped midsentence. She held the test at arm's length from her eyes, then brought it in for a closer look as her jaw fell to the floor and her eyes unbolted to their farthest extents. "Oh, fuck."

CHAPTER 26

**Rocket Center (formerly Allegany Ballistics Laboratory)
Mineral County, West Virginia
Friday, December 10th. Present day**

LAUREN GAZED IN CHILDLIKE WONDER at each of the four walls of the room, barely able to believe her eyes. They were painted an eggshell color, practically spotless, and were adorned with framed photographs of buildings, some of which she recognized, others she had never seen before. An American flag was mounted inside a frame and hung on the wall over the bed, and there were portraits of Naval officers on either side, all high-ranking, all bearing solemn, chiseled expressions in their full-dress blues and white caps.

She looked up at the ceiling to the clear, glass globe of an electric light fixture, very much alight and burning brightly, casting its incandescent hue over everything in sight. She folded her arms and leaned against the wall behind her. "This is some dream," she said, reaching over and feeling for the wall switch. She flipped the rocker, turning the light off and then on again, while shaking her head in utter amazement. "Unbelievable."

Too exhausted upon arrival the previous night to do any exploring of the complex, Lauren had gone to bed only minutes after being assigned quarters and stepping foot inside. She'd utilized what little light had been available from the corridor, letting it leak into the room through the open door enough for her to locate the bed and dive into it.

She had fallen asleep only moments after, too tired to allow random thoughts any consideration. The likelihood of the power being on in this facility hadn't even occurred to her. But why would it have?

Lauren continued to manipulate the switch. She flipped it off and then on, off and on again, and after several cycles, left it powered off for a moment, allowing her eyes to adjust to the darkness while she searched for signs of light creeping through cracks or crevices. Then she remembered where she was, several stories belowground. At least, according to the buttons she had seen Dave Graham press in the elevator car that had transported her and the others here.

Lauren smiled in amusement at herself and powered the light back on. She shrugged. "The elevator works here. There's lights in the hallway, and the light in my room works. So either we went back in time into another dimension, or there's a backup power system around here somewhere."

She dragged her bare feet over the soft wool Berber carpet from the entrance to the adjoining lavatory and reached in to feel for yet another set of light switches. She flipped the first one her fingers met, then felt for the second while glancing at the ceiling, assuming switch number two was meant for the exhaust fan mounted over the shower stall, but still tested it to make certain.

Lauren stepped into the bathroom and slid the shower curtain over. She reached for the faucet and turned it as far counterclockwise as it would travel toward the red *H*. The faucet jerked, and the pipes rattled, and for a moment, she didn't expect anything else to happen. It had been ages since she'd seen water pour from a faucet, and had long ago gotten over having any faith in such amenities. But sure enough, a few seconds later, a steady stream of water emerged from the tap and began flooding the tub. It even gave off a chlorinated odor.

Lauren beamed in astonishment. "Unbelievable. Looks like I'll be able to shed at least a couple of layers of filth after all."

She extricated two towels from a shelf, which were fashioned into spa-style rolls, and dropped them on the tile floor near the tub, then arranged her personal items around the sink. Her shower would be a respectable one, complete with soap, shampoo and conditioner, body wash, and a loofah, of all things. "This is just too much. Dave said we were coming to a former government installation. He never said it was going to be decked out like a Marriott." She chuckled. "Explain yourself, Lieutenant Graham."

Lauren glanced over her shoulder at the queen-sized bed in which she had slumbered the previous night, unable to remember enjoying a better night's sleep in a legion of days. Then she tugged on the belt of her bathrobe to unravel the knot, allowing it to fall free from her shoulders and onto the floor.

She had grown accustomed to taking cold showers ever since her move to the cabin and fully expected this one would be no different. But, upon noticing that steam was now rising from the tub, she hesitated before stepping in.

With inquisitive regard, Lauren reached forward and placed two fingers under the flow. "Ouch! Shit!" She recoiled backward from the scalding hot water. She examined her fingers as her body tensed and shuddered in unison with her senses. "Okay…I wasn't expecting that."

Lauren adjusted the faucet so the water would be less likely to inflict third-degree burns. Then, stepping in finally, she closed the shower curtain behind her and pulled on the plunger to divert water from the tub faucet to the showerhead. She stood motionless underneath the cascading streams in a veritable trance of blissful enjoyment, allowing them to soak her face, head, and neck. Then she ran her fingers through the lengths of her hair as the water gradually saturated it.

Lauren's eyes tracked downward into the tub, seeing the water at her feet had already turned a shade of muck, and rivulets of clear liquid were now scurrying down her stubbly legs in rows amidst small patches of dirt and grime. "Criminy. You are one disgusting ball of gross, Lauren Jane Russell," she mused. "How did you allow this to happen? How did you become so hideous?" She sighed. "It's going to take some work to get you looking halfway presentable again. But, since I've clearly been bestowed with the requisite tools, short of a razor and some decent shave gel…I think I might be willing to go the distance."

Lauren hoisted a pint-sized purple bottle of shampoo and rotated it so she could read the directions for her own recreation. "Lather a dollop of shampoo in your palms and massage into scalp. Now, rinse and go show off those hydrated locks." She giggled to herself. "I don't think a dollop is going to be nearly enough for these locks. There might be some lather, wash, rinse, and a lot of repeat in there somewhere."

Lauren shook the bottle before squirting its contents into her hand. "It might take everything left in this bottle."

Her shower completed, Lauren got out of the tub and wrapped herself with a towel, using the second to swathe her sopping wet mane. She then brushed her teeth and grabbed a hairbrush, taking it along with her as she exited the bathroom.

While brushing the knots out of her hair, made simpler by the use of conditioner, Lauren got dressed and then exited her room, turning right into a long narrow corridor dimly illuminated by lighting mounted at waist level on the walls. Barely able to remember her way around, she soon found her way to the large conference room where she had last seen the others the previous evening before turning in.

The door was closed, and Lauren could hear chattering coming from inside. She contemplated knocking, but instead, impulsively pushed the door open and stepped in.

There, she found Dave Graham, Woo Tang, Tim Reese, and several other semi-familiar faces huddled around a bench. Upon noticing her entry, the discussion they were having ceased, and each man turned to look at her.

"Sorry, I didn't mean to interrupt," Lauren said as she ran the brush through her hair. "I didn't exactly know where to go this morning. I figured this was as good a place as any."

Dave looked away without saying a word, returning to his business-as-usual bearing.

Staff Sergeant Tim Reese, the arm below his injured shoulder bandaged and suspended in a sling, used his other arm to wave. "No worries, Miss Lauren. It's good to have you with us. I take it you've found the accommodations to your liking?"

Lauren smiled and nodded, her face aglow. "Hell yes, it's to my liking. A lot better than anything I ever expected."

"Did having electricity catch you off guard?" the tall sergeant asked.

"It did…but not nearly so much as the hot water. That about scared the shit out of me."

The soldiers laughed and one by one returned to their discussion while Woo Tang broke from the group and strolled over to her.

"The entire complex used to run on solar," Tim explained. "Now it's just a couple of buildings, including this one, and a hangar we use for storage. There's a field of panels out there, most of which still work. It's one of the reasons Dave decided to…take it over."

"Take it over?" Lauren asked, her eyes squinting.

"Commandeered," Dave grunted. "And repurposed for our use."

Lauren nodded. "Oh, you mean tactically acquired," she said, smirking.

"Something like that."

"What happened to all the people who worked here?"

Dave peered over at her momentarily. "They don't anymore."

With a rarely seen snarky grin, Woo Tang leaned in and sniffed the air inches away from Lauren's hair. "Yes, this is much better. I approve. The scents I was able to detect the other day when we found you were nowhere near this becoming."

Lauren tossed her hair over her shoulder and continued to brush. "Why, Mr. Woo Tang, sir, if I didn't know any better, I'd say you were flirting with me."

Woo Tang erased the grin from his face. "I would like to believe you know better, because I would not dare. But that is not because I do not find you attractive. I have always considered you stunning, but I maintain the deepest respect for you, and for your father, as well."

Lauren cocked her head to the side and put her hand on Woo Tang's shoulder. "Jae, it's okay. But being honest, that is probably the sweetest thing anyone has ever said to me in my life."

Woo Tang leaned in closer to whisper in her ear, "To add to that, while I am aware it is hard for most to recognize…because I simply do not look it, I also happen to be more than twice your age."

Lauren giggled. "I know. And that's okay, too," she whispered back to him, then resumed brushing her hair. She gestured over Woo Tang's shoulder to the others. "What's going on over there? Looks intense."

"What makes you say that?"

"The air is so thick in here, you could slice it with your sword."

Woo Tang nodded slightly. "We are finalizing plans for the next op. Our final assault of the month."

"And the year?"

"That, too."

Lauren sighed, lowering the brush. "I was really starting to like this place. Electricity, hot water, soap, conditioner, a comfy bed. I mean, you guys even had toothpaste and a damn hairbrush for me. Alas, all good things must come to an end, I guess."

"I need to get back," Woo Tang said, motioning to the group. "It is crucial for me to be on the same page with the other team leaders." He turned to walk away, only to stop and reach out to her. "Care to join us?"

"Are you sure it's okay? I don't want anyone here to be mad at me for being somewhere I shouldn't be."

"There is no other place for you to be," said Woo Tang. "What we are about to do might necessitate some youthful intuition. And seeing as how you happen to be the youngest in present company, I do not see how it could hurt."

Dave bayed from his position at the bench, "Tang? Janey? Are you two just going to stand there all day chitchatting and wasting my damn time? We got a ton of stuff to go over. I'd appreciate a little urgency on both your parts, if you don't mind."

Lauren followed Woo Tang's invitation to the bench and joined the others. The discussion commenced, and she listened along while the soldiers used terminology and acronyms she wasn't familiar with. She did her best to follow along while studying a topographical map that had been unfolded and stretched across the bench.

The map had been marked on with pencils and chalk to display locations of buildings and other targets, and one particularly noticeable circle labeled 'detention area'. The map itself had been titled with the word *stalag*.

Lauren recognized the word. She knew it was a contraction for the word *Stammlager*, a term used for Nazi prisoner-of-war camps during World War II. She reached forward, placing her finger on the map. "Guys, I'm sorry to interrupt, but what is this place?"

The discussion now halted, Dave removed a well-worn ballcap and set it down on the bench nearby, then wiped his forehead with his sleeve. "It's a prison camp, but not like the one we found you in. It's nothing like the one in New Creek, either." He turned away with a grave expression, unwilling to look Lauren's way.

"So it's one of the *other* camps, then," Lauren filled in, the look on her face cloning his. "The ones you mentioned but have yet to go into detail about. The ones where they're keeping the children. Right?"

Dave didn't respond immediately. He fidgeted a moment as if he had become decidedly uncomfortable with the topic of conversation, or perhaps the audience. "I'm not going to lie to you, Janey. Potentially, there's some downright atrocious things occurring in this place. We've known about it for a few months now, and we've been sending recon units there periodically to bring us intel ever since we discovered it."

Lauren's expression slowly turned mordant. "What does that mean? What do you mean, atrocious? What are they doing with the children?"

"We don't know the full answer to that," growled Dave. "And part of me is thankful we don't. We just know it's contemptible, and those kids shouldn't be there. Personally, that's all I need to know in order to fuel my desire to stomp the entrails out of some hostile ass."

"Fuckin A," Tim Reese added.

Lauren passed Dave an angry look. "This is some sick, twisted shit, isn't it? Like continuance of a bloodline or controlled breeding… the eugenics premise I've read about, where some sick perv tries to generate a master race while killing off those less desirable. Is that why you labeled it a stalag?"

"Janey, calm down."

"Don't tell me to calm down," Lauren scoffed. "Jesus—who in God's name are these people?"

Dave sighed and backed away from the bench. "Listen, kid… something inexplicable happened back on *the day*. These folks didn't just turn bad all at once. Near as we can figure, a few thousand inmates somehow got released from their cells…from a half-dozen maximum-security penitentiaries in and around western Maryland and the Mountain State. That's who these people are. Ex-cons. Murderers, kidnappers, armed robbers and thieves, and rapists. The worst of the worst, some of whom were no doubt serving life sentences. That's who took you and your friends prisoner. That's who we're fighting."

Lauren put a hand to her mouth while remembering the ominous sights she had seen on the day her father had taken her to visit North Branch Correctional Institution. "Dear Jesus…"

Dave continued. "We're not sure if the EMP somehow caused it, if some bleeding hearts cut them loose, or if something else entirely was to blame. But once they got their taste of freedom, they did what escaped convicts tend to do…the same shit that got them locked up in the first place. They massacred thousands."

"And you've been fighting them ever since?"

"We don't see any other way around it," Dave said with a shrug. "We can't achieve forward progression with them in the way. So far, we've cancelled hundreds of them and dismantled quite a few of their camps, but this one is a bit different. They've seized a former West Virginia National Guard base and taken possession of their armory as well. It's going to be a tough nut to crack. But I made a promise to take these fuckers out before we rang in the New Year, and I intend to keep that promise."

"So when are we going?"

Dave stepped closer to Lauren and placed a hand on her shoulder. "We?"

"Yes, we."

"This isn't going to turn out like one of those movies where everybody makes it home safe and sound and gets a happy ending, Janey. There's no champagne and confetti and no ticker-tape parade. This is the real deal, and it is not going to be pretty. There's going to be a lot of booms and bangs, and a lot of blood on the ground. If I were you, I would stay behind on this one."

Lauren looked at Woo Tang, who didn't return her stare. Then, in a circular pattern, she shared stares with everyone in the room before returning a stone-cold glare to Dave Graham. "There is no way in hell I'm not going to go. In fact, I dare you to try to leave me behind."

Dave nodded and placed his cap back on his head. "I figured you'd have something to say along those lines. Fine. I'll *allow* you to go along... but here's the deal, so listen up. The prospect of collateral damage on this one is immense, and I wouldn't put it past these cowards to use human shields. So, as a provision to my usual Norman Schwarzkopf-esque shock and awe routine, we will be relying heavily on our snipers, placing them in these locations all along the perimeter." Dave used an index finger to indicate the spots. "If going along is your intention, this is where you'll be planting your ass, far away from the kill zone. No questions." He paused to adjust his posture. "We'll hit them early in the boogie dark and scare the living daylights out of them; then we'll pick them off with precision fire, and I mean *precision* fire. No funny business, no fucking up will be tolerated, or my boot gets surgically inserted in someone's rectum. Can you still shoot?"

Without hesitation, Lauren nodded. "Damn right I can."

"Very well."

"Can I team with Sanchez?" Lauren asked.

Dave sighed and folded his arms while the others moved away from the bench and stirred. "If Sanchez agrees, I don't see why not."

"He's never told me no." Lauren turned away and resumed brushing her hair, heading toward the exit. She stopped just before reaching for the door handle. "You know, I'm confused…why didn't you come right out and tell me this? Why did it have to wait until I came barging in asking questions? Are you trying to protect me somehow?"

Dave sighed. "Janey, I will always do whatever I can to protect you. After finding you again and hearing what you told me, I'm obligated. There are certain things happening in this world that should not be allowed, and quite frankly, it bugs the tar out of me as a God-fearing man that the big man upstairs permits them to happen. And that is why *I* cannot permit them to happen."

Lauren turned to him and moved closer, concern building in her eyes. "Elaborate."

"I'd be happy to. Once a soldier has seen combat, certain things that occur in combat simply cannot be unseen. Sometimes, it changes him forever. It changes the way he views the world. And regardless of supernatural beings and whether or not they truly exist, it has become undeniably evident to me that a war is being waged behind the scenes. The forces of good and evil are continuously going toe-to-toe. It is a never-ending battle, and if God can't put all the evil down with his great vengeance and furious anger, then it's up to people like us to do it for him."

Lauren nodded, ruminating over Dave's words, taking them all to heart. "You never said when we were going."

"That's correct. I didn't. Major pain and his militia boys are set to join us over the weekend, and we have some gabbing and a lot of serious training to get in. So I'm figuring two weeks from today."

"Um…that's Christmas Eve."

"I am cognizant of that fact," replied Dave.

"Lauren Russell," Woo Tang began as he turned his head her way, "evil knows no holiday. And no evil I have ever encountered has ever taken a day off. Should we be any different?"

Lauren stood there, nearly thunderstruck. She removed the brush from her hair and took turns looking into the eyes of each of the tenured soldiers in the room, doing so until an answer occurred to her.

When she went to offer a reply to the sword-wielding Korean-American soldier in her midst, she stopped herself, having come to the realization that a response wasn't required. If any one of these men believed she felt any other way, they wouldn't be involving her, and she wouldn't be standing among them.

CHAPTER 27

North of WV Army National Guard Camp Dawson
Preston County, West Virginia
Friday, December 24th. Present day

IT WAS A FEW HOURS BEFORE the sun would expose its face over the horizon to the east. The temperature had dropped to below freezing overnight, causing the dew clinging to the earth and vegetation to change state into a layer of frost.

In the bitter cold predawn hours of Christmas Eve, Lauren shadowed Sanchez in pitch darkness along a barely perceptible trail to the position he had chosen as his sniper hide for today's assault.

Both were wearing a PVS-7 single-tube night-vision device. They had been distributed to the unit the evening prior, and the two were now using them to light their way along the path.

Lauren's PVS-7 extended outward from a flip-up mechanism mounted to a ballistic helmet she had been assigned and instructed to wear, something she was only now starting to get used to. She knew it was for her own protection, but it was foreign to her, and the contraption felt clunky on her head, and she knew she had a long way to go with it.

While getting accustomed to the greenish-hued, nearly two-dimensional reality the monocular provided, she remained on alert, her senses invigorated by the chill in the air. She glanced left and right continually, same as she had always done while traveling on foot through the forest.

Occasionally, Lauren would look ahead at the tall Hispanic man leading her and reminisce about the first time she had met him and trained with him. The drag bag he had draped on his shoulders looked like the same one he had brought with him that day. With countless new routines to get used to since her decision to remain with the unit, the familiarity was comforting to her.

Sanchez turned broadside and pointed ahead to the edge of a small rock ledge overlooking the area below, just as a half dozen or more thumps blasted off in the distance.

Lauren's attention diverted upon hearing them, and she looked to the sky as it lit up in a nearly overpowering glow. "Shit." She covered the lens with her hand. "Dammit."

Sanchez quickly turned to face her and whispered, "*Que pasa?*"

Flipping the monocular upward, Lauren gestured her head in the direction of the signal flares. "I think I just broke my night vision."

Sanchez shook his head. "PVS-7s are pretty tough, *chica*. It's not the newest tech, but the tubes are auto-gated, and there's an automatic cutoff to keep that from happening." He trudged onward and began the process of unloading his gear and setting the position up. The first rifle he slid from the drag bag was the same one he had instructed Lauren with at Point Blank Range years ago. "Okay, I usually don't do this, but I'm going to give you a choice today."

Lauren approached him cautiously while her eyes readjusted to the darkness and she fumbled with her NVD. "Choice?"

Sanchez lit a cigarette and began methodically assembling the rifle. He attached an optic and threaded a suppressor onto the muzzle. "That's right, choice," he said, glancing up at her, then returning his attention to the weapon. Smoke billowed from his nostrils. "Spotter or shooter?"

Lauren moved closer and got down on one knee, setting her AK on a patch of grass next to her. She shook her head and tapped herself on the temple with a smirk. "Wow, I'm an idiot. I should've known what you meant."

Sanchez set the rifle down and continued arranging the hide. He had an animated look on his face Lauren had never witnessed before, but it didn't take away from his ever-present charm. "You're right, you should have, but that's okay. I know you've been through a lot, *chica*, and this decision of yours to tag along with us isn't helping." He glanced up at her with his dark, penetrating eyes. "Do me a favor...just watch yourself, especially after that blow to the head. Trust me, I know what I'm talking about."

"I will," Lauren said, snapping the NVDs over her eyes again, verifying their operation.

"So what's it going to be?"

"Shooter."

One of Sanchez's eyebrows shot up from behind his goggles. "You're sure?"

Lauren pointed to the rifle. "How could I say no? You even brought the M40A6...the one without the safety. It's the same one you had at Point Blank. I'd recognize it anywhere."

Sanchez cracked a slight smile. "You remember that day, huh?"

Lauren's response was interrupted by explosions booming off in the expanse. It was a sound she had heard before, recalling it from the morning Zero Dark Armageddon had begun, at least insofar as she was concerned. It was an event that would exist forever in her memoirs...the moment when the good guys showed up in all their glory and put down a mob of malicious hellhounds. It was the point in time when things had finally started to take a turn for the better, and it seemed to somehow mark the beginning of Lauren getting her world back.

"NVD still working?" Sanchez asked.

"Seems that way."

"Think you can shoot with it on? It'll be hard to focus at first... might take some getting used to."

Lauren shrugged. "Just like everything else I've been doing lately. If you see me struggling, tell me and I'll hand the rifle off. I won't be offended."

"Fair enough." Sanchez butted his cigarette out and gestured to the camp below. "The round will be over in a minute. Then it'll get real dark again. Let's get situated."

Lauren moved into position per Sanchez's instructions. She got down prone and lined up with the rifle, feeling the added weight of the suppressor. She snapped the legs of the bipod down and began adjusting them for proper height. Then she took in a view of the landscape through her optic while managing the added burden of aligning it through the NVD. "How far are we out?"

"How far do you think we're out? How far does it look to you?"

"I'm not sure. It's been a while since I've done this."

Once Sanchez was prone, he moved closer to Lauren with a spotter scope in his hands pulled close. "If the PVS-7 is screwing with you, take it off," he said. "Dave was adamant about using them for this op, but in my humble opinion, they aren't needed. They limit your field of view and keep your natural senses from homing in. If you feel you can see well enough to shoot with your naked eye, do so. Copy?"

"I copy."

"I know you've probably had smoke blown up your *culo* before, *chica*, but you won't get any of that shit from me in a combat setting. I always thought you were a natural. If the world hadn't gone crazy like it did, when it did, I think you might've missed your calling."

Lauren turned her head away from the scope for a second to gauge Sanchez's expression, what she could see of it. "Looks about somewhere between six hundred and seven hundred yards. But that's just a guess."

"You're not that far off," Sanchez uttered, making some adjustments on his scope. "I range it six-eight-eight meters. That's around seven hundred fifty yards. The optic is good…let's eyeball our sectors."

"Okay."

"From the far nine o'clock to those buildings, we'll call sector alpha. Sector bravo will begin at the far edge, and end at the stockade. Both alpha and bravo look like target-rich environments to me. From the stockade to the far three o'clock, all the way to the river, is sector charlie. Charlie has the most real estate, but there's not as many targets there."

Lauren could hear Sanchez ramble on, but she wasn't listening. Once in her view, she couldn't help but be transfixed on the stockade. She simply couldn't take her eyes off it.

Lauren reached for the optic's magnification ring and clicked it as far as it would go, then allowed her eyes to focus on the scene. There were the soiled, saddened, demoralized faces of what looked to be fifty to a hundred children of assorted ages, some as old as their mid-teens, others as young as preschoolers. It was heartbreaking to witness and a scene Lauren never could have prepared herself for.

"Hey, *chica*," Sanchez barked under his breath. "You still with me?"

"Yeah, sorry about that."

"Sorry about what? I was talking to you, and I got nothing back. Did you black out?"

"No, I didn't black out. My attention was…diverted for a second. It won't happen again."

Sanchez faced her. "If you can't handle this, I need to know now. Shit's about to get real."

"I can handle it."

"And if you're with me and you didn't black out, you need to respond to me appropriately, just like I trained you."

Lauren gritted her teeth and moved her viewpoint away from the stockade and the faces hiding behind the primitive bulwarks. "I'm affirm on all sectors." A pause. "Shooter ready."

Explosions continued to level portions of the camp while sending the camp's occupants scattering wildly in all directions. A battle had begun, and as she watched the scene play out, Lauren's lower lip began to tremble, and she could feel doubt begin to creep into her mind.

Then a strong hand gently touched the back of her neck.

"Listen to me, *princesa*. Hear my voice. I know what's down there. I know what's on the line today, and I'm with you, stuck to you like gum on a boot until the end. It's that end we need to concentrate on right now. So let's get this dirty business over with and get these kids back home so we can all enjoy better days. It's up to us now."

Lauren turned to look at Sanchez and was surprised to see him looking her way. He had locked his NVDs upward, and his charcoal eyes were glistening as if he had begun tearing up. It was easy for Lauren to feel the emotions he was exuding, and she tried her best to smile through her own. "It's always been up to us," she said, easing back into position.

Sanchez nodded, placing the scope back to his eye. "Target. Sector charlie. Tall gunman, green jacket, firing westward."

"Identified."

"Range seven-seven-five. Wind zero."

"Roger."

"Fire."

Lauren exhaled and squeezed the trigger, and the rifle burped through the suppressor, sending a round downrange, striking the gunman near his collarbone. He went down almost immediately, his hand attempting to plug the entry wound to no avail. Lauren reloaded the rifle in a rapid motion.

"Target down," the Marine emitted proudly. "*Muy bueno.*"

"He's not dead. Should I hit him again?"

"You hit his carotid. He's leaking like a stuck pig. Save the ammo."

The pair worked together to successfully delete numerous targets while other snipers contributed from their respective hides, their suppressed shots barely audible above the enemy's chaotic cries below.

Sanchez's body went rigid as he rotated right. "Shit. Sector charlie again, pivot double quick. Target at the stockade, reaching for the gate. Tall and skinny."

"I got him," said Lauren, already on the move, bringing the target into her sight picture. She lined the reticle just underneath his right ear, then let out a breath and squeezed the trigger, but the rifle failed to erupt.

"Shit!" Lauren grabbed the bolt and cycled it, sending the dead round out of the chamber. In that moment, she also realized she was out of rounds.

Sanchez turned to her, eyes wide. "Misfire?"

Lauren pulled away frantically from the rifle while looking to and fro for options. "Yes, a goddamn misfire! Can you believe it?" Her voice was panicked, signifying she had reached the edge of her comfort zone.

"Calm down," Sanchez said softly, handing her a fresh box magazine. "I've got you."

Lauren quickly sent the magazine home and chambered a fresh round. "Thank you." Peering into the scope, she reacquired her target, noticing the man had already opened the gate.

With a gun in one hand and a flashlight in the other, he waved them around wildly, ordering the children to follow him as they cried and screamed and fought to escape. Then, yards behind, three more men were closing in to join him.

"Multiple tangos approaching. Looks like we have ourselves a party now," Sanchez mused. "Fire at will, *chica*. Send them all screaming back to hell."

Lining the reticle up on the screaming man, once again Lauren exhaled a breath to allow her body to settle, and squeezed the trigger. This time, the rifle thumped, and the slug struck her target true, sending him flying to the ground under its energy. Lauren cycled the action while she acquired target number two, and without a second's hesitation, she put him down for the count. She repeated the motions for the final two men before allowing herself to breathe again.

"That's what I'm talking about," Sanchez said. "Talk about good shot placement. Nice shooting."

Lauren didn't say anything. She was in the zone. She scanned the area below, looking for additional evil men to bury, only able to see the terrified faces of young people, all of whom had no idea what to do or where to go.

Most of them streamed back into the stockade, as it had been their only place of refuge. But two of them, in particular a boy approximately ten or eleven years old and a feeble girl possibly half his age with thin, curly hair, had other ideas in mind.

Lauren watched in a daze as the boy reached for the girl's hand and led her directly into the center of the camp—right where most of the targets still were, and where most of the incoming fire was being sent.

"Jesus Christ," Lauren shrieked. "What the hell are they doing?"

"Who? What sector?"

"Moving into bravo…those two kids. They're headed right into the middle of hell."

Sanchez pivoted to see what Lauren was referring to, yet remained on point. "There's nothing we can do about that. Just try to keep an eye on them. Try to stay focused."

"Focused? Are you kidding me right now? We can't just ignore them, Sanchez. We have to do something! They'll both be killed!"

Sanchez added compassion to his tone while remaining matter-of-fact. "*Chica*, listen to me. We are doing everything we can to save them, but you must come to grips with the gruesome fact that there's no way we can save *all* of them. I'm sorry, it's just the way it is."

Lauren relinquished the M40 rifle and rose, causing Sanchez to recoil to the side. She threw her pack across her back and grabbed her AK. "Bullshit!" she screamed. "I can't accept that—I won't accept that." She darted away, directly down the steep embankment, heading right for the danger zone. "Cover me!"

Sanchez stared blank faced at her as she departed, his mouth agape. He abandoned the spotting scope and retrieved the rifle, then moved himself into position. "Women…"

With no regard of any kind for her own welfare, Lauren ran down the mountain in the predawn darkness, and it didn't take long for her to learn the limitations of the PVS-7 night vision she was using. In addition to objects appearing two-dimensional, her depth perception was dangerously limited, and while struggling to focus, she found herself running into all sorts of things. She slammed into trees, tripped over rocks and roots jutting up from the ground, and nearly injured herself a handful of times along the way down. At one point, Lauren felt a twinge of pain from her ankle, figuring she had tweaked the sprain she'd sustained months before, an injury she had spent so much time strengthening and regaining her confidence in. While providing her the ability to see in the dark, the NVD also provided a lengthy catalog of limitations.

Once she arrived on flat ground, Lauren watched the flurry of machine-gun tracer rounds flash by in green streaks, burning brightly at first as they entered her field of view, only to dissipate and vanish seconds after. Before moving again, she removed an infrared light stick from her hip pocket, brought it to life with a snap, and attached it to the MOLLE webbing on her pack. It was still plenty dark enough outside for most, if not all, of the shooters to be using their night vision, and she hoped the ChemLight would give her a better chance of not being hit by friendly fire.

From there, Lauren brought her rifle up and sprinted to where she had last seen the boy and the little girl. The fact that she was in a hostile environment now, one of the worst possible places to be, and there were enemies practically everywhere, both hidden and in plain sight, didn't even register to her as factors. All she concerned herself with at this very moment was getting to the two young souls who had been foolish enough to leave their only place of sanctuary.

Lauren knew deep within herself what it was like to make foolish decisions. She had been there a time or two before, both as a child and as a young adult, and she understood beyond a shadow of a doubt that this particular decision would be more than frowned upon. But it didn't matter to her. Lauren only knew she had to act.

Seeing two men she didn't recognize several yards ahead in her path, Lauren unleashed a burst of full-auto fire from the AK, sending both limply to the ground. She dropped to a prone position, and while stuffing her fingers into her ringing ears to nullify the rapid cracks of gunfire for a moment, she surveyed the scene, finally discovering what she'd come for. After taking in a few deep breaths, she darted off in their direction.

Spotting her approach, the boy turned to face her while he situated the little girl behind him, then held up a hand, trying his best to look aggressive. "Don't come any closer!" he yelped. "We're not going back there; I don't care what you do to us. You can shoot us both if you want to, but we're not going back in that cage." He paused, turning his head away to whisper something to the girl. "All we want to do is leave. Can't we just leave? Can't you just let us go home? All my sister and I want to do is—"

Lauren smiled and held a hand up to silence his pleas. "I'm not taking you back there. I came here to get you out." She moved slightly closer. "It's okay…I'm not with them. I mean, not with the people who took you. I'm one of the good guys. There's an army here now. We've come to save you and the other kids."

The boy cocked his head and gave Lauren a disbelieving look. "Who are you?" he asked, eyeballing her up and down, scrutinizing every attribute. "You said army, but you don't look like a soldier. You look more like a robot."

Lauren locked the night-vision monocular in its upright position on her helmet so the two young people could see her face. "I'm not a soldier or a robot. Just someone who's here to help."

The boy's sister displayed a set of tormented eyes, then pulled on him and whispered into his ear.

"My sister wants to know…if you're a superhero."

Lauren's features softened—the question nearly taking her breath away. She hesitated a moment, not knowing how to respond. "No, I'm not," she said, her tone faltering. "I am definitely not a superhero."

The young boy continued to scrutinize her in the darkness as if his eyes were capable of X-ray vision. His protective grip on his sister remained solid and unwavering.

"I need you guys to do a favor for me," Lauren said, finding as much calm as she could muster while moving in closer to the pair. "I need you to follow me over to that building over there. But you have to stay as low as you can the whole way."

"Why?"

"Because it's safer. We're going to stay there until the shooting stops."

The boy's murky, dirt-covered skin wrinkled a bit as his expression twisted. A second later, he nodded his understanding and got down on his knees while helping his sister do the same.

"That's it, perfect. Now, can you crawl? Can you crawl on your hands and feet the whole way over there and keep your head low at the same time?"

The boy nodded almost instantly and then turned to his sister to make certain she understood Lauren's instruction. He whispered something in her ear, and a second later she nodded affirmation.

Once Lauren's eyes had acclimated to the darkness, aided by brief flashes of sporadic gunfire, she led the way. The boy and his sister followed her diligently, and moments later, the threesome met with the building's cinderblock exterior. "Good job, you two. It'll be a lot safer here with bullets still flying around. We're much less likely to get hurt here."

"I don't want to get hurt at all," the boy said. "And I never wanted my sister to get hurt, either. But these people don't care. All they did was yell at us and hurt us, especially her." He gestured to the young girl with his head timidly. "I think they liked doing it. I tried to stop them, but they just didn't care. Nobody cared."

"Well, I'm here now, and I care. And as long as I'm with you, I won't let anybody hurt you. And I won't let anyone harm your sister, either."

The boy gawked at her and some innocence returned to his expression. "You promise?"

"I promise."

He held up a hand with his pinky finger sticking out. "Pinky swear?"

Lauren smiled slightly at the gesture, remembering its popularity in her youth. "Pinky swear, of course." She hooked her pinky finger around his. "I'm Lauren."

"I'm Daniel. And my sister is Lily. We were trying to run away before you came. I saw *goliath* coming, and I didn't want him to grab my sister again."

"It's nice to meet you, Daniel. And you, Lily." Lauren cocked her head slightly. "Who's goliath?"

"He's the big man," the boy said, hesitating as his eyes stretched and darted around. "Bigger than anyone I've ever seen. I hope you never meet him. Or the weird man, either. They're the worst."

Lauren thought a moment, her grip tightening on the AK. "Does goliath talk a lot?"

The boy shook his head. "No. He only makes noises. I don't think he knows how to talk. I think he's half-witted."

Lauren nodded after spending a couple of seconds deliberating who this 'goliath' could be, and it wasn't long before a rendering of her old pal Gus popped up in her mind's eye.

CHAPTER 28

LAUREN HUDDLED IN CLOSER WITH Daniel and Lily as a startling round of explosions went off not far away. A pair of others boomed together a few seconds afterward, both feeling even closer than the previous ones.

Lauren helped them guide their fingers into their ears, Lily first, followed by her brother; then she plugged her own as the thundering blasts became persistent.

Daniel looked to her, fear amassing in his eyes. "Who's doing that? The good guys or th—"

Another bellowing explosion sent them all cowering as the sky lit up in a blinding flash and fragments of debris showered them.

Lauren pondered the boy's question while recalling what Dave had said about this particular camp, that hostile forces here had sequestered an armory. "I don't know. But our plans don't change, okay? We need to stay calm and wait it out. This is all going to be over soon, I promise."

"I'm scared, Lauren," Daniel said, his terror noticeable now.

"I said I wouldn't let anything happen to you, and I meant it."

After an extensive blitz of back and forth artillery fire, it wasn't long before the outbursts came to a close. Lauren unblocked her ears, then used her NVDs to survey the camp. Bodies were strewn about as far as her eyes could see, and the weapons their foes had been using during their ephemeral counterattack lay peacefully on the ground amidst scattered fires, plumes of rising smoke, and piles of rubble. The stillness that had taken over the expanse was nearly deafening.

"Daniel, where exactly did you last see goliath?"

The boy didn't offer an immediate response. After a second, Lauren turned to him while reaching to remove her helmet, and upon doing so, she saw the horror in his eyes achieve apogee.

A hard smack to the back of her head sent Lauren face-first to the ground in a daze. Before she could react, someone with incredible strength reached in and grabbed an oversized fistful of her hair, twisted it and entangled it between his fingers, then hoisted her off her feet and pulled her backward and away with ferocious force.

Lauren shrieked and lost control of her M70, the rifle tumbling to out of her grasp as both of her hands flailed and reached for the enormous fist in a desperate attempt to free herself. She could feel the pain around the knot on her head begin to throb as he dragged her, kicking all the while. She tried with everything she had to free herself while looking beyond to the eyes of the young boy and girl as they stared helplessly back at her, wide-eyed, faces pale white, screaming for her and for the man to release her.

"Please don't! Please let her go! Don't hurt her!" Daniel yapped. He reached for his sister while she cried in fright, and told her to stay put; then he stood and started closing the distance.

Lauren gave Daniel a stern look through her agony. "No! Daniel, don't! Stay…back!"

The boy heeded her request and second-guessed his decision. Then his eyes caught sight of the stray AK-47 where it had landed.

Lauren couldn't see Daniel go for the rifle. Her neck was being jerked and craned in multiple directions, and she was in far too much pain to even think her situation through. The sequence of events was moving in fast-forward now while the brawny man continued to drag her farther and farther away.

Breaking free a hand, she made a frantic grab for her Glock 19, which in spite of her hysterics, remained safely holstered on her left thigh. As she made a move to retrieve it, she received another vicious tug.

The sudden surge of pain was overwhelming, and both her hands flew instinctively above her head, attempting to pry his hands from her hair. There was nothing she could do to stop him. Nothing she could do to quell the immense pressure within his grasp.

Then Lauren heard something zip through the air narrowly above her, followed by a loud *smack*. The man's grip turned to jelly in seconds, and he let go of her hair. She rebounded quickly, turning just as the man fell, watching him land on his side. He gasped for air while reaching for a fresh, hemorrhaging bullet wound in his chest.

Lauren struggled to gather herself as best she could. She slid away from the man in a panic, her heart pounding out of her chest, her breathing shallow and rapid. She extricated her sidearm, and while taking a second to scan for additional threats, she gradually rose to her feet and approached the bleeding man.

"Unbelievable," Lauren spat incredulously. "I had a feeling I'd run into you somewhere along the way." She stepped closer, gripping the Glock with both hands, aligning the tritium sights with the man's massive head. "Looks like someone finally had you put down." She paused, exhaling slowly. "It's been a long time coming, hasn't it, Gus?"

While reaching for the bullet hole in his chest, the burly man grunted and groaned while making faces at her, but he didn't say anything—having chewed his own tongue off many years before.

Lauren moved to within a couple of feet of Gus, the man who had hit her from behind and taken her to the camp that had almost killed her and her friends. The man who had spit in her face and laughed at her and who no longer had the upper hand. "Did you ever see the movie *Old Yeller*?" she asked him, her tone bearing zero sentiment. "I cried like a baby the first time I saw it. It's about two brothers and a stray golden retriever who protects them and earns their love and trust. The dog ends up getting rabies and attacks the younger brother, and the older brother has to put the poor pup out of his misery." She paused before continuing.

"That's where I first started to learn about responsibility and having to do what's necessary. Sometimes you have to cast your feelings to the wayside. After I watched that movie, I told my dad I would never be that person—I would *never* take aim and shoot a dog even if it needed to be done." She paused, widening her stance. "You know what he told me? He said never say never, because no one knows what the future holds. He said if I ever had to, it would be justified, and he'd forgive me for it. And so would God."

Lauren's expression deadpanned. "Dogs are beautiful animals. I've never had one myself, even though I always wanted one. And I've never put one down. Until today."

Lauren leveled the Glock and pulled the trigger three times in succession, sending a trio of slugs into Gus's chest and head. She watched as his body convulsed into tremors; his breathing slowed and ultimately ceased. She sighed. "Now, I just have to find your owner so I can tell him the bad news." Lauren leaned over and spit on Gus's mangled face. "Play dead…and stay that way."

There were about twenty possibilities where the shot that had begun the process of sending Gus to meet his maker could have come from. Lauren assumed it had come from Sanchez, theorizing he had never taken his eye off her since the point she'd decided to run off on him.

Lauren held a hand aloft, palm facing outward, in the direction of the sniper hide she'd abandoned. A second later, a red dot from a high-intensity weapon-mounted laser appeared on her palm. The dot disappeared and reappeared, and at first, the sequence escaped her, until she realized the sender was repeating a word using Morse code.

She read out the visually sent dits and dahs, deciphering them to spell out the word *okay*.

"Looks like Neo was right again," she said, smiling broadly and sending her grateful stare to the hide. "Thank you, homeboy. *Te amo mucho*." She made sure to mouth the words well so her guardian angel above could lip-read. "And I'm sorry for being a dumbass—I just had to save them." She looked to her palm again and the laser rattled off additional characters in code. *Okay* was sent and repeated, followed by a long pause and five more letters spelling out the word *alive*.

Lauren nodded, a firm yet humble look in her eyes. "Yes, I am." She pointed to Daniel and his sister, watching them as they drew near, taking hasty, cautious steps. "And so are they."

Daniel handed Lauren her M70, and she press checked it, returning her hand to the vented foregrip. The symphony of gunfire had begun to die down, and she returned with them to their location of safety from whence they came.

"Are you okay?" Daniel asked, the fear in his eyes still evident. "Did goliath hurt you?"

Lauren patted his head. "I'm okay, thanks for asking. No girl likes to have her hair pulled like that."

The boy's gaze fell to Gus's dead body. "Those things you said to him…it sounded like you knew him."

"We've met before. He tried to hurt me and my friends a couple of weeks ago. Now his days of hurting people are over." Lauren eyeballed the boy's sister, who seemed entranced, almost catatonic. She was using her right index finger to draw outlines of flowers and butterflies in the loose dirt beside her foot. "Once the shooting stops, we're going to walk together to somewhere safe, okay? Does that sound good to you?"

The boy nodded slightly, his eyes remaining transfixed on Gus. "It does sound good. Anywhere is better than this."

Lauren picked up on how closely Daniel was studying the deceased. "If it bothers you to see him like that, we can move to the other side of the building."

The boy bit his lip. "It's not difficult, and it really doesn't bother me. It's just that…I'm wondering."

"Wondering what?" Lauren asked, smirking. "If he's dead or not?"

"No. I'm wondering where the weird man is."

A chill ran up Lauren's spine, and she adjusted her position, placing her back to the wall of the building. "What weird man?"

"The one who's always with goliath."

"You want to tell me about him?"

"He's strange…looks weird and talks weird, and he's almost always right beside goliath. We saw him run away right when the shooting started."

Lauren shuddered. "Daniel, what does he look like? Can you describe him for me?"

The boy looked away from Gus's body. He nudged his sister on the shoulder. "Lily…show her. Show her the weird man."

Lily looked up innocently before her eyes sagged downward. She wiped clean the soft dirt canvas with her hand, erasing the flower bed and insects she'd been working diligently on. With her index finger, she drew a circle, then placed two dots inside to represent eyes. She drew in a nose, which was generously larger than what would be considered typical, and then added a crooked mouth and a set of ears. Then Lily drew a set of circles around the eyes and connected them with lines and finally ran a line from the edge of each circle to an ear.

Lauren didn't respond until the girl removed her hand from the image in the dirt. "Son of a bitch. It's him."

The boy cocked his head. "You know the weird man, too?"

Lauren nodded, turning her head away. "Yes. Unfortunately, I do."

"Did he try to hurt you? Like goliath did?"

"No, he didn't hurt me. He tried, but my friends came and stopped him." Lauren paused. "I got lucky."

Lily finally spoke, her voice inundated with trepidation. "That man is scary, and I don't like him. I don't like him at all. He says mean things, and he—"

Lauren reached for her, pulling her close and stopping her midsentence. "Hey, you don't have to say anything, okay? No matter what it was, it wasn't your fault. You don't have to say anything else at all. I get it."

Daniel's face contorted, and his expression filled with ire. "My sister wasn't as lucky as you were."

Lily's eyes welled up with tears, and she took Lauren's hand, while Lauren ran her hand through the dirt to erase the likeness. "Daniel, you said you saw him run off…which direction did he go?"

"I think he was headed back to his house."

"What house?"

"He doesn't stay here with the others." Daniel pointed beyond to a hill displaying the back side of a small wooded neighborhood not far away, on the other side of the river and just outside the encampment. "He stays over there. It's in a subdivision."

"Does he live there alone?"

The boy looked at her curiously.

Lauren rephrased. "Does anyone go with him or stay there…to guard the house?"

Daniel nodded.

"People with guns?"

The boy nodded again. "I think so."

"Terrific," Lauren spat. "What does the house look like?"

"It's a brick house—not the red brick, though, the lighter color. The windows have black shutters. It's at the end of the…cull d…cul de—"

"The cul-de-sac?"

Daniel rolled his eyes. "Yeah cul-de-sac. Sorry, it's a weird word. It's a pretty big house, it just doesn't look like it…from the outside."

CHAPTER 29

LAUREN KNEELED AND OPENED HER arms to Lily, who bashfully turned away. She shuddered a bit. "Come on, sweetie, it's okay. It's over now. I promise, no one is going to hurt you ever again. I won't allow it."

Her head lowered, Lily gradually turned until most of the freckles were visible on her soiled face. She soon skittered into Lauren's arms and placed the side of her head between Lauren's shoulder and neck.

While holding his sister tightly with one arm, Lauren stood and carried her, then reached for Daniel's hand, and the three walked together to where the unit had gathered with the other children, offering them comfort.

Woo Tang was the first to see them approach. He looked upon Lauren sharply at first, but upon seeing her condition, the resolve in her expression, and the children accompanying her, he thawed his composure. "Glad to see you are still breathing, Lauren Russell. Especially after hearing about your most recent escapade. And who have you brought along with you?"

"Jae, this is Daniel, and this is his sister, Lily."

Daniel stared at Woo Tang strangely, while his sister barely peered out from under her hair.

"Guys, this is my friend Jae. His friends call him Woo Tang. He's a good guy, like me. We're on the same team."

Woo Tang held out his hand after kneeling, and the boy took it with a lopsided head. "It is nice to meet you. Please join us. We have refreshments…and hot chocolate."

Daniel nodded slightly. "Why is your name Woo Tang?"

Woo Tang smiled, his lips slightly apart. "Why do you ask?"

"Because it's a weird name."

"That is true. But it is also unique in much the same way."

Lauren tapped Lily on her back and gently set her down, allowing her to rejoin her brother.

Daniel tilted his head. "You're leaving us?"

"I have to," said Lauren. "I still have some work to do."

"Work? You're going to visit the weird man, aren't you?"

Lauren nodded. "He got away once, and I can't let him do that again."

Daniel turned his head away when his sister reached for him. Lily put her mouth to his ear while staring Lauren's way.

"My sister says thank you for everything you did, and please be careful."

Lauren smiled broadly over her apprehension of what she was about to face. "You tell her she's welcome, and I will. I'll see you guys soon. I'll check in as soon as I get back."

Daniel took his sister's grip and walked away with her while Woo Tang regarded Lauren with a somber, judgmental look on his face.

Lauren held up a hand. "Jae, wait. Before you say anything or start chastising me for what I did, there's something we need to talk about."

It took a moment for Woo Tang's expression to mellow, but eventually his vexation evaporated. "Go on."

"This isn't over yet," Lauren said, looking around. "The leader from the camp where you guys found me…he's here."

The former Navy SEAL scowled while cradling his M4. "I take it he is not among the dead?"

Lauren shook her head.

"Approximate grid coordinates?"

Lauren pointed to the small group of houses in the distance. "According to the little boy and his sister, he stays in a house up there. They saw him run off when the shooting started, along with a few others."

"And you are certain it is the same person?"

"I'd bet my life on it," said Lauren. "Lily, the little girl, she confirmed it. She drew a likeness of him in the dirt like a sketch artist."

Woo Tang looked away and regarded the group of homes through his NVD. "We are losing cover of darkness rapidly. The sun will be up soon. I will take you at your word, but this must be done now." He pressed the push-to-talk button on his throat mic. "Yellow team, converge on me, pronto." He turned his head to Lauren, engaging her firmly. "I assume there is no point in asking you to remain here."

"Not this time," she replied, shaking her head. "If it was anybody else, I'd consider it. But this man is different, Jae. I could see it in his eyes when I met him."

"You could see *what* in his eyes?"

Lauren bit her lip. "Evil. I've seen it before, I know what it looks like. He has to be put down. If he gets away, this shit will never be over."

"Fine. You can accompany us," Woo Tang said, in clear protest with himself. "But we will need to locate you some body armor."

Lauren looked herself over briefly, then nodded with tightened lips, recalling the heft of the plate carrier Grace had given her and how good it had felt to rid herself of it after hefting its mass halfway up a mountain during her short-lived getaway.

Woo Tang's expression grew dark. He lowered his head, turning away. "There is more I feel I must ask you…to suppress my uncertainties."

"Ask away," Lauren said.

"Do you call to mind…the times we trained together? And all of which I have…imparted unto you?"

"Of course I do. Why?"

Woo Tang turned his head away momentarily as his squad closed in. "Because you are making the choice to directly oppose an iniquitous enemy." He dropped his pack to the ground. "And bearing that in mind, those recollections may be compelled to bolster you today."

Woo Tang addressed his team as they neared. "Gentlemen, we have a dwelling to clear and a potential HVT. Strip down your kits. Close-quarters weapons only, swift and silent." He looked to Lauren. "That goes for you, as well…prepare yourself for the ride. Your body will experience rapid changes in blood pressure and heart rate, and blood flow to major muscle groups will be hindered, conceivably making simple movements problematic or impossible. Rely on muscle memory. You may encounter visual difficulties as well, and your focus may suffer as a result." He paused, extracting a KA-BAR fighting knife from his pack. "Do not let fear overpower you. Channel it into aggression and stay in control." He handed her the knife, still enclosed in a Kydex sheath. "And never lose track of this blade."

Under the cover of waning darkness, Lauren followed Woo Tang and his team to the home she had indicated. Several men, all armed with rifles, were found to be standing guard outside. One stood with conviction on the concrete patio before the front door, casually smoking a cigarette; others were in random locations around and along the home's boundaries.

Using only hand signals, Woo Tang instructed each member of his team to form a circle around the house and locate themselves behind cover. He locked open his NVDs and turned to Lauren, who was kneeling behind him, motioning for her to come closer. "Ambient light will overload our night vision soon, but be ready to use them when we go inside. Chances are, it will be much darker there." He handed Lauren a Beretta pistol with a suppressor attached to the barrel. "Remember, swift and silent, emphasis on silent. No noise, Lauren Russell. Control the distance—and stay glued to my six."

After Lauren nodded her understanding, Woo Tang turned away to face the home, pressing the PTT on his throat mic. "This is yellow one. Danger close—strength seven, my count," he said, barely above a whisper. "Yellow two, yellow three, hold your positions and maintain perimeter. Yellow six will be overwatch. Four and five with me; one has point." A pause. "Six, do you have eyes on the stogie?"

"Roger, yellow six has the stogie."

"Stogie first, then others. On my go." Woo Tang held a hand aloft with three fingers in the air. A second later, he lowered his ring finger, leaving two to remain. His fingers reduced again to one and finally zero, and a flurry of suppressed gunshots popped off from hidden locations around the house in chorus. Each shot struck a target true, and the collection of men outside collapsed one by one.

With his M4's buttstock pulled to his cheek, Woo Tang placed two fingers to his earpiece as he began receiving whispered reports from the members of his team.

"Target down, yellow two clear."
"Yellow three is clear, tango down."

"This is yellow four...all clear."

The remaining men in the squad rang in their reports in the same fashion. Then Woo Tang pressed the PTT on his throat mic once more, whispering the words, "Yellow one moving with Orchid, standby to standby." He turned to Lauren once again. "Remember. Glued to my six."

"I got it," Lauren replied in a whisper, then press-checked the Beretta and swallowed over a lump in her throat. She was apprehensive, felt miles out of place, but she wasn't afraid. She refused to be.

Several of Woo Tang's men moved in closer to the house as instructed while others remained in their positions. One of the men signaled, and Woo Tang ran to the house in a high crawl with Lauren following in tight formation. He jumped into the door, kicking it in and shattering it into splinters.

Lauren snapped her goggles down, and the green-hued reality flooded her vision. She watched Woo Tang move in and buttonhook to the left, his M4 leading the way. Two men entered seconds later and quickly overtook her, crisscrossed, then moved through the house methodically in every direction, one gliding into the kitchen while the other covered him before they switched positions and swept the hallway.

Woo Tang turned and motioned for Lauren to stand by the door, while sounds of doors being kicked and rooms being cleared filled the home. "Watch the entrance. The house appears empty, but that could change at any moment."

Lauren nodded and slowly backed away, then turned and scuttled to the door. Several minutes later, after several shouts of 'clear', Woo Tang gathered with his team in the living room.

"There's no one here," the taller of the two said.

The second nodded. "That's confirmed...not even a trace. This place is empty—like a keg of Natty Boh in a frat house." He turned to Lauren, resting his carbine against his shoulder. "Where did you acquire your intel?"

"That is inconsequential," Woo Tang interrupted, preventing Lauren from proposing an answer. "We encountered armed resistance prior to the breach, which serves as indication."

"Sure, indication. But indication of what?" the second questioned.

Woo Tang glowered. "It is likely our HVT withdrew upon sensing commotion outside."

"This isn't making any sense," Lauren said, shaking her head in distaste. "He has to be here. I can feel it in my gut."

The taller man in black ACUs chuckled. "I used to get those feelings too, back when I was scared of the boogeyman."

"That will be enough," said Woo Tang. "You two—outside. Link up with the others. Hold the perimeter pending exfil."

The two men nodded their accord and followed each other out the front door.

Lauren sighed and wandered into the home, taking cautious steps. She turned on the IR illuminator on her PVS-7, thereby adding brightness to her view. Then she took a right turn and proceeded down the hallway.

Woo Tang called her from behind. "Lauren Russell, could there be another house we need to check?"

"We can check all of them if you want. But he's here, Jae. I'm telling you, he's here." She continued into the first room on her right and scanned it fully before exiting and entering another. "Daniel said it was a big house. Bigger than it looks from the outside. But it only looks like a single-level ranch…four bedrooms, two bathrooms, a kitchen, dining room and a living room."

"I am sorry this did not work out the way you preferred."

"You mean leaving this psycho at large? Trust me, I don't like it any more than you."

Woo Tang cocked his head and watched Lauren scour the home, the IR illuminator of her NVD visible like a concentrated starlight through his own. "Is there something in particular you are searching for?"

"I'm looking for a door. A hatch or something. Don't all houses like this one have a basement or a crawl space?"

Woo Tang pressed the push-to-talk switch on his throat mic. "Two, this is one."

"*Go for two.*"

"Verify dwelling for exterior exits—possibly leading to a basement or crawl space." He stepped closer to Lauren. "The team is on it."

A moment later, Woo Tang received a reply.

"*Yellow one, this is two. That's affirm. We got a small metal door on the west face. Appears unlocked. Ascertaining now. Wait one.*"

"What did he say?" asked Lauren.

"The team located a door in the foundation. They are checking it now."

A sensation punched Lauren in the gut and a hot wave of anxiety brushed over her. "Jae, no! Tell them not to! You don't know this guy... the door could be—"

Interrupting her midsentence, a crash, then the jarring resonance of an explosion rumbled from outside the house, shaking it all the way through to its core. Lauren ducked and cried out while Woo Tang reached for her, pulling her to the floor with him, using his arms to cover her as dust and debris shot from all directions. Defunct light fixtures came apart, and chunks of ceiling fell from their moorings, coating them both in shards of broken glass and a fine sheen of powdery gypsum dust.

Lauren grabbed for the shemagh around her neck and pulled it over her nose as she gasped and coughed out inadvertently inhaled breaths of dust.

After snapping his NVD in the up position, Woo Tang reached to Lauren's helmet and repeated the motion with hers. "Are you okay?" he asked, his concern mounting in sequence with his displeasure.

Lauren nodded in between coughs. "I'm...fine. But dammit, Jae, what about your men?"

"I am about to find out."

"Not without me, you're not."

The couple made their way to the rear of the home to discover four members of the team had been killed, their bodies mutilated and mauled in ways difficult to describe.

While Lauren stood guard, watching both the woods around them and the hole recently punctured in the foundation by the explosion, Woo Tang verified each of his men for vital signs. He pushed on his radio's PTT again. "Yellow six?"

"Go for yellow six," the voice bawled through Woo Tang's earpiece.

"Advise status."

Yellow six replied abrasively at a volume far beyond the routine covert threshold. *"Fuck...I'm solid, one. What the hell happened? I saw fire—debris...smoke's still rising..."* He trailed off, panting. *"I see... four men on the ground. All of them...down."*

"Report contacts."

A pause and then, *"Negative contacts—just you...and Orchid."*

"Copy that. Stay frosty. Break. Net, this is yellow one actual. I have casualties. Four K-I-A, I repeat...number four, all K-I-A." A pause. "Tango remains at large. We will be continuing in."

Woo Tang glanced at Lauren with narrowing eyes. Slowly and meticulously, he rose, removed his helmet, then regarded each of his fallen men. "Till Valhalla, brothers. I will see you all there, someday. Rest easy." He stepped away and turned to Lauren, his expression incinerating with angst.

Lauren approached him carefully, her tone grave and succinct. "Jae…"

"Yes?"

"Who's Orchid?"

The Korean-American frogman morosely smiled at her. "I was not aware my earpiece was so flagrant."

Lauren returned his faint, overcast smile. "Our overwatch is flustered…I heard everything he said. But you said it earlier too."

"I suppose I did." He hesitated. "It is your code name. The one we… chose for you."

"I don't understand."

"There is a modest explanation. You are the Ghost Orchid because you are both rare and endangered. There are other rationales, but those are the two I consider most prevalent."

Lauren rolled her lips between her teeth, nearly quivering at the sentiment. "I don't know what to say."

"Then say nothing; we can chat about it later all you like." Woo Tang took in a deep breath and exhaled little by little while strengthening his posture. "At present, I must admit to you that I am feeling rather… infuriated. I am inclined to *finish* this."

Her feeling of sorrow passed by in a flash as Lauren scanned the ground where the recently departed lay, finding herself quickly overcome by an abrupt urge for vengeance. "I'm right behind you."

Woo Tang nodded. After refastening his helmet, he moved swiftly, slipping through the hole in the foundation with Lauren following on his heels.

Once inside, the two shined their flashlight beams in every direction, discovering that the crawl space wasn't a crawl space by any means. It was spacious enough to be a basement or even a bunker of sorts. Directly before them stood a cinder-block wall with two doorways, one on each of its far sides.

"Well, that's life for you," Lauren said, breathing out a sigh. "What's it going to be? Door number one, or door number two?"

Woo Tang shrugged, his suppressed M4 pulled tightly to him. "I am casting my vote for door number neither. What is stopping this mongrel from setting up pitfalls behind every object we touch?"

Lauren's jaw set, and her fists tightened. "The fact he's a coward," she said. "He values his own life far too much to bring this whole house down on top of him. Hurting other people doesn't inconvenience him one bit, but I think…he's just as scared of dying as the next man."

Keeping his torch aimed at the door before him, Woo Tang turned his head. "Do you think this is the case? Or know it is? Remember the difference. We are not immersed in a training exercise at Point Blank, Lauren Russell, and this is far from being a controlled environment. One wrong move can mean death for either…or both of us."

"I appreciate your concern," said Lauren. "And I love you for it. But ever since this whole…thing started for me, not one day has gone by when I haven't told myself that." She stepped away, and with her pistol at the ready, approached the door on the left, placing her flashlight between her teeth. She then reached for the handle. "On your go."

He sent her a bleak smile. "Before we separate, I would like to pass something along to you. In my initial conversation with your father, he tried expressing to me how brave you were." Woo Tang came within reach of the other door. "His explanation was in metaphor, making it difficult for me to accept it as true." He paused. "I did not realize until this moment…how right he was about you."

Removing the torch from her mouth, Lauren sent the beam down the narrow corridor while her heart pounded away. She looked high and low, but the hall was empty aside from another closed door at the far end. She doused her light and placed it in her back pocket, then brought her NVDs down over her eyes, illuminating the darkness in front of her.

Lauren inched her way through, careful not to make a sound with every step she took, and every breath she inhaled and blew out. She could hear her pulse beating in her ears, and she could feel it throbbing in her throat, and it seemed to worsen the closer she got to the door.

She took in a deep breath before grabbing the handle and shoving it open, and the door's hinges creaked loudly as it swung inward.

With the muzzle of the Beretta leading the way, sweeping from one side to the next, Lauren stepped into a large storage room with benches and empty wooden and wire shelving mounted to the walls. She turned right and then pivoted left on the bare concrete, her heart jumping upon setting eyes on the one she had come for.

He had his shirtless back turned to her, wore nothing to cover his body other than a pair of torn denim jeans, and stood motionless as a mannequin. It was the leader of *the absolved*, the man who had spoken so eccentrically during their encounter. The bald, diabolical, sonnet-parroting man who wore glasses lacking lenses.

Lauren tiptoed closer. Once his hairless head was aligned steadily in her sight picture, she opted to announce her presence, using a manner with which her foe could identify. "Thou'st spoken right. 'Tis true," she said, her tone razor sharp, her eyes set to kill. "The wheel is come full circle. I am here."

The leader's neck muscles twitched. He turned his head somewhat to the side while keeping his back turned to her. "Cordelia…" he murmured, drawing out the name. "What an enchanting surprise. And here, I thought I had lost you for good…yet here you are, once again right beside me, in my realm." He paused to scratch his nose. "I see you have brought along friends today."

"The time for talking is over."

"On the contrary…I believe it's only begun. Tell me, why doth thee approach from behind in rabble-rousing fashion? With a gun pointed at me, no less?"

Lauren pulled the M9's trigger, firing a round into the cinder-block wall inches from her target, sending a cloud of silica dust bursting into the air. "And it's *loaded*, no less. That hole in the wall could've been your head."

"Perhaps it should have been." He paused. "Incidentally, I would like to point out, while you quoted your lines impeccably, it was not Cordelia who said them. Rather, it was Edmund."

Lauren took a step closer. "I know whose lines they were. I used them only because I felt them appropriate."

"Ah yes, I see. The wicked one is attempting to teach me a lesson of sorts." The leader held his hands aloft and to his sides. "Tsk-tsk. Are you able to see that you have found me unarmed?"

"That changes nothing today."

"Fine. Go on then…get your revenge. Take it if you must. As I've said before to you, child…do your worst."

Lauren gritted her teeth. She was gripping the Beretta with such force that she could feel the sweat of her palms wring out between her fingers. "The worst is coming. I lost friends today because of you."

The bald man laughed through his nostrils. "I am sorry to hear that, child. But it appears...so have I."

"You should've picked better friends." Lauren paused for a second. "I know why you chose to call me Cordelia. You had me imprisoned and wanted to hang me. And had things gone the way you'd intended, you would've been right. Prophesy fulfilled."

"Oh? Quite the confession, child. Yet the clock still ticks."

Lauren shuffle stepped to the side, making sure to keep a safe distance. "Cordelia and I have something else in common. There's a part in the play where she admits being deliberate with her actions, but not so much with her words. I take it you know the part."

"Heh—act one, scene one, page ten. So many similarities—both your lives being so tragic in essence. It must pain you to quantify that," he hissed. "I myself have been primarily the opposite for the majority of my life. My words have always held more clout than my actions, until recently, ever since my absolution."

"I get it," Lauren said. "Not everyone is capable of standing alone. Some of us need to hide behind other people and use them to fight our battles for us. Like you, for instance. You relied on Gus's small brainpan... his size and inclination to hurt people and take lives without exclusion." A pause. "That interdependence is finished, as of today."

"Oh? And why is that?"

"Gus is no longer with us. I had him put to sleep. For good."

A long pause. "Is...that so? Well, wicked one, if such is the case, you leave me with little options left over from which to choose." His body began to tremble. "I warned you...I *warned* you, before...that I wasn't in my...perfect mind."

In a flash, the baldheaded man turned, shouted, and charged at Lauren while screaming improprieties in prose.

Lauren gasped and reacted, backing away at the onset of his advance. She fired two succinct shots, one striking him in the clavicle, the other hitting him dead center mass. He shrieked in agony upon feeling the impact of the blazing hot copper-jacketed rounds piercing his skin, but the slugs failed to stop him.

Lauren fired several more times, and the shots went wild just as he ran into her. His strength, fueled by uninhibited rage, was enough to force her to the concrete floor beneath him. In seconds, his wiry hands found their way to Lauren's neck, and he began choking her.

She tried angling the Beretta between his body and hers for a point-blank shot to his midsection, but the suppressor's added length was preventing her from getting a clean shot. Lauren soon tossed the M9 away and shoved both her hands upward into Sir William's chin, attempting to force him off her, but it was no use. He was latched on to her now with the ferocity and crushing pressure of a snapping turtle, and he had no intention of letting loose.

"And never lose track of this blade," Woo Tang had said.

Lauren felt for the KA-BAR, relieved to find it was still there. Her helmet and NVDs now only a hindrance to her, she had been forced into a position where she needed to fight her attacker off without seeing him, and she could feel time was quickly running out for her. The leader's grip was so strong now, she couldn't utter a sound even if she tried.

As she extracted the knife and maneuvered it in her hand, preparing to shove it deep within her attacker's midsection, his grip on her neck went loose, and his body was jerked off her and violently away into the shadows.

Lauren gulped air, now able to inhale a breath. She reached for her helmet's chin strap and removed it, tossing it free from her head, then sat up and slid herself backward on her rear to gain distance from the attack. She could hear a vicious scuffle between two combatants occurring directly in front of her, but the room was completely devoid of light, preventing her from seeing anything.

She traded hands with the knife and reached for her flashlight, clicking it on with a button press. The beam projected outward, casting a shadow of both men on the adjacent wall, in time to see Woo Tang draw back his jingum and run it through the leader's chest. He pushed hard, forcing it in all the way to the handguard, then twisted it, perforating the bald man's heart and lungs.

The man winced and squealed in pain while trying to fight off Woo Tang's unyielding strength, attempting to extricate the sword from his body. But his struggles were fruitless. As blood seeped from his wounds, the leader, his face glazed with agony, turned to face Lauren.

He smiled at her grimly, then uttered several inaudible words with what little breath he had left. Then, dramatically, he closed his eyes, let out a final breath, and slithered to the concrete.

Woo Tang held both hands tightly on his jingum's handle and allowed it to glide from the man's chest. He snapped his NVDs upright while keeping his eyes fixed on his most recently cancelled enemy, then removed the glove from his right hand, sliding the blade between his thumb and index finger to expunge the blood and polish the blade. He wiped his fingers on his pants before returning the jingum gracefully to its scabbard.

He turned to Lauren. "Sorry I am late. I promise it will not happen again." He bolted to her, reaching for her hand, and pulled her to her feet. "Are you hurt in any way?"

Lauren shook her head and started rubbing the soreness in her neck and throat. "No, I'm good. You got here just in time. I was about ready to kill him myself." She held the KA-BAR knife aloft as proof that she had only been seconds away from using it.

Woo Tang smirked at her. "That is…comforting." He gestured to the bald man bleeding out on the floor. "If it makes you feel better, you can kill him again, if you prefer. I promise I will not tell anyone."

Lauren hung her head a moment and shook it in the negative. "I think you killed him enough for today." She sheathed the KA-BAR and reached for Woo Tang, embracing him. "I owe you."

"Call us even. This battle is over now, Lauren Russell. Same as many others before it. As such, you and I should take our leave of this place."

Lauren pulled away from him and smiled, taking one last look around before retrieving her helmet and the Beretta M9 from the floor. "I'm right behind you."

CHAPTER 30

WHEN DANIEL AND LILY SAW Lauren drawing closer, they abandoned the other children and sprinted to her with arms wide open.

Lauren barely had time to prepare herself for the tackle, much less the hugs. She knelt just as Lily ran into her and nuzzled her face into Lauren's chest. Overlapping his sister, Daniel put his arms as far as they would go around Lauren's neck while his sister simpered and cried out in joy.

"I knew you'd come back," Daniel said, pulling away with an enquiring look on his face. "Did you…"

Lauren nodded. "We got him," she said, and gave Lily a squeeze. She palmed Daniel's shoulder. "You don't have to worry about him anymore."

Lily bounced up and down with excitement. Reaching for her brother, she mouthed something into his ear again.

"Okay, I'll tell her," Daniel said, gently pushing her away. "Lily says it's okay that you're not really a superhero, because you still look like one."

Lauren smiled graciously. "Thank you, Lily. After the day I've had, that means a lot to me."

Lily pressed her lips to her brother's ear again.

"Why can't you just tell her? Sheesh," Daniel griped, then pushed her off his ear, rolling his eyes. "She says she knows what superheroes look like. She says she's seen them in real life before."

Lauren beamed. "I'll try my best to live up to the crusader standard. No guarantees, though." She reached for the siblings, pulling them in for another round of hugs just in time to see Dave Graham on the approach. "Listen, do me a favor and run along for a little while. I think my boss wants to have a chat with me."

Once Daniel and Lily moved out of earshot, Dave didn't waste any time. He moved in and glared at Lauren while rocking on his heels and giving her the most choleric look she'd ever seen. Then he muttered her name, "Janey…"

"Dave…"

A brief pause while he scanned her with sour eyes. "It's a shame about Tang's men. It goes without saying, they'll be sorely missed. But it also goes without saying, I'm pleased to see the two of you made it out of the suck." Another pause. "I take it your hostile was dealt with appropriately?"

Lauren nodded, pushing her hair away from her face.

"Very well. I heard some radio chatter 'bout a minute into the second wave…some lunatic friendly was hightailing it through the middle of the kill zone with an IR ChemLight flopping around on her back," he griped, his tone flooded with torment. "A couple of the men said they thought it looked an awful lot like you. I didn't want to believe it at first, so I had a chitchat with your spotter. It's since been confirmed." Dave positioned himself toe-to-toe with her. "Listen, I can't have any rogue elements in my unit. Everyone here has a job and a responsibility to themselves and to each other, meaning we work together or not at all, do you copy? What you did was idiotic and could've easily gotten you killed."

"I know, and I'm sorry, but—"

"No buts, no excuses," he interrupted. "You're one of the smartest young people I've ever met. Damn intelligent. I've always known you to be very bold and deliberate, capable of amazing things…but also capable of making some very imprudent decisions. The one you made today almost won you the gold medal in that category." Dave crossed his arms and leaned in. "It's probably the stupidest thing I've ever seen or heard anyone do. But in all fairness, it was also one of the bravest."

Lauren went slack-jawed. "What?"

Dave backed away with a strange contented smirk stretching across his face. "You heard me," he said. "I suppose it's pointless to be miffed with you. Had I been in your position, I would've been conflicted…and had a real hard time holding back from doing the same." He pointed to the children being cared for by his men. "This is what it's all about, Janey. This generation. Back before the world fell to pieces, they were already a posterity of lost souls and broken homes with no sense of family. Many of them impoverished, most of them undereducated, with parents too busy to worry about them, raise them properly, or even show them the love they deserve. Too much work to do, too many bills to pay, and too much of life's complications to deal with…and far too little time at home. It's a misplaced generation of forsaken young hearts left to fend for themselves. If they were lucky enough to make it out of their mother's womb, they were raised by the state, not by the two loving parental units who should've been there." He paused. "And now whatever semblance of the life they once had is gone, torn to shreds. It's a shame."

Lauren watched the children contemplatively. After a moment, and grasping just how much she had in common with them, she nodded. "You're right, it is."

Dave put all his weight on one heel and settled back into his stance. He folded his arms, his expression softening as he fell into a rare state of reflection. Lowering his head, he tilted the brim of his boonie hat in parallel with the ground. "I never really knew either of my parents. My father died when I was little, and my mother left us not long before that. They got married too young…about a year before my dad left for war. Vietnam was primed and ready to shift into high gear, and when he signed his enlistment papers, my mother couldn't hack it. She loved the partying life too much and ran off on him, only to come back when he got sent home, hoping he had some sort of bankroll to offer her. A few years, a couple of separations, and about a thousand fights later, she left him. But not after making a couple of babies, both of whom were left for my grandmother to raise."

"I never knew that," Lauren said.

"It's not common knowledge. And Kim might not want you knowing all this, so kindly exercise some statutory OPSEC," Dave said, then continued. "Our grandmother was a tough old gal. Hard as nails. A real survivor. And my grandfather was a West Point grad. I remember seeing the framed black-and-white pictures of him in uniform on the wall in their hallway. He got his captain's bars not long after he graduated, and he served in the Second World War and portions of Korea before he retired. He died not long after of some nasty disease, and I never got a chance to know him, but I've heard plenty of stories. I was told he was an honorable man. He loved his country and always made an effort to do right by others. He lived by a code, you see, and my dad wanted to be just like him." Dave peered over. "You can stop me anytime if I'm boring you."

"You've never told me anything about your past before," Lauren said. "You're not boring me at all."

Dave nodded approval. "My father nose-dived into the infantry just in time to experience the battle of Khe Sanh under Westmoreland in sixty-eight. Over seventy-seven days of complete fuckery just to protect some half-destroyed munitions base. Tet came about ten days later after Keh Sanh was hit, and the Viet Cong coordinated attacks on a hundred cities in South Vietnam, catching us with our pants down around our ankles." Dave paused. "Anyway, his platoon got pinned down pretty bad, and he had to fight his way out of a losing battle, but he rescued two fellow infantrymen in the process. He was christened a hero, sent home with a Purple Heart and a MOH, but it cost him…both of his legs. My mother didn't exactly provide him much support when he got back. She was always coming and going, and she vanished into thin air not long after Kim was born.

"Coming home from the war wasn't easy for any soldier back then, wounded or otherwise, and my dad was no different. My grandma used to tell me he'd cry a lot and talk to her sometimes about the things he'd seen and heard, the atrocities and such. She told me that saving those men was the only force keeping his pride intact. They were his brothers, and a selfless act tends to benefit a man's sense of dignity.

"Things changed rather drastically for him…when one of them died as a result of a malignant brain tumor. About a year later, the other got killed in a car crash, hit head-on by a drunk driver. After that, my dad just sort of lost himself. He hung on for as long as he could, came home to a disjointed country that hated him and despised what we were doing in southeast Asia, mostly due to misunderstandings and the war's overall lack of popularity. He got shit on by so-called peaceful protestors and labeled a baby killer, amongst other things. You've probably seen movies or documentaries about it, so you can imagine what it looked like. I know I have, only, I just can't imagine...how it must've felt.

"When my mother left, he found comfort in drugs and the bottle and wound up drinking himself to death. I don't know for certain, but he must've felt completely abandoned, by his wife, and by his country. And I imagine that was pretty damn hard to swallow. He was a man of honor, like my grandfather before him, regardless of his faults."

Dave took in a deep breath. "Sure as I stand here today, my father was a hero. He saved two men's lives in spite of himself, and he always tried to do what was right, even when he didn't know what the right move was. When in doubt, he followed that little voice inside him. He followed his heart, Janey. The same way you do." He paused, smiling at her. "Take some pride. You did good today, and I think you found your fight. You found something worth fighting for...like this country, and the republic for which it stands. Or maybe it's just for the ones who can't fight, like those children over there."

Lauren smiled and nodded as her eyes welled up. "Or maybe it's all of the above."

"Could be," Dave said. "I heard someone say before that every man in this world has to die, but not every man ever truly lives. Take a good look around you...this is why we bleed. This is why we fight. Without these kids and this generation, there is no country, there's no republic—no future worth fighting for. *This* is our future, and I'm investing in it with my life." Dave stepped closer to her and lifted Lauren's chin with his hand. "Seems to me you've made the decision to do the same."

Lauren nodded her head shamefully. "I've been so selfish," she said. "Ever since all this started, all I've been concerning myself with has been me...my family, and *my* world. I never gave any thought to anyone else or how others were being affected outside those boundaries, much less these kids. But now I know why I had to go with you. I know why I'm here, and I know why this had to happen. This...is what's left of my world. I have to do whatever I can to rebuild it."

Dave nodded. "It's *our* world—yours, mine, and theirs. You're not alone, kid. I know you were there for a while, and you probably still feel like it sometimes, but you're not anymore. You have a new, very well-armed, well-trained extended family now."

"It feels so good to hear you say that."

Dave moved several steps away, digging the toes of his boots into the ground as he walked. "Just don't go forgetting it anytime soon." He paused. "So…any idea where you want to go from here? Think it's time to head home?"

Without hesitation, Lauren shook her head and glared at him. "No way. We still have a lot of work to do."

Dave smiled. "Roger that. My back hurts just thinking about it."

Lauren ruminated a moment, then gestured to the children. "What happens to them? If my world is broken, theirs is in shambles. I know *we* have a place to go when we leave, but where do *they* go from here?"

"We do what we can for them, Janey. There's been some happy endings, and as you can imagine, we've also seen our share of sad ones. We make every attempt to reunite these kids with their parents, but this isn't the same world we used to live in, and circumstances have made that an impossibility for quite a lot of them. We reunite the ones we can. And the rest, we find…other options." Dave paused a moment. "There's some folks we know, an older couple. Met them when we liberated a small camp over near Franklin. They're two of the most generous folks I've ever met, and they own a large farm out in Pendleton County, right along the Potomac River. It's a ton of land out there, mostly field, but some forest too. They've got livestock, gardens, orchards, you name it.

"After we helped them out, they told us if we ever needed anything, they'd return the favor. So, once every month or so, we make a trip out to visit them. We've delivered a few bunches of refugees to them already and they've welcomed all of them in with open arms—even asked when we were planning on bringing more of them. I suppose they really enjoy the company." He paused, using his finger to take a quick head count. "Looks like we're about due to make another trip."

"Pendleton County, huh?"

"That's affirm."

"I've spent a few hours there."

"So I've heard," Dave remarked. "The farm is near a spot called Germany Valley, a several klicks south of Seneca Rocks. I think you'll like it. It's a prospering, well-protected area, replete with hardworking folks—lots of good guys, Janey. There's even a righteous militia there—they call themselves the Sons of the Second. They've been protecting those acres for decades, living rather primitively at that, and the collapse really didn't change much for them. Thanks to the magic Neo's been making on the radio, we've been getting to know them."

"You know, tomorrow is Christmas," Lauren said, taking in a breath. "What an incredible gift that would be for the kids, to bring them somewhere they can call home, with people around who can care for them, protect them, and maybe raise them." She paused, giggling. "Maybe we could exchange gifts. We do have our own personal Santa."

Dave nodded. "You took the words right out of my mouth."

CHAPTER 31

Pendleton County, West Virginia
Saturday, December 25th. Present day

SEVERAL MILES INTO THE TRIP after leaving Route 220 in Petersburg, the convoy passed through the long-abandoned town of Hopeville and crossed over into Pendleton County just as it started to snow.

The feathery showers of flakes had made it the first white Christmas Lauren could recall in a number of years. She had chosen to ride shotgun with Santa on this trip and had her window rolled down so she could catch snowflakes, allowing them to smack into her hand and melt into moisture immediately thereafter.

The vehicle Santa had chosen as his own was a 1977 Ford Bronco wagon, in amply distinct baby blue, the same one Lauren had used to seat herself while she'd gorged on the first filling meal she'd had in days. It was a true, well-maintained, vintage automobile, having no electronics or computerized anything to speak of. As such, it had remained undamaged by the effects of the electromagnetic pulse that had sent so many modern models to their final resting places.

From the ignition on the steering column dangled a set of keys and a photo keychain bearing a snapshot of a man with silvery hair standing with a woman who appeared to be his wife. A picnic table sat in the background and was covered in paper plates littered with food. The man was wearing a uniform with a chrome badge pinned to it, while his wife wore a simple sundress with a flowery print and had on a pair of glasses, the frames of which coordinated well with her dress. Both were smiling like they had been two of the happiest people on earth, and while Lauren considered the photo, she wondered what their fate might have been.

Santa reached for the climate-control knobs and fiddled with them. "Miss Jane, would you kindly roll that window up? I'm on the verge of freezing my nuts off."

Lauren giggled.

"Hey, that shit's not funny," Santa said, squinting his eye at her. "When we get to the farm, I'm going to get underneath the hood and see why this heat ain't worth working worth a damn. No way I'm putting up with this all winter."

Lauren pulled her arm inside and reached for the handle to roll the window up. "The last Santa I spoke with told me he liked the cold…you know, being from the North Pole and all."

Santa eyeballed her from his peripheral. "That Santa sure as hell wasn't me. I grew up in gulf coast Florida near Clearwater. One of these days, I'm taking my happy ass back there. I don't know how anybody deals with the weather at this latitude."

Lauren shrugged and wiped the wetness from her hand on her pant leg. "You might as well get used to it. Winter just started. It's only going to get colder."

Santa sighed. "Guess I'll have a talk with Dave, then. I might have to book a flight and head south for the winter."

"Really? And leave me here all by my lonesome?"

"Hell no. You'd go with me…if you wanted to go, that is. I could use a good sidekick down there. We could beach every day and work on our tans. And you could keep me out of trouble."

Lauren sniggered. "That's a full-time job."

"Darlin', you ain't shittin'."

The convoy continued for several miles along the slippery, untreated road, which was becoming more precarious by the minute as the frozen precipitation continued to fall at an enhanced rate. At times, the squalls would blow across the road under the power of gale-force winds, spawning whiteout conditions and bringing the overall speed of the convoy to a crawl.

Upon reaching a sign on the left that read 'Little Germany Farms and Orchard', the convoy turned onto a narrow gravel driveway while making cavernous track marks in the snow. They passed through an open gate and continued along the lane through a dense apple orchard until reaching the end of the driveway, stopping at a large brick colonial-era farmhouse with a tin roof and a massive red-painted barn out back.

There were fields as far as one could see on either side and behind the house. Beyond the field in the rear was a tree line marking the boundary where the Potomac River meandered through the property. The entire farm shared a westward-facing backdrop with North Fork Mountain and was enclosed by the Monongahela National Forest on all its flanks.

Santa shut the Bronco's engine off, and Lauren hopped out so she could get a feel for her surroundings. It didn't take any time at all for the snow to cover her clothing and hair.

The bearded one got out and popped the hood on the truck, shutting his door behind him. "The mister and missus should be out to greet us before long," Santa said. "It never takes them more than a few minutes, even when they're up to their ears in work, which is most times."

Lauren stepped to the front of the truck and turned to him, a curious look adorning her face. "Where is everyone else? The place looks vacant."

Santa shrugged. "I don't know. It's Christmas. They could be in the house or in that barn over there or out in the fields somewhere." He pointed over the hood of the truck to where a row of olive green military surplus tents had been set up in the field not far away. "That's where the kids have been staying."

Lauren's eyes followed his gesture to the tents, all of which had chimneys busily puffing out wood smoke from their respective tents' apexes.

A party comprised of Dave Graham, Woo Tang, Sanchez, and a few others approached from behind. As they marched by through the blanketing snow, Dave tapped Lauren on the shoulder. "Come on, walk with us. I want you to meet these fine folks."

Lauren followed the group across the snow-covered grass and walkway to the front porch of the farmhouse. She could hear a dog's rowdy bark inside, signaling their approach. When they reached the first step, the barking switched to a mixture of whining and heavy panting. The front door drew inward, the storm door was thrust ajar as if unlatched, and a medium-sized brown retriever took off like a shot through the entryway and lunged at the group of visitors, his tail wagging with delight.

The dog tackled Dave first, jumped on Woo Tang, licked Sanchez's hands, then bolted past Lauren in the direction of the convoy.

An elderly man made his way briskly to the porch, yelling, "Dammit, Cyrus! Get back in here, crazy mutt!"

Lauren didn't hesitate. She turned and gave chase. "I'll get him."

The old man squinted and neared the edge of the porch. "Thank you kindly." He had on a pair of glasses with paper-thin lenses that hung on the tip of his nose, and was wearing well-worn, soiled coveralls that draped over a pair of scuffed-up, marred hiking boots. Underneath a green John Deere brand baseball cap, his face displayed a toothy grin, bushy eyebrows, and plenty of wrinkles. "Well…what do we have here?" he asked in a brisk, youthful-sounding voice. "Visitors? On Christmas? At this hour?"

Dave ascended the stairway to the porch and strode to him with an outstretched hand. "We were in the neighborhood. Figured you could use the company."

"That so?" The old man took Dave's hand. "Well, I suppose today is as good as any other day. Merry Christmas to you."

"Thank you. Merry Christmas to you and yours as well."

The older man angled his hat backward after bidding identical greetings to the others. "The militia boys didn't give y'all any trouble on the way in, did they?"

Dave squinted. "I was meaning to ask you about that. We didn't see any sign of them. Did you give them the day off or something?"

The old man placed his hands on his hips and chuckled. "I declare—they probably saw the snow coming and said heck with it. They've been working hard lately, even more so than usual. There's been a few skirmishes in the past week or so, nothing too awfully precarious. No casualties, thank the good Lord. But still enough to get our hearts pounding. Especially my better half's."

Dave nodded his head and tensed. "Barring what the weather decides to do, we'll be hanging around for a few days, so if there's anything we can do to help out while we're here, just let us know. And if you wouldn't mind letting the Sons know we're here, I'd appreciate it. I don't want any misunderstandings."

The elderly man nodded his head. "No problem at all. I'll put the word out. You gentlemen make yourselves at home. Ruthie and the girls have a big Christmas dinner planned this evening with all the trimmings, or at least as many of them as we can muster. You're all welcome at our table, Dave, you know that." He paused, casting a stare at the convoy parked in his driveway. "I take it you brought me another load of expats?"

"That is affirmative."

"What's the head count this time?"

Dave gave him the figure.

"I see," the old man said, licking his teeth. "That's quite a few more mouths to feed." He paused. "But each mouth comes with two hands we can use around the farm."

"I apologize for the timing. If I had my choice, I would've picked any other day," Dave remarked.

"David Graham, as I've told you before, it's not a problem. You'll always have a place here. You bestowed upon us something awful special…a debt that can never be repaid. You and your men put your lives on the line for us. There's no greater sacrifice." He paused. "So enough jawin'. Let's get those kids inside and warm 'em up. I just put a fresh load of wood in the stove, and it's pipin' hot."

After chasing the rambunctious dog all the way to the final vehicle in the convoy, Lauren caught up with him at the point he decided to take a dive and roll around in a snowdrift. She belly-flopped beside him, and he jumped on top of her, noticing he had a new playmate.

The animal put his pinkish nose in Lauren's face and pushed her backward, then proceeded to lick every inch of her face and neck while he made gentle, playful growls.

"Oh, boy," Lauren squealed, pushing his face away. "You're a mess! But you're so pretty, aren't you? Sorry, I mean handsome." She sat up and rubbed his coarse brown fur, pulling on his face and ears while he offered her his paws. "Yes, you are. Shiny teeth, too. And you have the softest furry ears I've ever felt."

Lauren rose and called to him, then ran back to the farmhouse, the dog following her through the snow in a full-on gallop.

Once they reached the porch, the animal ran up the stairs and jumped on his master. The old man pulled a treat from his pocket and coerced him indoors with it. "Sorry about that…he's only about a year old, so he's just as full of stupid as he is energy. I appreciate you goin' and gettin' him."

Lauren examined the old man curiously. Since the point he'd opened his mouth and began to speak, she knew she'd heard his voice before. Watching his movements and gesticulations, she started to recognize him.

As the elderly man's eyes turned and intercepted her gaze, they grew wide with astonishment, and that was when Lauren knew without a doubt who he was, because she could see that he recognized her, too.

Dave held out an open hand. "Lauren, I want you to meet—"

"Bernie," Lauren blurted out. "It's Bernie, isn't it?"

The old man nodded after a moment as his mouth fell open, displaying some missing teeth. His wrinkly eyes welled up. "That's right. Good gracious me…I can't believe my eyes right now. I mean, how can this possibly be? This is just…it's just too hard to believe." He held out a trembling hand to her. "Lauren…"

Lauren smiled and nodded her head while reaching out to shake Bernie's hand. "Yeah. That's me."

The old man's eyes filled with tears. "Well, I'll be damned. I will be *damned*. Wait until Ruth sees who came to visit us on Christmas."

While looking back and forth between the two, Dave said, "I take it the two of you have met before?"

Both Bernie and Lauren nodded.

"A couple of years ago," Lauren explained. "We met on a backpacking trip in Dolly Sods."

Bernie held up a finger to Lauren. "Hang on a second, sweetie—just wait right there. Let me go grab Ruthie. She's not gonna believe this."

Lauren watched Bernie disappear back into the house, the storm door smacking the frame behind him. Through the faded, blemished screen, she could see young people milling about busily inside.

A moment later, a frail older woman wearing an apron poked her head into the door's frame. Her hair was as white as the snow falling outside and was pulled back tightly into a bun. She pushed the door open and stepped outside while wiping her hands on a kitchen towel. "Oh, my word," Ruth said. "I thought the old fart was pulling my leg. It really is you, isn't it?" She reached for Lauren and pulled her in for a hug that Lauren reciprocated. "My goodness, child. What on earth brings you to these parts? You're not in any trouble, are you? Please tell me you're doing okay."

Lauren nodded her affirmation while being embraced by Ruth's strong, yet thin, sinewy arms. "I'm alive. Things have been rough, but I'm here now and amongst friends, and I'm thankful for that."

"Well, praise God. Thank you, Jesus." Ruth pulled away, wiping away thin tears. "I haven't the faintest idea how you managed to find us after all this time, but welcome to the farm and to our home. Oh... good heavens...I'm sorry. Merry Christmas to you, Lauren. It's so good to see you again."

Lauren smiled, feeling her sentiments catch up with her level of surprise. "Merry Christmas. It's good to see you, too, you and Bernie. Who am I kidding—it's taking my breath away right now. When Dave told me about this place...a farm in Pendleton County, I never could've imagined any of this."

Ruth nodded. "It's a small world. My daddy always told me that... that's why he also told me to treat people the way I wanted to be treated, because you never know when you might run into them again." She placed her leathery, callused palm onto Lauren's icy cheek. "You are still so beautiful. Grown up a little bit, though, haven't you? I can see it in your face and in those splendid chestnut eyes of yours. You look like you've matured...maybe even become a woman, since the last time we saw you?" Ruth winked at her.

Lauren grinned sheepishly. "Maybe."

Bernie interrupted them, reaching for his wife's shoulder. "Don't be meddlesome, Ruthie. And don't hog all her time, neither. She just got here. Let's get them settled in before we start in on them. Dave said he brought us a lot more mouths to feed for Christmas dinner tonight, so we're gonna need all hands on deck."

"Slave driver," Ruth jeered.

Bernie pursed his lips. "And then some. I wouldn't be if you'd stop testin' my patience..."

"Mind if I help?" Lauren asked, letting a giggle slip out.

"Not in the least," replied Ruth. "We need all the help we can get." She opened the storm door and gestured for Lauren to step inside and that she would follow. "After you, dear. The kitchen is at the end of the hallway, past the living room on the left and the dining room on the right. It's a big house, but don't worry, I won't let you get lost."

Lauren was impressed by the abundance of the dinner Bernie and Ruth had been able to provide their newfound extended family, which included at least seventy young people of all ages, along with a large segment of Dave's unit. Despite the better part of the country being immersed in trying times, they had followed through with a plan and had not only survived the tribulations, but were thriving in the face of them.

Lauren had always known that Bernie and Ruth were good-hearted, genuine people. She'd gotten a good feeling from them on the day she'd encountered them, and she knew that feeling was one shared by her father, someone who had been capable of reading people and deciphering human nature better than anyone Lauren had ever known.

Despite having an overabundance of mouths to feed, everyone had a turn at a seat somewhere in the house and was able to enjoy a larger-than-average plate of food, which included proteins like venison, wild turkey, grouse, and fish, and vegetables like corn, cabbage, carrots, green beans, and brussels sprouts. The options available to them in this day and age baffled Lauren, especially since the majority of the foods she'd been eating as of late were of the dehydrated, freeze-dried, and ready-to-eat variety. Everything served for Christmas dinner in Bernie and Ruth's home was fresh, having been raised in a pasture, grown from a garden, or caught in a river, and she considered herself extremely blessed for being able to partake of it.

After dinner was over and the younger audience made their way elsewhere to frolic, Bernie offered glasses of homemade sour mash from his private stock to anyone he considered old enough, bearing in mind that the laws regarding alcohol consumption were no longer in effect.

Not long after, and not wanting to be outshined, Santa disappeared to his truck and brought some of his own inside, adding it to the mix. While the children and younger attendees played games, sang, took turns playing Ruth's piano with Dave, and enjoyed multiple snowball battles outside, the older generations enjoyed an evening of fellowship, reflection, and reprieve. A well-deserved one.

Lauren had been offered a drink by both Bernie and Santa, but she wasn't feeling it today. Despondency had taken her over, and she was beginning to feel dismal and glum. Immersed in deep thought, she began feeling homesick. She hated being so far from home, so far from the ones she loved on Christmas.

In an effort to pacify her thoughts for a while, Lauren took her leave of the adults and wandered outside to join the children, soon finding herself wrangled into several intense snowball fights. She chose to join the team that Daniel and Lily had been playing on, which also happened to be the team with the scrawniest players in the lot. Lauren couldn't help but root for the underdog, and with her help, the team pummeled their opponents a handful of times.

Just over a foot of powdery snow was caked on the ground, and it just kept coming with no end in sight. There was no technology available, no forecaster to offer advice, no radar indicating how much was on the way or when it would stop. The only thing anyone could do now was sit back, relax, and find the best way to enjoy it.

The snowball battles were competitive and exhausting, and it wasn't long before Lauren reached the point of feeling beleaguered. She excused herself amidst jeers, challenging catcalls, and chants begging her to return. She kindly refused, stressing the need to rest and be alone for a while.

Lauren bundled up tightly in a new Arc'teryx parka that Santa had found for her and went for a walk along the riverbank, trying her best not to allow her ever-increasing sadness to get the better of her.

The sun had set behind the four-thousand-foot-tall Alleghenies to her west hours ago, and nearly all natural light had disappeared, making the use of a flashlight a necessity. The whiteout conditions from the heavy snowfall only made seeing all the more difficult. The snow heartlessly reflected her flashlight's beam back into her eyes like a mirror, and at times, the showers fell in waves so thick, it was like walking through a wall.

She trudged through the piles of drifting snow while feeling it cake onto her pant legs and through the tops of her boots. She took careful steps, but halted occasionally to look up and catch the frigid snowflakes on her tongue.

Once Lauren was far enough away that she couldn't hear the chants and cackles of the children playing and the sound of the river's current became the only noise lurid enough to overcome the ambience, everything began hitting her all at once.

The precariousness of her life in the valley, and how hard it had become to protect herself and the ones she loved. The heinous acts of government agencies supposedly tasked with protecting people like her. People she knew, including one of her closest friends, becoming deathly ill from poisoning, of all things. Her decision to leave John and her family behind and encountering the most brutal of her enemies to date. Being captured, only to escape, and be captured again and imprisoned. The sensation of hopelessness and the feeling that she was going to die.

She recalled the look on Woo Tang's face when he saw her, and the feeling she got upon realizing they were saved. How unnerving it had been to talk to Dave Graham again for the first time in forever, and having to explain everything to him. The heart-rending feeling she got upon learning about the children…and the look on Christian's face when she told him she wasn't going home.

Her considerations crashed in on her all at once, like the storm surge of a hurricane slamming into a shoreline. The emotional fire inside her that had been burning for as long as she could recollect was smothered, and consumed by a raging flood of emotion, and Lauren just broke down. It couldn't be helped.

Lauren cried, nearly hysterically at first. She looked to the sky in desperation while the merciless snow fell in swathes, sticking to her face, nose, and lashes. She exhaled moist breaths into the dry air as her reflections simply devoured her. "I'm sorry," she whimpered under her breath. "I'm sorry I'm so far away. I'm sorry I didn't come home, and I know I shouldn't be here right now. I should be there…in the valley with all of you, where I'm happy, where I'm warm, and where I'm loved. I'm such an idiot…I don't know why I do the things I do sometimes."

Lauren wiped a mixture of tears and snow melt from her face. "I'm sorry for hurting all of you—I never meant for any of this to happen. I miss you, Mom, and I'm sorry I make things so hard for you. It's never been my intention. You've become so strong since all this started, since Dad's been gone, and I know I've never told you before, but I am *so* proud to call you my mother. You told me one time that I was irreplaceable, and you have no idea how hard it hit me. I need you to know I feel the same way about you. And I love you to the moon and back."

Lauren took in a deep breath and rubbed her eyes as more tears flowed in, replacing those wiped away. "And Grace, jeez…you can be such a righteous pain in my ass, and you're a freakin' bull in a china closet sometimes. I swear, you could probably screw up a two-car funeral if you tried…but you know something? You are, by and far, the most beautiful person I know, inside and out. You always find ways to surprise me and make me laugh, and you're so mysteriously strong in all the ways I'm not. I'm lucky…so lucky to have you as my sister."

Lauren hesitated. She sniffled and coughed as her sobbing became tumultuous. "And…John. Oh God, John, what have I done? I left you all alone…this isn't how I wanted things to be between us. I never wanted to push you away or separate myself from you. I have to find a way to make all of this up to you, somehow, and I promise…I will. I'll fix us. I'll fix everything when I get back. I love you with everything I am. Dammit—I love *all* of you. I pray that all of you are well…and everything is getting back to normal finally. I miss you all. And I'm just…I'm just really sorry."

Her throat drying up, Lauren tried hard to fight away the remainder of her tears. It was as sorrowful and nostalgic as she had felt in months, and now, she was a hundred road miles from home on Christmas Day, spending time with strangers, a group of people she felt she hardly knew. "You're such a horrible person, Lauren," she chided. "A class act. A bona fide magnificent, fucking tragedy."

"Who are you talking to out here all by yourself?" an older man's voice called out from behind her.

Sniffling, Lauren jerked her body around. While one hand fell instinctively to the Glock holstered on her thigh, she aimed her flashlight to find Bernie's face amidst the whitewash of heavily falling snow. Cyrus the Labrador was at his side, and once he saw Lauren, he bounded through the snow and jumped on her.

She grabbed his ears and petted him, brushing the snow from his head. "I wasn't talking to anyone."

"Oh, okay. Heard Cyrus whining about something…so I followed him and thought I heard somebody crying. I didn't mean to intrude, even though I tend to do it more by accident lately than anything else."

"It's okay. Really…you didn't do anything wrong," Lauren said, going nose to nose with Bernie's dog.

"He botherin' you?"

Lauren shook her head. "No…no way. He's amazing."

"You're sure? I know he can be a pest," Bernie said. "Me and that mutt got a lot in common…we both forget where we're at sometimes. Thank God he's got a good sense of direction, because I sure as thunder don't. Sometimes I forget where I was headed, even where I was coming from. The better half says I got signs of dementia, but like I keep trying to tell her, last time I checked, she didn't have a degree in neurology. I prefer to call it…*old-timer's*. It's kind of a play on words, you see. Sounds like Alzheimer's, but it's old-timer's instead. I'm not sure if I can claim it or not though, because damned if I can remember whether or not I made it up myself." He paused, scratching at his temple. "See? Must be the old-timer's."

Lauren chuckled inwardly through her sorrow, which seemed to fade away with each lick of Cyrus's soppy tongue. "That's funny…I suppose, and yes, I'm sure. You're no bother to me, and neither is this puppy of yours."

Bernie sucked on his teeth and nodded. "Okay. I guess you were talking to yourself out here, or maybe praying…either one, or neither, it's all fine, well, and good. We don't discriminate against anyone's beliefs around here."

"I was just thinking out loud," Lauren said. "I wasn't praying, even though I probably should. It's been years since I prayed."

Bernie smirked. "It does a body good, you know—prayer, that is. Believe it or not, the better half and me have been doing quite a lot of it as of late. After we lost power a while back, seemed like the right thing to start doin', you know?"

Lauren smiled warmly at him. "I tend to think out loud when I'm alone. I don't know, maybe God considers it prayer in some way."

"Young lady, you might be onto something," Bernie said. "He's always listening." The old man took a few steps closer, the dimness of his flashlight beam reflecting off the snow. He picked up on the redness in Lauren's swollen eyes. "I'll be doggone. You *have* been crying."

Lauren hesitated, turning her head away. She sighed. "Yeah. I guess I have," she said, almost in a whimper.

"What on earth for? Something you ate didn't agree with you?"

Lauren chuckled through her nose. "No, it's not that. Dinner was remarkable. Best I've had in a long time." She paused. "It's just that it's Christmas…and I miss my family. I could've gone home to them a few weeks back and I didn't. I decided, instead, to go with Dave and his crew."

"Why did you do that for?"

She shrugged her shoulders. "I guess there was something inside me I needed to figure out."

Bernie squinted and leaned over, an inquisitive look on his face. "You don't say? Did you get it all taken care of?"

Lauren nodded. "Yeah. Yeah, I think so."

"Well, that might explain the melancholy, then," Bernie said. "It's easy to hold back on what really matters when you got other things blocking the road your emotions want to take. Life's funny like that sometimes." Bernie acted like he was going to walk away, but stopped after taking a couple of steps. "Lauren, I got a question hanging on the edge of my thoughts that I've been meaning to ask you, but I don't want to pry, and I don't want to bother you about it. But it's something that's been on my mind since you got here today."

Lauren sniffled and looked to him with interest. "You can ask me anything you want. Especially after that dinner." She poked at her stomach.

Bernie nodded, and his mouth unbolted, exposing his toothy grin. "I'm very glad you enjoyed it. We don't get to have those kinds of spreads too often, but when we do, we pull out all the stops. Adds normalcy to the mix. And it's good to feel normal every once in a blue moon." He paused, looking away a moment. "Now, like I said, I don't mean to pry, but I'm a curious person by nature, and when I see something that ain't quite right, I tend to ponder it until I lose sleep."

"I'm the same way."

Bernie scratched his head. "Well, you see—I'm confused. You mentioned a minute ago that you missed your family…and I've been wondering why you showed up at my doorstep today with Lieutenant Graham and his soldiers, of all people. Where is your dad and the rest of your family, Lauren?"

Lauren glared at him sharply. She was growing tired of offering explanations and answering questions about her father, but she knew, just like so many others, it wasn't his fault for asking. "My mom and my sister and my boyfriend, John, and his family…and pretty much everyone I know and care about are all back in Trout Run Valley, near Wardensville. We moved there a few months after the collapse when some really bad things happened in our neighborhood. As luck would have it, though, we've had to fight to keep everything and to stay alive, even after our move. Things have been getting progressively worse for us ever since, and it reached a point a few weeks ago that if it weren't for Dave and his crew, you wouldn't be talking to me today."

Bernie pursed his lips as a look of trepidation washed over him. He folded his arms across his chest and rocked on his heels in the snow while it continued to pile around his legs. "I see," he said. "You've been through a lot. I'm sorry to hear of it. How's your dad been handling all this?"

"I wish I knew. He...never made it home."

"He never made it home? What exactly does that mean? Where was he when the stuff hit the fan?"

Lauren shuddered a bit, both at the chill in the air and the bitterness in Bernie's inquiry. "At work. In the city."

Bernie cocked his head. "Where? The District? Washington?"

"Yeah..."

"In that federal building near the White House?"

"What? What federal building?" Lauren quizzed, her face tightening.

"The one he *told* us about."

"*What?*"

"'Deed he did. Last time we spoke, he gave us the scoop," Bernie explained. "Said he'd be working in some federal building. Department of State, methinks...two blocks away from the White House—the president's residence. Seemed awfully concerned...told us he had a plan, though. He had everything worked out if something were to happen, and proposals laid out to get himself back home even if his car didn't work."

Lauren rocked her head back and forth as if trying to awaken herself from a dream. "I'm sorry...now I'm the one who's confused. This isn't making any sense."

Bernie slapped his hip. "Lord Jesus, I'm sorry, sweetie. Damn this old-timer's. I just assumed you knew."

"You assumed I knew what?"

"I assumed you knew about the plan."

Lauren's eyes narrowed. "What plan?"

Bernie's features softened, and the genuine smile Lauren had seen him offer her and her father on the day they had first crossed paths extended across his face. "His plan to keep you safe, dear. His plan to protect you and your family in the event something unforeseen came to pass."

Lauren didn't say anything. She could feel her pulse quicken as her mind raced through the possibilities. She felt like she had somehow been betrayed, like she'd missed out on something somewhere along the way. What did all this mean? She wanted to know more. She needed to know everything.

Bernie continued. "I don't know all the details, of course. I just know that he had us planning for something—something real big. Something your father had a premonition about…and he just *knew* was on the horizon." He paused. "Ruthie and I came to that same conclusion a long time ago ourselves. As such, we started making our own plans way back when. I'm sorry about this, Lauren. This wasn't how I envisioned this conversation was going to go. I can tell I've made you feel uncomfortable, and that wasn't my intention."

Lauren's face contorted as she brushed the caking snow from her shoulders. "Uncomfortable doesn't describe half of what I'm feeling right now."

"Want me to go on? Or stifle myself and leave you be?"

"No!" Lauren snapped. "By all means, go on."

"Okay. Well, this whole thing just sort of fell together before our eyes," Bernie began. "I suppose it might've been the mention of the farm that caught his attention. Maybe it was the valley or the river, or the fact we're far enough west and away from population that did it, not exactly sure. But we exchanged information and met back at Dolly Sods on a Sunday and had quite the conversation over some tasty chai tea he brought along. Then we left and drove down to a little mom-and-pop café not far down the road and had coffee. Your dad bought us lunch…grilled cheese, from what I recall, and we had ourselves a grand conversation…found out we were the same type of people. The like-minded type."

Lauren squinted. "Like-minded?"

Bernie nodded. "Yes, ma'am. Like-minded. Folks able to think for themselves and read between the lines. Good-hearted and genuine, who share an understanding with one another so they can lean on each other if and when hard times come around...if you catch my meaning."

Bernie pushed through the snow and put his hand on Lauren's shoulder. He could see that she had become exasperated and tried thinking of ways to lighten the mood a little. Then it dawned on him. "Part of your dad's plan was coming here eventually. In fact, he brought some things here, quite a bunch of stuff, actually. For you and your family. We set aside a spot in the barn just for it."

Lauren perked up slightly, but still looked perplexed.

Bernie scratched his temple again. He removed his cap and smacked it on his leg, clearing off the snow. "We didn't ask him what he brought, even though he insisted on it. Called it full disclosure. I told him a handshake was fine, and it wasn't a real estate deal, but that didn't matter to him. He didn't want to put us out in any way. Your dad is something else, I tell you. I think he wanted us to know the contents of all them boxes and crates so Ruthie and I could use it for ourselves if something happened and y'all never made it, even though we never would've. We're not those type of folks." He paused, patting his leg for Cyrus to come to him. "Want to see for yourself? You could pretend it's like opening gifts....it *is* Christmas."

Lauren sniffled a few times and wiped her nose. "I do. But only if you don't mind."

"Sweetheart, it's your stuff, not mine. Your father made arrangements with us to keep it here because he wanted options for his family for the future. And somehow you made it here today, and darn near as I can figure, the future he was planning for has somehow become our present." Bernie shifted to the side and held his hand out to Lauren, motioning her to follow him. "Come on. Let's you and I get out of this weather before we get buried alive in it. It'd be a shame to have that etched on my grave."

Lauren followed the old man through two sets of boot prints, which the snow had already halfway refilled. They travelled back toward the house along the riverbank while Bernie used his flashlight intermittently to light their way.

At the point they'd almost reached the house, they turned right and walked to the barn. There, Bernie slipped on his leather gloves and, with a bit of effort, slid open the barn door. They stepped inside, their eyes met only by vast darkness, and noses met by the smell of hay, feed corn, and manure.

"That's it over there," Bernie said, pointing his flashlight's beam to a stable in the corner, its upper and lower half doors closed and locked. "We had a couple horses living in them a while back, but they got too expensive for us to keep up with. We sure do miss them, though. The stable with all your dad's stuff in it belonged to my thoroughbred, Bart. Ruthie had a mare in the one beside his. If memory serves me correctly, her name was Chicory, or something like that. Then again, chicory might've been her favorite snack."

Lauren looked at the old man strangely, then strolled away from him and up to the stable. She reached for the hasp on the upper door and slid it across while it creaked loudly at her, then did the same with the lower door's hasp. She pulled the upper door open, then peered inside the stable at several towering stacks of boxes and tubs lining the wall. "Oh my God," she muttered as her eyes studied the interior. She gestured to a rectangular metal box nearly as tall as her. "Is that a gun safe?"

Bernie inched his way up to the stable beside Lauren. "Indeed, it is. My hernia starts acting up just looking at that damn thing. Your dad brought it up here on a Saturday, summer before last, I think. I told him he was plum crazy, and if it weren't for the help he'd brought with him, we would've never gotten that behemoth off the truck."

Lauren glanced over at Bernie, who was now picking his teeth with a toothpick. "He brought someone with him?"

"Yep. A fella about the same age, or thereabouts. Real nice guy. I think his name was Norbert, or Nolan—"

Lauren smiled. "Norman."

Bernie snapped his fingers. "That's it. Norman. I never forget a name or a face. Yep, between the three of us, we wrangled that beast off the truck and onto a dolly, then rolled her on over to where she sits to this day."

Lauren beamed cheerfully now, on the outside as well as in. Before Bernie had showed up tonight, she had felt so alone, so far away from home, surrounded by people she didn't truly know. And now she was finding out things she hadn't known about—that her father had been developing a relationship with Bernie and Ruth and making plans with them for the future existence of his family. And he'd even brought Norman along for the ride at some point. It truly was a small world.

Lauren pointed at the safe. "Any idea what's in it?"

Bernie tilted his head and shrugged. "Guns, I imagine," he joked. "Being completely forthwith, as far as I know, the damn thing's empty." He peered over at Lauren with a sly grin and winked at her again. "But isn't that what I'm supposed to say? Hell, the better half and I lost all our guns in a tragic boating accident. What a catastrophe."

Lauren giggled. It wasn't the first time she'd heard that line before. "This is surreal. And a welcome surprise. I didn't mean to sound unappreciative earlier, and I'm sorry if I came across that way. I just didn't know what was going on."

"Darlin', you need not apologize to me. I know you've been through hell. And I can't imagine what it must feel like for you to not know where your dad is. I do pray you find each other someday soon." A pause. "It's been my experience, when two or more join in prayer, the Lord answers. Just food for thought."

Lauren nodded, closing her eyes a moment. "I'll remember that."

"I know you will. For now, though, I'm gonna head inside and give you a little privacy." Bernie lit up a wall with his flashlight and reached for a lantern hanging on a hook nearby. Lifting the globe slightly, he lit the wick with a match, adjusted it for adequate brightness, and handed it to Lauren. "There's enough fuel in that thing to run it for about an hour or so. Just be careful with it...don't drop it, or anything. It'll give you enough light to see but if you drop it, we'll all have more light than we'll know what to do with." He paused. "Now, get in there and have yourself a look around. I hope you find something that helps you complete the puzzle." He headed off to the barn door and stepped outside, pulling it to within a crack of being closed. "Ruthie set up a room for you upstairs in the house. It'll be yours as long as you stay, and stay as long as you like. I'll see you at the breakfast table in the morning. Merry Christmas to you, Lauren."

Lauren reached for the lower door of the stable and opened it, taking a step in. She closed the door behind her and turned around, leaning her arms over it, and sent a smile in Bernie's direction. "Merry Christmas to you, too, and Ruth also. And thank you."

Just before Bernie pushed the door closed, he said, "Lauren...no one knows the future, not a single soul on this earth. The only one who knows what's going to happen from day to day is the big man upstairs.

Now, I don't have the foggiest idea where your dad is, or what he's doing, or why it's taking him so long to come around and show his face, but I'm telling you, he's out there somewhere. For what it's worth, I believe he's still alive, and he's still trying to make it back to you. So hold on tight to your hope, and don't give up on him. Because I guarantee he hasn't given up on you—not for a single second. No father who loves his daughter as much as your dad loves you would *ever* give up on her. Trust me on that. I know from experience."

EPILOGUE

A LATE AFTERNOON SEVERE THUNDERSTORM HAD gusted through Winchester from the west and could now be heard rumbling its way over the Blue Ridge Mountains, heading for Northern Virginia underneath a towering, churning anvil-shaped supercell.

In its wake, portions of town and surrounding neighborhoods had been left without commercial power, and the tempest had left behind a sticky, tropical feeling in the air. As the sun breached the waning cloud cover, the ambient temperature, which had dropped several degrees during the deluge, beelined swiftly upward to the sweltering summer norm, while residual moisture could be seen evaporating from the paved roads and driveways.

Alan Russell stepped out the front door and took a moment to study the storm's aftermath. Michelle and Lauren moved past him to the car, leaving him by his lonesome.

He tapped his smartphone, bringing the screen to life. "I take it there's no way to convince you two to stay?" Alan asked. "The last text I got said this one might last a while. I can get the generator going; that'll get things back to normal for you…posthaste."

"Alan, no," Michelle replied in refusal, her back turned to him. "Every time there's a power outage, you play this…game, and we usually play along with you. But right now, your daughter and I just want to get out of the house for a change of pace."

"Sure. Just like everyone else in the world when the power goes out. No one can stand being home for more than a few minutes anymore when the grid goes down. Imagine if it lasted a day…or a week or—"

"Dad, can you not be *that* person right now?" Lauren poked, cutting him short. "Please?"

"What person?"

"Just get in the car, Alan," said Michelle.

A full minute passed before Alan surrendered. He locked the door behind him, muttered a few choice words under his breath, and dragged his feet through the muggy air to the car.

Once inside, he was met with an even hotter, drier air mass, superheated by the unrelenting summer sun. "I really need to buy one of those damn sun shades for the windshield." He pressed the engine start button and turned the air conditioner on full blast. "I'm not sure how much help it would be on a day like today, but it has to be better than this."

Michelle snapped her seat belt in place. "Well, dear, it's no different than all the other things you tend to talk about incessantly and not actually *do*. Maybe if you stopped procrastinating for once, you could actually make it happen."

"Maybe I will, then."

"No, you won't," Lauren called from the backseat while tugging at her shirt collar. "Some things never change, Dad. You'd be better off sticking with a simpler option…like leaving the windows down."

"Sure. Ventilation works great when abetted by a thunderstorm." Alan shifted the car into reverse and slowly backed down the driveway, choosing to utilize the vehicle's rear camera. He typically preferred to look out the back window per the method he'd been taught when he learned to drive, only he didn't aspire to see the patronizing look on his daughter's face. "I love how you two always seem to know the right things to say to keep me motivated."

Michelle chuckled, facing Lauren. "Can you hear the gears turning? I can guarantee you, the moment we get to the mall, your dad will have his phone out ordering a sunshade on Amazon."

Alan peered over to his wife. "Why the jokes, Momma? I'm considering doing it right now. I could have Alexa order it for me while I drive."

The small talk and razzing continued while Alan piloted the car across town. After fighting his way through several sets of powerless traffic lights rendered inoperable by the storm, he pulled in to the mall parking lot, finding it teeming with other drivers on the hunt for places to park. "Guess that means the mall has power."

Michelle's face showed signs of enthusiasm. "Perfect. And that means Victoria's Secret is open."

"Is that sale still on, Mom?"

"Sure is, toots. Till tomorrow, I think."

Lauren nodded approval. "I'm going to check it out, then. I'm in dire need of some new bras...the ones I have are getting too tight."

"Jesus Christ," Alan cursed with a scowl. "I should've just let the two of you go alone."

Michelle patted him on the thigh. "Just park the car...honey."

Alan navigated through the swarm of impatient drivers, soon coming across a parking space not too far from an entrance. The family then gathered their things and headed into the building.

Once inside, Michelle excused herself first, as she usually preferred to shop alone, never wanting to have anyone wait on her. She was a finicky shopper, preferred taking her time, and it typically made her feel overly self-conscious knowing others were waiting around while she was on task.

Alan gave his wife a hug, kissed her on the cheek, and told her to text him if she needed anything.

"Where will you guys be?" Michelle asked. "I shouldn't take too long, but you never know with me."

Alan looked to Lauren, and she returned his gaze with a shrug. "Anywhere you want to go in particular, L? Other than Victoria's Secret?"

Lauren giggled. "I can go there with Mom after she gets back. I won't torture you."

"Okay, I guess we'll head down to the food court area and wait for you there," Alan said. "Maybe we can play a game or two at the arcade while we're waiting."

Michelle tilted her head to the side, giving him a funny look. "You two stay out of trouble."

While strolling along in the opposite direction his wife had gone, every so often Alan peered down at his youngest, realizing just how much she'd grown up in the past couple of years. He couldn't help but be impressed. "That's some good body language you got there, kid."

Lauren gazed over from the corner of her eye. "What do you mean by that?"

"You're walking with poise, and you have a certain look in your eye…the kind that makes people think twice before crossing you. It makes you look tough and not easily victimized."

"Okay…"

"I'm serious. It's the equivalent of having an ADT security system sticker on your house." He paused. "Did Dave teach you that?"

Lauren laughed. "Dad, you're funny, and no, Dave didn't teach me. It's something else us millennials have taught ourselves…maybe you've heard of it. It's called 'resting bitch face'."

"Oh," Alan said, nodding. "I believe I have heard that term before. I just never knew what it meant until now." Alan tried to grimace and imitate the look that Lauren was giving off, with some added overemphasis. "How's mine coming along?"

Lauren turned her head to see. "I don't think you're entirely grasping the essence of it."

The two continued to walk side by side until they reached the food court, noticing that it was much more hectic than usual. Restaurants had people waiting in long lines, and there wasn't a table in sight with an empty chair, even in the recently renovated additions.

"I guess the storm sent all the rats running inside for cover," Alan mused. He placed his hands into his pockets and sighed. "I really hate this, L. I've never been a fan of crowds, or rats. Or maybe it's being in tight places with a lot of people."

"Yeah, I know, Dad," Lauren said, pointing. "Look, there's a table over there…let's go snag it before someone else does."

"Good eye."

Taking her seat, Lauren unslung her purse from her shoulder and set it on the table, immediately pulling out her cell phone. She busily tapped on the screen, scrolling through several social media and messaging applications in the blink of an eye.

Alan's eyes darted around, taking in the scene of bustling mall patrons. "I know you're a popular young lady, L, busy as hell all the time, with lots to do and a reputation to uphold, but do me a favor and don't forget where you are right now, okay?"

Lauren hesitated, then set her phone on the table. She toyed with her hair, intertwined her fingers, and glanced up innocently at her father. "I'm getting pretty bad at that, aren't I?"

Alan shrugged. "You're nowhere near as bad as most people I've seen, including adults. Do me a favor, put that away and take a look around you. How many people are doing what you just were?"

Lauren took a moment to fully engage the scene. If a smartphone, tablet, or other screen device wasn't glued to their faces, people were carrying them in their hands or had them half-holstered in their back pockets. Most had a set of earphones jammed in their ears. Conversations with family members and friends were carried on halfheartedly at best, while the crowd's overall primary focus seemed magnetized to the glowing device screens.

"You're looking at the planet's newfangled social interface. We stand side by side, yet we find it essential to have miles of wires and radio waves to stay connected all the time and communicate. These days, everybody has their face buried in a screen. They stumble around aimlessly like real-life walking zombies. It's like people have totally let go of the fact that we're surrounded by a real world...and they've become hopelessly infatuated with the virtual alternatives. Being honest, I've never worried too much about you because you've shown so much interest in tangible, non-technological things." A pause. "Remember that saying about the day that technology will someday surpass human interaction...and how we'll then be stuck with an entire generation of idiots?"

Lauren giggled. "Yeah. That misquote even ascended to meme status."

"Meme status?"

"The one with the young mom at the airport. She's on her cell phone and her baby is lying on a towel at her feet."

Alan nodded. "Come to think of it, I have seen it. Misquote, meme or not, the photo itself is pretty damn authentic, making the point a valid one. Humanity is waning while technology is deliberately gaining ground. It's a shame. There's entirely too much real world still out there for us to ignore."

Lauren nodded her acknowledgment. "I know, Dad. And don't worry about me. I know technology has its place. It's useful and fun, but I can keep it in check."

"Then you should also know how to live without it."

Lauren's smile dimmed a few lumens. "Alas, getting to that level might take a little bit more time for me."

Alan reached for her hand. "Take all the time you need. Live your life. Just don't overlook what you've learned or what I've told you, and don't forget to stay vigilant."

"Situational awareness, I know. And I won't forget."

Alan sat back in his seat and folded his arms, watching as his daughter mimicked him in doing the same. A moment passed before he said anything. "So, what are you doing right now?"

"Well, since I'm *not* on Snap, Facebook, or Insta, I'm studying the layout of the mall. Marking my exits."

"If something popped off, where would you go?"

"I wouldn't, at first. I'd stay put, get low, and watch where everyone else was going. Then find another way."

"Good girl."

Lauren smiled and tossed her hair. "I'm also people watching and eavesdropping on some funny conversations. Watching hands, eyes, and body language, but mostly eyes. Eyes can sometimes tell you everything you need to know."

Alan slowly nodded. "See anything suspicious?"

"Not really. Lots of young people running around on their own unsupervised, and lots of families, mostly. Nothing dangerous or threatening."

"What about behind you?"

Lauren's eyes darted around until she found a pane of glass ready to lend a hand. "I can see behind me by looking at that window over there. It's not easy, but it helps."

"Anything is better than nothing. And I guess I don't need to ask you this, but I will anyway," Alan began. "Are you carrying today?"

Lauren smiled and nodded. "G27, extended mag, one in the hole. Two spare mags in my purse."

Alan smiled coyly. "That's my girl, L. You have definitely learned how to impress the shit out of me. You've taken what I've taught you and what you've learned elsewhere and become quite the…weapon." He paused, leaning forward. "Your mom will be back soon. And if you're okay with it, there's a few things I'd like to say to you before she gets back."

"Why can't you tell me when she's here?"

"It's not that I can't, just that I prefer not to," Alan said. "Your mother is just as important to me as you are, but it's no secret that she has a slight tendency to be jealous over the relationship you and I have, not to mention the time we spend away from her. I don't want to make it seem like I'm rubbing it in."

Lauren nodded. "Okay, I get that. So what's up?"

Alan wavered a moment. "Nothing much. It's just that…I've been meaning to tell you how proud I am of you, L. Proud of who you are and what you're becoming. Proud of the decisions you're making and the fact you remain capable of thinking for yourself amidst all of life's… distractions. I'm proud to see you're becoming a leader, not a follower… and that you've turned into quite the *anti-millennial*. You're growing into the young woman I always wanted you to be. That's it, nothing big. I don't get the opportunity to talk to you as much as I used to, and I sense those opportunities slipping away more and more as you get older. And I just needed you to know."

Lauren turned away and subtly rubbed at her eye. "Okay, that's enough, you have to stop it. Jesus, Dad. I love you, but don't make me cry in public. That's not cool."

"I'm sorry. I suppose I have a tendency to be overly sentimental."

"Yeah. And you do it a lot."

Alan nodded. "Point taken. I don't want there to be any stones left unturned between you and me. I've heard so many stories about regret, where a person becomes separated or loses someone they care deeply about, and they dwell on the things they never said, never did, and wish they had. I don't want to have any regrets with you. I'm just a dad trying to hold onto his daughter for as long as he can."

Alan held out his right hand in a gesture Lauren easily recognized, and the two performed a secret handshake of sorts that had been shared between them for years. "I've always thought you and I were indivisible, L. There's nothing I wouldn't do for you if I had the means. If some opposing force tried to keep us apart, I'd stop at nothing to find you and get back to you. I mean that."

Lauren shared his thoughtful gaze. "I believe you. You do scare me sometimes, but I like it when we have these little impromptu…heart-to-hearts. Thank you. For everything."

"Ditto. And you're welcome for everything."

ABOUT THE AUTHOR

C.A. Rudolph is a self-published novelist who lives and writes within the pastoral boundaries of Virginia's northern Shenandoah Valley. He spends most of his limited spare time frolicking out-of-doors and planning adventures with his family. He is an avid backpacker, proud gun owner, and an amateur radio operator with a predisposition to splurge on his hobbies.

His first book, What's Left of My World, published in December 2016, became an Amazon post-apocalyptic and dystopian best seller.

To be briefed on Mr. Rudolph and his books, his life, and future exploits, find him loitering outside the wire on Facebook, Twitter, Instagram, and via his website at http://www.carudolph.com

Stay apprised. Subscribe to the Preferred Reader's List

Made in the USA
San Bernardino, CA
13 November 2018